Bittersweet

Miranda Beverly-Whittemore is the author of three novels, including *The Effects of Light* and *Set Me Free*, which won the Janet Heidinger Kafka Prize, for the best book of fiction by an American woman published in 2007. A recipient of the *Crazyhorse* Fiction Prize, she lives and writes in Brooklyn and Vermont.

Also by Miranda Beverly-Whittemore

The Effects of Light
Set Me Free

Bittersweet

MIRANDA
BEVERLY-WHITTEMORE

THE BOROUGH PRESS

The Borough Press
An imprint of HarperCollins*Publishers*
1 London Bridge Street
London SE1 9GF

www.harpercollins.co.uk

This paperback edition 2015

1

First published in Great Britain by
The Borough Press 2014

Miranda Beverly-Whittemore asserts the moral right to
be identified as the author of this work

A catalogue record for this book
is available from the British Library

ISBN: 978-0-00-753667-2

This novel is entirely a work of fiction.
The names, characters and incidents portrayed in it are
the work of the author's imagination. Any resemblance to
actual persons, living or dead, events or localities is
entirely coincidental.

Set in Adobe Caslon by Palimpsest Book Production Limited,
Falkirk, Stirlingshire

Printed and bound in Great Britain by
Clays Ltd, St Ives plc

MIX
Paper from
responsible sources
FSC C007454

FSC™ is a non-profit international organisation established to promote
the responsible management of the world's forests. Products carrying the
FSC label are independently certified to assure consumers that they come
from forests that are managed to meet the social, economic and
ecological needs of present and future generations,
and other controlled sources.

Find out more about HarperCollins and the environment at
www.harpercollins.co.uk/green

For Ba and Fa, who shared the land,
and Q , who gave me the world

February

CHAPTER ONE

The Roommate

B EFORE SHE LOATHED ME, before she loved me, Genevra Katherine Winslow didn't know that I existed. That's hyperbolic, of course; by February, student housing had required us to share a hot shoe box of a room for nearly six months, so she must have gathered I was a physical reality (if only because I coughed every time she smoked her Kools atop the bunk bed), but until the day Ev asked me to accompany her to Winloch, I was accustomed to her regarding me as she would a hideously upholstered armchair – something in her way, to be utilized when absolutely necessary, but certainly not what she'd have chosen herself.

It was colder that winter than I knew cold could be, even though the girl from Minnesota down the hall declared it 'nothing.' Out in Oregon, snow had been a gift, a two-day dusting earned by enduring months of gray, dripping sky. But the wind whipping up the Hudson from the city was so vehement that even my bone marrow froze. Every morning, I hunkered under my duvet, unsure of how I'd make it to my 9:00 a.m. Latin class. The clouds spilled endless white and Ev slept in.

She slept in with the exception of the first subzero day of the semester. That morning, she squinted at me pulling

3

on the flimsy rubber galoshes my mother had nabbed at Value Village and, without saying a word, clambered down from her bunk, opened our closet, and plopped her brand-new pair of fur-lined L.L.Bean duck boots at my feet. 'Take them,' she commanded, swaying in her silk nightgown above me. What to make of this unusually generous offer? I touched the leather – it was as buttery as it looked.

'I mean it.' She climbed back into bed. 'If you think I'm going out in that, in those, you're deranged.'

Inspired by her act of generosity, by the belief that boots must be broken in (and spurred on by the daily terror of a stockpiling peasant – sure, at any moment, I'd be found undeserving and sent packing), I forced my frigid body out across the residential quad. Through freezing rain, hail, and snow I persevered, my tubby legs and sheer weight landing me square in the middle of every available snowdrift. I squinted up at Ev's distracted, willowy silhouette smoking from our window, and thanked the gods she didn't look down.

Ev wore a camel-hair coat, drank absinthe at underground clubs in Manhattan, and danced naked atop Main Gate because someone dared her. She had come of age in boarding school and rehab. Her lipsticked friends breezed through our stifling dorm room with the promise of something better; my version of socializing was curling up with a copy of *Jane Eyre* after a study break hosted by the house fellows. Whole weeks went by when I didn't see her once. On the few occasions inclement weather hijacked her plans, she instructed me in the ways of the world: (1) drink only hard

4

alcohol at parties because it won't make you fat (although she pursed her lips whenever she said the word in front of me, she didn't shy from saying it), and (2) close your eyes if you ever have to put a penis in your mouth.

'Don't expect your roommate to be your best friend,' my mother had offered in the bold voice she reserved for me alone, just before I flew east. Back in August, watching the TSA guy riffle through my granny underpants while my mother waved a frantic good-bye, I shelved her comment in the category of Insulting. I knew all too well that my parents wouldn't mind if I failed college and had to return to clean other people's clothes for the rest of my life; it was a fate they – or at least my father – believed I'd sealed for myself only six years before. But by early February, I understood what my mother had really meant; scholarship girls aren't meant to slumber beside the scions of America because doing so whets insatiable appetites.

The end of the year was in sight, and I felt sure Ev and I had secured our roles: she tolerated me, while I pretended to disdain everything she stood for. So it came as a shock, that first week of February, to receive a creamy, ivory envelope in my campus mailbox, my name penned in India ink across its matte expanse. Inside, I found an invitation to the college president's reception in honor of Ev's eighteenth birthday, to be held at the campus art museum at the end of the month. Apparently, Genevra Katherine Winslow was donating a Degas.

Any witness to me thrusting that envelope into my parka pocket in the boisterous mail room might have guessed that humble old Mabel Dagmar was embarrassed by the showy decadence, but it was just the opposite – I wanted to keep the exclusive, honeyed sensation of the invitation to myself, lest I discover it was a mistake, or that every single mailbox held one. The gently nubbled paper stock kept my hand warm all day. When I returned to the room, I made sure to leave the envelope prominently on my desk, where Ev liked to keep her ashtray, just below the only picture she had posted in our room, of a good sixty people – young and old, all nearly as good-looking and naturally blond as Ev, all dressed entirely in white – in front of a grand summer cottage. The Winslows' white clothing was informal, but it wasn't the kind of casual my family sported (Disneyland T-shirts, potbellies, cans of Heineken). Ev's family was lean, tan, and smiling. Collared shirts, crisp cotton dresses, eyelet socks on the French-braided little girls. I was grateful she had put the picture over my desk; I had ample time to study and admire it.

It was three days before she noticed the envelope. She was smoking atop her bunk – the room filling with acrid haze as I puffed on my inhaler, huddled over a calculus set just below her – when she let out a groan of recognition, hopping down from her bed and plucking up the invitation. 'You're not coming to this, are you?' she asked, waving it around. She sounded horrified at the possibility, her rosebud lips turned down in a distant cousin of ugly – for truly, even in disdain and dorm-room dishevelment, Ev was a sight to behold.

'I thought I might,' I answered meekly, not letting on that I'd been simultaneously ecstatic and fretful over what I would ever wear to such an event, not to mention how I would do anything attractive with my limp hair.

Her long fingers flung the envelope back onto my desk. 'It's going to be ghastly. Mum and Daddy are angry I'm not donating to the Met, so they won't let me invite any of my friends, of course.'

'Of course.' I tried not to sound wounded.

'I didn't mean it like that,' she snapped, before dropping back into my desk chair and tipping her porcelain face toward the ceiling, frowning at the crack in the plaster.

'Weren't you the one who invited me?' I dared to ask.

'No.' She giggled, as though my mistake was an adorable transgression. 'Mum always asks the roommates. It's supposed to make it feel so much more . . . democratic.' She saw the look on my face, then added, 'I don't even want to be there; there's no reason you should.' She reached for her Mason Pearson hairbrush and pulled it over her scalp. The boar bristles made a full, thick sound as she groomed herself, golden hair glistening.

'I won't go,' I offered, the disappointment in my voice betraying me. I turned back to my math. It was better not to go – I would have embarrassed myself. But by then, Ev was looking at me, and continuing to stare – her eyes boring into my face – until I could bear her gaze no more. 'What?' I asked, testing her with irritation (but not too much; I could hardly blame her for not wanting me at such an elegant affair).

'You know about art, right?' she asked, the sudden sweetness in her voice drawing me out. 'You're thinking of majoring in art history?'

I was surprised – I had no idea Ev had any notion of my interests. And although, in truth, I'd given up the thought

7

of becoming an art history major – too many hours taking notes in dark rooms, and I wasn't much for memorization, and I was falling in love with the likes of Shakespeare and Milton – I saw clearly that an interest in art was my ticket in.

'I think.'

Ev beamed, her smile a break between thunderheads. 'We'll make you a dress,' she said, clapping. 'You look pretty in blue.'

She'd noticed.

CHAPTER TWO

The Party

THREE WEEKS LATER, I found myself standing in the main, glassy hall of the campus art museum, a silk dress the color of the sea deftly draped and seamed so I appeared twenty pounds lighter. At my elbow stood Ev, in a column of champagne shantung. She looked like a princess, and, as for a princess, the rules did not apply; we held full wineglasses with no regard for the law, and no one, not the trustees or professors or senior art history majors who paraded by, each taking the time to win her smile, batted an eye as we sipped the alcohol. A single violinist teased out a mournful melody in the far corner of the room. The president – a doyenne of the first degree, her hair a helmet of gray, her smile practiced in the art of raising institutional monies – hovered close at hand. Ev introduced me to spare herself the older woman's attention, but I was flattered by the president's interest in my studies ('I'm sure we can get you into that upper-level Milton seminar'), though eager to extract myself from her company in the interest of more time with Ev.

Ev whispered each guest's name into the whorl of my ear – how she kept track of them, even now I do not know, except that she had been bred for it – and I realized that somehow, inexplicably, I had ended up the guest of honor's guest of honor. Ev may have beguiled each attendee, but it was with me that she shared her most private observations ('Assistant Professor Oakley – he's slept with everyone,' 'Amanda Wyn – major eating disorder'). Taking it all in, I couldn't imagine why she wouldn't want this: the Degas (a ballerina bent over toe shoes at the edge of a stage), the fawning adults, the celebration of birth and tradition. As much as she insisted she longed for the evening to be over, so did I drink it in, knowing all too well that tomorrow I'd be back in her winter boots, slogging through the sleet, praying my financial aid check would come so I could buy myself a pair of mittens.

The doors to the main hall opened and the president rushed to greet the newest, final guests, parting the crowd. My diminutive stature has never given me advantage, and I strained to see who had arrived – a movie star? an influential artist? – only someone important could have stirred up such a reaction in that academic group.

'Who is it?' I whispered, straining on tiptoe.

Ev downed her second gin and tonic. 'My parents.'

Birch and Tilde Winslow were the most glamorous people I'd ever seen: polished, buffed, and obviously made of different stuff than I.

Tilde was young – or at least younger than my mother. She had Ev's swan-like neck, topped off by a sharper, less exquisite face, although, make no mistake, Tilde Winslow was a beauty. She was skinny, too skinny, and though I recognized in her the signs of years of calorie counting, I'll admit that I admired what the deprivation had done for her – accentuating her biceps, defining the lines of her jaw.

Her cheekbones cut like razors across her face. She wore a dress of emerald dupioni silk, done at the waist with a sapphire brooch the size of a child's hand. Her white-blond hair was swept into a chignon.

Birch was older – Tilde's senior by a good twenty years – and he had the unmovable paunch of a man in his seventies. But the rest of him was lean. His face did not seem grandfatherly at all; it was handsome and youthful, his crystal-blue eyes set like jewels inside the dark, long eyelashes that Ev had inherited from his line. As he and Tilde made their slow, determined way to us, he shook hands like a politician, offering cracks and quips that jollified the crowd. Beside him, Tilde was his polar opposite. She hardly mustered a smile, and, when they were finally to us, she looked me over as though I were a dray horse brought in for plowing.

'Genevra,' she acknowledged, once satisfied I had nothing to offer.

'Mum.' I caught the tightness in Ev's voice, which melted as soon as her father placed his arm around her shoulder.

'Happy birthday, freckles,' he whispered into her perfect ear, tapping her on the nose. Ev blushed. 'And who,' he asked, holding out his hand to me, 'is this?'

'This is Mabel.'

'The roommate!' he exclaimed. 'Miss Dagmar, the pleasure is all mine.' He swallowed that awful *g* at the center of my name and ended with a flourish by rolling the *r* just so. For once, my name sounded delicate. He kissed my hand.

Tilde offered a thin smile. 'Perhaps you can tell us, Mabel, where our daughter was over Christmas break.' Her voice was reedy and thin, with a brief trace of an accent, indistinguishable as pedigreed or foreign.

Ev's face registered momentary panic.

'She was with me,' I answered.

'With you?' Tilde asked, seeming to fill with genuine amusement. 'And what, pray tell, was she doing with you?'

'We were visiting my aunt in Baltimore.'

'Baltimore! This is getting better by the minute.'

'It was lovely, Mum. I told you – I was well taken care of.'

Tilde raised one eyebrow, casting a glance over both of us, before turning to the curator at her arm and asking whether the Rodins were on display. Ev placed her hand on my shoulder and squeezed.

I had no idea where Ev had been over Christmas break – she certainly hadn't been with me. But I wasn't lying completely – I'd been in Baltimore, forced to endure my Aunt Jeanne's company for the single, miserable week during which the college dorms had been shuttered. Visiting Aunt Jeanne at twelve on the one adventure my mother and I had ever taken together – a five-day East Coast foray – had been the highlight of my preteen existence. My memories of that visit were murky, given that they were from Before Everything Changed, but they were happy. Aunt Jeanne had seemed glamorous, a carefree counterpoint to my laden, dutiful mother. We'd eaten Maryland crab and gone to the diner for sundaes.

But whether Aunt Jeanne had changed or my eye had become considerably more nuanced in the intervening years, what I discovered that first December of college was that I'd rather shoot myself in the head than become her. She lived in a dank, cat-infested condo and seemed puzzled whenever I suggested we go to the Smithsonian. She ate TV dinners and dozed off in front of midnight infomercials. As Tilde turned from us, I remembered, with horror, the promise my aunt had extracted from me at the end of my stay (all she'd had to do was invoke my abandoned mother's name): two interminable weeks in May before heading back to Oregon. I dared to dream that Ev would come with me. She'd be the key to surviving *The Price Is Right* and the tickle of cat hair at the back of the throat.

'Mabel's studying art history.' Ev nudged me toward her father. 'She loves the Degas.'

'Do you?' Birch asked. 'You can get closer to it, you know. It's still ours.'

I glanced at the well-lit painting propped upon a simple easel. Only a few feet separated me from it, but it may as well have been a million. 'Thank you,' I demurred.

'So you're majoring in art history?'

'I thought you were majoring in English,' the president interrupted, suddenly at my side.

I grew red-faced in the spotlight, and what felt like being caught in a lie. 'Oh,' I stammered, 'I like both subjects – I really do – I'm only a first-year, you know, and—'

'Well, you can't have literature without art, can you?' Birch asked warmly, opening the circle to a few of Ev's admirers. He squeezed his daughter's shoulder. 'When this one was barely five we took the children to Firenze, and she could not get enough of Medusa's head at the Uffizi. And Judith and Holofernes! Children love such gruesome tales.' Everyone laughed. I was invisible again. Birch caught my eye for the briefest of seconds and winked. I felt myself flush gratefully.

After the president's welcome toast, and the passed hors d'oeuvres, and the birthday cupcakes frosted with buttercream that matched my dress, after Ev made a little speech about how the college had made her feel so at home, and that she hoped the Degas would live happily at the museum for many years to come, Birch raised a glass, garnering the room's attention.

'It has been the Winslow tradition,' he began, as though we were all part of his family, 'for each of the children, upon reaching eighteen, to donate a painting to an institution of his or her choice. My sons chose the Metropolitan Museum. My daughter chose a former women's college.' This was met with boisterous laughter. Birch tipped his glass toward the president in rhetorical apology. He cleared his throat as a wry smile faded from his lips. 'Perhaps the tradition sprang from wanting to give each child a healthy deduction on their first tax return' – again, he was met with laughter – 'but its true spirit lies in a desire to teach, through practice, that we can never truly own what matters. Land, art, even, heartbreaking as it is to let go, a great work of art. The Winslows embody philanthropy. *Phila*, love. *Anthro*, man. Love of man, love of others.' With that, he turned to Ev and raised his champagne. 'We love you, Ev. Remember: we give not because we can, but because we must.'

CHAPTER THREE

The Invitation

O NE TOO MANY GLASSES of champagne, one too few canapés, and an hour later, the overheated room was swimming. I needed air, water, something, or I felt sure that my ankles – bowing under my body's pressure upon the thin, pointed pair of heels Ev had insisted I borrow – would blow. 'I'll be back,' I whispered as she nodded numbly at a trustee's story about a failed trip to Cancún. I teetered down the long, glass-covered walkway leading into the gothic wing of the museum. In the bathroom, I splashed tepid water on my face. Only then did I remember I had makeup on. But it was too late; the wetness had already wreaked havoc – smeared lips, raccoon eyes. I pumped down paper towels and scrubbed at my face until I looked like I'd slept on a park bench, but not actively insane. It didn't matter anyway – we were just going back to the dorm. Perhaps we'd order pizza.

I traipsed back up the hallway, a woman made new with the promise of pajamas and pepperoni. I was surprised to discover the great room already empty – save the violinist packing up her instrument and the waiters breaking down the naked banquet tables. Ev, the president, Birch, Tilde – all of them were gone.

'Excuse me,' I said to one of the waiters, 'did you see where they went?'

His eyebrow ring caught in the light as he raised his brows in a 'why should I care' I recognized from my own nights working late at the cleaner's. I went to the ladies' room and peeked under the bathroom stalls. Tears began to sting my eyes, but I fought against them. Ridiculous. Ev was probably headed home to find me.

'Goodness, dear,' the curator tsked when she caught me in there. 'The museum is closed.' Had Ev been by my side, she wouldn't have said it, and I wouldn't have quickened my departure. I plucked my lonely coat from the metal rack in the foyer, and plunged out into the cold.

There, in sight of the double doors, were Ev and her mother, their backs to me. 'Ev!' I called. She did not turn my way. The wind, surely, had carried off my voice. So I approached, concentrating on my steps so as not to twist an ankle. 'Ev,' I said when I was close. 'There you are. I was looking for you.'

Tilde snapped her head up at the sound of my voice as though I were a gnat.

'Hey, Ev,' I said gingerly. She did not answer. I reached out to touch her sleeve.

'Not now,' Ev hissed.

'I thought we could—'

'What part of *not now* don't you understand?' She turned toward me, rage on her face.

I knew well what it was to be dismissed. And I knew enough about Ev to know that she had spent much of her life dismissing. But it seemed so incongruous after the night we'd had – after I'd lied for her, and she'd finally acted like my friend – and so I remained frozen, watching Tilde steer Ev to the Lexus that Birch brought around.

She didn't come home that night. Which was fine. Normal, even. I had lived for months with Ev with no expectations of her – not of friendship, or loyalty – but by the next day, her dismissal was gnawing at me, rubbing me raw, like the heels she'd lent me, making blisters I should have anticipated, and tried to prevent.

Despite pulling on her boots and letting them cup my arches; despite allowing myself to wish, with every step I took, that the previous night's unpleasantness had been an anomaly, the day turned worse. Six classes, five papers, four midterm projects on the horizon, a thirty-pound backpack, the onset of a sore throat, pants sodden with snowmelt, and a hollow, growing loneliness inside. Trudging up our hall as evening fell, I could smell the telltale cigarette smoke whispering from under our door and remembered our RA's offhand comment about how next time it happened she'd be in her rights to fine us fifty bucks, and I allowed myself to feel angry. Ev had returned, but so what? I had asthma. I couldn't survive in a room filled with smoke – she was literally trying to suffocate me. My asthma medication's one benefit – justification for the extra weight I carried – wouldn't do me any good if I were dead.

I gritted my teeth and told myself to be strong, that I didn't need the damn boots. I could just write to my father and ask for a pair (why hadn't I done that already?). I didn't need a Degas-bestowing supermodel snob lying around my room, reminding me what a nothing I was. I gripped the doorknob and told myself to say it how Ev would say it, formulated

17

'Fuck, Ev, could you smoke somewhere else?' (I would make my voice nonchalant, as though my objection was philosophical and not an expression of poverty), and barged in.

She usually smoked atop her desk beside the window, cigarette perched in the corner of her mouth, or cross-legged on the top bunk, ashing into an empty soda bottle. But this time, she wasn't there. As I dropped my bag, I imagined with delighted gloom that she'd left a cigarette smoldering on the bedclothes before heading out to some glamorous destination – the Russian Tea Room, a private rooftop in Tribeca. The whole dorm was doomed to go up in flames, and I would go down with it. She would be forced to remember me forever.

And then I heard it: a sniffle. I squinted at the top bunk. The comforter quivered.

'Ev?'

The sound of soft crying.

I approached. I was still in my drenched jeans, but this was electrifying.

I stood at that awkward angle, neck craned up. She was really under there. I wondered what to do as her voice began to break into a full, throaty sob. 'Are you okay?' I asked.

I didn't expect her to answer. And I certainly didn't mean to put my hand on her back. Had I been thinking clearly, I never would have dared – my anger was too proud; the gesture, too intimate. But my little touch elicited unexpected results. First, it made her cry harder. Then it made her turn in the bed, so that her face and mine were much closer than they'd ever been and I could see every millimeter of her flooding, Tiffany-blue eyes; her stained, rosy cheeks; her greasy blond hair, limp for the first time since I'd known her. Her mouth faltered, and I couldn't help but put my hand to her hot temple. She looked so much more human this close up.

'What happened?' I asked, when she'd finally calmed.

For a moment it seemed as if she might start sobbing again. Instead, she fished out another cigarette and lit it. 'My cousin,' she said, as if that told the whole thing.

'What's your cousin's name?' I didn't think I could stand not to know what was breaking Ev's heart.

'Jackson,' she whispered, the corners of her mouth turning down. 'He's a soldier. Was,' she corrected herself, and her tears spilled all over again.

'He was killed?'

She shook her head. 'He came back last summer. I mean, he was acting a little strange and everything, but I didn't think . . .' And then she cried. She cried so hard that I slipped off my parka and jeans and got in bed beside her and held her quaking body.

'He shot himself. In the mouth. Last week,' she said finally, what seemed like hours later, when we were lying beside each other under her four-ply red cashmere throw, staring up at the cracked ceiling as if this was what we did all the time. It was a relief to finally hear what had happened; I had started to wonder if this cousin hadn't walked into a post office and shot everyone up.

'Last week?' I asked.

She turned to me, touching our foreheads. 'Mum didn't tell me until last night. After the reception.' Her nose and eyes began to pinken in anticipation of another round of tears. 'She didn't want me to get upset and "ruin things."'

'Oh, Ev,' I sympathized, filling with forgiveness. That was

why she had snapped at me after the party – she was grief-stricken.

'What was Jackson like?' I pushed, and she began to weep again. It was so strange and lovely to be lying next to her, feeling her flaxen hair against my cheek, watching the great globes of sorrow trail down her smooth face. I didn't want it to end. I knew that to stop speaking would be to lose her again.

'He was a good guy, you know? Like, last summer? One of his mom's dogs, Flip, was running on the gravel road and this asshole repair guy came around the curve at, like, fifty miles an hour and hit the dog and it made this awful sound' – she shuddered – 'and Jackson just walked right over there and picked Flip up in his arms – I mean, everyone else was screaming and crying, it, like, happened in front of all the little kids – and he carried her over to the grass and rubbed her ears.' She closed her eyes again. 'And afterward, he put a blanket over her.'

I looked at the picture of the gathered Winslows above my desk, although it was as silly an enterprise as opening the menu of a diner you've been going to your whole life; I knew every blond head, every slim calf, as though her family was my own. 'This was at your summer place, right?'

She pronounced the name as if for the first time. 'Winloch.'

I could feel her eyes examining the side of my face. What she said next, she said carefully. Even though my heart skipped a beat, I measured my expectations, telling myself that was the last I'd hear of it:

'You should come.'

June

CHAPTER FOUR

The Call

D O THEY KNOW WE'RE coming?' I asked as Ev handed me the rest of the Kit Kat bar I'd bought in the dining car. The train had long since whistled twice and headed farther north, leaving us with empty track and each other.

'Naturally.' Ev sniffed with a trace of doubt as she settled, again, on top of her suitcase under the overhang of the stationmaster's office. She regarded my orange copy of *Paradise Lost* disdainfully, then checked her cell phone for the twentieth time, cursing the lack of service. 'And now we'll only have six days before the inspection.'

'Inspection?'

'Of the cottage.'

'Who's inspecting it?'

I could tell from the way she blinked straight ahead that my questions were an annoyance. 'Daddy, of course.'

I tried to make my voice as benign as possible. 'You sound concerned.'

'Well of course I'm concerned,' she said with a pout, 'because if we don't get that little hovel shipshape in less than a week, I won't inherit it. And then you'll go home and I'll have to live under the same roof as my mother.'

Her mouth was set to snarl at whatever I said next, so

instead of voicing all the questions flooding my mind – 'You mean I might still have to go home? You mean you, of all people, have to clean your own house?' – I looked across the tracks to a tangle of chickadees leapfrogging from one branch to the next, and sucked in the fresh northern air.

An invitation marks the beginning of something, but it's more of a gesture than an actual beginning. It's as if a door swings open and sits there gaping, right in front of you, but you don't get to walk through it yet. I know this now, but back then, I thought that everything had begun, and, by everything, I mean the friendship that quickly burned hot between me and Ev, catching fire the night she told me of Jackson's death and blazing through the spring, as Ev taught me how to dance, who to talk to, and what to wear, while I tutored her in chemistry and convinced her that, if she'd only apply herself, she'd stop getting Ds. 'She's the brainiac,' she'd started to brag warmly, and I liked the statement mostly because it meant she saw us as a pair, strolling across the quad arm in arm, drinking vodka tonics at off-campus parties, blowing off her druggie friends for a Bogart movie marathon. From the vantage point of June, I could see my belonging sprouting from that day in February, when Ev had uttered those three dulcet words: 'You should come.'

Over the course of the spring, in each note scribbled on the back of a discarded dry-cleaning receipt, in each secretive call to my dorm room, my mother had intimated I should be wary of life's newfound generosity. As usual, I'd found her warnings (as I did nearly everything that flowed from her) Depressing, Insulting, and Predictable – in her way, she assumed Ev was just using me ('For what?' I asked her incredulously. 'What on earth could someone like Ev possibly use me for?'). But I also assumed, once my father reluctantly agreed to the summer's arrangement, that she would lay off, if only because, by mid-May, Ev had peeled her Winloch photograph off the wall, I'd put the bulk of my belongings into a wooden crate in the dorm's fifth-floor attic, and my summer plans – as far as I saw them – were set in stone.

So the particular call that rang through Ev's Upper East Side apartment, the one that came the June night before Ev and I were to get on that northbound train, was surprising. Ev and I were chopsticking Thai out of take-out containers, sprawled across the antique four-poster bed in her bedroom, where I'd been sleeping for two blissful weeks, the insulated windowpanes and mauve curtains blocking out any inconvenient sound blasting up from Seventy-Third Street (a blessed contrast to Aunt Jeanne's wretched spinster cave, where I'd spent the last two weeks of May, counting down the days to Manhattan). My suitcase lay splayed at my feet. The Oriental rug was scattered with sturdy bags: Prada, Burberry, Chanel. We'd already put in our half-hour jog on side-by-side treadmills in her mother's suite and were discussing which movie we'd watch in the screening room. Tonight, especially, we were worn out from rushing to the Met before it closed so Ev could show me her family's donations, as she'd promised her father she would. I'd stood in front of two swarthily paired Gauguins, and all I could think to say was 'But I thought you had three brothers.'

Ev had laughed and wagged her finger. 'You're right, but the third's an asshole who auctioned his off and donated the proceeds to Amnesty International. Mum and Daddy nearly threw him off the roof deck.' Said roof deck lay atop the building's eighth floor, which was taken up entirely by the Winslows' four-thousand-square-foot apartment. Even though I was naïve about the Winslows' money, I already understood that what summed up their status resided not in their mahogany furnishings or priceless art but, rather, in the Central Park vistas offered from nearly every one of the apartment's windows: a pastoral view in the middle of an overpopulated city, something seemingly impossible and yet effortlessly achieved.

I could only imagine how luxurious their summer estate would be.

At the phone's second bleating, Ev answered in a voice like polished glass, 'Winslow residence,' looked confused for an instant, then regained her composure. 'Mrs Dagmar,' she enthused in her voice reserved for adults. 'How wonderful to hear from you.' She held the phone to me, then flopped onto the bed, burying herself in the latest *Vanity Fair*.

'Mom?' I lifted the receiver to my ear.

'Honey-bell.'

Instantly, I could smell my mother's pistachio breath, but any longing was pushed down by the memory of how these phone calls usually ended.

'Your father says tomorrow's the big day.'

'Yup.'

'Honey-bell,' she repeated. 'Your father's set the whole thing up with Mr Winslow, and I don't need to remind you that they're being very generous.'

'Yup,' I replied, feeling myself bristle. Who knew what

Birch had finally said to get my reluctant, sullen father to agree to let me miss three months of punishing labor, but whatever it was, it had worked, and thank god for it. Still, I found it borderline insulting to suggest my father had had anything to do with 'setting the whole thing up' when he'd barely tolerated it, and was reminded of how my mother always sided with him, even when (especially when) her face held the pink imprint of his hand. My eyes scanned the intricate pattern of Ev's rug.

'Do you have a hostess gift? Candles maybe? Soap?'

'Mom.'

Ev glanced up at the sharpness in my voice. She smiled and shook her head before drifting back into the magazine.

'Mr Winslow told your father they don't have service up there.'

'Service?'

'You know, cell phone, Internet.' My mother sounded flustered. 'It's one of the family rules.'

'Okay,' I said. 'Look, I've got to—'

'So we'll write then.'

'Great. Bye, Mom.'

'Wait.' Her voice became bold. 'There's something else I have to tell you.'

I absentmindedly eyed a long, thick bolt on the inside of Ev's bedroom door. In the two weeks I'd slept in that room, I'd never given it much thought, but now, examining how sturdy it looked, I was struck with wondering: why on earth would a girl like Ev want to lock out any part of her perfect life? 'Yes?'

'It's not too late.'

'For what?'

'To change your mind. We'd love to have you home. You know that, don't you?'

I almost burst out laughing. But then I thought of her burned meat loaf, sitting, lonely, in the middle of the table, with just my father to share it. Microwaved green beans, limp, in their brown juices. Rum and Cokes. No point in rubbing my freedom in. 'I need to go.'

'Just one more thing.'

It was all I could do not to slam the receiver down. I'd been perfectly warm, hadn't I? And listened plenty? How could I ever make her understand that this very conversation with her, laden with everything I was trying to escape, made Winloch, with no cell phones or Internet, sound like heaven?

I could feel her trying to figure out how to put it, her exhalations flushing into the receiver as she formulated the words. 'Be sweet,' she said finally.

'Sweet?' I felt a lump rise in my throat. I turned from Ev.

'Be yourself, I mean. You're so sweet, Honey-bell. That's what Mr Winslow told your dad. You're a "gem," he said. And, well' – she paused, and, despite myself, I hung on her words – 'I just want you to know I think so too.'

How could she still make me hate myself so readily? Remind me that I could never undo what I had done? The lump in my throat threatened to well into something more. 'I've got to go.' I hung up before she had the chance to protest.

But I hadn't caught my tears in time. They flowed, hot and angry, down my cheeks against my will.

'Mothers are such lunatic bitches,' Ev quipped after a moment.

I kept my back to her and tried to gather my strength.

'Are you crying?' She sounded shocked.

I shook my head, but she could see that was exactly what I was doing.

'You poor kitten,' she soothed, her voice turning velvety, and, before I knew it, she was wrapping me in a tight embrace. 'It'll be all right. Whatever she said – it doesn't matter.'

I had never let Ev see me walloped, had felt sure that, if she did, she would be fruitless in her comforting. But she held me firmly and uttered calm and soothing words until my tears weren't so urgent.

'She's just – she's not – she's everything I'm afraid of becoming,' I said finally, trying to explain something I'd never said out loud.

'And that may be the only way that your mother and my mother are exactly the same.' Ev laughed, offering me a tissue, and then a sweater from a bag on the floor, azure and soft, adding, 'Put it on, you pretty thing. Cashmere makes everything better.'

Now, I looked across the Plattsburgh train depot and swelled with indulgent love at Ev's grumpy scowl.

'Be sweet,' my mother had said.

A command.

A warning.

A promise.

I was good at being sweet. I'd spent years cloaked in gentleness, in wide-eyed innocence, and, to tell the truth, it was often less exhausting than the alternative. I could even see now, looking back on how Ev and I had gained our friendship, that sweetness had been the seed of it – if I wasn't good, why on earth would I have dared to touch Ev's sobbing self?

There was no sign of anyone coming to meet us. Ev's mood had settled into inertia. It would be dark soon. So I headed south along the tracks, in the direction of a periodic clanging I'd heard for the past half hour.

'Where are you going?' Ev called after me.

I returned with a greasy trainman, toothless and gruff. He let us into the stationmaster's office before trudging away.

'There's a phone in here,' I offered.

'The Dining Hall is the only place at Winloch there's a phone, and no one will be there at this hour,' she snarled, but she dialed the number anyway. It rang and rang, and, just as even I was beginning to lose hope, I spotted, through the dusty, cobwebbed window, a red Ford pickup rolling up, complete with waggling yellow Lab in the truck bed.

'Evie!' I heard the man's voice before I saw him. It was young, enthusiastic. As we stepped from the office – 'Evie!' – he rounded the corner, opening his tanned arms wide. 'I'm glad you made it!'

'I'm glad you made it,' she huffed, brushing past him. He was tall and dark, his coloring Ev's opposite, and he looked to be only a few years older. Still, there was something manly about him, as though he'd lived more years than both of us combined.

'You her friend?' he asked, fiddling with his cap, grinning

after her as she wrestled her suitcase in the direction of the parking lot.

I shoved *Paradise Lost* into my weatherworn canvas bag. 'Mabel.'

He extended his rough, warm hand. 'John.' I assumed he was her brother.

CHAPTER FIVE

The Journey

JOHN'S FOUR-DOOR PICKUP WAS old, but it was clear he took great pride in it, second only to his yellow Lab, who barked triumphantly from the flatbed at the sight of us. Ev struggled to toss in her suitcase until John lifted it in one hand – mine was in his other. He placed them down beside the giddy canine, who was, by then, doing her best to lick Ev's ear. 'Down, Abby,' John commanded as he strapped our luggage flat. The dog obeyed.

Ev let herself into the front seat, a scowl tightly knit upon her brow. 'It stinks in here.' She pointedly rolled down her window, but it wasn't lost on me that she had smiled under Abby's lapping attention.

In the backseat, I checked the dog over my shoulder. 'She's okay?'

John turned on the ignition. 'She'd whine if we brought her in.' As the engine growled to life, his hand hesitated over the radio dial, then dropped back onto the steering wheel. I would have liked music, but Ev put up an arctic front.

We drove ten miles in silence, the country road canopied in electric green. I pressed my head against the glass to watch the new maple leaves curling in the breeze. Every few turns offered a tempting glimpse of Lake Champlain's choppy waters. I turned over in my mind which brother

John might be. He seemed less the type to donate to the Met, so I decided he was the 'asshole' to whom Ev had referred – she clearly had a strong aversion to everything of his, save Abby.

'Aren't you going to apologize?' Ev asked John when we pulled into line at the ferry that would take us from New York State to Vermont. I hadn't known there was going to be a boat ride, and I was doing my best to hide my excitement as the muddy smell of the lake wafted up to us. Being on open water seemed just the thing.

John laughed. 'For what?'

'We were at that station for two hours.'

'And it took two hours to get there,' he countered warmly, turning on Elvis. I had only seen men capitulate when faced with Ev's indignation.

Once onboard, I clambered up to the passenger deck. It was a clear evening. The western sky began to orange, and the clouds turned brilliant as fire.

I was glad to have left John and Ev in the pickup, figuring they could use some privacy to iron out their sibling rivalry. I opened *Paradise Lost*. My conversation with the college president at Ev's birthday reception had secured my spot in the upper-level Milton course, and I was planning to have the book 'under my belt' by the fall, when I could read it with a professor who could tell me what it meant. It might as well have been written in Greek; it seemed to be all italics and run-on sentences, but I knew it was Important, and I loved the idea of reading a book about something as profound as the struggle between Good and Evil. I also felt an affinity for Milton's daughter, forced to take dictation for her blind, brilliant father. It was my girlhood, but glamorous, trading sumptuous words for other people's dirty clothing.

But just as I began the first line – 'Of Man's First Disobedience, and the Fruit / Of that Forbidden Tree' – I heard a bark and lifted my eyes to see John and Abby climbing onto the deck. Beside them, a sign read NO DOGS, but a man who worked the ferry patted Abby on the head and shook John's hand before moving belowdecks. John strode toward me, into the gusting air, one hand on Abby's collar.

'Where you from?' he asked over the roaring wind.

'Oregon.' A seagull streamed by. My hair, whipping, stung the sides of my face. 'But I know Ev from school.' We looked out over the water together. The lake was oceanic. I released my finger from the book, watching the pages flutter violently before it closed on its own.

'Is Ev okay?' I asked.

He let Abby go. She settled at his feet.

'Is she mad because of the inspection?' I fished.

'Inspection?'

'The inspection of her cottage. In six days.'

John opened his mouth to say something, then closed it. 'What?' I asked.

'I'd steer clear of all that family stuff if I were you,' he said, after a long moment. 'It'll make it easier to enjoy your vacation.'

I'd never been on a vacation before. The word sounded like an insult coming from his mouth.

'You don't seem like the other girls Ev's brought,' he added.

34

'What does that mean?'

His eyes followed the seagull. 'Less luggage.'

That was when Ev appeared, bearing ice cream sandwiches. Her version, I suppose, of an apology.

Back on land, finally close to Winloch, worry about the inspection slipped through my fingers. The roadside hot dogs were flabby, the mosquitoes ravenous, and Ev was still grumpy, but we were in Vermont, together, on an open road winding through farmland. Dusk shrouded the world.

We filled up at the only gas station I'd seen for miles, and a knackered Abby joined me in the backseat, promptly laying her heavy head upon my knee and curling into sleep. We drove on, past a shuttered horse farm, signs for a vineyard, and an abandoned passenger train car, and finally, as dusk gave way to night, onto a two-lane highway that streamed south under a starry sky. At one point, the road broke out into a causeway that looked like something out of the Florida Keys – or at least pictures I had seen of the keys – and the moon burst forth from behind the clouds. It lit a yellow ribbon on the water and cast the dark outlines of the distant Adirondacks against a purple-black sky.

'How's your mother?' Ev asked. At first I thought she was speaking to me, but then, she knew how my mother was; she'd comforted me about her only the night before.

In the gap made by my racing mind, John spoke. 'Like always.'

Oh wait, I realized, he's not Ev's brother.

I wanted them to go on. But Ev didn't ask any more questions, and we crossed the causeway in silence.

On the other side of the glistening water, we were once again plunged into darkness. A sudden forest swallowed what became a gravel road. Birch trunks glowed ghostly in the moonlight. John's headlights gave us glimpses of barns and farmhouses. He took each turn with the reckless speed of someone who has driven it a thousand times. Ev unrolled her window again to let the sweet night in, and we were embraced by the soft chirping of crickets, their pulse growing louder as we drove into a vast meadow. The moon greeted us again, a milky lantern.

We slowed after a particularly skidding turn – I could feel the rocks kicking out from under our tires. 'We're here,' Ev sang. Outside stood dense forest. Nailed to one of the trunks was a small sign with hand-painted letters spelling out WINLOCH and PRIVATE PROPERTY. Our headlights pointed onto a precarious-looking road hung with warnings: NO TRESPASSING! NO HUNTING – VIOLATORS WILL BE PROSECUTED! NO DUMPING. This bore no resemblance to the grand estate which Ev had described. The skittering sound of the leaves brought to mind a movie I'd once seen about vampires. I felt a prickling up my spine.

It occurred to me then that my mother was probably right: Ev had brought me all the way here only to leave me on the side of the road, an elaborate trick not unlike the one Sarah Templeton had played on me in sixth grade, asking me to her birthday party only to disinvite me – with a roomful of classmates looking on – the moment I materialized on her doorstep, because I was 'too fat to fit in any of the roller coaster seats.' The doubt my mother had been planting began to spread through me – I was a fool to think Ev had actually brought me to her family's estate for a summer of fun.

But Ev laughed dismissively, as though she could read my thoughts. 'Thank god you're here,' she said, and the warmth of her cheer, and the softness of the azure cashmere, brought me back to my senses.

John flipped on the radio again. Country. We plunged into the forest as a man mourned his breaking heart.

We braked once, abruptly. A raccoon blocked our way, his eyes glowing in the glare of our headlights as he waited, front paw lifted, for us to hit him. But John flipped the lights and radio off, and we sat with the engine purring low as the animal's strange, uneven body scurried into the scrub lining the road.

We cut our way past a smattering of unlit cottages, then tennis courts and a great, grand building glowing white in the moonlight. We turned right onto a side road – although it could hardly have been called more than a path – which we stayed on for another quarter mile before sighting a small house set at the dead end.

'No dogs allowed, but I'll make an exception for Abby,' Ev offered as John pulled up in front of the cottage.

'Don't do her any favors.'

'It's not a favor,' she replied, eyes skimming John.

He took Abby toward the woods to piddle. The night came rushing in: the rhythmic cricket clamor, the lapping of water I couldn't see. The moon was behind a cloud. Beyond us, I could sense an expanse which I took to be the lake.

'What do we have to do before the inspection?' I asked Ev quietly.

'Make it livable. Now we only have six days until my parents arrive, and I don't even know what state it's in.'

'What if we can't do it that fast?' I asked.

Ev cocked her head to the side. 'Are you worrying again, Miss Mabel?' She looked back at me. 'All we have to do is clean it up. Make it good as new.'

The moon reemerged. I examined the old house before us – an indecipherable sign nailed to it began with the letter *B*. The building looked rickety and weatherworn in the moonlight. I had a feeling six days wasn't going to cut it. 'What happens if we can't?'

'Then I move in with my witch of a mother and you spend the summer in Oregon.'

My lungs filled with the chemical memory of perc. My feet began to ache from a phantom day of standing behind the counter. I couldn't go home – I couldn't. How could I explain my desperation to her? But then I stepped into the night, and there Ev was, in the flesh, smelling of tea roses. She threw her arms wide to envelop me.

'Welcome home,' she murmured. 'Welcome to Bittersweet.'

CHAPTER SIX

The Window

WHEN MY EYES OPENED that first morning in the cottage they called Bittersweet, shadows of tree branches danced across the bead board ceiling in time with the glug of water in the cove below. Out the window, I could see a nuthatch hopping up and down the trunk of a red pine, chirping in celebration of his grubby breakfast. The Vermont air was cool and I was alone.

Arriving under cover of darkness had given a disappointing first impression, made worse by the threat of Birch's inspection and my fate in the face of our failure. The house had seemed all dingy fixtures and shabby, unmatched furniture, touched everywhere with the scent of mildew; all I saw was work.

But I understood now, as I took in the shining brass beds in the morning, the crisp cotton duvet covers, and the faint scent of coffee wafting in from the kitchen, that this was a quiet place, a country place, a place of baguettes and pink grapefruit and spreadable honeycomb, idyllic and sun-drenched in a way I had never known, but of which I had long been dreaming.

Ev's bed, the twin of my own, lay empty under the opposite window, rumpled sheets cast aside. From the light and birdsong, I could guess it was no later than eight. In the nine months I had lived with Ev, I had never once seen her up before ten. I called her name twice, but there was no reply. I puzzled for a few moments over her whereabouts, before lying back and closing my eyes, willing more delicious sleep. It refused me.

I felt a hint of desire. I listened long and hard. I was truly alone. And so I (shyly, bravely) put my hand down between my legs and felt myself grow wet. I knew there was a risk Ev might barge through the door any second, so I told myself to hold still, to move only one finger, to feign sleep. It is strange how such restrictions heighten one's desire, but there it is. Soon my fingers were buried deep and I was in another world.

I tried to remember to listen. But there were always a few moments in which even I could not be cautious enough to subdivide my mind. I threw off the covers and felt that private wildness inside me rise up and carry me over a great, shivering chasm of joy, the only unbridled pleasure I knew.

It took time to recover myself. Afterward, I lay there, legs splayed, eyes closed, grateful for the warmth inside of me, until I felt the particular sensation of being watched. I lifted my eyes to the window just above Ev's bed.

There, framed by wood and glass, was the face of a man.

His eyes were glazed over.

His mouth was agape.

I screamed. He ducked. I covered my whole self with the quilt. I laughed, horrified, nearly suffocating under the duvet. Almost burst into tears. Peeked out from beneath the quilt again. The window was empty. Had there really been someone there? Oh god. A new level of humiliation. I would never forget the look on his face – a mix of lust (I hoped) and horror (more likely). He'd been freckled. Dirty blond hair. I could feel myself blushing from head to toe. When I got up the nerve, I strode to the window, wrapped in the comforter, and wrestled the resistant, dusty blind down into submission before dressing myself with nunlike modesty. Maybe they'd kick me out of Winloch before we even got to the inspection.

Ev returned an hour later, moss tangling her locks. She smelled like a child who'd been playing in the forest, and her face bloomed with a smile she was doing her best to hide. Eager for distraction, I offered to cook, but she insisted I sit at the oilcloth-covered kitchen table and let her do the work for once, a dubious allowance, since I knew that she could hardly boil water without setting the kettle on fire. As she bustled about the white metal cabinets, art deco refrigerator with a heavy, ka-thunking door pull, and dirty seafoam-green linoleum curling up at the edges, my fingers traced the repeating, once-vibrant pattern of blackberries and gingham that had protected the table during someone else's breakfasts, lunches, and dinners.

The kitchen had once been the short part of the L that made up the porch, and it retained the casement windows from its earlier life as a sunroom. Because the waist-to-ceiling panes overlooked the Bittersweet cove, what might have been a gloomy room glittered, making it the most beautiful spot in the cottage. But I resisted the view, keeping my back to the woods and water, remembering, with fresh embarrassment, the feeling of that man's eyes upon me. He was out there, somewhere. What was to keep him from telling? The hairs on the back of my neck stood on end.

'Galway said he met you this morning,' Ev mentioned, casually clicking on the stove's pilot light to heat the green enamel percolator set on the back burner. My pulse began to race. That man in the window was the only person I'd seen all day. Did she know? Had he told her? Had she read my mind?

'He's pretty awkward,' she said apologetically. She glanced at me for a moment, catching the expression on my face. 'Was he awful to you?'

'What'd he say?' I managed to squeak.

Ev rolled her eyes. 'Galway doesn't say anything unless it serves his own political gains.' I breathed a sigh of relief as she babbled on. 'Don't worry, he's only coming up weekends.' She rolled her eyes conspiratorially, as if I had any idea what she was talking about. 'Now you know firsthand why he's terrible with women,' she chirped, as I resolved simply never to see Galway again, whoever he was, while Ev went on to tell me how ill-equipped her brothers were for any kind of love, even though two of the three of them had managed to find wives. But Galway would be a bachelor forever, although she was almost positive he wasn't gay, he seemed extremely hetero to her, mostly because he was an asshole, and if she was going to pick one of them to be gay she would have picked fussy Athol, although Banning was such a pleasure seeker (this is how I gathered, with horror, that Galway was her brother) – and then she served me a burned scrambled egg and lukewarm, bitter coffee, rendered drinkable only after I added a healthy slug from a dented can of condensed milk found on the shelf above the sink, and gave dictation on the provisions and products we would need John to pick up in town for the coming days of cleaning.

Even then, I was glad I'd come.

CHAPTER SEVEN

The Cleanup

T HE COTTAGE EV STOOD to inherit had been inhabited, until her demise the previous summer, by Ev's
great-aunt Antonia Winslow. Although Ev insisted the
ancient woman hadn't actually died in the house, it was easy
to imagine that the yellowed piles of papers that lined every
room, or the permeating combination of animal urine and
mildew that radiated from the furniture, or the sulfuric smell
bubbling from the pipes every time we turned on the water,
might well have conspired to bring about her end.

I expected Ev to be overwhelmed in the face of such
disrepair, but she seemed energized by the challenge of it.
I thought I'd be the one to teach her that newspapers and
a touch of vinegar were best for windows, or that you diluted
the Pine-Sol in a bucket of warm water, but her years spent
getting into trouble at boarding school had taught her plenty
about deep and thorough cleaning. Covered in dust after
spending three hours sorting and binding the papers from
the living room, I asked her, 'Why do you have to clean
this place?' After all, the Winslows could afford the help;
this backbreaking labor seemed to contradict everything that
photograph above my desk had appeared to promise.

'We believe in hard work,' she said, tucking a piece of hair
back into the bandanna she'd tied over her head. 'It's tradition:

when we turn eighteen, we're each offered a cottage – usually the oldest, dirtiest one available. And then it's up to us to make it livable. To prove ourselves.' She frowned. 'It's been the big joke that when it's my turn I won't be able to hack it.' And then she met my eyes. 'But they're wrong, aren't they?'

Her vulnerability hit me in the gut. I knew what it was to be doubted. To need to prove yourself. 'Of course they're wrong.' And so, for the next six days, we both went to town on that cottage and its five little rooms – bedroom, bathroom, living room, kitchen, sunporch – as though our lives, and not merely our summers, depended on it.

Once we'd cleared away the superficial mess (even if the backbreaking labor didn't feel superficial), it became apparent that Bittersweet was a tidy cottage, good-boned after a hundred years, even if its musculature showed its age. On blustery nights, the wind sang through invisible gaps between the casements and their frames. The off-white bead board walls had been slapped with paint dozens of times, rendering the grooves between some of the slats all but nonexistent. What furniture we were able to salvage was mismatched: in one corner of the living room, a wooden chair with a fraying straw seat waited humbly before a nicked mahogany desk that had once been part of a grander household, while in the other corner, a sagging red chair with cotton spilling from its split corduroy upholstery held the distinguished position as most coveted reading spot in the house.

On our second afternoon, John returned with the groceries we'd ordered. He had delivered our box of cleaning products the previous day with what I took to be silent grudgingness, but when I'd asked Ev about it she'd replied, 'It's his job,' which was how I'd found out he was a servant.

Lest Ev confuse me with the help, I let her and John unload while I sank into the red chair with a glass of lemonade. I watched Abby drop a browned, balding tennis ball onto Bittersweet's uneven floorboards, painted a flaking Portuguese blue. The ball rolled in a straight line toward the crumbling brick fireplace, with its tarnished brass andirons, before inexplicably turning around the curve of a faded rag rug and heading north, toward the dimly lit wooden bathroom, with its stained sink and pull-chain toilet.

Abby's ears twitched with excitement as she traced the ball's trajectory. She panted as though it were alive, but I held her back, fascinated to see where it would end up if we left it alone. Sure enough, it hit upon a burl, cascading east again and nearly into the cottage's bedroom before plunging, along the line of a sunken floorboard, straight south toward the cove, back across my path, through the close living room, and into the jewel of the kitchen. I jumped up and followed. The old ball pinged against the metal cabinet that housed the deep porcelain sink, then through the doorway that separated kitchen from living room. On this new, northwest course, it headed into the screened-in porch, with its worn wicker couch, half-patched screens that allowed in the whistling breeze, and private view of the watery cove below.

The ball landed at John's feet as he stepped through the yawning screen door. He picked it up and tossed it outside. Abby gamely followed. 'Why'd you let her in here?' he asked crossly.

I hadn't.

John dumped the last bag on the kitchen table and headed back out onto the porch just as Ev came through the doorway. Her body blocked his way. She jutted her hip out playfully. He sidestepped, pretending to ignore her, lifting a piece of mail off one of the many stacks of newspapers, rain-warped and moldy, that lined the porch.

'Antonia Winslow,' he intoned in an attempt at a Waspy voice, before dropping the paper back onto the pile and making a move toward the door, then reached for his jacket pocket. 'Right, I forgot.' He pulled out three bolts just like the one I'd seen on Ev's Manhattan bedroom door.

A cloud passed over Ev's face. 'You're not serious.'

'You want to get me fired?'

Ev sighed. John left to get his tools from the truck.

'What're those for?' I asked once he was gone.

Ev rolled her eyes. 'My mother is terrified of bears.'

John returned and set to work, drilling holes and turning screws into the wooden frame. The muscles in his arms rippled as he worked, and I realized Ev and I were watching him in mutual, unabashed wonder. The glazed expression on her face reminded me of what Galway had looked like at the window, and I slipped into the kitchen as I felt myself turn scarlet.

It wasn't until later that night, long after John had whistled to Abby and gunned his engine into the afternoon, that I noticed the other two bolts now installed on the insides of the bedroom and bathroom doors. Bears? Really?

With every inch of Bittersweet I cleaned, I came to know it as my own. I shoved armfuls of Antonia Winslow's personal papers into garbage bags already filled with decades of other abandoned piles: calendars, shopping lists, newspapers. I sorted the magazines into their own pile, aching for the day I could flip through them. I lugged the garbage bags down to the crawl space below the porch to store them until we could make a trip to the dump and properly recycle them.

'Just think of when we're old ladies,' Ev said, as she scrubbed at the grout around the kitchen sink, knuckles bleeding. 'We'll sit on the porch and drink martinis.' My heart leapt when I realized what she was promising – a lifetime of Winloch. And so I joined her. As I scraped flaky paint from the windowsills, I admired our view out of the warped windowpanes, through which the straight trunks curved and parried whenever I moved my head. I braved rickety chairs to poke a rag-covered broom handle at the decades-old cobwebs hanging above the fireplace book-shelves. I bent before the cabinet underneath the bathroom sink, sorting through glass bottles and aluminum jars that held dried-up calamine lotion and the lingering camphor of Noxzema. We were positively nineteenth century, bundling up all the linens and sending them out to be washed, concocting strange recipes to use up the canned peas, Spam, and cream of mushroom soup that had been stashed on the pine shelves in the kitchen long enough to accumulate a thick layer of dust. Ev gobbled down the expired food as if it were caviar. Whereas for me, such meals brought up bad memories, for her, it was a point of pride – for the first time in her life, she was eating what she had earned.

48

CHAPTER EIGHT

The Stroll

O N THE FOURTH DAY, it rained. The constant patter was comforting, the best memory I'd brought from the Pacific Northwest. Though the cottage uttered small complaints against the gusts buffeting up from the cove, the roof did not leak (save for a spot in the bathroom, but that was nothing a rusty, pinging Sanka can couldn't fix), and the damp air wafting in from the screen porch somehow made our cleaning feel all the more appreciated.

It was good to roll up my sleeves and see results. But it wasn't lost on me that part of why I was burrowing, so gamely, into the cleaning – beyond the time alone with Ev and what my elbow grease might secure for me – was that it gave me a reason to hide. I could taste the humiliation anew every time I thought of Ev's brother's face in the window. Saturday loomed, when Birch would descend and give us the thumbs-up or -down. As the week drew to a close, I comforted myself in knowing I wouldn't have to step beyond the walls of Bittersweet at least until after our inspector arrived.

But on the fifth day, after Ev tromped in from her morning walk and declared, 'I've decided that I'm much better as an early bird than a night owl, so from now on, I shall go to bed at ten o'clock sharp' (which we both knew was a lie but which we nodded at together in fiendish denial), she further announced, 'And I'm going to scrape the porch on my own today, so you're free, free, free!' I realized that what she was saying in her Ev way was that she wanted the cottage to herself, and, although I took the news somewhat grudgingly, I had known all along that I'd have to leave Bittersweet someday. It was Friday morning. If Ev was right about Galway only coming up on weekends, then he wasn't at Winloch yet. A stroll through the woods wouldn't do me any harm, and I'd get to finally explore the place I'd been dreaming of and, yes, researching, for months.

Although Vermont is frigid in the winter, its summertime shimmers. That's stating the obvious to anyone who knows New England, but it was my brave new world. The mud season that begins in March and lasts well through May buffers one's mind from winter's ravages, so that, by the glorious day when neon-green leaf buds first appear on every tree, one can barely remember the bitter February winds streaming off the lake in great, frigid sloughs. Every year, the lake freezes solid around the shoreline, groaning and cracking under the push of the shifting wind, but, in the century-long life of Winloch, the winter had been heard only by the workingmen, men called in to plow the roads, or plumb frozen pipes, men who had the north country in their blood and the dried-up curl of French Canadian on their tongues. Winloch was a summer place, built of pine and screen and not much else, and the Winslows its only, rarefied, inhabitants.

It had been that way for over a century. Ev's great-great-grandfather Samson Winslow, 1850–1931, paterfamilias

– captured in black-and-white photographs, arms akimbo, on the deck of a sloop, in front of a bank, beside his blushing bride – looked at once a dinosaur and a modern man. Only the clothes set him back. The shape of his face – high cheekbones, wry smile – was full of twentieth-century vigor. His mother was Scottish, his father a Brit, and his was iron money, invested in coal money, invested in oil money. Once Samson had made himself a good fortune, he moved his young family to a grand manse in Burlington proper, washed the coal dust and sticky oil from his hands in the limpid lake, and bought himself a tract of farmland that stretched beside its waters. The lake, laid out at the foot of the Green Mountains that gave Vermont its name, reminded him of the lochs of his mother's homeland. He married that name with his own, and called his paradise Winloch.

Even though the tract Samson obtained was only fifteen miles from town – practically next door, in our car-choked era – in his day, getting there required a migration. White winters were passed in the banks of Burlington and Boston, tranquil summers on sailboats that skimmed the depths. And in between, a twice-yearly trek, first in buggies, then in Model Ts, of wives, sons, daughters, dogs, dresses, chairs, apples, potatoes, novels, tennis rackets. And a twice-weekly delivery of groceries.

Samson envisaged a village peopled with Winslows in the land he named Winloch. He had hundreds of meadowed and forested acres to work with, and set out to build the Dining Hall with his own two hands (he was helped by those same workingmen who braved the roofline and replaced burst pipes, but to mention them was to lessen the

Winloch mythology). The cottages sprouted up, in turn, around the great hall, like the plants they were named for – Trillium and Queen Anne's Lace and Bittersweet and Goldenrod and Chicory – and were soon peopled with Samson's descendants and their companions: a parade of loyal, soggy Labradors, Newfoundlands, Jack Russells, and a few memorably morose basset hounds, ears permanently sodden from their daily wades.

Soon, dinghies littered the low-lying sandstone outcroppings and the rocky beaches of the shoreline. As more land became available, Winloch acquired it, so that, by the time Samson's great-great-great-grandchildren were learning how to swim off the docks that stretched like fingers from the thirty-some-odd cottages into the water, the compound occupied two miles of the shore of Lake Champlain in sheltered Winslow Bay, a favorite of the mooring yachts down from Canada.

I had gathered a few of these snippets from Ev and her nonchalant boarding school friends who'd visited us during the spring, but those conversations had mostly centered on which of Ev's cousins was cutest or the nearest place you could drive for underage booze. Once I felt sure Ev's invitation was airtight, I conducted my own research, a stealthy interlibrary loan with the help of my friend Janice the librarian, and *Samson Winslow: The Man, the Dream, the Vision* and *The Burlington Winslows* both found their ways from northern libraries into my hands. I'd spent one damp March weekend in the gothic Reserve Room of the college library, poring over photographs of Winloch in the early part of the twentieth century, as rain lashed the windows in a satisfying thrum. Samson had been aptly named – his hair was so positively mane-like toward the end of his life that one couldn't help wonder if his idyll would have crumbled had his locks been cut. He seemed to my imagination to be the sort of man who'd loom large in family stories, but the few times I dared prompt Ev for a really great Samson tale she'd rolled her eyes and muttered a 'You're so weird.'

It had stopped raining, but I slipped on Ev's muddy rubber boots at the back door and made my way down the narrow path that led to Bittersweet Cove, our private bit of lake. It was a small cove, hugged on three sides by wooded, rocky land. A stairway cut down to the small beach directly below the kitchen, or one could take a more precarious route – continuing along the left arm of the hug on slippery pine needles (and, after a rainstorm, diminutive mudslides) and, finally, out onto a low, flat rock just above the waterline that offered one a magnificent view of the outer bay. That was my intended destination, but, as I slid and cursed, the rubber boots offering no traction, I was startled at the sight of a slender, magnificent creature skimming along the surface of the larger lake, then alighting, soundlessly, upon the very spot I'd been aiming for.

The bird stood perfectly still. A great blue heron. We'd had them at the river back in Oregon, but they'd always looked so scrappy. This one belonged here. Long lines, calm face, elegant – a Winslow. The heron regarded me coldly, reminding me of how Ev had merely tolerated my presence in the early months we'd shared a room, before Jackson's death had brought us close. I watched until the bird's long wingspan silently lifted it away. I dug my muddy toes in and climbed back up the embankment, backsliding with nearly every step.

I resolved to climb down again when the land was dry. As soon as the wind was warmer, and didn't send me goose bumps off the surface of the water, I would swim off the heron's rock. Even though it seemed hard to imagine it would ever be hot enough to want to swim – the summer was still newly born – I'd liked the running Ev and I had done in New York, and the new strength in my legs. I needed a bathing suit, and the confidence to pull it over flesh that had never known the sun, because this was the kind of place where one swam boldly, daily, and made a body one had never had.

I set out back up the dirt road John had driven us down that first night. It curved more sharply than I remembered, so that soon Bittersweet was out of sight, and all I could see were maples, pine, and sky. The fresh leaves shook down drops of water in little bursts, and crows cawed at each other somewhere atop the trees – a jarring, comical sound, too common for this beautiful place. I had worn the cashmere, but soon it was tied around my waist. The rain had washed the world clean. Rafts of freshly cut grass began to filter down the road, followed by the sound of a lawn mower.

As I caught sight of the Dining Hall – which I now knew was the great white structure looming at the intersection of the Bittersweet driveway and the main Winloch road – I saw a phalanx of workingmen sweeping the tennis courts, cinching the nets, mowing the lawn, and hammering at loose nails on the wide wooden steps leading up to the building. Two compact white pickups were parked along the side of the road, their flatbeds filled with tools and gathered branches, matching insignias painted on their doors: a yellow dragon, with the talons of an eagle, grasping a set of arrows. The coat of arms matched the flag that one of the men was now hoisting up the Dining Hall pole. I stood in the middle of the road and watched him pull it into place.

I was just deciding whether I wanted to cut back into the woods beyond the Dining Hall when three dachshunds, yapping sharply, appeared from the undergrowth on the other side of the road. They surrounded me, their assault ridiculous. At first. But every time I tried to step away, they growled and shifted to form a new circle of containment. They were small, and I wasn't afraid, but there was nowhere to go.

'Come back, assholes!' Soon, from out of the forest, burst a tall, sharp woman, Ev in another life. A good fifty years older, the woman was not as striking as Ev, and she wore a god-awful hand-crocheted poncho that Ev wouldn't have been caught dead in, but they were unmistakably related.

'Oh dear god,' she barked, marching toward me full steam, bending down and yanking the ringleader by the collar. 'Fritz, leave the goddamn girl alone,' she commanded, and Fritz ceased yapping at once, which quieted the other two dogs. Soon they were snuffling through the newly mown grass as though I didn't exist at all.

She started laughing, big and raucous. 'That must've scared the shit out of you.'

'I didn't think anyone else was here.'

'Drove up last night,' she confided, taking my arm in hers. 'Come to tea.'

CHAPTER NINE

The Aunt

Ev's aunt linden – who introduced herself as Indo – lived to the right and over a hill, in a part of Winloch I didn't know existed, a long, well-trimmed meadow where the oldest cottages sat, four in a row. At the farthest end of the meadow was the largest house I'd seen at Winloch; white, with multiple stories and a porch that stretched around its four ample sides. I recognized it from the picture that had hung in our dorm room. The other three cottages were siblings of Bittersweet, each small and block-like, one story high. Transplanted white pines tastefully disguised the poles carrying electricity to each home.

It wasn't hard to guess which house was Indo's. Cherry red, with a moss-covered roof, the first little cottage leaned to the left upon its foundation. A bathtub planted with impatiens occupied its small front lawn, mowed from the meadow. According to the faded, hand-painted sign pasted in the window of the door, it was called Clover.

'Leave your shoes,' Indo indicated as she let me into a kitchen smelling of sandalwood and cayenne. Fritz and his compatriots trotted right past me, faithful in their owner's assessment of my trustworthiness. I pulled Ev's boots off, balancing them upon a tangle of clogs in the corner.

From the peaked roof above me hung a dozen baskets covered in thick dust. A glass-fronted cabinet, propped up on one side with a stack of shims, overflowed with china. Clipped atop it was the room's sole light, a bulb set inside an aluminum funnel, with which a construction crew might have illumined a work site. The kitchen itself seemed haphazardly collected, as though Indo had gone into a handful of homes with a hacksaw and helped herself to an Edwardian porcelain sink here, a particleboard shelving unit there. And where the impulse, under someone else's directive, would have been to use the cutout above the sink to pass food between the kitchen and living room, in Clover, it served as a repository for more stuff – two dozen wooden spoons, a precariously stacked collection of teal earthenware, and a great green tin of Bag Balm.

I followed the older woman into the living room, watching her long gray braid snake across her back. 'It's not much,' she prattled, 'but it's all I have. Must sound melodramatic to a pretty young thing like you. But I'm afraid it's true, this eyesore is everything to me. And who knows how long it'll be before it's taken from me too. What's that saying? "It's not whether you get screwed but if you have fun while it's happening." Something like that, but pithier.'

She spoke as though we had known each other forever, and I hid my discomfort with such unearned intimacies by taking in the rest of her home. Clover's walls, like Bittersweet's, were made of bead board, but whereas Ev's cottage was painted a silty white, Indo had embraced color: scarlet paint on the walls; an indigo, batiked cloth tossed over a sofa whose fourth leg was a stack of water-rippled paperbacks; a chair upholstered in seventies tangerine floral. Through two sets of French doors along the second and third of the living room's adjoining walls, the screen porch looked out over the lake.

'But listen to me, going on about myself. It's you I want to hear about. You look sparky. I like that about you. Do you need to pee? No, that's fine. Right through that door on the left.'

I followed her directions into a short hallway that led to two small bedrooms. I peeked into both of them in search of the toilet, and was surprised to discover that whereas the rest of Indo's home seemed funky and youthful, her pastel bedroom looked like it had been decorated by the old woman she seemed to have avoided becoming. Mosquito netting modestly shielded the bed, which was draped with a chenille spread. Framed lithographs of local flowers hung on the pink walls.

I found the cottage's only bathroom, painted a glossy magenta, and learned quickly it was a primitive affair, with a cracked, too-high mirror and two sinks – the working one of which was turned on by a permanently affixed set of pliers – and a decoupaged toilet that swayed dismayingly whenever weight was set upon it.

Throughout Clover, the wooden walls – no matter their color – were decorated with black-and-white pictures, either framed and askew or curled up toward the tacks that pinned them. A few of the photographs depicted landscapes (some of which I could recognize right out the window), but, for the most part, the subjects were children: blond, sinewy, strong. I scrutinized the faces, recognizing

Indo herself as a young girl, and a tall, proud boy who had Birch's eyes.

'You like my pictures?' Indo chuckled through the kitchen cutout as she busied herself over the stove.

'You took these?' My eyes ran over the taut bodies sunning themselves in old-fashioned bathing suits.

'My mother bought me a camera for my tenth birthday. I was a hobbyist.'

'And now?' I asked, discovering a newer photograph, of a beaming toddler who might have been Ev.

'Art is for the young,' Indo declared, and a long silence fell upon us for the first time.

Every nook and cranny of Indo's living room was filled: books, masks, and little carved boxes from all over the world. A collection of birds' nests was displayed on what she called a whatnot shelf of driftwood and wind-felled pine. The sheer quantity of accumulated goods was no far cry from my mother's Hummel figurines and salt and pepper shaker collection. Whereas breezy Bittersweet felt like a foreign country, Clover, with its alarmingly creaky floors, damp smell, and myriad collections, made me feel homesick for the first time.

Indo emerged from the kitchen with a clinking tea tray. She ordered the dogs down to their ancient pillow on the living room floor, in front of the cold woodstove, then led me onto the side porch, where a long table and moldy wicker chairs awaited us. It was brighter out there, and I squinted as my eyes adjusted to the glare of the sun upon the lake. She served a strong pot of smoky Lapsang souchong beside rye toast dripping margarine; if I'd known her well, I would

60

have teased her that it had taken her so long to make such a simple snack.

She seemed to read my mind. 'I'll be pleased as punch when they open the goddamn Dining Hall – I am not a cook. And the Dining Hall's free. Only good part about the Winloch Constitution – all you can eat. Oh, but look at you, poor thing, I've made you glum. Well, I won't be the one to tell you Winloch is anything but heaven on earth.'

'You should eat with us,' I proposed.

'Might want to ask Ev first,' she warned, but when I blushed as I remembered my place, she was tongue-tied for the first time. 'I meant— Oh dear.' She placed her hand over mine as if we'd known each other for years. 'I meant to say that Ev doesn't like me much.'

But I found that hard to believe. Indo was a character, sure, her mismatched socks and moth-nibbled man's sweater told you that right off the bat, but she was irreverent and honest, traits which I had seen Ev love in others. As soon as she found out I was a reader, she wanted to talk books, and, seeing my goose bumps rise in the broad southerly wind coming off the bay, she brought me an afghan off the back of the couch. We passed the afternoon on *Wuthering Heights* and *To the Lighthouse,* my limbs wrapped in the scratchy wool. I told her about my mother's love of line dancing – it wasn't much, but it was more than I'd ever told Ev – and, in turn, she described her junior year abroad in Paris and the love affair that had ended with a kiss beside the Seine. I gathered she was lonely and, in the way of those the world has left behind, fiercely attached to her solitude while quick to blame the world – and her family – for her isolation. But I didn't mind being in her company. My week as Ev's scullery maid had made it lovely to simply enjoy someone without the threat of impending expulsion. We drank many pots of tea, and I made many trips to Indo's jury-rigged toilet in the exuberant bathroom, and it wasn't until I noticed the long shadows moving across the lawn that I realized the day was almost gone.

'I think we've become friends,' Indo said when I told her I should be going. 'Do you feel that?'

'Of course,' I replied.

'It may be "of course" to you, but I don't have many friends. Don't get me wrong, that's my own goddamn fault, but it means I'm afraid I don't often get the chance to connect with people like you. People who are trustworthy, and kind and—'

'Thank you.' I felt myself grow hot under her compliments.

But she went on. 'You see, when you find you don't have anyone to trust, it makes you greedy. Here I am, in this little rat's nest of mine, gathering my things around me, sure at any minute it'll all be taken from me—'

'I can't imagine anyone taking this from you. It's your home.'

'Who'd want it, right?' She laughed, gesturing to the chaos around her. 'Who indeed. Perhaps you're right. Or perhaps a friend will climb out of the woodwork and present herself to me, help me in my time of need, just when fate comes to screw me after all. A friend like you: brave and bold.'

I squirmed in my seat as her eyes bored into me. 'I'm neither of those things. Really.'

But Indo wasn't deterred. 'I guarantee that if your mettle was tested you'd be surprised. Indubitably surprised at how resourceful you are.' She sat back. The wicker creaked underneath her. 'And you know, you might be surprised what you'd gain by even trying to help someone like little old me.'

I knew I was being manipulated into asking, but I couldn't help myself. 'Like what?'

She smiled. Spread her arms wide, indicating all her possessions, and the house around her. 'Like this.'

'Like your house?' I asked incredulously.

She nodded.

'But it's your house. The one you're afraid someone is going to take from you. And anyway, you don't know me. And what do you need help with?' I sounded irritated, I knew, but I was beginning to feel trapped by her rhetoric.

'After this afternoon spent together, I know you infinitely better than any of my nieces. I can see that your mind moves like quicksilver, and I admire that. And you know when to bite your tongue.'

'You're being very kind,' I said, scooting my chair out so I could stand. I felt dizzy, as though a spell had been put on me.

'It's not kindness. It's fact.'

'Really,' I protested, my voice rising without my permission, 'I'm not the kind of person you think I am. I'm not. I'm not brave at all. I've been tested, I promise you I have.' I stopped myself from going on.

But I'd said enough for Indo. She leaned back in her chair and narrowed her eyes at me. 'I see.'

63

'This was such a nice afternoon.' I gathered up the dishes. 'Let's do it again soon.'

She shook her head. 'I didn't peg you as a girl plagued by self-doubt.' She rose from the table, muttering. 'Well then, perhaps it's better – yes, it's better to let you find your own way.'

'Thank you so much for your hospitality,' I said primly, striding back inside.

She caught up with me in the kitchen as I stepped into Ev's boots. 'Mother always told me I shouldn't force what takes its own time.' She caught my arm. Her fingers gripped me with a strength I couldn't have guessed at. It was then that I noticed six locks lining the inside of the back door, chains dangling, bolts pushed back, padlocks undone. I would have chalked them up to Indo's eccentricities if I hadn't seen John install the bolts in Bittersweet.

Indo followed my gaze and took in the locks as though she, too, was seeing them for the first time. Quickly, she pushed the door open, hustling me outside.

'I've been looking for a friend like you for a while,' she persisted. 'Someone interested in stories. You're interested in stories, aren't you? You see, I've been trying to locate a manila folder . . . I'm sure you're aware we have a family collection of artwork . . .'

'Yes,' I answered, glad to be outside again. She was still talking, but I was distracted by the softness of the late afternoon. The drone of the mower continued from over the hill – the landscapers were still at it.

'The Winslows have pretty incredible tales,' she pressed on. 'They're just sitting up there, in the attic of the Dining

Hall, waiting in boxes. Samson's papers, his son's, it's really worth looking at. You could keep an eye out for that folder I need, and find an interesting tale or two to make your own.'

'Sure,' I said, 'okay,' eager to placate her as I waved good-bye, even if I had no idea what she'd meant by 'that folder,' wondering if Ev was worried about me. We had so much to do before the next day's inspection.

A damp and droopy Abby, tongue lolling from a day in the water, met me on the Bittersweet road. She gamely licked my hand, but it wasn't until I got to Bittersweet that I noticed John's truck, parked behind the cottage, out of sight.

'Hello?' I called.

The screen door swung open, and John strode down from the porch, brushing past me. 'You guys had a leak,' he said, not looking me in the eye, calling Abby to him, hopping into the truck and gunning the engine. He was off in a matter of seconds.

'What was that about?' I asked when I found Ev on her hands and knees scouring the porch, her hair tied back in her bandanna.

'Huh?' she asked dreamily.

I pointed in John's direction, noticing, with disappointment, that the porch was in the exact state I'd left it that morning.

'Oh, right. We had a leak.'

CHAPTER TEN

The Inspection

THE WINSLOWS DESCENDED THAT third June Saturday like bees to the hive. The sun was high in the sky by the time Tilde and Birch arrived at our door. Ev and I were sprawled on the porch couch, exhausted – we'd finished mopping at 4:00 a.m. and allowed ourselves only a few hours of sleep, lest we miss the knock. At the sound of nearing footsteps, Ev perked up, grabbing a copy of *Catcher in the Rye* and focusing on a random page with rapt attention. I put down *Paradise Lost*, bookmarking the page I'd been trying to decode for a good hour. My heart was in my throat.

Birch had seemed easygoing the first time I met him. I had a hard time imagining him a harsh critic, but I was nervous nonetheless, if only because Ev seemed to be. 'Hello, Mr Winslow,' I began, adopting a formal tone, as he knocked his boat shoes against the doorframe. I assumed he wouldn't remember me, but he strode into the house and slung his arm about me immediately, insisting I call them by their first names, boasting to Tilde about my GPA before even looking in Ev's direction. Left to each other, Ev and Tilde hugged perfunctorily, as though terrified their bodies might actually touch. Tilde's passing glance over her daughter's unbrushed hair made me glad I'd gotten dressed.

'You smell like dog,' Ev said, wrinkling up her nose as she pulled back from her mother.

I winced. When my father was provoked, he spewed venom. I held my breath, waiting for the same from Tilde.

But instead of lashing out, Tilde seemed cheered. She turned to Birch and demanded, 'Can't Indo be made to keep those horrible creatures on lead?'

Birch strode into the kitchen. The whole cottage seemed to sigh under the weight of his footsteps. I held my breath as I watched him go, praying he'd be impressed by the Windexed windows, the lack of clutter. 'I don't think Indo can be made to do anything' was his answer when he returned with a cup of coffee. I was glad I'd been the one to brew it that morning.

I smiled, thinking of Fritz and his compatriots surrounding me.

'I see you've met my sister.'

'She's certainly a character,' I answered, feeling an ounce of betrayal as a mocking tone crossed my lips.

'It's not hard to be a responsible pet owner,' Tilde remarked sourly. 'Madeira and Harvey come when we call, and when our angels are on the rocks, we leash the poor creatures. Besides, I think it's torture to bring a dog that isn't a swimmer here, but what do I know? We've got dachshunds and corgis and greyhounds up the wazoo. Whatever happened to a good old-fashioned water spaniel, that's what I'd like to know.'

Birch shook his head. 'I'm not about to waste the next year of my life on a leash bylaw that'll be fought by more than half the board.'

'Anyway,' Ev chipped in, 'everyone loves it when Abby shows up – we wouldn't want her leashed.'

Tilde arched one eyebrow.

'Abby is our handyman's yellow Lab,' Birch explained, thinking he was filling me in. 'Come to think of it, she's a lot like John – loyal—'

'Dumb,' Tilde added.

'Mum!' Ev harrumphed.

'Temper temper,' Tilde scolded, lifting her eyes to the ceiling. They narrowed. I followed her gaze – she'd found the only cobweb we'd missed. As Ev fumed beside me, I watched Tilde take in the porch – windows, floor, ceiling – and realized that Birch wasn't the one doing the inspection. Oh sure, he'd stay, and he'd be the one to issue the verdict. But this was Tilde's game. She nodded approvingly at the already installed bolt, and I thanked John silently for taking that into his own hands. But her foot touched on a loose board and she frowned.

'Would you like to see the kitchen?' I asked, gesturing into the house.

'I'm glad one of you remembers your manners,' Tilde sniffed, and, as I followed her off the porch and into the house, I turned and shot Ev a look that meant buck up and start smiling.

Tilde declaimed. The kitchen needed new appliances and a new floor, 'and for god's sake, get rid of this hideous table.' The living room furniture was 'unlivable,' the beds were probably crawling with 'god knows what kind of vermin,' the bathroom was 'atrocious.' As the list of 'necessary fixes' reached a page and more, I noticed Ev begin to disengage. Weariness replaced annoyance. By the time we were back in the living room, from the defeated look in Ev's eye, I half expected her to toss the keys to her father and volunteer to give up Bittersweet herself. Birch looked on with a distracted smile, nodding when prodded, agreeing with Tilde as she shook her head at the sad state of affairs, offering a sympathetic pat to Ev before he excused himself to the bathroom.

'Aren't you going to offer us a cold beverage?' Tilde demanded when we'd covered every square inch of the house. I retreated into the kitchen, grateful for a break. That woman made my mother look like a carefree soul.

'Have you been in for a dip yet? Is it cold?' she queried as I brought in a tray of lemonade and Ritz crackers, placing it on the rickety bench we'd pulled from the side of the house. There wasn't enough seating, and Tilde had taken the armchair for herself, so I sat beside the food. The bench swayed precariously. Birch had been in the bathroom for a while, relieved, I imagined, to get a break from the female politics.

'I have,' Ev responded. 'I don't think Mabel's much of a swimmer.' I opened my mouth to protest – I had shivered my way through a waist-high wade during one of Ev's dawn forays – but, before I could say anything, Ev demanded from me, 'Have you thought about changing your name? Even just to Maybelle, and then we could call you May for short; it just suits her so much better, don't you think, Mum?'

Only one person had ever called me Maybelle. Involuntary

tears filled my eyes. I crammed a Ritz into my mouth. Salt. Butter.

'It's Winloch,' I heard Tilde respond. 'She can go by anything she wants.'

I told myself to get it together. Chew. Swallow. Sit up straight. Be sweet.

Ev took a sip of coffee. 'When's Lu coming?'

'Our baby girl,' Birch explained, returning from the bathroom.

'You have a baby?' I asked. Ev had mentioned only older brothers.

Tilde's laugh erupted sharply. 'Well, it's not outside the realm of possibility.'

'Jesus, Mum,' Ev said, 'not everything is a comment on how old you look.'

'She's in Switzerland, dear,' Tilde replied testily. 'At tennis camp.'

'The one you sent me to?' Ev asked in an innocent voice. 'Where that twenty-five-year-old deflowered me?'

I nearly choked on my coffee. Birch pounded me on the back, and, by the time I'd regained myself, Tilde was already out the screen door and Ev had shut herself in the bedroom.

'You girls coming for dinner tonight?' Birch asked cheerily, popping a Ritz into his mouth. 'We're having a spur-of-the-moment get-together.'

'Did we pass?' I blurted, unable to help myself, sure my rude question was the final nail in the coffin. But he didn't answer. Just gave my shoulders an affectionate double pat and followed his wife out the door.

Twenty minutes later, Ev emerged from the bedroom, face stained with tears. I watched her pull the bolt closed on the front door. When she shut herself back into the bedroom, I heard the bolt slide closed there too. She didn't say one word.

CHAPTER ELEVEN

The Brothers

'S EE?' EV SEETHED LATER that afternoon. 'See? She's a psychopath.'

We were strolling down 'Boys' Lane,' a side road that angled off from the main thoroughfare near the Dining Hall and led to a string of three of the ubiquitous Winloch cottages.

'But when will they tell us if we get to keep Bittersweet?' I asked, gagging at the memory of my mother's chipped beef on toast, the first meal I'd be met with if I had to go home.

'You never get to know anything important, not when my mother's concerned.' Ev sighed. I bit a nail. She pulled my hand from my mouth. 'Don't worry so much!' she insisted. 'She'll be onto something else by tomorrow and forget we ever existed.' She slung her arm over my shoulder and snuffled my ear until I smiled. I understood the sentiment well: hoping your mother forgot you walked the earth. It was the one thing Ev and I shared in spades.

We came upon the first cottage, smallest and farthest from the water. 'This is Queen Anne's Lace,' Ev said. She made a face. 'It's Galway's.' My heart started pounding, and I was grateful to confirm the place was devoid of life, for his predicted absence was the only reason I'd dared accompany his sister to this side of camp.

I eyed the house – it was unpainted, the wood gray and weathered. 'I thought he came up on weekends.'

Ev rolled her eyes. 'Too busy saving the world. Don't despair, you'll see him again soon if he doesn't make it for the Midsummer Night's Feast,' but before I could ask her what that was, she sniped, 'Can you believe he chose this shack? Such a hovel. He could have had Banning's' – pointing to the cottage sitting ahead at the left end of the road – 'I mean, he is the second-born, but he can't appreciate natural beauty or something. The views are to die for over on this side.'

Soon we were before Goldenrod and Chicory, the house on the right standing at attention in crisp white, the one on the left saggier and tea-colored in a dirty, unintentional way. Beyond the cottages, through carefully thinned woods, lay a wide view of Winslow Bay – not nearly as impressive as Indo's, but something to admire. Before them, matching SUVs were piled high, hatchbacks open. Two towheads, an older boy and a younger girl, ran in shrieking circles, chased by a pair of game, harmless golden retrievers.

A tall, handsome man emerged from Chicory, his frame nearly filling the doorway. 'Hey, Sis.' He strolled over and pecked Ev on the cheek, then introduced himself as Athol.

'This is May,' she blurted. I was tongue-tied; firstborn Athol was better-looking than I'd prepared myself for, perhaps because Ev had described him as all serious business. Samson's cheekbones, crystal-blue eyes, six-foot frame – out of a propaganda photo for eating organic or running Ironman. As he extended his hand, I realized that he was the spitting image of a young, lean Birch, although he didn't radiate his father's charisma.

Athol picked his little boy up and tossed him in the air; the four-year-old shrieked in laughter. To the chubby toddler at his feet, he cajoled, 'Do your parents know you're out here?' and she huffed with resignation toward the other cottage. Soon they had all come out to greet us, Athol's equally tall and tanned wife, Emily, who explained that the baby was napping; the little boy, Ricky, being gathered by his auburn-haired, foreign au pair for an afternoon swim, water temperature be damned; Ev's other brother, Banning, balding, rotund, pulling Ev into a sloppy hug; his wife, Annie, an air of messiness in her curly hair and round face, bearing the chubby little girl, Madison, out on her hip and asking the au pair if it wouldn't be too much trouble to take Maddy along too. There were dogs too – I had begun to realize there would always be dogs: Banning and Annie's two simple-looking golden retrievers (named Dum and Dee, although, like their namesakes, they were only ever mentioned in the same breath, giving them a collective identity) and Quicksilver, an old greyhound who stuck close to Emily's side until he spotted an unfortunate squirrel and took off up the road, toward Galway's.

'Be careful,' Ev said, watching the dog's pursuit. 'Mum's on about leashes again.'

'All well and good for her,' Athol snapped. 'She doesn't have a greyhound.'

'Don't shoot the messenger,' Ev bit back, matching her eldest brother's tone.

I could already see a few fault lines in their siblinghood, but I couldn't help but feel a pang of jealousy. It was impossible to imagine being known this way, teased, taken for granted. And Ev would never ask me what it was like with my brother, because, as far as she knew, I was an only child.

Athol and Emily's summer cottage was far nicer than the year-round home I'd been raised in, and Emily proudly took me on the grand tour, explaining how over the winter the whole foundation had been lifted onto steel beams, and then, naturally, they'd decided to repaint, and redo the kitchen with Sub-Zero and Wolf appliances. The home was modernized, with every possible extravagance, although that was not the word Athol and Emily would have used to describe the chrome garbage can that opened with the wave of a hand, or the flat-screen television hung on the wall in the 'library.' Every surface in that cottage was dust-free, and, when the baby awoke, I noticed that she, too, was a perfect, tidy creature, smiling down from her mother's arms like a dewy baby bird. I liked Emily in an abstract way, but she was the kind of tall, athletic person who lived in a different stratosphere, hardly looking below her shoulders. I wondered if she'd even recognize me the next time we met.

We stepped onto Chicory's whitewashed, screened-in back porch for a bottle of Prosecco and a view of the water and the other cottage. Banning lived a jovial, disheveled life in comparison to his toned and crisp older brother, and Goldenrod seemed a messy second to the elder brother's summer home. The paint on Banning's house and porch was peeling, the screens sagging, loose with age. Plastic ride-on toys were already scattered over the back lawn, and Annie huffed around them, trying, in vain, to minimize their tacky effect upon the landscape, her hair flying up and out like some kind of alive thing. I imagined Athol and Emily had strong opinions about spending their summer so close to his brother's life and wife, and I wondered how on earth Banning had passed his mother's inspection.

Below us, at the water's edge, the poor au pair tried to keep Ricky's and Maddy's little bodies from drowning. Every few moments there was a splash of exuberance or a sharp yelp, but none of the other adults paid the sounds any mind. Nor did they help the girl when, arms laden with wriggling children and sodden towels, she trudged up toward us through the woods. Only when Quicksilver, Abby, and Dum and Dee careened at top speed down the forested embankment toward the overburdened girl did Emily stand and yell, 'Stop. Come.' On the other porch, Annie looked up obediently, as though one of the dogs herself. Quicksilver emerged hanging his head, but it fell to Annie, carrying a giant plastic ball under her arm, to rescue the au pair and the children from the rest of the exuberant canines.

Seemingly oblivious to the domestic hubbub, Athol took Ev and me into the master suite to show us the last bit of renovation. He crossed his arms skeptically and surveyed the neat, tight room. 'We wanted to expand,' he said, 'but the footprints are protected. Can't build up or out.'

'Mum doesn't want anyone's house to be as big as hers,' Ev said to me.

'Don't be petty, Genevra, it doesn't become you,' Athol scolded. He was tilting his head, scrutinizing the floor. 'It's crooked.' He turned to me. 'Doesn't it seem crooked?'

'It looks fine,' Ev said.

76

Outside, Abby wandered by. Athol's eyes followed the dog as she passed the window. 'I hate having to use John.'

'He works hard,' Ev responded evenly.

'I don't see why Father doesn't just send him off. When I'm in charge, I won't confuse backwards tradition with loyalty,' Athol grumbled, his jaw growing tight.

Out on the road, Ev fumed. 'I always think I'm going to love it here, and then I come back and I remember what they are – arrogant and thoughtless and moneygrubbing.' I nodded and agreed, and did not say that the floor had, in fact, looked a little crooked to me.

CHAPTER TWELVE

The Painting

D INNER THAT NIGHT WAS held at Trillium, the white, multistoried cottage Samson had built on the spit of Winloch beyond Indo's, on the peninsula that lay between the outer bay and Winslow Bay, with a 270-degree view of the lake. Standing on the whitewashed porch, one felt as if on a boat, ever on a set course southward. Trillium was grander than the other Winloch homes – along with its three stories and the best view, it boasted a wide, mown lawn. It had passed from man to man, father to firstborn son, through the generations: Samson to Banning the first, to Bard, then Birch. Someday it would be Athol's, and then little Ricky's. How disappointed the Winslows would have been if they'd had only daughters.

Tilde stood by the door, the first to greet us. At the sight of her, my mouth went dry – I didn't know if I could bring myself to ask someone so intimidating to give me my fate. She was dressed impeccably – crisp ivory shirt, pressed raw silk capri pants in a stunning turquoise, luscious pearls around her throat. 'Care to put on a sweater, dear?' she asked as she eyed Ev's décolletage, prominent in her coral sundress.

'Jesus, Mum.' Ev huffed past her mother and into the room within, where a crowd had already gathered. I handed Tilde the corn muffins I'd baked, each topped with its own plucked daisy. Tilde took the platter from my hands as if it was a foreign object.

'How . . . thoughtful,' she said, looking down at the muffins.

My tongue stuck against my palate – my mother had taught me one could never go wrong by bringing something to a dinner party, and Birch had used the term *spur-of-the-moment*. Besides, Ev should have said something to save me from committing a faux pas. I almost offered to take the muffins back, but just then Birch emerged from the party and clapped his hands as if in delight at the sight of me.

'Tilde! She brought cupcakes!' he exclaimed, heartily grabbing one and tearing into it with his teeth.

'You aren't supposed to eat the flower,' I apologized as I watched a petal disappear into his mouth.

He laughed heartily, clapping Tilde on the back, and, as though she were a windup doll on the fritz, her smile returned mechanically. I felt faint – I knew I had to ask them, straight out, whether Bittersweet would be ours for the summer. I didn't think I could step inside another Winloch cottage until I knew.

I cleared my throat. 'Do you mind if I ask—' I began, my voice coming out thin and shaky. 'I just mean, if I need to buy a ticket home . . .'

'You're not thinking of leaving us?' Birch looked stricken.

'Oh no,' I said, 'I wouldn't want to, just, if I need to.'

'Why would she need to leave?' Tilde asked as though I wasn't there.

Birch waved his hand dismissively. 'Nonsense.'

Tilde handed Birch the platter, then turned to take in

the view, lifting a pair of binoculars from a side table that sat beside the door. The porch was scattered with twiggy rattan furniture painted white, in stark contrast to the jewel-toned Adirondack chairs that were sprinkled across the lawn below. At the far end of the porch, I admired a twin-size cushioned swing upholstered in navy ticking, comfortably appointed with an abundance of peachy pillows. It looked like the perfect place to curl up with a book and drift into a sun-dappled nap. But no, I couldn't love it until I knew.

'So you were pleased, then,' I pressed. 'We passed the inspection.'

Birch's eyes lingered over me for a long, odd moment. He frowned, dismissing my words, before turning back to the water. 'How many do we have?' he asked. I followed his gaze out to Winslow Bay as Tilde counted aloud, noticing, for the first time, a tangle of masts, bobbing like a floating forest.

'Do you know much about yachts?' he asked.

I shook my head, thoughts racing. They hadn't told me I had to leave. Which meant they were going to let me stay. I almost laughed aloud with relief but for the serious tone Birch used as he pointed out toward a moored boat with two masts. 'That's a yawl – the mizzenmast, which is the second mast, is behind the rudderpost. And that' – he moved his hand to the right – 'is a ketch – the rudderpost is behind the mizzenmast. The rest are sloops – single masts.'

'Twenty-six,' Tilde said crisply.

'Give her a chance to look,' he said, and she handed me the heavy binoculars. I wasn't even sure what I was supposed to be looking for, but I held the glasses to my eyes. The magnification moved so quickly across the suddenly close landscape that I felt dizzy. Finally I found the fleet of moored boats in the water right before us. In the golden light I could make out a family swimming beside one of the yachts. On the deck of another, a couple sipped martinis.

'Canadians,' Birch said in a mocking tone.

'They sail down just for the weekend?' I asked, impressed that so many people were living such luxurious lives.

'Twenty-six is far too many,' Tilde said. 'They'll keep us up half the night.' Then a look of delight flitted across her face. 'Perhaps one will get stuck on the reef.'

'We don't want that – then we'd have to help them.' Birch laughed, and, much to my surprise, Tilde joined him. I'd never seen her amused, and the sound was much lighter and looser than I would have imagined. Birch turned to me again, and Tilde's laugh cut itself off, midair. He hardly seemed to notice, but I could feel her disdain.

'I curse the crows when they wake me up,' he declared, 'but I praise them when they wake the damn Canadians.' He held up the platter of muffins. 'Shall we find a place to put these?' I was grateful for his graciousness, and to leave Tilde behind.

Birch led me into the room just inside the screen porch, the finest I'd seen at Winloch; if this was the summer room, I wanted to know what the rest of the house looked like. Upon the honey-colored floor stood antique wooden sideboards and a large mahogany table. An exquisite burgundy Oriental rug tied the furniture together, ending before a large fireplace sporting a brass fender and matching andirons. Canapés were arranged in colorful formations upon hand-painted porcelain platters: crab cakes and mini-lobster rolls and demitasses of chilled pea soup. Never before had I been at a 'spur-of-the-moment' family dinner of this caliber – now I understood why my corn muffins had been in error. Birch found a spot for them, a spot I kept my eye on as the night progressed, praying someone would finish the stupid things so I might be absolved of my blunder.

As more Winslows arrived, I filled a china plate and nibbled at the far wall, watching them pass before me – an older woman, a little boy, the well-dressed mothers, the chiseled men – all with their alabaster skin, scrubbed clean of dirt and imperfections. They were a perfect, particular breed of animal, like racehorses or hounds, thin-ankled and groomed. It was easy to tell those of us not related by blood – we were almost all shorter and darker, but there was something else: we hung back.

Elegant Ev checked in on me more than once; apprehensive Annie sought me out for company; blundering Banning spilled his daughter's apple juice all over my sandal, making my left foot moist and sticky for the rest of the evening. But otherwise I was left alone. As the soiree progressed, a herd of blond children thundered in and out of the room, raiding the crackers and cheese. They were shooed out onto the porch intermittently by a clucking mother, and, more than once, I thought to follow them, longing for their honesty. As the summer room grew too small to contain the sheer number of Winslows inhabiting it, the party spilled out onto the porch, and I made my way to the other side of the room, thinking I'd go in search of the toilet, when my gaze settled on an alcove built into the wall, out of sight of my previous post. Inside the alcove hung the most beautiful painting I'd ever seen.

True, I hadn't seen many paintings in my life; the reproductions in the art books at the library had, at best, been murky sketches of the real things. In person, Ev's Degas had impressed me; I'd known, just by looking at it, that it was Important. Still, that small, predictable work of art called forth a far less rousing sensation than the gasping good fortune I felt as I took in the great painting hanging before me.

It was a Van Gogh.

I couldn't call up the painting in my memory, so perhaps I'd never seen it reproduced. It was unmistakably one of his, if bigger than I'd ever guessed a Van Gogh to be.

A landscape – his telltale cypress trees in rich greens and blues, reaching up toward a night sky. Above, stars. Below, yellow and green grasses, purpling in the distance. If there was a distance; it was hard to hold on to the perspective in any of it, for just as the eye would settle on a horizon line, a glance to either side would reapportion the whole thing, casting one's first impression into doubt. But far from causing frustration, as such an effect would have elicited from a lesser artist, the result was exhilarating, pulse-quickening. The painting heightened emotion as only great art can.

For the first time that evening, I forgot about the Winslows. I stepped slowly toward the feverish brushstrokes as though they were calling to me, until I was mere inches away. Had the same work of art been hanging on the wall of my parents' house (however laughable that possibility), I'd just have assumed it was a cheesy reproduction bought at a mall shop and set in a spray-painted frame. But as the evening light filtered in from the bay, I felt proud, as though somehow, being here with this piece of history, I had already made something of myself.

'It's magnificent, isn't it?'

I turned to find Indo right beside me. I could only nod, enthralled. 'Is it really . . . ?'

She nodded, a smile forming on her lips. 'My mother loved art.'

'She was a collector?'

She took a good while to answer. 'It's mine.'

'Oh?'

'My financial inheritance was smaller,' she said, gesturing to the grand house around us, 'because I was a girl. So Mother gave me the painting. I was the only one who loved it the way great art must be loved. But then my brother magically came up with some heretofore unknown bylaw which apparently gives him the right to march into anyone's home and seize her personal property like some kind of dictator. So here it hangs, when I was the one who was prepared to do what was right on its behalf, to—'

'Can I get you girls something?'

I turned, surprised, to find Tilde standing on my other side, smiling falsely, glass of sherry in hand.

'We were just discussing . . .' I gestured back to the Van Gogh.

'She asked,' Indo said.

'Oh, Indo, I'm certain the poor girl did no such thing.'

I stepped back and out of the sandwich they'd made

84

around me. Something was happening that I did not understand. Yes, Indo was spilling family gossip, but she was a good person, and Tilde just seemed mean.

'It's beautiful,' I offered. Something sharp passed between the older women that I could not name.

A little girl ran up and tugged on Tilde's arm. 'Auntie T., can we do sparklers down on Flat Rocks?'

'I'll bring them right out.' The girl squealed and ran out into the tangle of adults. Tilde turned to us. 'If you'll excuse me, the angels call.'

'It's creepy to call children angels,' Indo said, as she glowered.

'And you know so much about it because of all your experience parenting,' Tilde replied.

Indo listed, and Tilde watched her, satisfied she'd stung.

'No, you're right,' Indo said, 'I should keep to my role as bitter eccentric.' But Tilde was already gone.

Cursing quietly, Indo gulped down her wine before charging in the other direction, opening a door into the rest of Trillium and slamming it shut behind herself.

I turned back to the painting, unwilling to let it out of my mind. But what had occurred between the two women – even if I didn't fully understand it – made it impossible to really see again. The beautiful space inside my head that the Van Gogh had created, that the promise of a summer at Winloch had warmed, was filled with the idle babble all around me, about the sad disrepair of the docks over on the far side of camp, and the best breed of hunting dog, and the name of the right contractor to hire for cottage renovation, so that even as I tried to hold on to the painting with my eyes, the cacophony pulled me away from it, rendering the artwork unfriendly.

Soon I found myself drifting, unnoticed, onto the lantern-lit porch and out into the night, where the children's sparklers made brilliant, swooping circles upon the lawn. Beyond them, the lights atop each of the twenty-six masts bobbed like fairies, reflected in the velvety black water below. That was when I remembered the sound of my brother's voice, carried along, like the heady smell of a thunderstorm, on the warm night wind.

CHAPTER THIRTEEN

The Inevitable

I GOT THE PACKAGE FROM my mother that Monday morning. From the way it crinkled, I knew it was lined with Bubble Wrap. John delivered the prize himself, along with a bag of apple-cider donuts.

'You remembered!' Ev clapped, jumping unabashedly into his arms when he appeared with the treats. He looked alarmed at the public display of affection, so I excused myself to the bathroom, smiling even more broadly to myself in private, giddy at the notion John was the one Ev was sneaking off to in the early morning hours.

Back in the living room, they stood over me eagerly like children at summer camp as I opened my mother's package. I noticed him link his hand briefly with hers as she hoped aloud for candy. But I knew what the envelope held without having to look: a stack of self-addressed, stamped envelopes that would lead straight back to Oregon.

'M.,' the letter began, 'Jeanne says you had a lovely visit. I forgot to ask you when we talked. Please call when you get a chance. We miss your voice. Please give Mr and Mrs Winslow our thanks again. Your father sends his love too.'

Six sentences. Easy enough to reply to. I had the envelopes, after all. But responding to my mother in kind always felt like lying. She was so good at playing her part; I was terrible at the role I was meant to uphold. And the alternative, to write what I was really thinking, was impossible, if wickedly fun to imagine:

Mom,

I'm glad to be almost as far away from you as this country allows. The Winslows are beautiful and rich, probably more than your imagination can muster. I know you're picturing gold candlesticks and infinity pools, but this place they made isn't decadent, no, it's rustic in the way only a rich person's place can be, with money flowing under it invisibly, so that they get to pretend they're just like the rest of us. They are characters, all of them, and I'm sure they must quibble with each other behind closed doors, but no one here walks around with the imprint of a ring scabbed onto their cheekbone. Funny, that. To a person, they are attractive, devoid of body odor, and not the least bit interested in me. Their dozens of children (nearly all biologically impeccable, with one adopted Chinese toddler for good measure) are precocious. Their dogs ignore me in the nonchalant way only overindulged canines can. They all – even the dogs – eat organic.

Ev has three brothers. The fat one, Banning, has a house made out of straw; the meticulous one, Athol, has a house made out of steel; and I'm fairly certain the third brother, Galway, is the big bad wolf. Ev's parents, Birch and Tilde (these people all have names only the rich can get away with), are, at once, enigmatic and gracious.

Birch has five living siblings, and they and their broods make up the bulk of the clan in residence at camp. (You're supposed to call it camp, even though no one is actually camping.) Most of the Winslows, with the exception of Birch's eccentric sister Indo (who I'm beginning to suspect may be of sapphic persuasion), have children and grandchildren.

Birch's oldest sister, Greta, has a husband and asexual daughters and a vague son, and three Teutonic grandchildren: Arthur Jr, Victoria, and Samson. Skippy is their Jack Russell, Absalom their golden.

Birch's younger sister Stockard (Ev calls her Drunkard), has a fat husband called Pinky, a divorced son, PJ, and soccer-loving teenage grandsons. Word is that PJ and his wife were driven apart by the death of their little girl, Fiona, years ago; apparently this loss has rendered them too sad for pets.

Birch's youngest, pseudo-bohemian sister, Mhairie, has an unremarkable family but for her Jewish son-in-law, David. Everyone has made a point of remarking on the fact that he's 'Jew-ish,' as they pronounce it, not that there's anything wrong with that. His children, as a result, are Jew-ish too: sharp Ramona, worried Leo, and silly Eli. They are too allergic for pets.

Then there's Birch's sister CeCe. She's the one whose son, Jackson, killed himself. She hasn't shown her face yet.

Each relative I've met wants to discuss Cousin Jackson's suicide, but discreetly (they adopt the same hushed tone as when they mention David's Jew-ishness), leaning, with *great concern, against their porch rails, asking Ev – even asking me, forgetting I'm no one – 'Have you heard how CeCe's doing?' 'Can't medication help with that kind of thing?' 'Do you think there was a way to stop it?' I wonder if Jackson knew they would talk this vividly about him, and if that's part of why he did it.*

Is it lost on me that a boy who blew his own brains out is the primary reason I find myself Genevra Winslow's personal guest in the sun-dappled Eden where she's spent every summer of her life? Not a bit. I have come to believe Jackson's death was a necessary sacrifice to the gods of friendship ('he died so that I may live'), and I tell myself it isn't selfish to believe so. After all, he was born into this bounty. It's his problem it wasn't good enough.

Give my love to Dad if you dare.

Okay, I wrote it. But I didn't send it.

Just one weekend spent amid the Winslow clan and I'd already learned a useful trick – if you didn't speak, they forgot you were listening. That's how I gathered that only a handful of Winslows had attended Jackson's memorial service back in February, where CeCe, Jackson's mother, had been inconsolable. Over the first lantern-lit dinners of the season, there volleyed a tingling, electric replay of the returning soldier's every act the previous summer, the last time anyone had noticed him.

He had been too skinny.

Too quiet.

Always buried in a book.

Angry about the Kittering boys borrowing the canoe.

Or no, when Flip was hit by the dock repair truck, he'd been empty of emotion, remember, hadn't so much as batted an eye, just carried the mangled dog into the grass and laid her down.

Wasn't there a broken engagement to some girl from Boston?

Hadn't he once yelled at Gammy Pippa in the Dining Hall?

As all of Winloch replayed the stammering timbre of Jackson's voice, the slight shake in his hands – which hadn't been there before Fallujah – our collective chatter crescendoed, filling Winslow Bay with the single, relieving point the Winslows could finally agree upon:

It was because of the war. A relief, someone uttered, to have a reason.

Beyond that, one couldn't blame anyone in particular, but it didn't escape me, as I listened invisibly, that those few Winslows who lived in Burlington and had four-wheel drive were doing their best to forget the unhinged pitch of CeCe's keening, not to mention the attention-sucking way she'd fallen, dramatically, to her knees beside her son's coffin (her histrionics, frankly, a bit much), as the snow fell outside the funeral home, blanketing the city in fresh, pure white.

It was times like these that one was thankful for tradition. At least that's how Birch Winslow began his toast that first Monday evening of summer, raising a glass of local ale before the whole of Winloch. It was the twenty-first of June, the Midsummer Night's Feast, held every year on the solstice upon the Dining Hall lawn, before the tennis courts, such a fundamental Winslow tradition that Ev seemed shocked when I needed it explained. A good hundred of us were spread before Birch on blankets and folding chairs in the soft, falling light, our collective contributions to the groaning board (the elite's name for a potluck, I'd come to learn) already picked apart on the tables made haphazardly of sawhorses and plywood. Stockard's russet potato salad, Annie's fried chicken, and my homemade blueberry pie were all long gone.

'We are missing one of our own,' Birch went on, and a sad hush descended upon us – even wild little Ricky stopped squirming – 'and the loss is a great hole in us that will remain unhealed.' Missing was any mention of Jackson's name; his family was absent as well. Rumor had it that Mr Booth had left CeCe for good back in April, and that she and her offspring would not be coming back. But Birch did not elaborate. We raised our glasses of artisanal beer as the Winslow coat of arms rippled above us.

Tradition held that the feast was dinner theater; the Rickys and Maddys of the family, too young to memorize lines, were dressed as sprites and fairies, outfitted in diaphanous wings, wielding Peter Pan swords and Tinker Bell wands, their faces swirled in glittery turquoise. It fell to the older boys (and the men who fancied themselves young) to perform the memorized parts of the rude mechanicals from Shakespeare's *Midsummer Night's Dream*. Star-crossed lovers Pyramus and Thisbe had courted each other through the reticent wall for nearly a century, and the Winslows still found it hilarious.

'O Grim-Look'd Night! O night with hue so black! / O night, which ever art when day is not! O night, O night! alack, alack, alack.' Pyramus was played by Banning in a pair of his wife's culottes. The audience cheered at the sight. His timing was good, actually, as though his premature businessman middle age was just a diversion from his true, thespian calling. He was all bluster and arrogance, a donkey in the clothing of a man.

As the prologue finished introducing our Pyramus, messy Annie accosted me on my blanket, digging her ample hands into my forearm, begging for help in a frantic whisper. Ev glared at us until I snuck off the blanket and followed Annie to Maddy, sitting on the bottom step of the Dining Hall, stuffing her tiny pink mouth with the remnants of a pan of brownies. 'She's swallowed walnuts! Walnuts!' Annie hiccuped like the Little Red Hen, and I spent a good ten minutes with the wiggling, sugar-high girl in the bathroom, helping her mother swab off the chocolate and watching her closely for anaphylaxis.

Crisis averted, I returned to our blanket. I had planned to spend the evening getting sloppy drunk with Ev, but where she'd been sitting, Abby now dozed. The Winslows were absorbed in the play. I put my hand on the dog's hot head, laughed at Banning Winslow, and couldn't believe my fortune that these people loved Shakespeare.

Then Thisbe entered.

Yes, it was a challenge to recognize 'her' – the red wig, the vintage dress. But the smattering of freckles over the cheeks, the pink, supple lips – every detail was sharpened by my shame.

His flounces were met with riotous laughter as he delivered his lines in falsetto. He was silly, yes, playing his own brother's female lover. But he was also electrifying. Not an eye strayed.

To have stood would have been to draw attention. Or so I told myself, rapt at his every move, until he stabbed himself, landing atop his brother's corpse, causing Banning to cry out, and the audience to give them a standing ovation.

After dinner, I escaped into the bustling herd of fairy children. They were free at last, from school, from the inhibitions necessarily placed upon city kids, finally able to run facefirst into that loose, early summer burst of wind and sun and sweat. It was better with children. They were either loyal or beastly, and it wasn't hard to tell the difference. We threw sticks for the dogs, and gathered tennis balls from the hedges, as dusk fell and the mosquitoes partook of their own feast, until, one by one, the angels were gathered up and carried home.

The crowd dispersed, it seemed safe to stroll back to the Dining Hall. Abby dreamed loyally on Ev's blanket, the only one left on the great lawn. I couldn't bring myself to wake the sleeping creature, even though the sawhorses were gone, the plywood stacked against the hall.

I found myself alone before the barnlike building. The soft sound of guitar filtered out the screened double doors and down the broad steps. I wondered after Ev – should I go back to Bittersweet and check on her? Instead, I climbed the stairs toward the tempting glow and peeked in through the screen, taking in the large space.

Round tables were scattered across a well-polished hardwood floor, with boards so wide they must have been original. Opposite me, another set of double doors led back down to the main Winloch road. To the right lay the industrial kitchen, separated from the main hall by a cutout wall on which food could be set. To the left, a stairway led up to a second floor, buttressed by a set of long, drab couches on which a small group of people were gathered. I worried I might be interrupting some sacred Winslow tradition, but it was only Indo and a few of the teenagers – Arlo and Jeffrey and Owen, all several years younger than I – who'd spent the better part of the evening on the other side of the tennis courts trying to build a bottle rocket.

Beside the teenage boys, his back to the door, a man played the guitar. The music was exquisite – all trills and fretting, a delicious melody laid forth. It was a song lifted from a warmer place, a place of dancing and the ocean, and I felt pulled toward it, the rhythm settling in my hips and pulsing in my collarbone. I allowed myself to step inside. The screen door yawned open, making a much louder sound than I'd intended.

Indo turned at the whine of the hinges. 'Mabel!' she cried.

The teenagers glanced up.

The music ended mid-strum.

Indo strode across the room and enveloped me in her patchouli-scented hug.

The man turned. Over Indo's shoulder, I recognized those freckles, the dirty blond hair. He was Galway.

'I'm looking for Ev,' I stammered, trying to extract myself. But Indo held me tight, drawing me toward the one man on the Eastern Seaboard I dreaded seeing.

'Have you met my nephew?'

Galway smiled. Stood. His eyes danced over me playfully. 'Yes.'

CHAPTER FOURTEEN

The Collage

I TURNED WHAT I CAN only imagine was a shade of crimson, feeling the intensity of Galway's gaze. 'I really should go.'

'Nonsense.' Indo gripped my arm. 'Now's a perfect time to show you the archives we talked about. Test your mettle. Oh, don't look so terrified, I'm kidding. Mostly. But really, can you resist? They're just up there, waiting for someone to do something with them, to reveal their secrets. Galway helped me box them up a few years ago, and since we are such good friends now, and my poor back won't allow me regular stairs anymore – don't grow old, you beautiful creatures . . .' And on she went, urging me up the rickety steps.

Much to my chagrin, Galway followed.

Indo flipped on the weak overhead lights and excitedly pointed out the mouse-nibbled cardboard boxes piled in the center of the immense, airless attic. 'Oh, I'm so pleased,' she said, clapping her hands together. 'Galway is such a help in these matters, and I know you two will have good fun tackling this together.'

I could barely think, so embarrassed was I to be near that man. I kept my head down and tried to focus on the sound of Indo's voice.

There were dozens of boxes, filled with clippings and

personal papers and business documents. The immensity of the task I had blithely agreed to that chilly afternoon the week before struck me – Indo wanted me to find something in this mess for her? And if I found it, she'd, what, give me her house? Fat chance.

'What exactly do you want me to find?' I asked, when I could get a word in.

'First order of business,' she pronounced, 'put your hands on that manila folder about my painting. Yes, Galway, I told her your parents took my painting – you know me, I can't keep my mouth shut. The folder's nondescript, I'm afraid, so you'll have to root around a bit, but that's half the fun now, isn't it? And keep your eyes peeled for good stories – you never know where you might find some material. She's a budding writer, did you know that, Galway? The quick mind of a detective. Especially, dear, especially keep your eyes open for anything about . . . Well, yes, all right, I'll let you find your own way.'

She then launched into a disquisition on her storied ancestors – 'They were visionaries! The leaders of their fields!' – until Galway asked me pointedly, 'Weren't you looking for Ev?' I considered him the enemy but saw the possibility for retreat so agreed apologetically that, yes, he was right, Ev had fallen ill at the picnic and I really should check on her.

'Oh dear,' Indo exclaimed, releasing me. 'You should have said something.' I hurried down the attic stairs as she called after me, 'If it's woman's troubles, tell her to find me; I've got fabulous herbs from my guy in Boston.'

I was back out into the moonless night in seconds, cursing

myself for ever stepping foot inside that building, cursing Galway for playing that guitar, and it wasn't until I was far from the Dining Hall that I realized I had no flashlight and only a vague notion of the direction I should be heading. 'Abby!' I called, but even the dog had abandoned me. I told myself not to think about vampires. The crunch of my feet on gravel was a good, if small, sign I was going in the right direction.

The Dining Hall was out of sight by the time the light glanced toward me. The beam flashed over me a few times, and I stopped, like a deer in headlights, grateful for the flashlight if wary of whoever might be bearing it. It was just as I feared – Galway, alone. He was winded.

He handed me the flashlight silently, and I was forced to thank him. There were two of us, and only one light. One of us would have to walk the other home. Since we were halfway to Bittersweet, we continued in my direction.

He cleared his throat. I thanked god for the darkness. We walked on together into the night. Finally, he said, 'I'm not going to tell anyone.'

I said nothing.

'It's kind of funny, actually, when you think about it,' he went on. It sounded like he was smiling.

I kept my eyes on the beam and prayed he was done.

'I was looking for Ev that morning,' he said, 'and I thought she might be sleeping and—'

'Okay,' I said, wheeling toward him, shining the light at his face, 'good.'

He put his hand up to shield his eyes. 'I just wanted to say—'

'I get it.' I kept the light pointed directly at his face, unable to restrain my anger at the oblivious, blithe way these people went about their lives. 'I get it, it's hysterical, and now you can hold it over me and humiliate me all you want, you saw me . . . doing that . . . but it isn't lost on me that you were the one spying on people, that you're' – I searched for the right word – 'a Peeping Tom, a pervert' – and with that, I left him. Didn't care that I had the only flashlight, or that he was the one who'd brought it to me.

Abby met me a few steps from a pitch-black Bittersweet, the night filling with her clacking tags and panting tongue. She licked my hand faithfully. I went straight for the crawl space below the porch, easily finding the one bag of recyclables I'd set aside, grabbing the three magazines on top. I listened for Galway's footsteps, but I could hear only the night.

We crept into the sleeping house. The bedroom door was closed, a relief, since Ev, who'd abandoned me for the evening, was the last person I wanted to see. I clicked on the lamp in the living room, pulled the pair of nail scissors from the medicine cabinet, grabbed a notepad and roll of tape from the supply basket, and settled before the cold hearth, letting myself open the September 1, 1961, issue of *Life*, an L.L.Bean catalog from 1987, a *Town and Country* from 1947. I knew exactly what pages I wanted, and ripped them expertly, already feeling calmer, letting my mind wander to the other periodicals waiting below the porch; this was just the beginning. I extracted what I loved: the *Town and Country* cover painting of a woman in a long dress leaning over a balustrade toward a sailboat, a picture of a fresh-faced Jacqueline Kennedy from *Life,* and the laughing blond family from L.L.Bean that I'd been waiting for since I noticed them. I'd use the scissors to do the detail work.

My anger ebbed. I kept going, cutting and taping, until I had a complete picture laid out before me. Only then did I sit back against the red chair. Abby laid her head upon my lap. I must have dozed off, because the next thing I knew, I heard an unfamiliar motor roaring off into the night, and the screen door nipping at Ev's heels. I sat forward, taking in the messy room, disoriented, irritated I'd been wrong about her whereabouts. She was standing over me before I had a chance to begin cleaning up.

'Was that John?' I asked.

Her pupils were dilated, her hair messy, lipstick smeared. 'Why on earth would I be getting a ride from John at this hour?' She prodded Abby with her foot. 'He should be taking her home at night.' That was when she noticed my collage. I wanted her to divulge her secrets, but instead, she plucked the paper from the mess and pored over it.

Blond family. The lake. Polo shirts. Sunglasses. Insignias. Rowboats. Beautiful people. Money.

'Is this us?' she asked, delighted. Before I could answer, she pulled two pushpins from the wall. Centered the collage above the mantelpiece and pressed the pins into its corners. Then stood back, and frowned. 'Or were you making it for your mom?'

'Why would I make it for my mom?' I balked.

She blinked at me. 'Because she sent you that package?'

I snorted. 'Please. I don't make anything for my mom.'

She edged back toward me. 'Why not? I mean, I know she made you cry before we came up. But she seems . . . nice.'

'Mothers always seem nice when they aren't yours.'

'Mine doesn't!' She guffawed, plopping down on the floor beside me. I laughed with her.

'She's only nice to show me I'm not,' I offered, once our humor had faded. Instantly, I felt guilty – my mother was the one who'd urged me to 'be sweet.' Maybe she really was as nice as Ev thought and it was only my own cruel mind that turned it to meanness.

Ev began to braid my hair. Silence settled over us. 'You think . . .,' she began, once she'd restarted the braid for the third time, 'you think it would have been better if I'd gone out with John?'

'Aren't you guys . . . together?'

'A girl can still have a little fun.' Her voice sounded sad, as though even she was disappointed in herself.

'But I thought . . .' Her fingers deftly wove the plaits she'd made. I realized no one had touched me for a good while. The words sounded so simple, so stupid, as they tumbled out, but I couldn't help myself: 'I thought you loved John.'

She paused as she considered my question. 'I do.'

'But he doesn't love you?'

She smiled proudly. 'John LaChance has wanted to marry me since I was six years old.'

'So what's the problem then?' I found myself growing irritated at the tug on my hair.

'It's complicated.' She pulled hard at my scalp. 'He . . . he can't give me what I need. Not all of it. Not now.'

'But that's not love,' I pressed, thinking her selfish. 'Love is sacrifice. Putting someone else first.'

'Exactly,' she said, 'that's exactly what I told him. I'm not asking for much, just that he keeps his word, you know?' She sat back, gripping the braid in her hand, and squinted her eyes in appraisal. 'You're so kindhearted, Mabel.' She let the braid go. 'I'm sorry to burst your bubble.'

I opened my mouth to tell her it wasn't fairy tales I believed in, just the tender way I'd seen John grasp her hand.

But she was already off to the next subject, nodding toward the collage. 'Tomorrow you can do your family.'

I watched her push the bolt into place on the front door. Together, we brushed our teeth, turned out the lights, and drew the bedroom door closed behind us. She locked the bolt there too.

I listened to her sink into sleep. It was best to let her believe the project had been spur of the moment. That it wasn't something I'd done hundreds of times before. I was proud of myself for biting my tongue. For not replying, 'No, Ev, I never do my family.'

CHAPTER FIFTEEN

The Girl

I HAD NO IDEA WHERE Ev was sneaking out to – or who her mystery 'other man' was – but as June edged on, she spent less and less time in Bittersweet. John, too, steered noticeably clear of us. I missed his shy charm, how Ev danced around the kitchen humming when she knew he would be coming by, the lap of Abby's tongue across my fingertips. But every time I asked about him, Ev's response was to pluck an Empire apple from the full bowl atop the kitchen table and disappear down the road. She returned in the evenings, and sometimes after midnight, tight-lipped as to her whereabouts. I kept my ears open for the growling, unknown motor I'd heard in the night, but she wandered in soundlessly from then on.

Dear Mom,
I'm beginning to realize I'm a person whom loneliness
follows. It's lazy to call my isolation a condition – I
know all too well how it has been my nature, for years,
to think of myself as an island. But I swear: this time I
thought it was different! I would be perfectly content
living as Ev's right-hand gal, even though it seems she's
already bored by me – what does that say about my
need? Am I unquenchable? Unable to take a hint? I

*wouldn't blame that on you, Mom, but Dad's a different
story.*

*Wait – I forgot – nothing real can pass between us. So
how's this?*

*The swimming's lovely. I bought a suit with Ev's
L.L.Bean card – don't worry, I'll pay her back – and I'm
able to tread water for a good two minutes before I need
a handhold. Sorry I'm not sending you this letter, but it's
best for both of us. I think you'd probably agree.*

When writing unsendable letters to my mother, cutting
pictures from magazines, half drowning and calling it swimming, or pretending to read Milton could capture my
attention no longer, I rolled up my sleeves in the Dining
Hall attic. Indo's treasure hunt gave me distraction, the
chance to chew up a few hours here and there during
which I could forget my solitude. But it also offered something more. Foolish as it may sound, Indo had whetted
my appetite. I couldn't resist the chance for access to the
Winslows' inner workings; after all, I was the girl who'd
researched them on interlibrary loan in the spring.

Did I forget how vehemently Tilde seemed to dislike
Indo, especially on the subject of the Van Gogh? Did I think
Tilde would really approve of my riffling through the family
archives? Well, no. But she'd been mean to Indo and to Ev.
And anyway, the 'archives' were only some abandoned papers
I was casually sifting through without direction.

There was something else – something I shouldn't have
dared to dream about but did all the same – Indo's offhand
suggestion that her house was up for grabs. Still, now,

mentioning that remembered hope brings a blush to my skin, because, really, who would be foolish enough to believe an eccentric old woman's ramblings? And I didn't even know what she was looking for, not really. Anyway, hadn't Ev already offered up the vision of us as old biddies sitting on the porch together? She had, certainly. But perhaps I had already started to doubt her constancy, to try to map out other ways I could keep Winloch mine. In any case, I know myself well enough to admit that once someone has introduced a suggestion to an imagination like mine . . . well, let's just say by the first day I sat down with the family archive, I had already pondered how much it would cost to have Clover's toilet replaced.

The moth-nibbled, mouse-nested Winslow papers made me sneeze. Their crumpled, knife-thin edges flaked off like autumnal leaves in late fall. They had acquired an ancient, musty smell from the many seasons they'd been waiting in the attic. Some of the papers were thick and heavy and marked with fading fountain-pen ink. Those old documents held crossed, European sevens and bore the imprint of typewriters, so that, as I ran my fingers over the backs of the pages, I could feel the ripple of backwards words set down a hundred years before. The newer pages were thin as onionskin and already yellowing. Some bore sickly sweet–smelling purple mimeograph ink; others were scrawled with handwriting that pointed to more recent failings in the teaching and execution of proper penmanship.

But regardless of whether the Winslow papers were young or old, the collection, as a whole, was in ruins. Coherent order was nowhere to be found. It took me a few half days to simply put the piles of paper in some kind of chronology. I roped Arlo, Jeffrey, and Owen, eager for action, into dragging a few unused dining tables up the creaky attic stairs, and we stacked the papers onto each one, decade by decade, before the boys scrambled off in search of greater adventure.

There were very few documents from Samson's day – a copy of the original Winloch deed, a half dozen sheaves from one or another of his companies – and then, from the era after Samson died, when Banning the first was coming of age, there was a slim pile of papers regarding war bonds, succession, a box of personal letters, and a few newspaper clippings that mentioned his sister Esther, who had become a physician. Someone had taken care to save those articles, and I read with great admiration about her bravery and determination.

There were some papers in there regarding a bankruptcy from sometime in the thirties – I couldn't tell if the smudge at the end of the year read '2' or '9,' but it seemed unlikely the Winslows would have gone bankrupt and held on to this paradise, so I set it back down on the pile, even as it burned a question mark into my memory.

It wasn't until Bard – Birch's father, Ev's grandfather – came to power, in the midthirties, that the papers grew voluminous. There were work orders, deeds, clippings, many more pounds of paper creating many more pounds of dust. On more than one of those June afternoons, I picked up the trail of a bought tract of land – apparently Bard was something of a land baron – followed it for a few years, and then, when the scent ran cold, shook my head at the sheer vagueness of my task, and at how well Indo, of all people, seemed to know me. I was just supposed to be looking for a manila folder. But she had been right – I couldn't resist a juicy tale.

I pulled myself away and wandered downstairs, bidding good-bye to Masha, Winloch's ample, white-haired, Russian cook. She took a moment from stirring her minestrone to answer with a gruff nod.

My favorite spot in all of Winloch lay at the lip of our cove, on the flat, smooth rock on which the great blue heron had perched the first day I ventured beyond Bittersweet. The rock was big enough to hold only one body, easily reached by swimming, or, if one didn't mind a bit of a scramble, by climbing down the ledged incline through scratchy undergrowth. I liked that the spot lay between private land and public. Basking on the warm swath, I could turn my head out, to the push and pull of the outer bay only inches away, where motorboats sped in toward Winslow Bay, and, in the distance, a marina flashed silver and white when the sunlight hit it; or I could turn my eyes in, toward Bittersweet, making out our small, sandy beach, even as the stairs, cottage, and the rest of Winloch was hidden from view. It was here that I felt the most in my element – hidden, but watching.

I believed I was the only one who knew about the spot, which was sheer folly, since I'd stayed at Winloch for all of three weeks and the Winslows had been there for more than a century. But one morning I clambered down through the forest, backpack full of snacks and reading, a morning of solitude ahead of me, only to discover someone already lying in my place. She was on her stomach, her long blond hair spilling down over her bare lower back, just brushing her apricot bikini bottom. I imagined her a selkie, that mythological creature of the Celtic lands, a girl who'd shed her sealskin to become human. But at the sound of me, she lifted her head, and I saw she was only a girl. A girl who looked as much like Ev as Indo did, but still a child – gawky, insecure, on the brink of beautiful.

She held up her hand to shield her eyes from the sun. 'Are you Ev's friend?'

I squatted down as she sat up. 'May.'

'Lu.' She stuck her hand in her bag and pulled out two cigarettes. She couldn't have been more than fourteen.

'No!' I must have looked horrified. She returned them to their original spot and pulled out two lollipops instead.

'You're Ev's sister?' I asked. It was hard not to scrutinize her face – it moved in and out of exquisiteness. She had one little mole on her right cheek – the only imperfection I noticed, if it could even be called that. 'I thought you were at tennis camp.' I sat beside her.

She snorted. 'Yeah, 'cause I'm so athletic.'

'There was a sit-ups requirement at my high school, and you can imagine how well I did.'

She looked me up and down – the full thighs, the soft belly – and genuinely giggled, but before her pleasure could grow into a full laugh, she caught it abruptly, her shoulders shrinking impishly by her ears. A look of delight flitted across her face as she pointed over my shoulder into the cove and, with the other hand, put a finger to her lips. 'We're not alone,' she whispered.

I turned, expecting a large creature – another human, a dog, perhaps – but, as far as I could see, there was nothing to note. Lu's finger pointed a path to what looked to be a dead head, a decaying stick making its slow way down to the lake bed.

'It's a turtle,' she whispered, and as I leaned forward in disbelief, the stick popped underwater. Lu let out a gleeful gasp. We scanned the cove for the surfacing head. It finally appeared, far to the left of where I was looking. Lu spotted it first. 'They swim faster than they walk,' she explained.

'What kind is it?'

'Probably a painted turtle. Could be a snapping turtle, but I'd have to see its shell to know for sure. Don't worry,' she said, noting the alarm on my face, 'they're much more afraid of us than we are of them.'

'What other animals live here?' I asked.

Her face lit up. 'We used to have otters – you could tell because, in the early spring, there'd be cracked-open mussels on the shore. And muskrats too – they made their nest in that little spot over there between the rocks. There are beavers inland – everyone's always in a fight over them damming the streams because it raises the water table. And let's see . . . ospreys. They don't live in the cove, but they fish here, and near the ledges, in the morning and the night. You see them soaring way up, and then they swoop down, making their bodies like arrows, and they'll catch small bass or minnows. Oh, and the wood thrush!' She closed her eyes then, dipping her foot into the water. 'She sings at dawn and dusk. The most beautiful melody.'

Catching herself, Lu looked up at me sharply, worry

furrowing her brow. I recognized in that look a child in possession of an inconveniently attuned mind, one she had learned to camouflage. I nodded once, and then she truly smiled, before going on, her knowledge of the natural world spilling forth as though, with that one nod, I'd given her a gift.

'Let's see . . . white-tailed deer? Sometimes you'll see a red-tailed fox for, like, a second, running across the meadow. And there are black bears – well, supposedly. I've never seen one. Quail families. Pheasant families in the forest. Quail are much more skittish, but if you can catch a glimpse of them, their babies are these tiny, adorable puffballs with little racing feet. And keep your eyes out for the pileated woodpecker.'

'What does it look like?'

'A dinosaur.'

I laughed. 'No, really.'

She nodded knowingly. 'You'll know it when you see it.' We both checked in on the turtle head, bobbing in the water. 'Daddy says there are catamounts – you can tell because you'll find a deer kill sometimes off the Winloch road.'

'What's a catamount?'

'An eastern cougar.' She shook her head to reassure me. 'But I've never seen one of those either.' We sat in silence, looking out at the small tufts the breeze was making on the quiet lake. 'You really love it here,' she observed, unwrapping her lollipop and sticking it in her cheek.

My eyes skimmed the dazzling water as I thought of all the vibrant life above and below. I wanted to tell her how lucky she was to call this hers. Instead I said, 'It's heaven.'

CHAPTER SIXTEEN

The Rocks

LUVINIA WINSLOW WAS THE first person I met at Winloch who I would have easily befriended elsewhere. She wasn't as cool as Ev, but whether that was character or lingering childhood was hard to tell. She was smart, and not afraid to boast about it – top of her class in math ('that's both boys and girls' she was quick to point out) – but also innocent in a manner not shared by any boarding school girl I'd ever met. And she was innately generous; in the first twenty-four hours I knew her, Lu picked wildflowers from the meadow for Bittersweet's kitchen table, mixed me a batch of sourdough starter, and taught me how to do the Australian crawl. From the few interactions I witnessed between them, I caught on that Ev treated Lu much the way she treated me – adoring one minute, blind the next – but instead of feeling jealousy, I found myself glad to live in the category of little sisters.

'Have you been swimming off Flat Rocks yet?' Lu asked as we sat together below Bittersweet, where we'd met each morning for the three days I'd known her. It felt like we'd been friends much longer than that.

'No.' Flat Rocks was the prized swimming area below the Trillium meadow, where the Winslows frolicked and splashed together – it was centrally located, a flat, smooth expanse of sandstone big enough for two dozen people, which allowed a sweeping view of Mt. Mansfield, the Adirondacks, and Winslow Bay. Although the spot had been mentioned to me by nearly every Winslow I encountered – from the teenage boys headed there to practice diving off the swimming dock to Emily and Annie and other young mothers herding their small children, water wings, sunhats, and many bottles of sunscreen up and over the hill – I had never been invited. It would have been easy to grab my towel and descend the Trillium steps to the broad plateau myself, but I had a clear sense that each Winslow would have stared up at me just a little too long, and even the thought of their collective watchfulness made me blush.

Lu insisted we go that instant. We found Ev still in bed. She scowled at my waking her, at my invitation, at the obvious closeness that had already grown between Lu and me. 'I've never been to Flat Rocks,' I said, tickling at her toes, 'and you've been god knows where all week. You owe me an afternoon.'

'I don't owe you anything,' Ev sniped.

'What's wrong?' I asked. I had resolved to ask nothing specific about her love triangle, and I knew she wouldn't volunteer anything in front of Lu.

She only sighed.

'Come on then,' I insisted as I gathered up *Paradise Lost* from our bedside table, brushing aside the irritation at her recent lack of interest in me. She should have been the one inviting me to Flat Rocks. Eventually she followed us out of the house, slumping in self-pity until Lu and I threatened to throw her in the lake, which brought an ever-so-slight smile to her face, turning her, briefly, back into her best self.

We descended the wooden stairs below the Trillium lawn just as the sun passed its midway point. We were laden with goods, including turkey sandwiches Masha the cook had slapped together on a moment's notice. One way in which Lu and I were not alike: while it never would have occurred to me to ask someone else to make my lunch, Lu had assumed it was our only option.

A few folks had scattered themselves across the rocks, but we were early enough that the teenagers and childless had yet to arrive, and late enough that those with small children had already come and gone, for noon lunches and nap time. We had ample room to spread our towels. I applied my sunblock in globs, then watched Lu skillfully rub a thin layer of the lotion into her golden skin. At the sight of my blotchy face she giggled, and her slender fingers evened me out. Ev rolled her eyes at us and settled into another nap on the warm rocks.

I donned my sunglasses and flipped open *Paradise Lost*, retucking the letters I'd penned to my mother, but hadn't sent, into the back of the book. Lu frowned at my reading choice as she flipped open her *People*. 'You're going to fall asleep,' she singsonged.

My official story – as if anyone was asking – was that I was on Book Three. But Lu knew me better than I imagined, because the truth was, I hadn't been able to read more than a page at a time before dozing off. Consequently, even though I'd devoted many cumulative hours to the cause, I didn't have any idea what was happening in the damn book (1) because it was smarter than I was, and (2) because I had no memory of what I'd read the day before.

I flipped, with dread, to the page I'd earmarked and began:

> *Thus with the Year*
> *Seasons return, but not to me returns*
> *Day, or the sweet approach of Ev'n or Morn,*
> *Or sight of vernal bloom, or Summer's Rose,*
> *Or flocks, or herds, or human face divine;*
> *But cloud instead, and ever-during dark.*

An *Us Weekly* tumbled over the top of the book, landing on my face. 'Thank me later,' Lu deadpanned.

I'd never been much of a beachgoer, and it took me a couple hours to understand that our business for the day would cover – and not exceed – swimming, reading, gossiping, and lolling in the sun. I kept wanting to stand up and do something, kept thinking of the Winslow papers waiting for me in the Dining Hall attic, but every time I stirred, Lu placed her hand upon my arm and insisted I enjoy myself. 'If you want, we can take a dinghy out,' she said, disdainfully adding, 'but that's mostly for the boys.'

After we ate our sandwiches, Ev declared herself parched, gathered up her things, and headed back up to Bittersweet. I guessed I was supposed to follow her – it was certainly what I would have done only a week before – but Lu shot me a look that told me to grow a backbone. So I stayed.

The boys arrived. Arlo and Jeffrey and a few of the

younger teens made a beeline for the water, splashing as they submerged themselves, butterflying to the swimming dock twenty yards out. I watched Owen set his things down carefully where the other boys had tossed their towels, then glance over his shoulder at us. It was a surreptitious look, meant to appear nonchalant, as though he were scanning the whole rocks, but I saw he was searching out an oblivious Lu, absorbed in her magazine.

'How's he related?' I asked as I watched him wade into the water.

'Who?'

'Owen.'

'He's not,' Lu said without lifting her eyes from the page. 'He's Arlo's best friend from school.'

So he was fair game. 'He seems nice.'

'Sure.'

'Have you talked to him?'

'Once or twice.'

'Lu,' I said sharply, 'I think he likes you.'

That got her attention. She drew herself into a sitting position. Watched him swim carefully to the dock, where Arlo and Jeffrey jumped and called his name. 'He's seventeen,' she whispered, awestruck.

'And cute.' He was the kind of boy I would have loved in high school – well-mannered, tawny, and lean. The kind of boy who wouldn't have given me the time of day. He was good-looking in counterpoint to the purebred Winslows; his ancestors, like mine, had probably been workingmen.

Lu lifted her magazine again. But I could tell, from the

glow in her cheeks, that she didn't mind the thought of Owen liking her.

My memory of the many afternoons I spent at Flat Rocks that summer is long and lingering, bound up with the reassuring sense of things always having been the way they were, and the belief that they would always be that way. As the afternoon wore on, more Winslows descended the steps, calling happily to one another, and I began to see the nonfamilial, simply familiar, connections between them, and understand that to sit upon the rocks and watch the world go by was essential to the definition of being a Winslow.

They liked to ride in boats: wooden canoes, rowboats, skiffs, dinghies, kayaks. Once the children were awake again, someone – an uncle, a cousin – would take a few little ones out on the Sunfish to teach them to sail. Birch owned a Chris-Craft, a wooden motorboat from the thirties, with teak decks. Every winter, the whole boat had to be stripped and revarnished, the chrome polished so that it gleamed anew. Come midafternoon, he'd take the teenagers out with a pair of water skis, and they'd zoom by us in great circles, taking turns whizzing atop the water.

The Winslows liked to discuss boats almost as much as they liked to ride in them: how loud the Boston Whalers were, how terribly accosting the buzz of the Jet Skis, the awful sound of new-moneyed Canadian French coming off the too-close yachts. To a person, the clan admired the beautiful line of a Friendship sloop, and the primary colors of the spinnakers as they came off the marina, speeding past Flat Rocks for the Thursday night races.

Then there was the constant hubbub about the dogs: who had rolled in deer scat, who had disobeyed on the walk, who was a good girl, who could be trusted with the children, who should be taken back up to the cottage. All of Flat Rocks – all of Winloch, for that matter – became permeated, as the summer went on, with the rancid tang of canines living in a constant state of dampness – a smell I never could have imagined I could tolerate, and came to love.

And finally, there were the angels, the dozen or so Winslow cherubim: pouring, toe-dipping, squatting at the edge of the water. The youngest were naked, the oldest in bathing suits, the five- and six-year-olds in water wings or life preservers so their mothers could chat one another up, scraping their aluminum chairs along the rocks as they found an even spot to sit. The offspring wore hats atop their sunblock-drenched bodies, and were periodically wrapped in damp towels that invariably ended up dragging, dirty and brown, upon the ground. Watching Lu's delight as she joined the little ones at the water's edge, I realized how recently she had been one of them. She was only a head taller than the eldest child, but something definitive had happened to separate her from them. And yet, it was not hard to imagine what she had looked like at the lip of the lake only a few years before.

As the afternoon settled into night, the watchful mothers called their angels home, and the rocks took on a cocktail tone, smelling of bourbon, Sauvignon Blanc, and Camembert, permeated with a momentary, smudged happiness that would descend, inevitably and all too soon, into the insistent night-time rituals of dinner, bathing, and sleep.

When the light began to fade, Lu and I gathered up

our things and marched back to the Dining Hall, where Indo and her dogs ate all their meals. During the day, the teenagers came for second lunches, and there was always an odd relative or two – an accompanied child who'd awoken late from a nap, an elderly uncle in for a few days – but at night especially, when it was just a handful of us, I couldn't help but feel a little sad for the great cavernous hall, built to feed a hundred Winslows, echoing now with our quiet conversations.

'Everyone has their own kitchen now,' bemoaned Indo one misty, late June night. We were huddled over our teacups. 'Used to be the Dining Hall was the heartbeat of Winloch.' She went on to regale us with memories of nightly dinners that fed a hundred, Friday evening talent shows, and illicit romances with the waitstaff. Two tables away, Arlo, Jeffrey, and Owen were discussing how to hot-wire a powerboat. I watched Owen glance repeatedly in our direction. His gaze lingered over Lu. 'My mother was a German,' Indo went on, 'so we had special "beer hall" nights, with Wiener schnitzel, and the waiters dressed in lederhosen, and, let me tell you, it's hard to tear lederhosen off in the heat of the moment!'

I was instantly desperate for a moment alone with Lu – had she spoken to Owen since we'd noticed him on Flat Rocks? – but she was summoned to Trillium in the interest of a small family meal.

'Let's meander your direction,' Indo insisted once we were alone. 'Fritz hasn't had his proper exercise today.' We rambled along toward Bittersweet at a dachshund's pace. 'So?' she asked. 'Have you given any thought to my offer?'

'Your offer?' I feigned ignorance in case she had forgotten.

'My house. The opportunity to inherit—'

'Of course I've thought about it,' I interrupted, relieved to be able to ask my questions, 'but I don't even know why you'd give me your house – it's your house. Are you even allowed to do that? Isn't there some rule in the bylaws about giving a house to a stranger? And I haven't even found your folder yet—'

'One thing at a time, goodness, calm yourself!' Indo chuckled at my questions. 'One thing at a time.' She stopped walking, then looked up and down the lane as though to check for spies. Satisfied that we were alone, she placed her two heavy hands on my shoulders and met my eyes. 'I don't just need the folder. I need solid evidence of anything untoward.'

As if that meant something to me. 'But how am I supposed to know—'

She lifted one finger in the air as if to scold me. 'I'm letting you take your own time, remember?'

'Yes, but "untoward"? What's that supposed to mean? And "solid evidence"? I don't know what that—'

Just then Ev charged around the bend. Indo dropped her hands from my shoulders, and I understood that my work on the Winslow papers was supposed to be a secret.

'I've been looking for you everywhere!' Ev flung her arms around me as though I was the one who'd been ignoring her all week. 'A few of us are going on a voyage tomorrow, and you have to come too.'

'Voyage?'

'On a sailboat.'

Another version of myself would have been terrified at the thought of sailing for the first time, but Ev was saying she needed me. Still, I'd made plans for an afternoon of swimming with her sister. 'Lu can come, right?' I pushed my luck, thinking of the chance to play matchmaker. 'And the boys?'

Ev rolled her eyes dismissively.

'Well, how many people are going?' I pushed. 'Is there enough room? I don't want her to feel left out.'

Ev grudgingly admitted, 'We could use the extra hands.'

Indo had wandered off. She picked at Fritz's burrs.

'Sorry, Indo,' Ev said disdainfully, 'it's for the under-twenty set.'

The momentary look of pain in Indo's eyes was so familiar that I almost begged out of the trip right there.

CHAPTER SEVENTEEN

The Voyage

B UT INSTEAD I STOOD on the rocking Winloch dock bright and early the next morning, Ev on one side, Lu and the boys on the other, keeping a lookout for the white sail and spinnaker betokening our ride. There were whitecaps. The wind coming off the water brought a shiver. I'd roused at dawn, long before Ev and Lu (who'd crashed on the musty porch sofa, barely denting it), and proudly made a picnic of chicken salad sandwiches.

'What do you think the whole point of the trip is?' Ev had teased when she'd emerged twenty minutes later than we were due on the dock.

I frowned, not understanding.

'We're going for lunch,' she'd said, giggling, pulling me into a hug. 'So serious, Mabel Dagmar.' I could hear the mocking in her voice but made an effort to laugh along because we'd finally be spending the day together.

I had never been on a sailboat before and was sure I'd do something disastrous that would capsize the lot of us. On the dock, Lu leaned up beside me like a grateful cat. 'Don't worry, the boys won't let us do anything anyway,' she said. Arlo and Jeffrey threw twigs into the lake, while Owen sat silently at Lu's side. As far as I could tell, not a word had passed between them, but then, I reminded myself, the girl was only fourteen, and I wouldn't do any better.

'There they are!' exclaimed Ev, waving at a distant white spot on the horizon. I still had no idea who was taking us out. As the speck became a boat, I didn't recognize either of the men on deck – one was tall and broad, the other round and bearded.

I kept my eyes on the craft as it approached, Lu explaining the actions of the men on board. 'They're coming in on a broad reach, so they'll take a tack in, which means bringing the spinnaker down.' I thought I understood what she meant – the boat was coming in a straight line from a long way off, but there was no way they'd reach us at the angle they were coming, so they were going to turn abruptly toward us – tack – and take down the great white balloon-thing I'd been eyeing at the front of the boat. 'See?' she said, as one of the figures jumped where she'd been pointing. 'He's climbing on the foredeck. Now down comes the spinnaker' – the figure gathered the big, white, mushrooming sail as the boat turned toward us – 'see, he's pulling it down with one arm, and with the other he's hooking the halyard to the jib' – which I took to be the smaller sail that he attached to the line which had formerly held up the spinnaker – 'and now they're going to heel as they come about.' Before I could ask what *heel* meant, I understood. The jib up and secured in place, all at once the boat listed dramatically to the right as it came across the wind and in our direction. I shrieked. 'It's not going to capsize,' Lu reassured.

The boat came about fifty yards off the dock, then tacked quickly straight toward us. The sails roared as they whipped about. I stepped back as the boat neared, until, as though in a choreographed dance, the men on board let the ropes in their hands go ('They're called sheets,' Lu shouted), the sails cursed as the boat zoomed straight for the dock, Ev and Arlo grabbed the rope at the front of the boat, and I was pulled on board.

I crouched and covered my head, shielding myself from the terrifying flapping, and the shouting all around me, until there was a collective pulling-up of lines. The fabric quieted above us. We were off at an alarming pace; by the time I lifted my head, we were already twenty feet from the dock. I couldn't believe they all looked so calm.

'You'll get the hang of it,' Lu said indulgently, but I could guarantee I wouldn't be doing this again anytime soon.

I finally let Ev coax me over to the wheel, where the two men piloting the craft stood. When I ventured a glance at the water, it seemed as though we were going hundreds of miles an hour. Ev urged me toward the men, and it dawned on me, through my queasiness, that this was a setup.

They were already grown. One of them, Eric, was tall and blond and handsome, and clearly, from the way Ev was eyeing him, meant for her. The other was named Murray. He was squat and pink-faced, the collar of his polo turned up against his hairy neck. He had the kind of disappointing beard that had taken weeks to grow – scraggly and sparse. Satisfied she'd found me a date, Ev canoodled with Eric.

'You from around here, May?' Murray demanded as he thrust a glass of champagne into my hands.

I shook my head no and looked for Lu, but she and Owen already sat side by side up on the bow, gazing silently together into our future. I selfishly wished I hadn't invited him.

'She's a beaut,' Murray bragged. I thought he meant Lu, but he knocked on the side of the boat and went on. 'Eric's dad bought her back in 'seventy-three, but you wouldn't know it – they've taken real good care of her, real good care.' He pointed to the varnished wooden detailing. 'Just look at that brightwork.' His puffy, pink lips flapped as he prattled on, and I learned that he and Eric were both the sons of prominent Burlington families. 'But nothing like the Winslows,' he declared with obvious admiration. It was clear he had a big man-crush on Eric, who looked like the over-drawn hero of a Disney film. Poor Murray, I thought, as I sipped my champagne, watching Eric wave him over to steer so he could take Ev belowdecks.

'I think they've been meeting in secret,' I mumbled, remembering the unknown motor roaring off into the night. I watched the cabin door close behind Ev.

'Doesn't surprise me.' Murray burped, offering me a wry wink. 'Eric knows how to close the deal.'

The minutes crawled by as Murray bragged about Columbia Business School and I watched a piece of food wiggle in his thin mustache (after much deliberation, I determined it must be soft-boiled egg). Lu wandered by with a beer.

'You shouldn't drink.' I sounded like a schoolmarm. I could see Owen over her shoulder, waiting for her.

She took a long draft, raised the bottle in salute, and winked. 'I know.' After she left me, I could think only of

Ev, down below my very feet, doing god knows what to Mr Disney. I guessed this must be what seasick meant.

'Land ho!' Murray cried at the shore growing before us. The teenage boys took his instructions until Eric appeared back on deck looking quite pleased with himself. Ev emerged a few minutes later, hair tousled, rubbing her nose. 'You look so cute today!' she squealed manically, clasping my hand.

I wanted to be away from her, for the first time in a long time, just as far away from her as I could get.

We disembarked. Lu's arm linked in mine.

I was grateful for the touch of kindness. 'So?' I whispered, trying to be fun. Before us, Owen and Murray and the teenagers were charging toward lunch. Ev and Eric were still on board.

'He held my hand,' Lu confided. I took her trembling fingers and squeezed them reassuringly, as if I had ever even kissed someone.

Poolside at the Mansfield Club were a handful of paunchy golfers drinking whiskey – Murray in twenty-five years. We were by far the youngest people there, and stuck out like sore thumbs, if only because three of us were girls. Eric strutted under the awning as if he owned the place, ordering us all Cokes at the outdoor bar and sneaking rum into his and Ev's glasses with a hidden flask. We settled down beside the turquoise pool.

'You happy now, baby?' Eric asked Ev. To me he bragged, 'She wouldn't shut up about this place, and since my dad's a member . . .'

'I'm getting the Caesar salad,' Ev declared. Her eyes looked crazy. I'd seen her on drugs before, but never in the middle of the day. She was like a car accident I'd driven past once on I-5: irresistibly distressing. I proposed to Lu we take a walk, but she seemed completely unfazed by Ev's altered state – either she was so innocent she noticed nothing or she was so inured to drugs that this hardly registered.

'Why isn't anyone here?' I asked.

'It's packed on the weekends,' Eric boasted. 'Friday afternoons are Adults Only.' He gestured toward Ev. 'Good thing we had this hottie with us or they wouldn't have let any of you kiddos in.'

Ev giggled, burying her face in his neck.

'They should have more "Adult" activities then. Let's get some strippers out here, am I right, boys?' Murray sneered, lifting his hand up for high fives with the teenagers, who guffawed in response. All but Owen. I liked that kid.

'I'll have a burger,' I said, getting up. 'With cheese fries.' Ev didn't so much as bat an eye at my diet-busting order.

Inside, the club was low-lit and carpeted. I'd expected something Adirondack and upscale, but I might as well have been in Texas in the seventies. I followed a long hallway in the direction of the double doors, which the waiter had told me would lead to the lobby bathrooms, wondering if the pair of Ev's flip-flops I'd slipped on that morning were up to the dress code. A busboy brushed through the doors and headed straight toward me. He had a tray of dishes balanced on his shoulder, and I almost went by without looking at his face. In the instant we passed each other, I did.

'John?' I said, stopping short, surprised and happy to see him.

His face froze as he took me in: shock, then anger. 'What are you doing here?' he demanded. I realized I'd never seen him anything but calm.

'We – we sailed over,' I said, as John scanned the hallway.

'You can't tell anyone you saw me,' he said.

'Okay.'

'If the Winslows found out I work here . . . it would be a disaster.'

'I get it.' I padded down the hallway toward the lobby. I could feel him watching me walk away. At the double doors, I swiveled. 'Ev's here with Eric, you know.'

He clenched his jaw involuntarily. So it was true – he loved her.

I thought of how wistful she'd sounded the night she'd discovered my collage, talking about him. Love was a force stronger than anything that could keep them apart – if they couldn't see that themselves, someone had to help them. 'You should be fighting for her,' I heard myself say. 'She deserves better than him.'

He looked down at the floor as though he were a little boy shamed. He nodded once before turning, with his tray of tinkling dishware, to stride down the hall.

CHAPTER EIGHTEEN

The Rescue

WE SAILED BACK ON a southerly breeze, after hours huddled by the wind-whipped pool. On the way home I watched Owen and Lu. Something had shifted between them; even though they were not touching, they were recognizably in each other's orbit, two magnets that could not be unstuck. I felt proud of my matchmaking abilities as we anchored well off Winloch and Eric popped open yet another bottle of champagne.

'Show's over, kiddos,' Ev declared, pointing at the water. I expected Lu to scoff, but instead she drew off her T-shirt and shorts, revealing her damp bikini, and dove in. Owen watched her with unabashed admiration, and jumped in behind her, fully clothed. Arlo and Jeffrey joined too, their flailing bluster disrupting the perfect vision of Lu's long, lovely limbs propelling her toward home.

'It's a long way to shore,' Murray said, raising a cocky eyebrow at me. I was well aware of this, calculating, as I had, that unless I strapped myself into a stolen life preserver, there was no way I was escaping this boat. Even if I had been able to flee, I couldn't leave Ev.

'Party!' She whooped, fist whipping the air, until Eric planted a messy kiss on her lips. Then she put her arms around him and kissed back, a long, slow, wet embrace that made my stomach lurch.

Murray leaned in.

'No thank you,' I said as politely as I could. He raised his hands in the air and stepped back, then strode to the stern and rolled himself a joint. So it was either spend the evening with lecherous Murray or chaperone the writhing, double-backed monster of Ev and Eric. In the distance, I made out Lu and the boys pulling themselves onto the dock. The light was dying around us. A cloud moved in.

I edged in on Ev and hovered there until she finally looked up at me.

'Can I steal her?' I said to Eric in a fake voice. 'Girl troubles.'

He let go of her with the same raised hands with which Murray had met my rebuke, a you-can-have-her-you-crazy-girl stance which angered me even as it satisfied my need to get her alone. Eric joined Murray at the stern, taking a long draw from the joint.

'What?' Ev said wearily.

'Don't you think we should be getting home?'

She rolled her eyes. 'Grow up, Mabel. Have some fun.'

I looked back at Murray. 'I'm not having fun with that.'

'Well I am,' she slurred, swaying. She tried to wave to Eric, but her hand got lost in the air. She was more messed up than I'd thought.

'What'd you take?' I asked. She stuck out her tongue in reply.

'Let's just ask them to take us home, okay,' I continued, 'and we can have a good dinner and—'

She lurched past me, managing, somehow, to get to her feet, stumbling toward Eric. Like a true Disney hero, he rushed to her aid, and she clung hard this time, wrapping herself around his barrel chest and smiling up at him. He pushed the hair from her face, then took her by the wrist and tugged her toward the cabin door. I headed that direction, to block their way, but Eric pushed right by.

'We were there to make John jealous,' I said.

Ev's eyes flashed, as though, for a moment, she had come back into herself. But her words lumbered out. 'I don't know what you're talking about.'

'Ev.' I tried to grab her arm.

'What are you, some kind of lesbian?' she spat, before disappearing down into the cabin.

Bitten and stunned, I watched her go, and in an instant I felt a hand clamp down on my shoulder, and another slide around my waist from behind. 'Hey hey hey,' Murray whispered into my ear, 'let's enjoy the quiet.' I tried to struggle against him, but I was going nowhere; he had pinned me from behind.

'Ev,' I called, but Murray's spidery hand moved from my shoulder to clamp over my mouth, taking my air. I tried to kick, to move away, any which way, but I was pressed between him and the closed cabin door. His breath smelled horribly of licorice and marijuana, and I could feel his erection boring through his clothes into my leg like some horrible rodent, and he was humming, growling into my ear as he writhed against me.

'Murray.' The voice was familiar and came from behind us.

Murray dropped his hands at once and stepped away, laughing, like a kid with his hand caught in the cookie jar. I turned and gasped, coughing for air, for freedom, and met Galway's eyes. He was walking carefully toward us along the boat's deck. I wondered if he'd been a stowaway this whole time. 'Heard you were having a little party,' he said grimly.

'We're having fun, right?' Murray really thought I might corroborate.

Galway held out his hand to me. I took it and realized I was shaking. 'Okay,' he said to Murray, 'you're going to go down and get Ev.'

Murray thrust his hands into his pockets and looked at the deck. I actually felt bad for him for a split second. Then I remembered the feeling of him behind me.

'Go down and get her,' Galway said, his smile gone, 'or I tell your mother who really embezzled the family trust.'

Murray wheezed. Disappeared into the cabin. As soon as he was gone, Galway turned to me. 'Did he hurt you? Did he do anything to you?'

I couldn't speak. Galway pointed to stern. 'My rowboat's tied up right there. Do you think you can climb down by yourself while I wait for Ev?'

I nodded a feeble yes. Clambered over the back of the yacht, lowered myself down the ladder and into the dinghy.

'Murray?' I heard him ask with authority. And then there was a sudden burst of sound, as Ev came tearing out of the cabin, cursing Murray and Galway, calling them assholes and worse, and the next thing I knew, Galway was forcing her down into the rowboat until we were untied and blessedly free, and, behind us, there was the scraping metal sound of the anchor chain lifting, and the yacht's motor coughed to life, and then we were rowing back toward shore – Ev seething, me shaking, and Galway silent and strong.

CHAPTER NINETEEN

The Discovery

I EMERGED FROM THE HUSHED bedroom just after dawn, clear-minded and angry. Ev was passed out in the same sprawled position she'd collapsed into in a fit a few hours before, but I'd awoken early from familiar nightmares – the horrible, driving sound of the frigid river; the hand grasping out into the open air. Fighting to forget, I banged the kettle onto the stove and cursed the pilot light until it took. Kicked the cabinet when it failed to yield any cereal.

I heard footsteps and gathered my strength for all the things I'd say to her, about how selfish she was, and stupid. I might even use the word *slut*.

'You okay?'

I turned to find a half-asleep Galway, tousled hair and bleary eyes, wrapped in the couch throw. 'You slept here?' I asked incredulously. The words came out mean.

He rubbed his eyes. Nodded. I tried to imagine anyone heavier than sylphlike Lu sleeping on the busted, ancient wicker porch couch – my back ached just imagining it. I returned to the cabinets. We had to have bread, Cream of Wheat, something.

'Don't you have work?' I asked in a clipped voice, slamming the metal doors as they revealed their uselessness.

I could feel him watching me. 'It's Saturday.'

There was nothing in the house. Finally, I turned to meet his eye.

'Did he hurt you?' he asked in a low voice. I was surprised at his anger. No one had been angry on my behalf in a very long time. I shook my head, even as I rubbed one wrist and felt tears well up inside me. I told myself I would not cry.

'Are you sure?' he asked, taking one step toward me.

I took an honest accounting of myself, every muscle, every inch of skin, and really felt. I was lucky, I thought, with a burst of recognition, and, like it or not, Galway had been my luck. 'It was terrifying,' I admitted. 'But I'm fine.'

'Murray used to come over to Winloch when we were kids. He was always trying to get me to murder frogs with him. One time, a rabbit.'

'Boy stuff,' I offered.

Galway shook his head. 'Those guys are sickos.'

The kettle shrieked. I moved it off the burner and opened its mouth, silencing it. I had wanted to wake Ev, but now I wanted her to sleep all day. I dreaded facing her hangover, her love triangle, and, even more, the helpless rage that had coursed through me all night and was stalling into defeat.

There came, at just that moment, a sweet and perfect birdsong from the woods. Galway and I each froze and listened as the notes cycled through four more times. The haunting melody brought back Lu's promises of what Winloch would offer. It was dawn. The wood thrush.

Galway's smile was kind and careful. 'You hungry?'

Masha made us omelets and home fries and thick-cut bacon. The salty aroma filling the empty Dining Hall sent me into paroxysms of joy. Apparently Masha had been cooking Galway hearty meals since he was a boy. They had an easy rapport, that of an aunt doting upon her favorite nephew, but it did not escape me that she was a servant and he a Winslow. Still, when the meal was cooked, Galway urged her to put up her feet. She showed us pictures of her apple-cheeked grandchildren in New Jersey and told a few embarrassing tales on Galway the boy. I found myself laughing, eating seconds, pushing aside the feeling of Murray behind me.

But after I'd cleaned my plate, when Masha was back in the kitchen making lunchtime chili and silence had fallen upon us, I found myself saying, 'I should get back.' Despair descended as I looked out the opened double doors at the gray day and anticipated a morning alone on the cold Bittersweet porch, trying to read *Paradise Lost*, avoiding writing another letter to my mother, while both waiting for and dreading Ev's awakening. Now that my stomach was full, I couldn't stand what Galway must think of me, between what he had seen in the Bittersweet window and what he had saved me from on the yacht. He was kind, I could see that now, which made me hate the idea of his pity even more.

'Indo said you've been making progress on the papers,' Galway said enthusiastically. He was immune to my mood, apparently, or willing to be its salve.

'What defines progress?'

'I spent some time with those papers a few years back,' he said. 'I'm embarrassed to admit I found it kind of interesting.'

'I haven't found Indo's folder,' I said miserably, remembering that she'd told me to search for even more than that, cursing myself for obediently looking. It stung to think of anyone in Ev's family considering me to be in the same class as Masha, but wasn't that exactly the roles we'd fallen into? Indo had told me to jump, and I'd asked how high.

Still, there was Indo's suggestion that she would share the wealth, that the papers might offer me the chance to earn the right to come back next summer. And Galway was trying to distract me, and it meant not having to face Ev, and maybe he'd have some idea of what would satisfy Indo's thirst for knowledge. We climbed the attic stairs. It was already stuffy up there, the timbers retaining a month's worth of heat, and Galway cracked the windows on either end of the great space to establish a cross-draft. I hung back as he set to work. His eager hands riffled through my piles as concentration settled on his brow. I was not used to being around people as in love with research as I was, and I felt suspicion rise through me. The way he tilted his head and displayed absorption was so like myself that I wondered, for a paranoid moment, if he was mocking me.

'Esther,' he said with admiration, shuffling a piece of paper up from the table on which I'd stacked what I could find from his great-grandfather's generation. 'She was a battle-ax.' He grinned, reading aloud from the brittle, yellowed newspaper clipping in his hand: '"Dr Esther Winslow spoke before the Smith College Society for Science and Medicine this Thursday past on the subject of Hysteria and the Female Temperament: 'I advise you ladies to put little stock in the misperception that our brains are any less formidable than those of the opposite sex. Experience has shown females much less likely to be swayed by the organs below their waists than our counterparts would have you believe, and certainly much less than our counterparts are.'"

I chuckled. Galway nodded. 'She was the rebel. Classic second child.'

'But not your direct ancestor?'

Galway rummaged out a hand-drawn family tree, made, I guessed, almost thirty years before, since it listed only Athol in our generation. Galway stepped up beside me and pointed to Esther's name, his arm so close to mine that I could feel the warmth from his skin. 'She was Samson and Bryndis's second daughter, of five. Banning was the only boy, born after her. Sometime around eighteen eighty.'

'And Banning was your great-grandfather.'

Galway nodded.

'So why aren't Banning's sisters' descendants here at Winloch?' I asked, casting my finger over the names of Great-grandfather Banning's sisters: Abigail, Esther, Katherine, Margaret, and Victoria. 'Didn't Samson build it for all of you?'

'Well, Esther didn't have any kids, or rather didn't let her female "organs" sway her, and I think her career was so intense that she hardly took a vacation. Abigail married and moved somewhere else – Maine, I think – where she had her share of summer residences. Katherine summered here, but she was a spinster.' I grimaced. 'I know,' he said. 'Awful word. Margaret' – he grinned – 'Indo once told me that Margaret was a lesbian who moved to San Francisco.'

'Shocking!' I gasped in mock horror.

'But that might just be wishful thinking on Indo's part. And Victoria?' He looked up to the rafters as if they offered some kind of answer. 'Boston maybe?'

'You know a lot about your great-grandfather's family,' I said, wondering if there was an untold reason all those women, Banning's sisters, had left Winloch, or if their departures could be chalked up to a different era, in which men inherited and women became part of the families they married into.

I followed Galway back to the table, still musing on secrets. 'How did you know that about Murray?' I asked hesitantly. 'About the embezzling thing?'

He raised his eyebrows. 'Thing about this family is, you stick around long enough and remember what you hear, you can piece together the truth about just about anyone. It's all said in other ways, usually about a boat or a dog or taxes. So you consider the source, and the information, why the information was leaked, and then you decode what it really means.'

He pulled a couple of dusty chairs from the eaves of the great room and settled in again at the papers. I started in at the table beside him, where I'd arranged the papers for Galway's grandfather Bard, head of the generation below Banning Winslow and his sisters.

'Did you know your granddad?' I asked, after consulting the family tree again.

'Bard? He wasn't much on kids. More concerned with money. The family trust. That kind of thing. He died when I was ten. But his sister, Gammy Pippa, she's still around.'

'Here?' I asked.

'She usually comes for a couple weeks. She's ninety-five. Feisty. Used to let me and Jackson drink beer on her back porch, where no one could see us. I think she liked the company.'

The specter of his cousin loomed over us. 'Were you close with Jackson?' I asked.

Galway put down the papers in his hand. 'He was intense. Even when we were little, he took everything personally. And then, you know, signing up for the Marines. I think he had a lot to prove.'

'About what?'

'He had Winslow blood flowing through his veins.' I thought of asking if that meant Galway felt he had a lot to prove too, but he continued. 'You know, I bet she'll be here for the wedding. Gammy Pippa.'

'Wedding?'

'The wedding. Tomorrow.'

I laughed. 'There's a wedding here tomorrow?'

'In the meadow beside Trillium. My cousin Philip is marrying his college sweetheart. I give it two years.'

'Is that a cynical view of them, or just your general take on marriage?'

He cleared his throat. I could feel his eyes on my face. 'I feel like I haven't made it up to you for spying.'

'Please – let's not.'

'I feel awful about it. And I've learned my lesson – I won't go peeking into other people's windows ever again.'

I smiled in spite of myself as I felt my entire body growing red with embarrassment.

'And then, the whole Murray thing. I'm not like him,

okay? I just want you to know it's not my habit to . . . to . . . to prey on innocent women.'

I nodded. My heart was pounding hard.

He was anxious, one hand rubbing the other. 'But I also want you to know – I hope this won't seem forward – I want you to know I didn't mind what I saw.' He held my gaze, then, hardly blinking, and I saw something glaze over him that I'd seen in the window, something warm and dreamy, his mouth opening, his eyes softening, and I felt my breath catch in my chest. 'It wasn't – it wasn't unpleasant, all right?'

I let out an involuntary, sharp laugh, fast and nervous, breaking his open gape. I turned my eyes back to the papers until a new silence, buzzing with something electric, descended upon us.

The papers concerning Samson's grandson Bard Winslow; his wife, Kitty; his older sisters, Pippa and Antonia; and his younger brother, Samuel (who had lived to the tender age of six), were voluminous but not particularly personal. This was less scrapbook material, more of a legal and financial nature. Ledgers, contracts, tax returns.

My eyes had started to blur by the time Galway moved to sit beside me. Instantly I felt alive again. We worked in silence for a while, handing papers back and forth, our fingers almost touching. I asked him how the Winloch board worked.

'Winloch is essentially a small country.' He laughed when I rolled my eyes but urged me to consider the metaphor. 'In Samson's direct line, the firstborn son of each firstborn son becomes "king" when his father dies. Then there's the board, a parliament of sorts. And then the general population.'

'So your father is a dictator.'

He grinned. 'Not exactly. There are checks and balances. He has to get at least two-thirds approval from the board to get anything passed.'

'How often is he overturned?'

Galway conceded his point. 'My father can be very convincing.'

'Could he just go into someone's house and take owner-ship of whatever he wanted?'

Galway sighed. 'You don't actually think they stole Indo's painting, do you?'

It wasn't until he asked me like that that I realized I kind of did.

'Indo is lovely, and emotional, and has a long history of being angry at my father,' he explained. 'The painting was never technically my grandmother's to give her. It belongs to the Winloch trust.'

'A trust your father – or any of the firstborn sons who come after him to rule this little fiefdom – can use to seize other people's property.'

'It's not like that,' he insisted.

'What's it like?'

'Yes, technically every bit of Winloch belongs to the trust. And, in theory, that means none of it is really ours, and, in theory, my father is the one making the major decisions, and, in theory, he could just wave his arm over everything and claim it for himself. I don't "own" Queen Anne's Lace and Ev doesn't "own" Bittersweet. But, for that matter, my father doesn't "own" Trillium either. It was a system built to make things evensteven, while also protecting the place from turning into some failed socialist experiment. No Winslow would ever unfairly seize something from another Winslow. It's a matter of honor.'

'Do children inherit their parents' cottages?'

'They often do, they just don't technically own them. Tradition is stronger than whatever is legally approved.'

'And who gets preference when inheriting? Sons or daughters?'

He sighed. 'Sons.'

I was beginning to understand why Banning's sisters had left Winloch. My heart was fluttering, but I had to ask one more question. 'Say someone wanted to give their cottage to someone outside the family. Say – a friend. How would that work?'

Galway shook his head. 'I think it would be up to the head of the family to approve. Where did you—'

'Oh, I read it in one of the papers.' I gestured vaguely toward one of the half-filled boxes to cover my tracks. 'Some cousin or something, I have a hard time keeping you all straight.'

'Honestly' – he shook his head – 'unless the inheritor had married in or something, I doubt it'd ever be approved. He'd have to be pretty convincing.' He chuckled. 'Or strong-arm his way in.'

The hairs on my arm stood up. 'Like by finding proof of a serious transgression?' Indo had told me to keep my eyes out for 'solid evidence of anything untoward.' Was she was expecting me to blackmail my way into Winloch?

Galway frowned. 'Can you find me that paper? I've never heard of something like that happening.'

I rubbed my eyes. 'Maybe over there?' I said vaguely. 'To tell you the truth, it's all bleeding together.' He started flipping through the box I'd gestured to. As he did, I seized upon the bankruptcy papers I'd discovered earlier. This wasn't just an effort to distract him. Something he'd said made me see the document with new eyes.

'Winloch is held in trust,' I repeated.

'That was Samson's vision.'

'Have you seen this?' I handed him the papers detailing the bankruptcy. He examined them for a while and frowned, then looked up at me questioningly.

'This is nineteen thirty-two, I think,' I said, looking at the numbers over his shoulder. 'Three years after the stock market crashed.'

He nodded.

'And this,' I said, handing him a financial statement that showed the Winslows to have hundreds of thousands in assets, 'is from only two years later.'

He pored over the document.

'Lots of families filed for bankruptcy and lost everything,' I continued. 'But I bet not many came out of the crash not only keeping a place like Winloch but even richer than they were before.'

He cocked his head to one side. I noticed the particular green of his eyes, tinged with a smokiness that reminded me of the ponderosas back home. 'So?' he said.

'Aren't you curious?'

'Curious about what?'

'About what your grandfather – third king of Winloch – did to keep this place.' It wasn't so much that I thought I would discover anything worth Indo's time, more that my mind had finally snagged something worth pursuing. I couldn't imagine letting it slip from my grasp. I could see him hesitating. 'Oh, come on, you think I'm hatching some diabolical scheme to bring the Winslows down?'

His eyes crinkled as he smiled. 'Of course not.'

'So then let's find out what happened.' I leaned down to his ear, felt my hot exhalation pool there. I felt powerful just inches from his skin. 'It'll be fun.'

CHAPTER TWENTY

The Wedding

Ev FINALLY SLUNK FROM our bedroom well past eight that night, her slender frame brittle and hunched. She was sober in body and spirit. Though I hated not confronting her right away about what a wretched position she'd put me in with Murray, I couldn't help but take pity on her pathetic, hollow-eyed self. I served her up Masha's leftover chili and sat with her at the kitchen table, looking down at our darkening cove as the bats darted for mosquitoes.

She finished her bowl in silence. 'More?' I asked.

She shook her head as her eyes filled with tears. I reached across the table for her tight hand, but she pulled it away. 'Don't be nice to me,' she sobbed.

'Would you rather I tell you Murray is a monster and you're a horrible friend for leaving me alone with him?'

She nodded, hiccuping through her tears. She looked like a child.

'What did you do with Eric?'

Her lips curved into a heartbroken smile. 'Everything he wanted.'

'You're better than that.'

She shook her head. 'It's like I'm infected, and everything, everyone I touch gets it. You shouldn't – you should just stay away from me, Mabel. I mean it. Go back to your family. Go home.'

My first reaction was to rail at her. But I stopped myself. I knew what it felt like to be Ev. To believe you were a pariah. A poison. A ruiner.

Like it or not, the memory of my mother's voice came back to me: 'Be sweet.'

I stood. Put my arms around Ev's shoulders. Held her until her tears dried.

Like little girls, we crawled into the same bed that night, brushed each other's hair, and made shadow puppets on the ceiling. The monkey lamp on the Hepplewhite table between our beds cast a comforting corona over the room. Ev whispered she was sorry, and awful, that she would buy me anything to make up for horrible Murray and his horrible hands. Her feet found mine. Her toes defrosted.

'Mabel Mabel Mabel,' she murmured as she drifted off to sleep, 'don't change a thing, I love you just the way you are.'

The next day was perfect for a wedding. Ev and Lu and I set out to pick wildflowers as ordered by Tilde with a pinched smile, and arrived back from the Winloch meadows with burred, laden arms – black-eyed Susans, tiger lilies, daisies – before heading into Trillium to help with the arrangements, which would be set along the pathway to the wedding tent ('Why they couldn't hire the florist to do this is beyond me,' Tilde griped). We were all in better moods – Ev, I supposed, for being free of the Eric drama; Lu because of Owen; and me because of what I'd discovered in the Dining

Hall attic and the person I'd discovered it with. In and of themselves the papers about the bankruptcy were nothing, but in contrast to the veritable wealth the Winslows had boasted only two years later, I knew they revealed a story, something secret, maybe even untoward, and my heart skipped at the thought of not having to discover that story alone.

Cousin Philip's bride-to-be was sweet as apple pie. She took me for a servant, but I could hardly blame her for asking me to find her another pair of panty hose; the phalanx of Winslow staff was impossible to track. In the second bedroom, the bride's future mother-in-law hemmed and hawed over which dress to wear, while, in the meadow below us, Tilde insisted loudly that the rental company absolutely must return to move the tent ten feet to the left for the sake of the ceremony view, and, all the while, the heady smell of sandalwood incense poured across the open meadow from Indo's downwind porch, until someone was dispensed to extinguish it. Ev and Lu rolled their eyes from the sidelines of this circus, but they and the other girl cousins, many of whom had married in, were warm to Philip's fiancée. I staved off jealousy, even though this was the day another girl was becoming a Winslow for good.

The wedding was to be held at five, followed by a cocktail hour on Flat Rocks, and then dancing under the stars. I stopped to pee at Indo's house after I changed into my dress at Bittersweet.

'I found something,' I mentioned. 'Bankruptcy papers from the thirties. Is that what you wanted?'

She was draped across the love seat in a kimono, a wet washcloth upon her brow. She lifted a finger to her lips.

I came closer. 'Why don't you just come out and tell me what you want me to find? It would save us both a lot of time.'

She pulled herself to sitting. It didn't look easy for her. 'You need to know what we're made of, my dear. What has made us Winslows.'

I sat down. 'Sure, right, you've pretty much already said that. I get it, you're all very fancy and mysterious and believe this is a little country that no one else can be a citizen of, but it's not lost on me that you Winslows aren't exactly friendly to outsiders. I imagine your brother wouldn't love the idea of me poking into your secrets.'

She patted my knee. 'Too bad I can't trust anyone else.'

'What makes you think you can trust me?'

She rose and drifted from the living room.

'I don't have to help you, you know,' I called behind her. 'I could just stop searching.'

I waited on her couch. It took her a good fifteen minutes before she revealed herself, wearing a dashiki I knew would make Tilde's head explode. 'Ah,' she intoned, as though the conversation hadn't paused for even a moment, 'but I know you won't.'

We ate well: whole lobsters, peekytoe crabs, risotto balls, oysters, quail and pasta primavera and grilled artichokes and more, followed by individual molten chocolate cakes topped with freshly churned ice cream. The feast almost justified the bride's father's jokey thirty-minute toast, which tried, in vain, to make up for the fact that he had obviously paid for none of this. The waiters wore bow ties. The wine and spirits flowed freely. Although this was a 'country' wedding (an adjective I'd heard Tilde deploy with a certain trace of disappointment more than once that day), I had never been at anything so fancy in my life.

At the first strains of music from the band, Ev and Lu and the rest of the young Winslows got up and danced to a song about lost love that I didn't recognize but everyone else knew by heart. I stayed in my seat, and was surveying the space when I felt a tap on my shoulder. I turned to find Galway standing above me, holding out his hand.

I took it, assuming he was asking me to dance. But instead he led me across the tent, past round tables festooned with rustic floral centerpieces and pillar candles, and to a table closer to the water, where a tiny white-haired woman held court. She was surrounded by a handful of rapt older gentlemen, Birch included, and I tugged against Galway's hand, shy to be introduced. He squeezed back in response and offered a reassuring smile.

'Gammy Pippa,' he said, crouching before the matriarch, 'I'd like you to meet my friend Mabel.'

The woman looked up at me, and, a moment later, joy overtook her face, which was already warm, open, and lined with wrinkles. Age had only enhanced her great beauty. She reached her hand up to take mine. 'Hello, dear.'

The men around us watched as I crouched before the old woman. I found myself flushing as Galway placed his hand on my lower back.

'I can see you're someone special,' she said to me, but I

could tell she was really describing me to Galway, as though giving her stamp of approval.

'She's Genevra's roommate,' Birch cut in from above.

Gammy Pippa's face registered a flash of irritation, but she didn't succumb to it. Instead she placed her hands on either side of my face. It was an intimate gesture, one I was not expecting. 'But we're keeping her, right?' What on earth had Galway told her?

'Pippa,' Birch admonished sharply, 'Let the poor girl go. She's not interested in us old folks.'

The woman withdrew her fingers from my cheeks as quickly as she'd put them there, and I instantly felt woozy. The room swam. I stepped back, stumbling on Ev's borrowed platform shoes, and Galway caught me. 'Are you okay?' he asked, but I knew they were keeping track of us, and what I wanted, in that moment, was to be invisible.

I pulled myself away from him and lurched toward the outside. As I left the tent, I heard Birch remark to the gathered quorum, 'Someone's been drinking.'

My face burned. I fought back hot tears. I couldn't put my finger on why, but I felt wretchedly embarrassed. What did that mean – 'keeping her'? I heard Galway call after me, but I raced ahead, nearly tripping on a root of the shade tree planted at the corner of the Trillium property. I gathered myself, and headed for the grand home.

Trillium was empty and unlit, thumping with the muffled sound of the party. I realized that my ears were ringing from the band, and that I was, in fact, a little drunker than I'd thought. I couldn't find a light switch, then remembered a flashlight I'd seen just inside the screen porch earlier in the day. With it, I found my way to the downstairs bathroom. I sat on the toilet and let myself shake, setting free all the strangeness of the interaction. Once my hands were still, I rose again to wash them. My face was a shock in the mirror – I had spent so many hours looking at Winslows that I expected aquiline features and a rosebud mouth. Instead, I was met with my moon face, my nonexistent cheekbones, my dull, small eyes set too far apart. My dress was too tight, too black, too polyester. I would sneak out the back door and back to Bittersweet.

My feet led me into the summer room, where Tilde and Birch had hosted their opening-of-the-summer party only a few weeks before. Through the open door, I could hear the crickets pulsing in time, vibrant laughter drifting in from the dance party. I remembered the uncomfortable moment between Indo and Tilde at the summer's opening dinner, meant, somehow, for me, but I pushed away the recollection in the interest of the Van Gogh. What I wanted now, to comfort myself, as a balm against the strange turn the night had taken, was just to see the magnificent painting in the shadows.

The wall where it should have been was blank. I cast my flashlight over the empty space again and again, searching desperately, but the Van Gogh wasn't there.

'They put it away for outsiders,' came a voice, and I jumped out of my skin. I thought of Murray first, and Galway second, but for better (or worse) it was neither of them. My flashlight revealed Athol sitting across the room, his sleeping baby in his arms. He'd been there the whole time. 'Sorry to frighten you,' he said, not sounding sorry at all.

'It's such a beautiful painting,' I said. 'I just thought I might be able to visit it.'

Athol blinked in the glare from the flashlight. I moved the beam from his face. I could hear his even inhalations, and the wheezing of the dreaming baby. 'Can I get you something, May?' he asked, sounding just like when he scolded little Ricky.

'No. No. I'll go find Ev.'

I made my way hastily onto the porch, my steps gaining momentum as I let the screen door swing shut behind me. I was grateful to be back in the world of the crickets. I started toward the party and ran smack into Galway. 'You okay?' he asked.

'I think your brother thought I was trying to steal something.'

Galway laughed. 'Which brother?'

'Athol.'

'The only thing he has to fear is time stealing his good looks,' he said loudly, as though he wanted Athol to hear. To me, he added, 'He takes everything too seriously.'

I realized my hands were trembling again, and let Galway take one of them. The touch of him stilled me. And then he said, 'I want to show you something.'

CHAPTER TWENTY-ONE

The Kiss

H E L E D M E S T R A I G H T behind Trillium, away from the music and people. It was even darker in the forest. I couldn't make out a trail, but he seemed to know the way, leading us around trees, pointing out roots to avoid, rocks to step over. His voice was gentle and his hand firm.

Then, abruptly, he stopped, reaching out to feel the trunk directly before us. I could sense its imposing size – it loomed, bigger than the other trees around it. Still, I was surprised when he began to climb it. He turned and instructed, 'Follow me.' I tested a two-by-four nailed sturdily into the wood. There was nowhere to go but up.

Galway climbed carefully, checking each rung as he ascended, and I stuck closely behind him, grateful that the darkness masked how far below we would find the forest floor. The footing was sure and secure, but as we got higher, I began to wonder how much farther up we'd have to go in order to reap whatever rewards were offered at the top. A view? A grand, secret tree house? A spaceship? Anything seemed possible.

Then, at once, the canopy gave way. We were close to the stars. I felt Galway scramble onto something wide above me. His arm reached down and guided me onto the platform on which he was standing. My heart raced as I vowed not to step an inch in any direction lest I plunge to my death. I held his elbow tight. But I couldn't help notice the stars, bigger and brighter above us. One of them streaked across the sky, leaving a bright line in its wake.

There was another one. And another. Magic, even though I knew it was just meteors. We stood beside each other with our heads tipped back, pointing and wordless, as each star tore across the sky. I took in the world below us too – the lake visible only where it reflected lights from the bay. And then, there came a burst of fireworks.

'Just in time,' Galway murmured.

They came quick and large from Burlington, bursting open the sky above us all. 'Are they for the wedding?' I asked, impressed.

'It's Independence Day.'

I'd completely forgotten it was the July Fourth weekend; I realized I hadn't seen any buntings or decorations anywhere at Winloch. 'Don't you guys celebrate?'

'Mum thinks it's tacky. We used to say we observed Bastille Day instead, but that just sounds pretentious.' The fireworks were still exploding above us – red, green, swirls of golden light. 'As if it isn't pretentious to call it Winloch Day and have everyone dress in white. It'll be next weekend.'

I nodded up at the sky, and felt Galway draw closer. We watched the fireworks in silence, listening to the booms ricochet and crescendo across the water. As the sky lit up, he stepped before me, took my face in his hands, and kissed me.

He tasted of blackberries. I forgot all fear that I might

not know how to do it right, and I kissed him back. And let me tell you, it was beyond what I had ever imagined, that first kiss, out of my dreams, under the stars, our bodies growing warm and together, a sweet truth surrounding us, the lake lying below us like glass.

Our bodies touched, but softly. I didn't know if he was being reticent for my sake, but I appreciated the quiet lust between us, nothing of Murray's aggression or need. We stopped to watch the finale. I thought he was going to kiss me again, but he spoke instead. 'I hate to do this, but I have to drive back to Boston tonight.'

'Oh.'

'Work stuff.'

'What is it' – I felt embarrassed not knowing already, but couldn't help myself, because the omission combined with Ev's disparagement had made me wonder if he didn't kill people for a living – 'what is it that you do?'

He laughed, brushing one hand through his hair. 'I fight for immigrant rights.'

'Oh, good.'

'Akin to being a hit man in this family.' As if he'd read my mind.

I took one last look up at the shooting stars.

'I'd like to stay,' he said wistfully, before swinging his foot back down into the open space in the floor. We made our way down the ladder carefully, his body just below my own, and, as I reached the bottom, he kissed the nape of my neck.

I spent the next few hours of the wedding reception dancing with Lu, oblivious to the adults who may or may not have been scrutinizing me. Ev had slipped off in the time I'd been with Galway, but even that I didn't care about – I embraced the numb bravery brought on by intoxication.

The music finally ended at two in the morning. My feet ached from dancing, and I was drunk and alone – Lu had wandered off with Owen. I clomped to the Dining Hall and swayed up the steps to my attic lair. I was too drunk, too happy, to really work, but it felt cozy in there, just the place to collect myself and take stock: I had had my first kiss, and it had been with Galway Winslow. As I touched his family's papers, I remembered all of it, his hands on my face, the taste of him, and I held still and closed my eyes, reliving each detail again and again.

My hands settled on the family tree we had looked at together, all the names of all the powerful men who'd passed this kingdom down to their firstborn sons. My eyes followed the bloodline of Samson Winslow and his wife, Bryndis Iansdottir, down to their firstborn son, Banning, and his wife, Mhairie Williams. Reading the family tree from the bottom up, the firstborns were again prominent: Athol had descended from Birch and Tilde; Birch had come from Bard and Kitty Spiegel.

But that was where the neat line of inheritance fell apart. For Birch's father, Bard Winslow, the second generation born into Winloch, was not his family's firstborn son. He'd had a brother older by two years. Gardener Winslow, born in 1905.

My first thought was that Gardener must have died as a child, a historically plausible explanation for altering the clear line of inheritance. I turned to the Winslow papers and searched for his name, almost giving up until I found a copy of a marriage certificate from 1938: Gardener Winslow and a girl named Melanie.

'So why didn't the firstborn son inherit?' I mumbled aloud, looking again at Bard, his younger brother, shining from the family tree.

I turned back to the other documents – the bankruptcy papers from 1932, the abundant bank statement from 1934, the family tree that listed Samson Winslow's death as 1931. They were telling me a story. According to the inheritance papers, Bard's father, Banning, was head of Winloch for only five short years, from his father's death in 1931 until 1936, and yet he remained alive well into the fifties.

What if – I thought, my heart pounding as the idea formed – what if Bard Winslow had done something so extraordinary to save his family's fortune that it had not only brought the Winslows back from certain bankruptcy but allowed him to both supersede his older brother's inheritance of the Winloch leadership, and depose his father decades early?

If Bard had done something tremendous to keep Winloch for his family, I wanted to find out what it was.

I bolted back down the stairs, into the great, empty hall. I raced for the phone. I found Galway's Boston number in the family directory. I dialed. He would be back home by now, and I could hear his voice.

The phone rang five times. I nearly hung up before a groggy female voice answered: 'Hello?'

'I'm sorry,' I said too enthusiastically for four in the

morning, 'I must have the wrong number, I'm calling for Galway Winslow.'

'He's not home yet,' the half-asleep woman answered, at which point I promptly hung up.

'He's not home yet.' Which meant it was her home too. Maybe he had a female roommate, or some other explanation. But the potential of what this meant itched at me. All at once, I felt exhausted and sad. The momentum I'd built dwindled. The connections my mind had made withered. I couldn't remember what had so excited me when I'd been upstairs only a moment before. My limbs were leaden, my tongue dry. I was no longer drunk, but the alcohol was still infecting me, making the distance to Bittersweet seem vast. I swayed out into the night alone.

Was it still even night? It's hard to remember, all these years later, but I can see myself picking my way to the road, as though I am a bird flying above myself, and I can make out my girlish limbs, my downtrodden form, without a flashlight, pressing toward the cottage, toward bed, so perhaps I was already touched by the good light of dawn.

I felt a wakefulness, a need to glimpse the water. I was quiet, quieter than I might have been, padding down toward the cove for a chance to peek at the lake on that night one last time.

When I was halfway down, a purple sound froze me in my place. I thought, at first, it was the cry of a dying animal, that of something feral caught in a trap. A moan, a yelp. But then, as I listened, I realized it was laughter. Human laughter. A yawning. Then more moaning. As I crouched, and moved to get a better glimpse of what was below me, on the rock where I had met Lu, I realized what I was hearing.

There, below me, a nude Ev sat astride the face of a naked man. She raised herself up in the early light and ululated into the sky, her breasts heaving, then brushing against his belly, with her rocking movement. I knew what he was doing, but I had never seen that, and certainly never done it. Her pleasure was contagious as she bucked atop his mouth until her voice rose into a fevered pitch of expressed pleasure, whooping up and up and then breaking. She collapsed atop him.

They lay still for a moment, his hands caressing her back, until she disentangled herself. And that was when I saw his face. Not Eric, as I had feared, but John. He turned her onto her back, and right there, on the rock, for any passing boat to see, he fucked her.

I was the only one watching, and I watched John and Genevra until the end, until, as he came, her voice broke into throaty sobs, and she wrapped her arms around his neck, called his name, and told him she loved him. She seemed desperate. She seemed happy. He knelt before her and lifted her up into his arms, burying his face in her neck. They sat like that, nude, wrapped around each other, until I noticed that the day was truly upon us and, unless I wanted to be caught spying, I should make my way to bed.

July

CHAPTER TWENTY-TWO

The Secret

I SWAM LIKE A FISH that first week of July, as though my life depended upon it. What I was swimming from, or to, I wasn't sure, but if the previous weekend's events were any indication of what could happen in two short days, I could not imagine what the rest of the summer might bring.

Every day, I did the crawl out to the floating dock off Flat Rocks, stopping long enough to pull myself up into the warming sun and let my bathing suit dry. I'd count the welted mosquito bites on my thighs and calves. The pink bumps itched like the devil, but my willpower had grown in direct proportion to the liters of blood that had been sucked from me, and I felt pride in my fortitude as I tucked my hands under my legs. Every day, I looked back to shore over my knees – I hadn't spent this much time with them since I was a child – blinking across the blinding, peaking water to watch those willowy Winslow bodies in profile.

Galway and I had not spoken since our time together on the platform in the tree. Periodically, I'd visit the murky sound of the woman's voice answering his phone in the near dawn, even as I sought out the drowning press of exercise upon my tired limbs. I hadn't dared call his number since, and by Tuesday afternoon, with my feet hanging off the gently rocking swimming platform into the sparkling lake, I had convinced myself that the kiss, and maybe even Galway himself, was a figment of my lonely imagination.

Then there was the lingering trace of Athol's threatening tone, almost laughable in the light of day, especially as I sat on the edge of the floating dock, shielding my eyes and looking back toward the water's edge, where Athol was teaching Ricky how to swim. The little boy kicked and splashed, shrieking between terror and pleasure as his father, tanner with each passing day, held him afloat. Birch watched from shore, and I remembered his sharp admonishment to Gammy Pippa, insisting I was only Ev's roommate when the old woman inexplicably took my face into her hands. In both interactions, I'd felt an unsettled strangeness in my gut, but I couldn't pinpoint the reason.

Beyond Athol and Birch and Gammy Pippa and Galway and the groggy 'Hello,' no matter how many watery meters I covered each day, I couldn't wash off the memory of John and Ev conjoined. I'd always found the phrase 'making love' so precious, but now I understood it. Even more, I longed for it. Was that normal? To watch people you knew mounting each other, riding each other, as though they were animals, and want what they had, even as you found yourself laughing at the mechanics of what one body was doing to the other? To feel a hand inside your most primal self grasping for what they had with a longing so deep you thought you might weep, or moan, or come yourself?

So I swam. I swam up and down, out and in, until I thought I could swim no more, and then I swam again. Sometimes Lu joined me, offering pointers about my arms or my foot placement, and I improved my form, grateful my hard work was beginning to show on my body. She talked of Owen in spurts of joy – they had kissed behind the tennis courts, he'd put his hand up her shirt and his fingers had felt like a promise. Then, on Wednesday, she whispered: 'I touched his . . . you know,' just as Owen and the boys leapt off the floating dock, leaving it swaying below us.

'Has anyone talked to you about sex?' I asked as the boys raced back to shore, splashing Athol and Ricky with no regard.

Lu sighed. 'Are you?'

'No, but you can get pregnant. You're fourteen, Lu.'

I expected her to make a dismissive comment à la Ev, but instead she wrapped her wet arms around me and kissed me, unexpectedly, on the shoulder. 'Thank you for worrying,' she said before cannonballing into the water. I could feel the kiss twinkling long after she'd made it back to shore.

Ev had departed early that morning with her suitcase in hand; I'd opened my eyes and croaked a 'Where are you going?' She'd replied, simply, 'Don't worry, it's not like I'll be having any fun.' But of course I had. I'd roused and fretted until I found the little note she left on the dining room table: 'Mum's kidnapped me for a "vacation" in Canada. KILL ME NOW and pray it's only tonight.' She'd been gone a few hours, and, while I felt liberated, missing her was another kind of trap.

Since there was no one waiting for me at home, I decided to stop by Indo's on the way back to Bittersweet. She'd gone to Boston for a few days right after the weekend, but I'd heard the familiar chug of her old station wagon I-think-I-canning over the hill and into the great meadow the night before. I marched toward her cottage, heart beating faster, as I thought of telling her what I had discovered in the attic. But once I thought about it hard, what it even was that I had found seemed to slip through my grasp, just as Galway's kiss had. Some papers about a long-ago bank-ruptcy? A subsequent positive financial statement? The revelation that Bard was second-born? These were details from a Nancy Drew mystery, probably not even news to the Winslows. Besides, I hadn't run across anything like Indo's manila folder. As a cool wind tousled my wet hair, I almost bypassed her cottage. She wasn't going to give me Clover – according to what Galway had told me, she couldn't.

But no, I thought, I want to see her, and ask her about the folder – there must be some detail I'm missing. Ever the optimist, Mabel Dagmar.

I was glad to find the station wagon parked before Clover. My hand fisted to knock when the door yawned open.

It was Birch. 'Hello hello,' he said with a cheerful grin. 'You here to see Indo?'

'Is she inside?'

'I'm afraid she just settled in for a nap.'

I heard the familiar scrape of nails across the floor as Fritz ran toward us, yapping like a lunatic, his compatriots at his heels. I knelt down, ready to scratch behind his ears. But when he was almost at the door, Birch's boat shoe moved as though of its own accord, tucking under the dog's low belly and sending him flying across the kitchen and into the cabinet below Indo's sink. The dog yelped, landing like a rag doll, as Birch stepped out and slammed the door behind himself, smiling all the while. 'Come to tea!' he said, adding, 'You can stop by after she's awoken,' clapping my bare shoulder and pressing me toward Trillium.

'You take milk? Sugar?' Birch asked as a woman carried a tea tray onto the sunny porch. One of the pair of water spaniels lying at the foot of Birch's wicker chair lifted its head and growled at the rattle of the dishes, but the maid paid him no mind, setting the silver service down and leaving us as soon as she'd come. The tray was laden with homemade chocolate chip cookies, and though I was trying not to eat anything made of butter, sugar, or wheat, they sent up a glorious smell and I felt, for the woman's sake, that I should taste at least one.

As I thought of Fritz sailing across Indo's kitchen, I squirmed in apprehension. Had Birch been lying in wait for me at Indo's? And if so, why? Had he discovered that Indo had offered me her house, that I was rooting around in his family's history? Under the scrutiny of his gaze, I felt naked in my bathing suit. I crossed my arms over my chest and hoped if he was going to banish me he would do it soon.

'Have you heard from Ev and Tilde?' I asked, grateful she wasn't here to scrutinize me too. I succumbed to a bite of cookie.

He shook his head. 'You know how girl time is. Too much shopping to call home.' I knew that Ev would rather do just about anything than spend time alone with her mother; what had her note said? *Kill me now.* I wondered if Tilde had discovered Ev and John's dalliance. Maybe that was why I was in trouble. If I was in trouble.

As if an internal timer had gone off, Birch deliberately poured our tea from the pot. He set a silver strainer atop paper-thin porcelain cups. The liquid was black and steaming. His hands worked methodically, ritually, always at a task. He rested only after he had taken his first sip.

'You know, my dear,' he said, settling back into his wicker chair, 'I don't think we've properly expressed how much we appreciate you looking out for our Genevra.'

'We look out for each other,' I said, nervously downing another cookie. 'She's a great friend.'

'You are the great friend.'

I sipped my tea. It was bitter. But I had already turned down the sugar.

'In fact . . .' He put down his cup. 'I hesitate to mention this, because I can't imagine creating tension between you two. You seem to have such fun together.'

I set my cup down too.

'At our first dinner of the summer, you mentioned something to me called, what was it, the "inspection"?'

'Yes,' I clarified, 'the Winslow tradition of making sure that when someone has inherited their house, they're doing the proper upkeep and—'

He held his hand up. 'I'm going to stop you right there. You see, my dear, there is no such thing as an "inspection" in the Winslow tradition. Once a home is passed to someone, we don't check over her shoulder. It's her private home, to decorate and care for however she pleases. Certainly you've seen Indo's hovel. I doubt it would pass any inspection, familial or safety or what have you, were such a bylaw in place.'

'But Ev told me . . .' My mind was trying to gather up the bits of what Ev had told me about the inspection. She'd first mentioned it on our arrival at the Plattsburgh train station.

Birch frowned. 'My dear, I'm afraid . . .' He sighed. 'You are an honest girl, I can tell that. Not used to people manipulating you to get what they want. We adore Genevra, but she's had her . . . troubles over the years. With honesty, among other things.'

My face felt hot. 'You're saying she made up the inspection? She tricked me? But why would she do that?'

Birch leaned forward. He put his fingers together against his lips and closed his eyes for a moment. 'Genevra is about to come into a good bit of money. Her personal trust. She turned eighteen, after all. But before she gets it, the transfer has to be approved by, well, the board, and then, as head of this family, by me. It's my belief that she meant you no harm. She simply wanted to put her best foot forward, to impress Tilde and myself with a beautiful home. And she believed that if she made up some elaborate tale about an inspection, it would . . . motivate you. Get you to work as hard as possible. So that when I saw the house I would see, once and for all, that she is ready to inherit what she believes she is due.'

I sat back in my chair.

'If it makes you feel any better, she's done something similar to just about everyone she loves. It's her nature. Although it doesn't make the experience any less painful.'

'I don't know what to say.' My mind was replaying every aspect of my friendship with Ev. Rekindling the suspicion my mother had encouraged me to undertake at the beginning of it. Reprimanding myself for brushing off my mother's warnings as paranoia. I couldn't believe that Ev could have just lied to me so effortlessly and threatened me with being sent home. But then, that was exactly what had motivated me to spend a week on my hands and knees scrubbing, wasn't it?

Birch went on. 'I fear this will sound overly permissive, but lying to you is really quite irrelevant in terms of the finances. I can't exactly stop my daughter's trust from coming in just because she made up a story. But that doesn't mean what she did doesn't have personal ramifications. Mabel, I want to extend an apology on behalf of my daughter. She is . . . a challenge, and I would understand completely if you wanted to pack your bags.'

'No,' I said quickly, panicked he was sending me away. 'No, I'm hurt, I'll need to work it out with her, but—'

'And this is the other bit of it,' he interrupted. 'I'm going to ask something, well; perhaps you'll think me too forgiving, but . . . you see, Mabel, I'm going to ask if we could keep this revelation of her dissembling between ourselves. Not because I believe Genevra's behavior is excusable. But because it worries me.'

'You don't want me to tell her I know she lied to me?'
He nodded.

Looking into the house, I could make out the maid doing something methodical – dusting, folding, polishing. Her arm waggled back and forth, diligently doing work my ancestors would have done. I wondered if she could hear us. I wondered if the Van Gogh was back on the wall.

I stuffed another cookie into my mouth. 'Why does her lying worry you?'

'She's always been somewhat troubled. Had a hard time separating fact from fiction. But the real risk is that she can be quite self-destructive. I'm sure, hearing what she did to you, you can hardly imagine how she could treat herself more poorly than she's treated you, but I can assure you, Genevra has tried to . . . well, to hurt herself on more than one occasion.'

'She's tried to . . . ?' I wondered if he was suggesting she'd attempted suicide. I shivered at the thought, but having seen how wrecked she was the day after our ride on Eric's yacht, I wasn't entirely surprised.

'She's our daughter. We hate the thought of her being . . . unkind . . . but we hate the thought of her hurting herself even more. I asked you here to enlist you. As my ally in this matter.'

I was relieved that he wasn't sending me away, that he believed I might be able to help them all move forward. 'I'll help any way I can,' I replied.

'This is awkward, I'm sure you must be aware of that' – I nodded – 'but I want to know if you'll inform me if you notice any strange behavior on Genevra's part. Oh, the usual shenanigans, forget about them, I just mean if you see her doing something . . . dangerous. Making decisions you worry aren't in her best interest. I hope you'll feel you can come to me. That you won't think of it as tattling.'

'Absolutely,' I said quickly, 'absolutely,' my body welling

with relief, even as I thought back over what I'd seen in the past week alone. But then, this was another world, and the Winslows seemed positively nonchalant about behaviors that would have sent my mother to an early grave. I wondered if I should ask Ev's father if he could define the concerning behaviors for me – outdoor sex? cigarette smoking? – so that I might at least know if I should be worried myself, but he spoke instead.

'Anything you need, Mabel, just let me know.' He cleared his throat. 'It can be uncomfortable to discuss financial matters, but rest assured, you are part of this family now, and we care for our own.'

Involuntary tears sprang forth – no father had ever spoken to me this way, least of all my own. But before I could muster up an appropriate response, Birch had stood. He took a long draft from his teacup, then set it down hard to rattle on its saucer. 'Now if you'll excuse me . . .' With that, he turned on his heel and disappeared into the house. The dogs woofed and shuffled off behind him. 'Bring some cookies to grumpy old Indo,' he called over his shoulder. And then he was gone.

I finished my tea alone, hopeful that Athol wouldn't find me there and accuse me of pilfering the china, then basked in the sun streaming onto the wide, whitewashed porch, free of unnecessary clutter, running my mind over how to handle Ev, grateful she was out of town so I didn't have to face her yet. It had become a perfect day – the wicker furniture, the view, the fullness in my belly. Briefly, I considered curling up and drowsing on the porch swing. I doubted Birch would mind.

It occurred to me that I couldn't hear the maid anymore. I peeled myself from the damp cushion and ventured into the summer room. The Van Gogh was back in its place. I was drawn, like a moth to the flame, back into its thrall, to the trees spiraling up toward the midnight sky. I had never known a piece of art to be something one could taste and smell and hear. I just wanted to be near it, consumed by it, undone in its company.

The maid reemerged, startling at the sight of me.

'It's a real Van Gogh,' I said softly.

Her eyes danced over the painting for the briefest of moments before looking down. Had I been someone different, who I am today, that look would have told me all I needed to know. But instead, I saw reflected in that woman's diverted eyes only the fact that I did not know how to speak to people like her without causing offense, and so I apologized.

She handed me an empty striped baker's bag. I filled it with cookies before glancing one last time up at that secret – not even knowing it was one – before finding my own way out.

CHAPTER TWENTY-THREE

The Book

THE NEXT DAY, EV was still gone. Clover was quiet when I knocked. A sour-looking Indo opened the door an inch. 'What's that?' she asked, suspiciously pointing to the baker's bag I'd resisted overnight.

'Cookies!' I said cheerfully, realizing I'd missed the smoky scent of Indo and her house. The sweets gained me entry.

Indo moved around Clover with greater deliberation than I'd ever seen, as if she were carefully placing one foot before the other, lest she tip forward into some kind of oblivion. She looked thinner than usual. When she moaned as she pulled herself down before the wide table on the porch, I asked, 'Are you okay?'

She took a bite. Closed her eyes and chewed with careful pleasure. In contrast to Trillium's porch, Clover's was damp and alive, its floorboards curling in places, dirty paint peeling off as though the color were the skin a snake was shedding. The furniture, too, was unpainted and moldy, the damp wicker threatening to collapse under either of us at any moment. It occurred to me that Indo didn't have anyone to help her. I tried not to think about what that boded for my own future.

'I hear LuLu's got a boyfriend,' she finally said, licking chocolate from her fingers.

'He's sweet.'

'He's a teenage boy.'

'Yeah, but I'm starting to think that's better than a grown man.'

'You, my dear, are wiser than you look.' I blushed at her backhanded compliment. 'And you?'

'Me?' I asked.

'Any crushes?' Her gaze was direct. I felt sure she already knew the answer to that question – anyone who'd seen Galway lead me across the tent to Gammy Pippa probably suspected there was something there. But I stayed silent. Finally she ended her scrutiny. 'Probably for the best,' she concluded. 'Save yourself some heartache. How goes your search through the Winslow archive?'

'Actually,' I said crisply, 'it would help to know what kind of information – proof, you called it? – I'm looking for.'

'Yes, yes.' She waved her hand as though bored with my requests.

'I haven't found anything like the manila folder you described. Is there anyplace it could be besides the Dining Hall?'

'There are dozens of places,' she answered breezily, 'most of them behind lock and key. It was a fool's errand, I'm afraid.'

'Is there anything missing from the archive?' I pressed.

'Whatever do you mean?'

The question had bubbled out as though of its own volition, but now that it had, I knew why. She'd been the one to send me to the papers, to make me promises based on what they would provide me, to beg me to help find proof of something she wouldn't name. The folder so obviously wasn't there. And now she was acting like it wasn't important. So maybe it wasn't. Maybe she was testing me. Seeing how tightly I could lock my jaws when I wanted something. 'I need another source. Another way to find whatever you're looking for. If you really want me to find it.'

The smile fell from Indo's face. She sat still for nearly a minute. Then stood, without a word, and left the porch. Fritz toddled off after her, while the other dogs snored on their moldering pillow. I couldn't hear her. I wondered what I should do – stay at her table? Leave? It seemed I had offended her. I stood and brushed the cookie crumbs from the table as Indo marched back onto the porch and placed a worn, old book with a tattered black cover into my hands. It smelled faintly of the earth.

'You should go,' she said firmly, her voice low.

'What is it?'

She squeezed the backs of my hands. 'Good girl,' she whispered. 'Hide it well. Trust no one.'

The next thing I knew, I was back on Indo's driveway, blinking into the sun, and wondering what, exactly, was now in my care.

CHAPTER TWENTY-FOUR

The Turtles

L U WAS WAITING FOR me on the Bittersweet porch, her feet dangling over the couch's wicker armrest. She sprang up at the sound of me. 'I have a surprise!'

I told her I'd be with her in a minute, that I really had to pee – it was the only excuse I could think of. Under the bathroom sink I found a holey towel I'd insisted on saving on our cleaning day. I wrapped the cloth around the black book I'd spirited from Indo's and tucked the package into the recesses of the cabinet, behind the sunblock and bug spray and unopened bubble bath.

'A surprise?' I asked, emerging.

'I made it!' She handed me a friendship bracelet made of embroidery floss – peacock, crimson, jade. I wasn't disappointed – it was as good a present as any I had gotten – but I suppose I'd come to expect Winslow presents to be, well, expensive. I hesitated a moment longer than I should have.

'You don't like it?' Lu asked, her eyes darkening into something liquid.

'No, I love it!' I said too enthusiastically, putting my foot up onto the couch and tying the bracelet around my ankle. 'Can I wear it here?'

'You can say if you don't like it.'

'I love it. I love that you made it.' But I could tell, from the way she stiffened as I kissed her cheek, that I had hurt her.

I spent the next hour dying to take a peek at Indo's book, distracted by imagining what it might be and say. But Lu wasn't going anywhere fast – her intractable presence in the cottage made that clear, and my distraction only rendered her more irritated, so I tried to make amends, pressing the girl for details about Owen. All I got in return were noncommittal shrugs and this, finally spat at me as though I had offered her poison: 'He's spending time with his friends today.' So that was why she resented me – because I was her only option.

'Aren't you lonely?' she asked. 'I thought you'd be lonely, with Ev gone.'

I realized that, for the first time in a good while, I wasn't.

'What can I do to cheer you up?' I asked after we had plowed through dozens of rounds of Spit, usually her favorite card game. Lu had beaten me every time, her hands stinging my own with harsh slaps as we sat cross-legged on the chilled floor of Bittersweet's diminutive porch. I'd cooked her a grilled cheese on rye, but she'd eaten it sulkily, leaving the crusts. She'd shot down all my ideas – no swimming, no baking, no walk. My heart sank as it occurred to me that spending the afternoon with her was just like babysitting the neighbor kids on my parents' block.

'Anything,' I pleaded, wanting my friend Lu back. 'I'll do anything to get you out of this funk.' If I was going to spend the day with her and not with the mysterious book

Indo had produced, the least we could do was have a good time.

Lu crossed her arms over her chest defensively and stuck out her lower lip in protest against what she took to be my condescending tone. But then she shifted, peeking out the screen at a handful of chickadees flitting between bush and tree just outside our door. 'Do you have any grain?' she asked, leaping up before I had the chance to answer. She emerged from the kitchen with a handful of oatmeal, stepping over our newly dealt game and out the screen door.

The little birds, a blur of white and black and brown, startled at the creak of the hinges. She scattered some of the oatmeal on the dusty ground at the base of the porch stairs, then sat on the bottom step, pulling her feet below her, and opened her palm. The remaining oatmeal pooled there. She held still as a statue.

The black-capped chickadees flitted over, calling to each other in loud voices, announcing the good news. They jumped from tree to bush and back again, gaining confidence, until one grew brave enough to hop down onto the dirt a few feet from Lu. She remained motionless. The bird pecked at the oatmeal, then called to its friends, who joined it. They circled Lu carefully, eyeing the feast in her hand. She didn't move or cough or sneeze. I was enraptured.

That first chickadee took the chance. It swooped down into Lu's palm, and then out again as quickly as it had come. But she had willed her body to be as another bush, and, confident that she would neither catch nor abuse them, the birds began to land gamely in her palm, picking up pieces of food, carrying them off to eat, and returning, until Lu was the only still point in a flutter of exuberant movement and sound. The chickadees ate it all. Only when they were done, and had skittered again, did she turn to me, beaming. 'I'm taking you to Turtle Point.'

We used a white dinghy tied up on the Flat Rocks dock. The last time I'd been rowed anywhere was when Galway had rescued me from Murray. I was grateful to be out with Lu on this day, and not still in peril on that one. She laughed at how tightly I gripped the life preserver ('You don't have to hold on to it, it's strapped to your body') and suggested I row, but I was content to close my eyes in the stern and pray for my life.

We went straight across Winslow Bay, through the sheltered area where the yachts were starting to moor as another weekend began. Women in bikinis jumped off the backs of their pristine boats. I turned to look over my shoulder. I could see Trillium and Clover growing smaller and smaller behind us, until the trees obscured the houses. It was late afternoon, and one of the young families emerged onto Flat Rocks, but I couldn't make out who they were. I watched Lu's face – there was a serenity to her focus, one I didn't want to break with conversation. She rowed fast and evenly, her back to our destination.

As we neared the other side of the bay, what I had always taken to be solid shoreline on the horizon revealed itself to be three long points, bisected by private coves. We cut toward the rocky ledges. It was quieter over here.

'Is this Winloch?' I asked as we entered a shadowed cove.

The water was shallow, and I could make out a shelf of sandstone below us, bass and minnows hiding underneath our boat.

'I think so,' she said. 'No one's ever bothered me.' I was struck that, as a Winslow, Lu had no idea what it felt like to be chased off someone's property. She went on. 'This is where the townie fishermen come early in the morning. They have these horrible trawling motors, like two- to three-horsepower, that they just keep on, and they throw in their lines and just, like, trail along, waiting for something to bite.' She rolled her eyes. 'Not a sport, if you ask me. And they're way too close to shore.'

As she used her oar to push us off the stranger's point we were skirting, I didn't have to wonder what gave us special privileges to lurk here, but neither did I defend the townies. 'Are there laws about that?' I asked. 'About being too close to shore?'

'Daddy always tells a story about some Canadian who ran his line to Flat Rocks, and Gammy Pippa came down and snipped the line with a pair of wire cutters.' She giggled. 'And then, you know, sometimes people skinny-dip, just, like, to give the boaters a fuck-you.'

'Or a free show.'

'Yeah, but I don't think anyone wants to see Aunt Stockard in her birthday suit.'

Dear Mom,
Whenever summer strikes, and I finally prevail upon
you to come down to the river with me, you insist on
covering as much square footage of your body as possible.

Shorts to hide your thighs. A button-down shirt to drape your arms. A hat and sunglasses, not for protection, but so no one will recognize you and invite you to swim.

Rich women are different. They're confident that people want to see them naked, even if they don't. Truthfully, I'd probably rather see most of them without their clothes on than see you.

The question is, who will I be? Wacky Aunt Drunkard, giving the boaters a show? Or Doris Dagmar, afraid of her own breasts? There must be some middle ground.

Lu gestured to the point before us. 'That's where the turtles live,' she said, and I felt genuine affection for her again. She was spoiled in ways that were mostly not her fault, that had to do with being fourteen and raised by the wealthy. Still, it felt dangerous that in only a few years she'd be on her own, blithely espousing her elitist opinions to the grown world. Hers was a strange brand of naïveté, and I wondered if anyone was going to help her with it.

We rowed across the next cove. The soft spot between the two points was a sandy beach, reedy and quiet. 'We used to play Indian Princess over here,' Lu said. 'Ev and I would row over with a picnic whenever Mum was in our hair.' I felt a flush of envy for a safe girlhood I'd never had.

Lu rowed straight toward shore. She hopped out and kicked the driftwood out of the way before pulling the boat up onto the beach, tying the painter around the trunk of a pine.

Once on shore, she was a chatterbox, capably leading me up a ten-foot rock face and into the woods, then down a rarely used trail that backboned the point. The mosquitoes had found us, and we waved our arms like lunatics as she spoke. 'Wild blueberries grow up here. I guess it's probably too early for blueberries, but when Ev and I were little we used to pick them and gather them in our hands, and then we'd bring them back to the lean-to we built – no, I'm serious, we built a lean-to out of driftwood – oh, May, I wish you could have seen it, it was just perfect, and up here is where the turtles nest, in the spring you can find their white shells right around the holes, we used to— Oh!'

Out of nowhere she yelped, cutting herself off and stopping short on the path. I nearly tripped over her. As the seconds passed, my emotions ran the gamut, from irritated – I couldn't see around her – to concerned – she doubled over, and I thought she might be sick – to confused – as she exclaimed, 'Oh no, oh no, May.' When she began to cry, I stepped off the precarious path and looked around her.

There, in front of her, lay the carcass of a turtle. It was big – its shell a foot in diameter. In death, it lay belly up, its four legs blackened and splayed, hardened like cured leather. Sharp-looking claws curled into the air from its toes, as though the beast had died fighting. Its head was gone.

'Oh my god,' Lu gasped, covering her mouth with her hand. A smell had begun to settle over us – rotting, salty – and I feared she would be sick, for then I would be too. I grabbed her by the waist and pulled her forward, around the dead creature. She ogled as we stepped over it, gagging. All we had to do was get to the end of the point and reassess. Animals died all the time.

As we made our way down the path, a strange sound settled in my ears. The loud, communal thrum was made by nature, but I had never heard anything like it. I led Lu toward the rocky point. It wasn't until the tree cover ended that my knees went weak and I felt myself swoon. I tried to turn Lu around before she saw, but it was no use. The girl let out a sobbing cry, and nauseous sorrow came over her as she took in the gruesome scene – a dozen turtles, or more, each in the same rigor mortis as the first, covered by a swarm of hungry, angry flies and squirming with maggots. The dead bodies were in various states of decay. A few were half eaten. Lu retched into a blueberry bush, but nothing came up. I took her hand and led her back the way we came. The whole terrible world seemed to be buzzing.

CHAPTER TWENTY-FIVE

The Evening

B Y THE TIME WE got back to camp, Lu was reasonable – there was no one to call now that it was past business hours, but first thing in the morning she'd go to the Dining Hall and phone the university. There had to be someone studying turtles.

'It's global warming,' she cried, her eyes rimmed with red.

'Didn't everyone say it was a very cold winter?' I asked. 'Maybe the water was frozen solid. Maybe they couldn't get back in.' She shook her head and started crying all over again.

I braced myself when I heard the car motor. Eric? John? Galway? But it was Tilde's white Jaguar, and soon Ev was upon us, arms laden with shopping bags. I was surprised by how hardened my heart felt when she stepped through the door, as I remembered how she'd lied about the inspection. Still, I was ready for reinforcements. She'd comfort Lu, pull her into bed, hold her until she slept.

But instead, she loomed over us, sneering. 'What's that smell?' To Lu she growled, 'Don't you have somewhere to be?' Hot, new tears sprang to Lu's eyes as the girl wordlessly rose and left the cottage, the screen door slamming behind her. Ev balked. 'What's wrong with her?'

'How was your trip?' I mustered.

'My mother has such wretched taste,' she complained, tossing a bag at me. 'I bought you a sweater.' And with that, she bolted herself in the bedroom.

I locked myself in the bathroom. The single lightbulb cast the roughly hewed pine boards that lined floor, walls, and ceiling in a dreamy red glow. Out the eyebrow window, the night sky faded to a deep purple. I ran myself a piping hot bath in the claw-foot tub, filling the room with the scent of sulfur – the hard water had to come all the way up from a well three hundred feet below. I was grateful to be immersed in a smell other than that of rotting turtle, no matter how strong or unpleasant.

Bath run, remembering Indo's warning ('Trust no one'), I felt for the book in its hiding place below the sink, half expecting it to be stolen. But it was right where I had left it, wrapped in its old towel. I didn't dare sit in the tub for fear of dropping the precious book in; instead I settled onto the brand-new violet bath mat Ev had spent far too much on.

The book was small – both covers only a little larger than my hands bookending it in prayer. The musty smell I'd first caught a whiff of when Indo placed it into my hands still lingered. The binding sighed a brittle complaint when I opened it. The paper was of heavier stock than used nowadays, its edges beveled.

The blank pages had been used to make a journal, filled with sloping cursive in the same black ink, from one cover to the other. I deduced it was a woman's handwriting even before I found the name inside the front cover: Katrine

Spiegel Winslow. My mind worked on the family tree, recalling what I could from memory. This was Kitty. Bard's wife; Birch and Indo's mother.

'Thursday, January 2,' the first entry read, 'a lovely New Year's present from B. to record our life together. He is back in Boston already for a fortnight. Easy to miss Mutti and Papa and Friedrich when the snow is falling. I felt sure B. and I were expanding our own little family, but the holiday brought unhappy news. Thankful for B.'s optimism and Pippa's company. The sister I never had. She comes to tea daily with tales of the world's misfortune. Is it terrible to take solace in finding oneself better off than the huddled masses?'

Kitty's voice seemed to fill the small wooden bathroom. I pored over the entry, trying to deduce the year. She might still be childless ('I felt sure B. and I were expanding our own little family') or she might have only one or two children, which, I supposed, could still be considered a 'little' family. So she might have started the journal anytime before her first baby, little Greta, was born, through the birth of her second child, Indo, in 1937.

I took the Pippa mentioned in the journal to be the old woman who had cradled my face – she had been young, and even more beautiful, whenever this was written. I thought back to the family tree I'd found with Galway – Gammy Pippa was Bard's sister. So I took the 'B.' in Kitty's entry to be her husband, Bard, making Pippa Kitty's sister-in-law.

I thought of my own family – one, two, three – at Kitty's mention of her parents and, presumably, her brother. I wondered what had brought Kitty so far from home.

I looked back through the entry for clues of when it had been written. Birch was easily in his seventies – vigorous, but aging – and given that his sisters Greta and Indo were older than he, that meant Greta had probably been born in the early to midthirties. I thought giddily of the money that had saved the Winslows from certain ruin as early as 1934 – if I was correct about Greta's age, and that 'our own little family' might just have meant a childless Kitty and Bard, then that money could have come in right around the time Kitty started this journal.

Another way to age the entry was the mention of the 'world's misfortune.' The Great Depression had already struck, or was striking. Which meant she had probably written this after Black Tuesday, in October 1929 – I'd gotten an A in Modern American History.

'Can I come in?' Ev asked from the other side of the wooden door, startling me.

'Ummmm,' I hedged, frantically wrapping the diary inside the towel, shoving it back into the cabinet.

'Are you pooping or something?'

'Just a second,' I called, ripping my clothes off and hopping toward the door. I slid open the lock and vaulted toward the bathtub, pulling the shower curtain around me. 'Okay,' I called out, plopping myself down into the water, wetting my arms.

Ev opened the door. 'What's the bath mat doing over by the sink?' I heard her tromp over and sit on the closed toilet. 'Why is the curtain closed?'

Because you called me a lesbian, I thought. Because I don't want to see you right now. Because you lied to me.

She peeked her head around the curtain. I could feel her eyes wandering over my naked flesh. 'Wow,' she said after a minute. 'You look fantastic!'

I frowned.

'Your arms are totally toned. And you're all tan. You look really . . . strong.'

I tried not to let her compliments work on me. But I looked down at myself and realized she was right. I did look good.

'I missed you,' she said.

I didn't reply.

Ev spent the next day firmly by my side. I'd planned to slip down to my favorite waterfront spot for a few hours alone with Kitty's journal, but Friday promised gray, beginning with a constant drizzle that rendered our summer quarters cold and close. I was concerned about Lu, and thought of heading over to Trillium to check in on her, but Ev wouldn't let me out of her sight ('Let's bake cookies!' 'Let's pick a color for the trim!'). She wanted to take me for a wet hike down to Bead Beach ('The clay from the lake gets washed up on the reeds and dries and makes these amazing little beads – oh, you'll love it!') or on a rainy, long row ('Have you seen the view from Honeymoon Cove?'), but I feigned illness from the couch, hoping she'd let me retreat to bed while she headed out for better company. She stayed put, wheedling me with a constant happy mood I found disconcerting. I wondered bitterly what John was busy doing that made her crave my company.

'Are you mad at me?' she asked when I made a face at the grilled cheese sandwich she'd made me.

Birch had told me not to say a word. And hadn't she been so nice ever since she got home?

I took a bite of the sandwich. It wasn't half bad. 'I guess it just hurt my feelings you didn't tell me you were going to Montreal beforehand.' As I said the words, I believed they described everything that was bothering me. I was hurt to know she could so easily leave me behind, simple as that.

She wrapped her arms around me. 'I know, sweet girl. Mum basically kidnapped me. At least I left a note, right?'

It was easy as that to forgive her.

It's sad and beautiful how a few hours can come to stand for the many others that never were. One looks back and holds up a handful of hours to prove, 'That was what it was, it was so perfect,' in spite of what one knows, in spite of all the other days that came before and after. In the intervening years, I've found myself awake in the wee hours, remembering the simple pleasure of that evening with Ev as I finally allowed myself to embrace it. Had the rest of the summer been uneventful, full of nights like it, I would have forgotten all we did – how she taught me her six favorite summer camp songs, and snorted unabashedly when laughing at my second-grade *Mayflower* joke. How we hauled up the bag of magazines I'd saved and, together, made collages for each of the Winslow family units – tidy for Athol's, messy for Banning's, hippy-dippy for the Kitterings – until we'd made a dozen to line our bathroom walls. We ate spaghetti sauce, hard-boiled eggs, and white rice for dinner. We made hot chocolate with little marshmallows. We listened to Sinatra and, when the music ended, rejoiced in the fact that the rain had stopped, and listened to the distant strains of 'La Vie en Rose' amplified off the water – someone, somewhere, was playing Edith Piaf.

I had thrown around the term *postlapsarian* in preparation for my Milton seminar, because it made me sound like an expert. The truth is, I had no idea what the word meant, not really. Sure, I knew that before Adam and Eve ate of the apple, they knew no sorrow. I knew that they lapsed by eating from that tree. I knew that God kicked them out of Paradise because of it. And that the rest of us came after that, prohibited from Eden.

Post (after). Lapsarian (the lapse).

We live in the world with sorrow in it, the world that Adam and Eve created the moment they tasted that apple. Each of us humans has a moment – if not many – in which we lapse. For some, the transgression involves sex. For others, simply, doubt or a rage so all-encompassing, it impels us to make irreversible decisions.

But whatever the transgression is doesn't really matter. What matters is that lapsing is our fate. We humans are doomed to it. Worse, it is our destiny to look back longingly, with nostalgia, at our world before we changed, at who we were Before.

We can never forget.

But we can never go back.

I remember that night with Ev, just the two of us, just happy. I remember because it was our last.

CHAPTER TWENTY-SIX

The Mother

I OPENED MY EYES THE next morning to the pocking sound of tennis balls. It was sunny once again, but my heart sank as I remembered it was the weekend. Galway would come, or he would not. I would ask him about the woman, or I would not. He would remember he had kissed me, or he would not. It occurred to me that this was why I had been so desperate to bury myself in Kitty's narrative; I didn't want to face my own life.

Ev rolled over in bed and rubbed her bleary eyes. 'What's wrong?'

I shook my head and offered a smile.

She fumbled for my copy of *Paradise Lost* on our shared night table. '"Awake, / My fairest, my espoused, my latest found,"' she read in a croaky voice, '"Heav'n's last best gift, my ever-new delight, / Awake, the morning shines, and the fresh field / Calls us."'

I heard the soft scratch of paper feathering out of the book. 'What's this?' she asked.

The letters to my mother. I sat bolt upright. 'Those are private,' I growled, grasping for the pieces of paper as I launched from my bed.

'Jesus,' she said, hands darting from my reach.

My mind was racing – what had I said about her in those

192

letters? Had she seen her name? I'd have to find a better hiding place.

I held my hand out. 'Can I have them?'

She relinquished them reluctantly, then sighed. 'We need to get out of here.'

She was right – it probably wasn't healthy to spend the day waiting for Galway to stroll up the lane. She tossed me my jeans. Next thing I knew, we were dressed and Abby was barking at us from John's pickup, idling outside our door.

It didn't occur to me I'd be the third wheel until we were already barreling past the Dining Hall in John's Ford. The two aging couples playing in their tennis whites watched us pass, their faces and rackets turning toward us as though they were sunflowers and we the sun. Ev and John gave them nothing to gossip about – they neither touched nor spoke – although I suspected none of that was necessary to start a Winloch rumor. I turned to look out my open window as we passed Galway's vacant cottage. My heart sunk a little further and stuck in something angry as Quicksilver darted out from behind Queen Anne's Lace and raced beside us for a stretch, his mouth holding something helpless and squirming.

'Where are we going?' Ev asked John once we were into the forest. She placed her hand on his leg.

John's truck forged through the woods, farther than I had walked, far faster than my legs could carry me, and I felt a burst of gratitude for all that Ev had brought me. I could hardly imagine that, two days before, I'd been subject to the mercurial passions of a fourteen-year-old, desperate to read some dead woman's journal. A family of seven pheasants darted across the road before us – six babies faithfully following their mother, bobbing back under cover before we drove on.

We started up again, but more carefully this time. Not yet out of the Winloch woods, John slowed.

'Wait, what?' Ev asked. Her body had gone rigid.

John turned the truck left, down a rocky path that cut sharply from the main gravel road that would have led us out of Winloch. 'We're going to have to do it sometime.'

'I want to talk about it first,' she replied.

'We did talk about it. We have to tell her.'

'Well I'm not ready.'

'Tell me what?' I asked. They both turned to me in surprise, as though they'd forgotten I was there.

'Not you.' Ev frowned. 'His mother.'

We drove in silence down the pockmarked path, the chassis groaning as the axles bucked in and out of potholes the size of our tires. Rain and ice had carried the gravel off the road and into the ditch beside it, leaving a hardened clay behind. Ev crossed her arms as John drove on, and I nearly asked 'Where's his mother?' when the road rose sharply to the right, revealing a brown cottage in disrepair. A beat-up two-door sedan sat in the driveway, beside some vicious-looking rusted farm equipment. Whereas Indo's cottage sat in a perpetual state of eccentricity, John's mother's house was of the kind inhabited only by the poor and rural.

John turned off the ignition and opened his door in one

fell swoop. In silence, we watched him and the waggling dog enter the diminutive cottage, until Abby's tail nipped inside.

'She hates me,' Ev said. The whole building seemed to rock under the sheer force of John's and Abby's footsteps, as if two more beings inside were too many.

I patted her shoulder. 'How could anyone hate you?'

It took ten minutes to convince Ev that if she wanted to make a good impression on Mrs LaChance, hiding in the car was not her move. She squeezed my hand as we approached the moss-covered door. It was the first time I saw her terrified.

She knocked. Abby's hot breath came snuffling through the screen. John's broad smile at the sight of Ev reminded me of Galway. I pushed away the memory of that man's kiss and followed them inside.

Mrs LaChance's house – called Echinacea – was architecturally similar to the rest of the Winloch cottages – a few rooms and a view. Built on the forested side of camp, the structure was the embodiment of what I had feared Bittersweet to be the night I first arrived. Every bit of Echinacea's structure that was exposed to weather – windowsills, roof, railings – was covered in thick, spongy moss. Dust gathered in the corners of the living room, peeking out from behind mildewed furniture that resembled the boulders scattered about the surrounding forest. It was clear there had been human attempts to stave off the encroaching wilderness – the scent of Lysol, the residue of Windex upon a mirror – but they were no match for the rot running under everything. The creeping scent of sickness reminded me of home.

I forced myself to smile as we followed John through an olive-green linoleum kitchen, circa 1963, harshly lit with a humming fluorescent tube, before we ventured onto the precarious porch that jutted out into thin air, overlooking the water. There we found a slender woman, impeccable in a crisp white uniform. The nurse stood with an exclamation, 'Genevra!' and exuberantly took Ev in her arms. She was tall. Her accent came from another world. Ev clung to her until the woman stood back, taking Ev's face in her hands. 'All grown up,' she sighed, disappointed and proud.

I watched John squat beside the old wheelchair, which Abby lay beside, and realized it was filled with a brittle body. The person – hardly recognizable as such – was facing the view: through thinned maples, a craggy sandstone cliff gave way to a shaded vision of the lake. It was a melancholy vista, barren of the easy escapism the Winslows enjoyed.

The only indication there was something human in that chair was the constancy of its breathing. Even at John's touch, the figure didn't turn its head.

Ev remembered me. 'This is May,' she said. 'And this is my old nanny, Aggie.'

'Who're you calling old?' Aggie teased, before introducing herself by pulling me into a tight hug. She smelled delightfully of pepper. I was on the verge of sneezing when she released me. 'Let me get you all a snack.' She looked fondly at Ev from the doorway and disappeared into the kitchen.

'Mama,' John said softly, as we all turned our attention to the figure in the wheelchair. 'Look who came to visit.'

He wheeled his mother around to face us. I had expected an old face, but hers was smooth, girlish in its lack of wrinkles. Her skin was almost translucent – I could make out the veins in her forehead. She had John's eyes.

'Hello, Mrs LaChance.' Ev did not reach out her hand or lean down to the woman's level, and I knew her tall, beautiful nervousness was easily mistaken for snobbery.

'Thanks for having us.' I squatted down and touched Mrs LaChance's hand. Her fingers squirreled under mine.

'Who is that?' Mrs LaChance asked in a vital voice, looking past me.

'That's May, Mama,' John answered.

'Her,' the woman said, her eyes on Ev all the while.

'I'm Genevra,' Ev said, eyeing John, 'I just stopped by to say hello.'

'No!' Mrs LaChance yelped, her voice now fierce. 'Aggie? Aggie?'

Aggie appeared in the doorway.

'Get her out of here,' Mrs LaChance growled. All the blood had drained from John's face.

'Pauline,' Aggie pleaded, approaching. 'Let's be kind.' As Mrs LaChance protested again, Aggie whispered to John, 'You've caught us before nap time,' and to me she commanded, 'Take Ev for a walk.'

Mrs LaChance's voice had grown more frantic; she was practically yelling, 'Don't bring her in my home!' Abby began to bark, only agitating the situation.

Aggie nodded me toward the porch door. I took Ev's arm and pulled her away in retreat as I heard the nurse chide, 'Now I know you don't mean that, Ev's a lovely girl.'

But we all knew Mrs LaChance had said precisely what she meant.

Ev was crying by the time our footfalls thudded onto the skinny trail running atop the cliff. 'See?' The view of the lake was less kind over on this side of camp. The craggy sandstone gave way to ragged boulders below.

I took Ev's hand in mine and tried to think of the right thing to say. 'She's not well,' I hedged.

'She always hated us,' Ev complained, pulling away, 'even when we were children.'

'Well, she worked for you, right?'

'What's that supposed to mean?'

I thought of my mother taking the abuse of a customer whose Burberry coat had been damaged by a steamer, my father losing a thousand precious dollars on a legal consult when one of his customers threatened to sue. 'It's not easy to serve other people.'

'Who do you think put a roof over her head when her husband died? Who pays for Aggie? Who keeps John employed and lets her live rent-free?'

'Maybe that's exactly why she doesn't like you.'

Ev rolled her eyes as my point sank in.

I walked to the end of the little path, a few yards farther. The way was precarious. The end of the peninsula – no wider than my two feet – was a good sixty feet above the water.

'He told me we were going to do something fun,' Ev complained.

I laughed. 'Not what you had in mind?'

She'd plopped herself down on a boulder and I joined her there. We watched a skiff sail by. 'She's never going to approve of us,' she said more calmly. 'I don't know why he even tries.'

'What's wrong with her anyway?'

'She had a total breakdown when her husband died. It was like twenty years ago. I mean, don't you think she'd be over it by now?' She narrowed her eyes at me. 'You didn't seem scared.'

I couldn't tell her my secret. Not yet. 'I used to volunteer with people like her.'

She picked up a stick and threw it over the edge of the cliff. We listened to it crack to smithereens. 'Will you get John? I have to get out of here.'

I considered saying, 'If you really love him, you'll have to face her someday.' But I kept my mouth shut and did her bidding. On the small footpath that led me back the way we'd come, I thought of the cold touch of Mrs LaChance's fingers under mine.

I heard John before I saw his outline on the porch, crouched beside his mother's chair. 'Mama, you have to give her a chance.' The wind was coming in my direction, carrying the low tones of his voice. Had he turned, he would have seen me, so I told myself I wasn't eavesdropping, even as I backed behind a tree and listened hard for his mother's response.

'Anyone who isn't one of them,' she croaked. 'Anyone else, and I'll say yes.'

'I deserve to have what you and Dad did,' he pleaded. 'Life is short. When you find love, you fight for it.'

'She is a Winslow,' Mrs LaChance enunciated, ending the conversation.

Through the trees, I could make out the peacock tones of Ev's sundress as she picked her way toward me. I darted back onto the path, heading for the house, and John emerged from the porch door, whistling Abby to him, letting the door slam shut behind him. 'Where's Ev?' He ran his hand over the dog's back as she snorfled after a chipmunk under the porch stairs.

As we sped out of the camp, I expected tension between John and Ev. But as soon as we passed out of the Winloch woods and into the meadow, the sound of our motor turning the world yellow as it scattered a dozen goldfinches into the air, he slung his arm over her shoulder.

'A sparkle of goldfinches,' she murmured.

'A siege of herons,' he replied.

'A murder of crows.'

'A murmuration of starlings.'

She nuzzled up in the crook of his neck. 'A host of sparrows.'

'An exaltation of larks.'

I was struck that they had known each other longer than anyone outside of my family had ever known me. 'A skein of geese,' she laughed.

'It's a gaggle.'

'A gaggle is when they're on the water. They're called a skein when they're in flight.'

'Fine then. But I call foul on your pronunciation.'

'Fowl?'

John cracked up. 'Puns are strictly outlawed in this truck.'

'It doesn't matter how I pronounce it,' Ev said vehemently, 'there's no points deducted for mispronunciation.'

His eyes crinkled at her solemnity. 'Okay, smarty pants, so what do you call a lot of quail?'

'A bevy.'

He shook his head in protest. 'A drift.'

On they played, leaving his mother, and Winloch, behind.

CHAPTER TWENTY-SEVEN

The Festivities

THE NEXT MORNING, EV and I were sipping coffee in our bathrobes when John arrived dressed in white from head to toe. His tanned skin looked even browner against the pristine cotton fabric – slacks, button-down, cap. I tried not to let my eyes linger too hungrily as Ev wolf-whistled.

He rolled his eyes. 'It is fucking ridiculous your mother makes the help dress like this too.'

She laughed breezily.

'Where are your whites?' He frowned at us.

I looked between them, bewildered, but Ev seemed to know exactly what he meant. They laughed at my bafflement until Ev chirped, 'It's Winloch Day – cheeseburgers, football, fireworks! Put on those white clothes!'

My heart stuck in my throat. The best I had was a T-shirt and a pair of granny panties. 'Look at her face!' Ev giggled, pointing at me. 'Don't worry! I got you something in Montreal!' She leapt from the table, squeezing past John with a chaste, if lingering, peck on his lips, and returned moments later with an ivory cotton dress on a hanger. I knew just by looking at it that it would fit me perfectly.

As I uttered my thanks, John wrapped his arms around

Ev and kissed her neck. 'Evie, you are the sweetest girl I know.'

'You have no idea.'

'Someday,' he said, holding her tight, 'someday I'm going to give you everything you want. A big house. Six bedrooms. One for every baby.'

Ev snorted.

'And plenty of bathrooms. A state-of-the-art kitchen.'

'I don't know who you think will be cooking in that kitchen.' Ev tried to twist from his grasp. He didn't let her go.

'I promise,' he said. 'Anything you want, Evie. Anything.'

'A carousel!' She was not going to let this get serious.

'Okay, a carousel then,' he said indulgently. 'What else?'

'A cotton candy machine.'

'I'm going to take care of us.' His voice was so low I could barely hear it.

She finally broke free. 'I have to shower.'

'Be my guest.'

She nodded toward my dress. 'I'm glad you like it.' Then slipped past him and into the bathroom.

'So you're the help today?' I asked.

'Lackey, Sherpa, at your service.' He took a sip of Ev's lukewarm coffee.

I asked what I'd been wondering for a while. 'How is working for the Winslows?'

He took me in so carefully that I felt the need to explain myself. 'My parents own a dry cleaners.'

The suspicion melted from his face as he considered my question. 'Seems like I've been working for them my whole life.' He wasn't self-pitying, just honest. I wondered if that was why he loved Ev – because it felt so natural to be looking after a Winslow – but the instant the thought flitted through my mind, I chastised myself. Who was I to judge why one person was bound to another?

'What about the other guys?' I asked, thinking of the men with farmers' tans I'd seen doing work around camp. When I first came to Winloch, I'd noticed them everywhere – the way they parked the small, white groundskeeping trucks off the beaten path, the sound of their hammers on the shingles atop the Dining Hall. I realized that, as June had turned to July, I'd become less attuned to their where-abouts, which meant that either they were doing less work nowadays or I'd become so accustomed to all my needs being met I wasn't noticing who was meeting them anymore. I had a sneaking suspicion it was the second. 'Where are they from?'

'Locals. Their fathers and grandfathers worked for the Winslows.' He was quiet then. We listened to the water streaming from behind the bathroom door. 'There's a lot to be done down there. You put in the docks, and the swim floats, repair the roofs, you know? Do all the mowing, all the planting. Then you've got to shore up the banks below the cottages to stop the erosion, so you haul rocks, bring in the backhoe, that kind of thing. Weed whacking. Tending to the leach fields, making sure they're clear of saplings and the sewage is evaporating. You replace sump pumps in the basements, and the wood beams of the foundations with steel ones. When the decks rot, replace them. And in the winter, you've got to close up the cottages, so that's shutting off the water, draining the pipes, sweeping off roofs, taking off the gutters, moving the furniture, repainting.'

I had never heard him say so much. 'Do you work on the woods?' I asked, wanting more of his voice washing over me like water.

'Oh sure. You thin out the softwood saplings – white pines, red pines – you want the hardwoods to grow. See, in my grandfather's day, it was all farmland down here, and what comes after farmland is the softwoods. But hardwoods are what give you good heat for stoves in fall and spring, so you thin out the pine so the maple and oak can get enough light to—'

'Hey!' Ev's chipper voice cut through his. She was standing in the living room, one towel wrapped around her lithe frame, the other like a turban on her head. 'Are you going to help me pick my outfit or what?' She walked suggestively into the bedroom.

John practically panted as he stood to follow her. 'Excuse me.'

I washed the dishes a few times until they were done.

That afternoon, dressed in our alabaster frocks, Lu and Ev and I stuck flags embossed with the Winslow crest at three-foot intervals along the border of the Trillium lawn as per Tilde's instructions. John backed in his full pickup. I watched Ev observe his interaction with her mother – John's cap in his hand, Tilde's words of instruction – and wondered how Ev felt. But as he hauled the bags of ice onto his shoulder and followed Tilde to the porch, neither he nor Ev acknowledged each other, so I kept my head down and pushed the next dowel into the soft earth.

'Do you think Galway's coming?' I asked as casually as I could muster, when we had finished up our task.

'He's probably with his girlfriend,' Lu said, flopping to the ground.

'He has a girlfriend?' I tried to sound calm.

Lu caught sight of Owen mounting the stairs up from Flat Rocks. She checked to make sure her mother was out of sight, then rushed to his side. Ev lay beside me, squinting at the teenagers as they embraced furtively.

'Have you ever kissed John like that?' I asked.

'In front of my mother's house?' Ev shook her head emphatically. The day had grown warm, but not unpleasantly. Bumblebees darted in and out of the tiger lilies that edged the grass. 'Why the sudden interest in Galway?' she asked.

The lie came easily. 'Oh, he knows I'm interested in the Winslow genealogy and—'

'Oh my god, you're such a nerd!' She slapped at me, and I scowled. She rolled onto her back. Her fair hair splayed across the close-cut grass and her eyes dreamily opened and closed as one hand lay open upon her stomach. 'I have some news—'

'Genevra?' Tilde's voice snapped Ev out of whatever she was about to say.

'Yes, Mum?'

'Have you gotten out the tablecloths? Look at you girls. Grass stains everywhere.'

Ev darted to her mother like a little girl.

The men lit the barbecue. The women set out the potato

salad and lemonade and ketchup. The white-clad guests arrived and relished the juicy jalapeño burgers topped with Cabot cheddar as a pack of dogs drooled below the children's table, hoping for a dropped morsel. The Winslows wore their summer's best white clothing – collared polo shirts, cotton sundresses – and I realized I had finally stepped into the picture that had hung in our dorm room. I closed my eyes and uttered up a prayer of thanks to Jackson Booth, my patron saint, the reason I was there.

I was standing on the porch beside Ev, deciding whether I could allow myself a second corncob rolled in butter, when she gasped and grabbed my arm. I followed her gaze out the screen. 'It's Aunt CeCe,' she said, abandoning her plate on the table and rushing into the house.

All I knew of CeCe Booth was that her only son had committed suicide, and that she had been devastated – embarrassingly so (at least according to the Winslows) – at his funeral. I had heard snippets of gossip – that her overprotectiveness was the reason Jackson had enlisted, that she had driven her husband away with unparalleled neediness – but I had taken the unkind assessments as idle chatter, the inevitable fallout of tragedy. I knew all too well how quickly the wolves gathered.

Standing outside Trillium, the woman looked undone by grief, as if all it would take was one touch and she'd disintegrate. Her brown hair was pinned back messily, her too-warm gray wool sweater too big, her hands wrapped around herself as if she might crack apart. I watched her approach her older brother's house. I expected to see her embraced. And she was – by her sisters Stockard and Mhairie, by her nieces, Lu and Antonia and Katie, and by the local family friends who had heard of her tragedy and now gathered around her, cooing in sympathetic tones. Far more instructive was to notice who did not open their arms. From my vantage point on the porch, the division was glaring, if the reason for the rift invisible. Birch didn't look her way, and her elder sisters, Greta and Indo, pointedly remained in their Adirondack chairs on the Trillium lawn. I was shocked by Indo's snub. She was eccentric, yes, but usually welcoming in her oddness, and I'd assumed she'd embrace the one person who seemed even more out of place at Winloch than she. But then, perhaps that was precisely it; perhaps Indo didn't want to be associated with someone perceived as weak.

Tilde swept across the Trillium lawn like an arrow, reminding the guests gathered around the grieving woman that there was cold beer on the porch and waiting until, one by one, they had moved away from CeCe to lean in close and whisper into her sister-in-law's ear.

CeCe's body tensed. In a desperate tone, she replied, 'I just want to join in the fun, Tilde. I'm not going to ruin anything.'

Tilde leaned in for another exchange, at which CeCe exclaimed, 'Well of course I'm emotional,' her voice getting louder as she said that word. Tears began to leak from her eyes.

Ev appeared beside me again, lifting her plate in a satisfied gesture.

'Is everything okay?' I asked.

Ev followed my gaze to her mother and aunt's conversation.

Tilde's hand was now on CeCe's arm, and CeCe was trying to remove it. 'She promised not to come,' Ev replied tersely.

'Why?'

'She'd just upset everyone. Which is exactly what she's doing.'

'Her son just killed himself!' I balked.

'For god's sake, Mabel, butt out,' Ev snapped. Then she disappeared into the crowd.

CHAPTER TWENTY-EIGHT

The Fireworks

CHASTENED, I ATE AND drank alone, observing CeCe's gradual admittance into the festivities, although she hardly looked festive. Without a second glance in my direction, Ev slipped off as the football game began. Athol and his wife, Emily, argued about who had forgotten the baby carrier, and, some moments later, Lu and Owen retreated down to Flat Rocks for a make-out session. Indo's Fritz and Tilde's Harvey got into a growling match over a squeaky toy, which ended in Indo barking at Fritz and leading him back to her house.

I uncapped my sixth beer – had I really had that much? – and decided to strike out on my own. I made my way through the summer room, drifting before the Van Gogh until I thought I heard footsteps and, remembering my interaction with Athol, darted out Trillium's front door. I wandered up the road that led through the meadow, past the two other cottages and Clover. Fritz appeared at my heels, yapping grumpily, as though I'd been the one to banish him from the party. Once I'd begun to crest the hill, he stopped short and woofed a couple of satisfied barks, as though to say, 'Take that!' before turning back toward Indo's.

It was dark in the woods, and I stumbled as I climbed but acknowledged, as I swigged the beer and began to hiccup, that that might have more to do with my drunkenness than with the coming night. I could have turned onto the lane leading down to Bittersweet, but, instead, I found my feet leading me past the Dining Hall on the main road and toward Galway's. I succumbed, quickening my pace until his cottage was in sight.

The little house was unlit and the driveway empty, but I still peeked in every window, taking the only parts of him I could get – a mug waiting on the kitchen counter, the bed made neatly in the sparse, small bedroom. I ran my fingers over the cottage's name, carved into a piece of wood hung up beside the door: Queen Anne's Lace. Galway was about the least lacy person I had ever met. That would be funny except it seemed as though he was never coming back.

I leaned my head morosely against the doorframe, then jerked it back up again as soon as I heard a shriek: high, intense, short. I froze. The sound had come from the direction of the other brothers' cottages. I thought of Ev and John. I didn't much care to see them at it again – more for my sense of self-preservation than anything else – so I told myself the sound was nothing and lay my forehead upon the doorframe once again. But then, I heard it: more of a scream this time. A woman's scream.

I thought of Murray – what he had tried to do to me. If someone was hurting another woman that way, I had to stop it. I lumbered off Galway's porch, then stopped for a moment to collect myself, slapping my cheek to regain relative sobriety. The point of impact stung, but the world still swam. I lurched up Boys' Lane toward the two cottages.

In the time it took to walk from Queen Anne's Lace to

Banning's and Athol's cottages, I didn't hear a thing. I began to doubt myself. The night was now almost upon me, and I considered just going back to the fireworks, expecting to hear them bursting above me at any moment. But there it was again – that sharp cry, and so I pushed on, moving off the gravel road onto the grass so that my steps were silent. As I approached, there were no clues to which house the sound had come from. So I chose Banning's, on the left, crouching down as I ran around its side, grateful for the cover of night. I stood on my tiptoes and peeked into the first window, sure I was about to see something horrifying, but the unoccupied living room was only messy. I crouched down, replaying the same scenario with the master bedroom.

It was then that I heard the scream again, quickly, and intentionally, muffled. It had come from Athol's. I surged with adrenaline, picking up a large stick from the lawn and creeping toward the back of the house, where I knew I'd be able to peek around to Athol's back porch. I could hardly breathe as I crept, wincing at every sound my body made, sure I'd accidentally tumble over one of Maddy's noisy toys and give myself away.

At the edge of the house, I got as far down to the ground as I could, and looked.

A single kerosene lamp flickered on Athol's back porch, but to my dark-accustomed eyes it might as well have been a hundred. There, upon the table, Athol lay on top of a woman, his hand on her mouth as he thrust inside of her. He was entering her over and over, ramming her head against the screen. Quicksilver lay to the side of them, sleeping, as though this were an everyday occurrence. I began to cry. It looked like he was hurting her. I had to do something.

And then I heard her laugh. 'I said "harder,"' she commanded, 'hold me down and do it harder.'

I saw her face. The au pair. Realized: she was choosing this. He wasn't hurting her – it was part of some game they were playing.

He returned her kiss with a probing tongue. My stomach turned. This was nothing like John and Ev. Nothing like love. This was just two sad people rutting in the woods. Quicksilver lifted his head as though he smelled me. I ran, sure at any moment I'd find that dog tearing at my heels.

I got back to Flat Rocks just as the fireworks started. I noticed Emily sitting on a folding chair, draped with her slumbering children, and wondered if she knew where her husband was. Just then, Ev slung her arm through mine.

'Sorry about before,' she whispered. The sky burst red above us. She pulled me over to a towel some way from the rest of the family, now oohing and aahing at the dazzling gold glitters falling above us. Emily's baby roused at the booms, her squalls carrying over the water.

'I have something to tell you,' Ev said quietly.

I was hungry for the fireworks, eager to feel them rumble through me, explode what I had just seen, destroy the knowledge I now had, about Athol, about the au pair. I wanted Ev to be quiet.

But instead, she whispered, 'I'm pregnant.'

CHAPTER TWENTY-NINE

The Enigma

I DID THE MATH: TEN weeks along by early July, Ev had conceived before we came north. That night, in our room, as she fantasized aloud about sewing a baby quilt and buying a safe car, I wondered whether John was the father. Unless he'd come to New York in early May, she was carrying someone else's baby.

I couldn't bring myself to ask her. 'Does John know?' was the closest I could get.

'Why do you think he wants me to kiss up to his mother?' I was glad the room was dark, so she wouldn't see me wince at the flippancy of her tone. 'I'm so glad I finally told you,' she gushed. 'I've been bursting, but he wanted to keep it just for us.'

'You'll start showing soon,' I replied neutrally. 'What will your mother say?'

'I'm not going to have to worry about her.'

I paused. 'You're not keeping it?'

'Of course I'm keeping it,' she said. But she didn't explain what she meant.

I wanted to scream: What about me? What about college? What about us old ladies sitting on the Bittersweet porch together? Did she know what childbirth consisted of? Was she taking vitamins? I slipped into a restless slumber, for once welcoming the suffocating distraction of my nightmares.

The next morning, when Ev returned to Bittersweet after her daily walk, she looked devastated. I hesitated to ask what was wrong, guessing it would be another lovers' spat and that she'd lash out at me for prying, but she seemed glad to spill her heart.

'Don't tell anyone,' she began as she sipped the cup of Earl Grey I placed before her, 'and please don't be mad.'

'What happened?'

'We've been planning to leave.'

'Who? Where?'

'Me and John, goose. Just to run away together. My father's going to sign off on my trust any day now. It's the chance to start a new life.'

'Wait,' I said, my distrust in her growing anew, 'you've been planning to run away with John? For how long?'

She grimaced. 'Since the summer began.'

It was all I could do not to walk out the door. To ask how on earth she could have brought me to this paradise knowing she was just going to abandon me here. She had pretended, for weeks on end, that we were settling into domestic bliss, while harboring this secret all the while? Threatening me with Oregon to get me to work harder, knowing that was exactly where I'd be sent once she had disappeared and the Winslows had moved on? But I didn't have to say a word – she could read the hurt all over my face.

'Well, you don't have to worry because it's not going to

happen after all,' she said, dissolving into tears, as though she was the one who deserved sympathy.

I sighed. 'Why not?'

She could barely speak through her tears, but managed to say, 'He says we have to bring his mother.'

'So?'

'So? I'm not going anywhere with that woman. She hates me. She will literally murder me in my sleep.' She shook her head. 'He doesn't understand. She'll never let us be happy. But he won't leave her. So we're not going anywhere.'

I took her hand. I thought she was being awfully melo-dramatic, but, then, Mrs LaChance did seem like a doozy of a mother-in-law. And anyway, wasn't I pleased to know her escape with John had been thwarted?

'It'll be okay,' I said, but my voice went up at the end, as though I was asking a question.

She nodded.

'He loves you.' As I said those words, I wondered if love was enough.

I spent that week with Kitty's journal. Indo's suggestion that I might someday own Clover had taken on a more urgent meaning in light of Ev's recent revelations.

John had to keep up the façade of normalcy while they figured out what to do next, so he worked morning till night. Ev was bursting with plans for the baby, and wanted to spend every minute John was occupied with me. But I needed space. I methodically cooked us healthy dinners or pretended I was absorbed in *Paradise Lost* until she wandered down to the cove for a swim or settled in for a catnap. Then I'd spring into action, laying my hands upon that familiar book in the towel in the back of the bathroom cabinet, unwrapping it into another world, until I heard her footsteps and had to hide it away again.

Scanning through, I'd surmised that Kitty's journal followed the course of a year, from the January entry I'd read that first day to a late December entry that read simply, almost sadly: 'First snow. Late this year. The Tannenbaum is decorated. I lit a candle and prayed.'

In between, the yellowed, smooth pages were filled with Kitty's perfect hand, sloped to the right, as though she was always pushing forward. She used black ink and a fine nib, and wrote her dates either like this: 'Monday, July 14th,' or without a day of the week: 'June 26th.' Never once did she mention the year.

From her first entry, I had gathered that she was writing sometime between 1929 and 1935, but, aside from occasional mention of the world's miseries, she did not elaborate much on what was happening beyond her sitting room. That was what disappointed me the most. I had thought the journal would prove illuminating, shed some light on one delicious secret or another, but the subject matter of Kitty's writing was positively navel gazing. She hardly seemed to lift her head from the page long enough to look out a window, so little did she mention what was happening in the rest of the world – the Great Depression, the gathering storm of what would become the Second World War. Instead she wrote of her silver pattern: 'B. is insisting I go down to New York for a look at Tiffany, but I have assured him I'll do just fine with his mother's choice'; her lapdogs: 'Fitzwilliam is a fine little pug, with a wheezy breath and hardy disposition'; and visitors: 'We are being joined this week by Claude, Paul, and Henri. B. and I are so looking forward to offering them shelter until they decide where to settle.'

By Wednesday I had gotten through my first pass. I had nothing to show for it. So I started again, rereading the entries out of order, trying to find something secret, about the unexpected money, or the bankruptcy. On the second pass, I did find one secret, but it was personal and filled my heart with pity: 'B. has been carrying on with one of the maids, P. He has assured me it's over, but it is a mess nonetheless, one I shall be paying for myself, that weighs heavily upon me.' I suppose it shouldn't have surprised me that Bard had cheated on Kitty with a servant. It was horrible to think about but not hard to imagine, especially as I thought of Emily and her children watching the fireworks while Athol hammered the au pair. Poor Kitty, poor Emily.

I was settling down for a third pass over the journal that Friday afternoon, Abby panting at my feet (John and Ev were in the bedroom talking seriously – his low rumble occasionally peppered by the bleat of her voice from behind the closed door), when there was a knock. I stashed the journal, cursing the intrusion, and strode blindly from the bathroom.

'Yes?' I said, as I came in sight of the figure waiting on the steps of the cottage, head turned toward the road. He swiveled back at the sound of my voice. Galway.

'Hello.' His voice was smooth.

I spoke to him through the screen. 'Hello.' Abby happily stuck her head out the door for a scratch.

'What's she doing here?' Galway asked.

'John's fixing the bathroom sink.'

He sighed. 'Sorry I couldn't make it for Winloch Day.'

I held my hands up in a gesture of liberation.

'I would have liked to see you,' he said carefully.

I shrugged.

'Can I make it up to you?' His hand started to fiddle with the doorframe a few inches from my arm. The ball was firmly in my court.

'No need.'

'Can I take you out?'

'Really, don't do me any favors.'

'You're upset.'

'Why should I be upset?'

He dropped his hand. 'Because I kissed you and then I disappeared.'

My face felt hot.

'Please,' he pushed. 'Tomorrow night? Something casual. Eight o'clock.'

'I don't know.'

'I found something,' he volunteered. I almost responded, 'A girlfriend?' but he went on. 'Something in the Winslow financial records.'

If I told him I had plans for something incredible tomorrow night, all he'd have to do was walk a quarter mile from his place and find me lying on our couch to catch me in the lie. Besides, even his company sounded better than another night spent untangling Kitty's journal, or enduring Ev's sudden mommy mode.

'All right,' I told him. Abby whined when I pushed the door shut on him. I walked into the kitchen, feeling his eyes on me the whole way.

CHAPTER THIRTY

The Apology

T HE NEXT MORNING, FRIGID air lifted off the water and squirreled through Bittersweet, creeping under our doors and around our windowpanes, as if the century-old structure was simply a lovely puzzle for the wind. I made scrambled eggs in the drafty kitchen with my coverlet wrapped around me while Ev tried, in vain, to start a fire in the woodstove. We ended up wreathed in smoke as Abby, whom John had left with us, barked incessantly. Our only recourse was to open the windows, which just made things colder. After that, we took to our beds.

'I have something to tell you,' I announced.

At the sound of my voice, Abby scratched against our door. When we didn't respond, she began to whine. Ev rolled her eyes and threw her pillow at the door.

'She's just taking care of you,' I said. 'She can probably smell the baby.' Abby had been following Ev everywhere, much to Ev's annoyance and my amusement.

'She's driving me crazy!' Ev yelled. The dog gave one last, pleading whine, then scuttled off, presumably to check her food bowl. Her nails tapped rhythmically across the wooden floor.

Ev flopped back down into bed. 'So what's the big news? You're pregnant too?'

I hesitated. There was no other way – she'd see me dressing, and press me for details. Even if I refused to tell her, he'd pick me up, so not saying anything would only make his appearance more awkward. And even if she didn't see his car, all she had to do was ask around and someone would have seen us leaving Winloch together. Better to just be up front. 'I'm going out with Galway tonight.'

Ev started giggling.

'I don't know why that's funny.'

'Wait, you're serious?'

'It's not a date or anything,' I said defensively, climbing from the bed. 'Just a chance to talk about the Winslow genealogy.'

'God, Mabel, you're obsessed with my family. It's creepy.'

'Believe it or not,' I heard myself snap, 'the research is for me. I know it's hard to fathom I'd do something for myself.'

Her response was an eye roll.

'Anyway,' I continued, 'the only reason I told you is I don't want you to get the wrong idea about me and Galway.'

'No,' she said sarcastically, 'why would anyone get the wrong idea about you and Galway?'

I dressed in silence, pulling on a couple sweaters. I'd go out in search of Lu and Owen.

I could feel Ev's eyes peering over her magazine. 'You should be careful.'

'I know my way around.'

'With Galway.'

'I'm not good enough to have dinner with your brother?' I scowled.

'I'm just saying he's complicated, okay? Don't get your hopes up.'

I turned to her, furious. 'You can't lie on your back,' I spat. 'You'll hurt the baby.' I stormed out of the bedroom, cursing myself for caring, for showing her I cared, for choosing to tell her about my date in the first place, but, most of all, for knowing she was right.

Since finding the turtle corpses, Lu had put in many hours with a bookish, bearded marine biologist from the university – first in multiple calls, on multiple days, and then, on a few occasions, when he'd driven from Burlington right up to Trillium, so she could row him across Winslow Bay to Turtle Point and he could see the horror for himself. They had gathered water and soil and flesh samples, and he'd called his colleagues at Fish and Wildlife, but, so far, no one had found an explanation for the turtle colony's demise. Lu's response to uncertainty was vehement determination, and I sensed, the one time I met the poor scientist, simply from the way his shoulders hunched when Lu asked him, for the fiftieth time, if he didn't really think that global warming was the cause, that he wished he'd never answered her phone call.

Still, I admired her fortitude. 'We are stewards of this land,' I had heard her gravely explain to her father. So when I finally found her and Owen down on Flat Rocks that chilly day, about to launch the dinghy out across the bay, even though the last thing I wanted was to be flung about on a blustery lake, I agreed to set out with them for another round of sample gathering.

Owen rowed. Lu sat behind him, in the bow, and I faced him. As we launched across the rocking water, I realized I had hardly ever heard him speak. He brushed his auburn hair off his forehead with his slender fingers, pinkening in my gaze; perhaps shyness was the reason he was so quiet.

At last, we arrived in the cove beside Turtle Point. They had cleared a spot on the beach where we could pull up easily. I wondered how many times they'd been there since Lu and I had discovered the dead turtles.

She darted over the point. Owen and I followed more slowly, cutting brush and grasses from the area where the turtles were – I didn't care to look closely to see how much they had decayed, but the stench of rot remained. We placed our cuttings in jam jars, labelless and washed clean, and then Lu gave us masking tape and we recorded the date and the approximate location of the plant we'd cut from. Lu's jaw was set, her eyes focused. Once we'd filled the canvas bag with two dozen samples, we followed her back down to the beach.

'Oh, I forgot!' she exclaimed, grabbing the last empty jar and darting off to the end of the point without further explanation.

I smiled at Owen. 'She's taking this very seriously,' I said, sounding condescending without meaning to. I suppose I already fancied I'd entered the realm of the adults, in which even the world-weary marine biologist believed one couldn't count on finding an answer, a solution, to everything.

'Turtles just don't die like that,' Owen replied. 'I don't know much about them, but she does, and I'll do anything I can to help.'

'It's good to help. But sometimes terrible things just happen and there's nothing you can do about it.'

'I don't believe that,' he pronounced, surprising me with his conviction. He looked up at Lu as she flitted along the point, racing through the trees, another sample in hand. 'No. I don't believe that at all.'

The shadows were growing long across the tennis courts by the time I got home, but Ev was still in her bed, and Abby was snoozing on the narrow rag rug below her. The dog lifted her head and watched me root through my drawers. Satisfied I had brought no steak home, she flopped back down with a disgruntled sigh.

'Pregnancy has turned me into a weird little hermit,' Ev said some minutes later. Her voice was thin. She hadn't spoken for hours.

'I shouldn't have snapped at you,' I apologized, turning to look at her.

'But you're right. I don't know anything about having a baby.'

I sat down on my bed. 'You'll figure it out.'

'I'm stronger than I look,' she agreed. She cleared her throat. 'Anyway, I'm sorry for butting into your business.'

'That's okay,' I said, surprised to hear her apologize. I'd never heard the words from her mouth. I suddenly wanted to tell her. 'He kissed me.'

'Was it nice?'

'Yeah. But when I called his house, a woman answered. So, you're right. Complicated.'

'Did you ask him about it?'

225

I shook my head.

'I'll see what I can find out,' she promised.

I kicked her bed playfully. 'Get up.'

'It's good in here.'

'But I've got nothing to wear and you have to do my makeup.'

CHAPTER THIRTY-ONE

The Date

B Y THE TIME GALWAY pulled up in front of Bittersweet, I was dressed in a pair of jeans and one of Ev's T-shirts, baggy on her but tightly provocative stretched over my torso. I had on a black bra and a matching sexy thong, and my hair was pulled into a low ponytail. I even had makeup on. Ev squealed at the transformation, then made herself scarce as her brother's wheels crunched the gravel outside.

'Wow,' Galway said when I met him on the stairs. He was dressed in a summer blazer and button-down shirt, slacks, loafers. I'd only ever seen him in his camp clothes.

'You look dressy.' My voice sounded harsh.

'You look' – his eyes wandered over me, lingering unapologetically on my breasts – 'great.'

I cleared my throat. 'I should change.'

He grabbed my hand. I'd forgotten how smooth his skin was. He tugged me gently toward him.

His car was impeccably neat – no garbage, no maps, nothing personal. It was a nice night but his windows were up. I worried a rolled-down window might muss my hair anyway, ruining the overall magic that Ev had wrought upon me. We drove in silence until we were out of Winloch, then headed south, toward Burlington.

He glanced at me a few times as we drove past rocky outcroppings and sheep grazing below shade trees. But he didn't say anything, and the silence started to grow into something meaningful. I couldn't tell if that meaning was romantic or uncomfortable.

He cleared his throat. 'So how've you been?'

'Oh fine.'

'Good.' We drove on.

He flicked on his blinker at the sign for Burlington, but, after exiting, he turned off the main road quickly, heading south again on Spear Street. I looked longingly toward the university, and Church Street below, where I'd spent one afternoon a few weeks back wandering aimlessly with Lu. My heart fell a little – I'd been looking forward to an evening in civilization. There was a casual French bistro on a corner of the walking mall. I had planned to order the steak frites.

'Where are we going?' I asked as the land fell away while we drove along a ridgeline. The sun was almost slipping behind the Adirondacks. Between the mountains and us the lake glimmered. I squinted down at the tiny triangle sails, skipping crisp and white across the gold-kissed waters.

'You'll love it' was all he said, as we turned again, plunging down the hill toward the lake, back under the maples.

We drove country roads for a few more miles, then over a covered bridge and past a house bigger than the one I had grown up in – although I understood it was only the carriage house – and into a grand estate that looked more like a park, or insane asylum, than someone's home. An arrow pointed the way to the Restaurant at the Farms, and we drove slowly and carefully, past beautifully mown lawns and large, sturdy buildings sporting copper roofs, now lichen green. We came up a rise and caught sight of a palace, for lack of a better word. It was grand in the way of country estates from Jane Austen novels, but American – red brick, copper roof, rounded walls – with an incredible view of the lake beyond it.

'This belonged to friends of Samson's.'

'This house?'

He gestured grandly. 'All of it.' It made Winloch look like the slums.

'And now?'

'It's a land trust. They have a children's petting barn, a dairy farm, they sell cheese, they have a garden, and trails, and house tours. They grow all the vegetables and raise the meat for the restaurant.' He opened his door. 'Shall we?'

He came to my side of the car and waited for me, then walked behind me with his hand close to the small of my back. This made it feel like a date. But the way he was speaking to me – without much content or interest – made me think I'd hallucinated the kiss, the chemistry, even our camaraderie before things had gotten romantic. There had been something tangible between us, and I feared it was gone.

We entered the foyer of the great house, which led directly into the restaurant. The maître d' dressed in a waiter's tuxedo raised an eyebrow as he caught sight of me. A tall brunette slipped from the restaurant, jangling her car keys. She was wearing a perfectly tailored black dress.

My heels clopped to a halt on the wide cherry floorboards. I looked down at myself. My bra was visible through my

T-shirt. My thong had ridden up and my jeans had ridden down. I realized that, inadvertently or not, Ev had made me a version of myself that made her feel better.

Oblivious, Galway strode forward without me. I couldn't hear his voice but watched with horror as he mentioned our reservation to the maître d'.

'Just one moment,' the man replied haughtily, disappearing into the restaurant after a pointed glance in my direction.

Galway turned back with a quizzical look. We couldn't have been more than twenty feet apart, but the distance felt unbridgeable. My feet grew roots as the violin filtering out from the restaurant became more passionate. He brought a menu over, mentioning a few choice items before he was even at my side: 'They've got an amazing butternut squash risotto with roasted pumpkin seeds. Oh, and the veal scaloppine is incredible.'

I shook my head like a child.

'Come on.' He reached for my hand again. 'The food's all locally sourced.' I pulled my hand away. 'What's the matter?' he asked, as the maître d' appeared again.

'You should have told me it was fancy.'

He waved his hand dismissively. 'It doesn't matter.'

'It matters to me.'

'You can borrow my jacket. But really, Mabel, you look fine.'

The first hot tear burned down my cheek. 'I don't want to look fine,' I managed to say, before turning and running toward the massive front door, gulping my tears. I hurtled myself against it before realizing I had to press down the latch. I could feel the maître d's eyes burning into my back.

I heard Galway behind me but quickened my pace across the parking lot, finding shelter sandwiched between his car and the next. There was nowhere else to go. I was trying, in vain, not to sob. Everyone could see.

'What's wrong?' Galway asked helplessly from beside the rear tire, and I wondered how I could possibly explain. I didn't know what was wrong, not in words. All I knew was I was humiliated. It reminded me of how strange I'd felt when he'd introduced me to Gammy Pippa – all those elite eyes crawling over me. Of how Indo had made vague promises before asking me to dig deep for her. Of how Ev had confessed she'd been planning to leave all along. None of them had ever known the embarrassment of not belonging.

'You should tell someone,' I bawled, 'when you're taking them somewhere nice.'

'I thought I did,' he mumbled.

'When you saw what I was wearing . . . I mean I look like a fucking joke, Galway. You could have said it was going to be like this.'

'I think you look beautiful.'

I crossed my arms over my chest. 'Don't lie to me.'

'I don't lie.'

'Then who is she?' I cried.

His face was blank. I would have to spell it out.

'I called your house in Boston the night you kissed me. She said you weren't home.' His expression told me all I needed to know. Shock, awareness, panic. He opened his mouth to defend himself, but I added, 'Remember, Galway, you don't lie.'

All the fight went out of him. He put his hands to his face, then leaned back against the car. He closed his eyes. Nodded. Just that, and the fight was out of me too. The clouds were skipping across the pinkening evening sky. A gust of wind swept over us from the direction of the lake, worrying the trees into a churning tizzy above.

'It's not what it looks like,' he said.

'Well, what is it, then?'

He laughed, defeated. 'I'm getting out of a relationship,' he said finally. 'That's what it boils down to.' He met my eyes. 'I should have told you. But I didn't think . . . Look, I know this is going to sound crazy, but I really . . . I like you. I felt something the first time we' – he laughed – 'well, not exactly the first time we met – I mean that was great – but the first time we talked. I felt like I knew you. Like I'd known you for a long time. It's crazy, okay, it's cheesy and clichéd . . .'

I knew exactly what he meant.

'And I didn't want to ruin it,' he went on, 'by delving into my own stuff, stuff that has nothing to do with you. She's . . . she's been a friend of mine. And we thought – I hoped – it could be more than that. But. Not anymore. Definitely not since I met you.' He stopped himself. 'I'm really sorry.' He moved closer. 'I really want to make it up to you.'

'You don't have to make anything up to me.'

'I said that wrong,' he said, putting his hand onto my arm. 'I meant: I really want to take you out. Because I think we could have fun together.'

An involuntary smile crept onto my face. 'Like we're having right now.'

He nodded vigorously. 'Oh, absolutely, this is exactly what I had in mind.'

At once, I was hungry. I glanced back up at the grand home. 'Okay,' I said, holding out my hand, 'give me your blazer.'

He shook his head and grinned, unlocking my door. 'We're going somewhere else.'

'I'm hungry now.'

'Yeah, well, tough.' His eyes crinkled when he smiled.

We drove toward town, but, almost to the university, we turned away from Burlington, crossed the highway, and followed arrows for the airport. A lit-up sign enthusiastically announced AL'S FRENCH FRYS, and we turned in to the parking lot.

'We weren't allowed to come here when we were kids,' Galway said, turning off the car. He popped the trunk and met me at my door with a hooded UVM sweatshirt. I put it on. The sleeves flopped down over my hands. I felt comfortable for the first time that night.

Red vinyl booths, milk shakes, a short-order grill – we gobbled the greasy food, sucking down the thick french fries two at a time. 'I thought you were a vegetarian,' I said, as he took a hearty bite of his second cheeseburger.

'Who told you that?' He laughed with a full mouth.

'You seem too . . . self-realized for meat,' I replied, which tickled his funny bone.

We drove downtown and got ice cream and strolled until the stores closed and it was just us and the street kids under the twinkling Christmas lights that entwined the branches above us. I checked my watch – it was eleven. There was nowhere else to go – I was underage, with no fake ID.

'What's your family like?' he asked. We found a bench in the middle of Church Street, and watched a hippie girl dance messily before her dog and a group of boys. They might as well have been in Pioneer Courthouse Square, in Portland – same hemp clothes, unwashed funk, and abandoned look in their eyes. Music thumped from a rowdy pub a block away.

'My family's not – they're not important.'

'The Winslows are rich,' he said, 'but that doesn't mean they're better than everyone else.'

'I think . . . more than what you are, is what you think you are. If you believe you're the most powerful man in the world, and act like it, people respond. If you think you're nothing, you are.'

'You don't think you're nothing, do you?' His voice quavered as if he couldn't bear the thought.

The hippie girl collapsed against a boulder. One of the street boys took her place. He was shirtless, with long, dreadlocked hair. His dance was a lament.

'I have a brother,' I replied, as though that was some kind of answer.

'Okay.' Galway was the first person I'd told since I came East. He nodded as though he understood it was grave news, even though he knew nothing of its content.

'And he . . . he taught me what I am. Not exactly that I'm bad, not exactly that, but that I can be. That I am capable of . . . what other people aren't.' I knew what I was saying was cryptic and hard to follow, but I also knew that I had to say it. Galway deserved an out.

He took my hand. 'Well, I know you're not nothing. And that you're not bad.'

It was too late. I had wanted him and now I was going to get him. There were so many things I could have said then, but they would have fallen from my mouth like burned ash, collapsing into sorrow, changing forever how Galway could know me. Instead, I decided to take what I wanted. I squeezed his hand back. We sat together and watched the boy fall upon the brickwork, in an ecstatic mock seizure, until he was replaced by another dancer, then another, then another, until the Christmas lights above us were switched off and Galway drove me to Bittersweet.

CHAPTER THIRTY-TWO

The Scene

L U KNOCKED ON THE screen door with the good news that the wind was gone. She managed to convince Ev to come too, and the three of us set out for Flat Rocks just as the midday sun broke through the cloud cover – Lu in her bikini, me in my L.L.Bean tummy tucker, and Ev in a button-down shirt to hide the baby belly I'd hardly noticed but she insisted, once Lu was out of hearing, would give her pregnancy away.

The day was made for Flat Rocks. The calm lake was warm enough to float in languidly for hours. There was plenty of dry rock, now that the waterline had fallen, for all the Winslows to spread their towels. And the sun cast enough heat so that one could spend hours on end outside, as close to naked as propriety would allow. As the summer had worn on, most of the young parents had grown relaxed about nap time, so the children played all afternoon, uninterrupted by their dozing chaperones at the water's edge. The little Winslows' high voices, the hilly hiccups of their laughter, were a sweet counterpoint to the sixth chapter of *Paradise Lost,* and, once I realized I'd reread the last page a dozen times, I succumbed to the heat of the sun, closing my eyes to a happy glow, and to the memory of Galway's hand in mine and the realization, all over my body, as the sun beamed down, that he and I were going to touch each other again, with more than just our hands.

'Hey, guys.'

I squinted up into the sun to see Galway standing over me. I blushed, at what I'd just imagined us doing together, and the warmth between my legs, and the hungry way he was looking at me spread before him. I sat up shyly as Lu and Ev mumbled their dreamy hellos. He pulled his shirt over his head and sat. I tried not to gape. He leaned his bare shoulder against mine in a private gesture of hello.

We spent the afternoon side by side, sharing a bag of chips, teasing his sisters about their fashion magazines, swimming out to the float and back. There was an elastic tether between us; no matter which cousin's towel he wandered to, or how far I swam out beyond the swimming dock, we each felt the tug of the other.

Flat Rocks buzzed that day – everyone seemed to be moving in concert with the summer afternoon. When Owen and the cousins backflipped off the swimming dock, we all cheered, as did the passengers on the twenty-two yachts bobbing in the bay. When Mhairie brought down a cooler filled with ice cream bars, she was celebrated.

We came to three o'clock. Tilde descended the steps, and a quiet cautiousness overtook us all. The boy cousins swam out to the dock. 'Well well well,' Tilde said, bringing a folding chair over to our little encampment, where Ev was feigning sleep. 'Looks like everyone's here.'

Galway stood, leaving the towel he'd been basking on most of the afternoon, and turning to Lu instead of me. 'I'm going in for a dip,' he announced.

'Mm-hm,' Lu answered absentmindedly, absorbed in her magazine.

'Stop mumbling,' Tilde scolded Lu as Galway made his way down to the water. I couldn't help watching him go. Out of the corner of my eye, I saw Tilde's hand swat the back of Lu's head.

'Ow.' Lu scowled, rubbing her skull.

'How many times do I have to tell you not to chew your hair, darling?'

Lu looked down at the soggy end of her braid. She'd been unconsciously sucking it for the better part of the day. 'Sorry.' She sulked, but Tilde was already standing.

'Put your suits on!' Tilde commanded in the direction of the throng of children gathered at the water's edge. They were oblivious to her instruction, darting back and forth with buckets of water. I sat up, shielding my eyes with my hand, following Tilde's hawk-like gaze as she called to them again, muttering to herself.

The children had been in various states of undress all day. Little bottoms had darted past our spot since we'd staked our claim, and Lu and I had remarked how adorable those twin pillows of the newly walking were. Perfect pudenda, quivering penises, the innocence and openness of children playing by water in the sun. Now, as I looked to the water's edge, I noticed one girl cousin around eight years old, who bore a strong resemblance to both Ev and Lu. She was a distant relative, visiting for a couple weeks. She was a head taller than the next oldest child, but still a little girl at heart, and, like many of the other children had been at one time or another that day, she was nude. Her back was turned to Tilde as she prattled excitedly about building a fairy swimming pool, her buttocks lit up by the light reflected off the water, when a hush descended over the crowd. Tilde was coming right for her.

'Hannah!' Tilde barked. Frozen shock descended over the little girl as she recognized the sound of an angry adult. Most of the other children had already run off to their parents, who were murmuring about the whereabouts of Hannah's mother. Soon, Tilde was towering over the girl. 'Put your clothes on, Hannah, you can't run around like that anymore. It's fine for the babies, but you're a big girl now!' Exasperated at the girl's helplessness, Tilde turned to the gaping adults, demanding, 'Doesn't anyone have a towel?' When no one answered, she marched to the nearest vacant chair, where a worn piece of terry cloth lay, and wrapped it aggressively around the girl. Hannah began to wail.

'What happened?' came a worried voice. Everyone turned to see Hannah's mother running down the steps. She cascaded toward her inconsolable daughter. Most of us turned awkwardly away. Ev stuffed her bag and stormed up the steps. Tilde tried to explain herself. I spotted Galway out on the floating dock and grabbed Lu by the wrist. We picked our way to the boat dock, away from the drama. As the women bickered, I squeezed Lu's hand tight and we ran down the long, wooden walkway, gaining speed, until we jumped together into the loud gasp of water, in pursuit of our boys.

CHAPTER THIRTY-THREE

The Swim

GALWAY, LU, OWEN, AND I stayed with the cousins out on the floating dock long after Tilde, Hannah and her mother, and the rest of them had turned toward home. We spoke little of what had occurred, but I guessed that was less because they were all surprised by Tilde's attack and more because they weren't. Mostly, Owen and the cousins discussed a moneymaking scheme they'd been dreaming up: 'So right after dark, we load the dinghy with cookies, coffee, beer, wine, that kind of thing, we row out, we knock on a few hulls—'

'We should have a menu, that way we can do a once-around and then come back.'

'Can we take Canadian money?'

'Where the fuck are we going to get wine?'

I lay in Galway's lap. He stroked my hair. I smiled, numb to potential criticism. I didn't much care who could see me out of Trillium's windows, or if they liked what they saw.

We all ate dinner together in the Dining Hall – Masha's brisket and mashed potatoes, along with a couple filched beers. The boys debated the fairness of inflating prices and whether or not they should sell batteries, and Galway found my hand below the table. By the time we made our way back to Bittersweet – we could cheer Ev, I was sure of it – I was happy and sated.

I noticed John's truck pulled up behind the cottage before anyone else did, and realized that I wouldn't have time to warn them we had visitors. Luckily, Abby caught wind of our gang. Whatever John and Ev had been doing when we were in the Dining Hall, they were perfectly platonic as the six of us climbed the porch steps – Ev reading quietly on the porch couch, John fiddling with the loose board he'd been promising to fix since June.

I had expected to find Ev upset, given how she'd left Flat Rocks. But she seemed as buoyant as I felt, and I was grateful our good moods were aligned.

'We've come to kidnap you,' I said. 'We're going skinny-dipping.'

Ev shook her head. 'Mum will kill you.'

'Precisely,' Galway said. 'What did she say after Jackson died? "The Booths skinny-dipped and look what happened to them."'

Even Arlo and Jeffrey chuckled, so giddy and enthralled were they with the idea of swimming naked with girls – even if two of the girls were their cousins and the third was me. Owen took Lu's hand. John wiped the sweat from his brow and rose from the floor. 'Well, I'm game,' he said.

We tiptoed down to the Bittersweet cove. The moon had risen, casting a silver dreaminess over the world. The crickets droned, and a few flashes, low over the water, promised fireflies. 'Oh, it's perfect,' Lu cooed to Owen, and I watched him lift her fingers to his lips. I found Galway's hand in the dark.

'I'll stay with the clothes,' Ev declared as we began to undress at the water's edge.

'Like hell.' John kept his distance. If they'd been alone, or with just me, he would have swept her into his arms.

'I'm cold,' she squeaked.

I guessed she was afraid they'd see her pregnant belly, but it was truly night, and I nudged her with my elbow. She reluctantly began to undo the buttons of her shirt.

We were a tangle of stripping limbs. The boy cousins were the first to jump in. Ev shushed them. They swam gamely for the flat rock at the lip of the Bittersweet cove, climbing atop it in the moonlight, and slipping into the outer bay on the other side. I tried to avert my eyes from their nakedness, but it was hard not to be curious about what their pink bodies revealed.

I faced Galway as I undressed, feeling his roaming eyes. I peeled my swimsuit off my top half, surprised at how easy it was to be shirtless. I kicked my shorts onto the ground. He was eager but polite, deftly pulling off his shirt as he watched me undress. The night wind was cool on my skin, and I raced to remove the rest of my swimsuit, ready to jump into the water. His eyes met mine as he stepped out of his swimming trunks. He was naked before me. His sex dangled a few inches from mine, a question and an invitation. I kept my eyes on his, but knew we were both pushing the breadth of our peripheral vision. He grinned widely, grabbed my hand, and pulled me toward the water.

We waded in, flopping forward as the rocky, clayed lake bottom squished under our steps, and swam, together, to the lip of the cove. Lu and Owen splashed in behind us, whispering happily, and soon John joined. Only Ev was on shore, still half dressed, reluctant.

Out from under the cove's tree cover, we could finally see the Milky Way, a startle of stars peppering the firmament. Galway pulled himself up onto the rock, then turned to offer me a hand. I pulled myself up beside him, and we stood, alone, together, at the edge of that great water, where sky met lake, like Adam and Eve. Then he dove in and I followed.

In the bay, the insistent chirrup of the crickets was quieter. The lilt of nighttime conversation filtered to us from shore. I floated on my back and took in the dazzling sky. *Sky* seemed an insufficient word – what I saw wasn't above us but all around, as though the water and air were one whole thing. Fireflies flickered like living stars.

Galway swam to me. His body was warm, his lips soft, wetter, lapping, and he treaded water for both of us as I wrapped my legs dangerously around his waist, feeling his hardening desire. I wouldn't make love to him, not here, not the first time. But it was thrilling to feel his longing, to know I could fulfill it. The younger cousins swam close. Galway kissed me one more time and let me go.

I swam back to the Bittersweet rock to rest and pulled myself up into the cooling breeze. I could make out the boys swimming as far as they could and realized, with pleasure, that Ev and Lu were floating on their backs, side by side.

I looked down to find John treading water below me. He pulled himself up onto the rock beside me. I tried to look away, but I had a flash of memory of the night I'd seen him and Ev together, and, matched with the hunger I'd felt in Galway, I found myself open, as though I were Ev herself – the Ev I'd met at school – desired and desirous of any attractive member of the opposite sex.

So I looked. And it was pleasing, to see how that man was put together. More muscular than Galway. Tanner. A fresh, ample cock, lolling in a nest of dark hair. I averted my eyes as he made his place beside me.

'Thanks,' he said, gesturing toward Ev. 'For telling me to fight for her.'

The breeze blew across my nipples, hardening them. 'She deserves to be happy.'

'Got that right.'

Galway and I cut across the Dining Hall lawn as the moon was setting. We hardly spoke; an inevitability had fallen over the evening that words would not change. I was not melancholy, but that was the closest emotion I had ever known to what I was feeling. This was it: tomorrow I would look back, and what was coming would be done.

Queen Anne's Lace was smaller than Bittersweet and cut, as though with a knife, into four equal pieces: bedroom, living room, bathroom, kitchen. When I had peeked in its windows on previous occasions, I had always taken it to be run-down, badly cared for, but now that I was inside, I realized it was probably the most historically accurate building at Winloch.

In the simple living room, the walls were rough-cut, the ceiling held aloft with beams made of tree trunks. Galway's guitar hung over a small woodstove that held up an old cast-iron pot with three legs, and around that central hearth sat handmade furniture, turned and cut from the living world around us – a rocking chair made of tree limbs, a simple table planed from felled wood. A linen-covered love seat held cross-stitched pillows. On the walls hung pewter plates; I leaned in toward one and noticed it bore the Winloch crest. Books were everywhere, and they were old; as Galway slipped into the kitchen, I examined one to find a bookplate bearing Samson Winslow's name.

I could hear already how Ev would snipe about the decoration, but, now that I knew Galway, I knew why the place felt so safe, and lovely, in spite of its aged quality. He had saved, and collected, all the things his relatives had discarded. Whereas they had revamped, he had preserved.

I took in the small bouquet of buttercups in a child's pitcher on the coffee table, and realized that he might have placed them there that afternoon in anticipation of my arrival. I felt a wave of desire at his confidence. 'Whiskey?' he asked, returning from the kitchen with a bottle and two glasses. I took a careful sip, and he sat beside me on the couch.

Silence burned over us like the alcohol in my chest.

'What's your place like in Boston?' I asked nervously, at the same moment he asked, 'What classes are you taking in the fall?' Our questions came out like swords against each other, creating a distance to mask the strangeness of what we were doing, here, alone, together, and we sparred back and forth, each insisting the other continue, neither of us with anything important to say, but feeling we must fill the silence, the knowledge of what we were about to do, with words, to delay it, to appreciate it, to acknowledge what was to come. It felt like this: a dance. Him, then me, him, then me, back and forth, until we were both laughing, and then we were looking at each other, and then he reached across the space between us and put his hand on the back of my neck, and then we were pulling toward each other, magnetically, kissing with a fury I didn't know I possessed, as though he was everything I had ever wanted in the world. Every touch between us, every space that disappeared, was filled with warmth. All I knew was the softness of his tongue against mine, and his hands running over my back, the strength of the muscles in his legs underneath my fingertips, and our chests pressing hard together.

My brain, the part of me that never turned off, just seemed to sail away. Instead I was all body. Hungry. On fire. Before I lost myself completely, I pulled back. 'You're not with her anymore,' I led. His last out.

'No,' he gasped, 'no,' as if he couldn't breathe without me, and he kissed me again, and lifted me, carrying me into his bedroom, where we stayed all night, wound around each other, meeting each other in a place I had never known. We made love again and again, until the planet tilted toward morning. The night was ours.

CHAPTER THIRTY-FOUR

The Morning

Ping. Ping. Ping ping. Ping.
A distant sound. Watery.

My unwilling eyes fluttered open. The world was still blue. Galway's body slept behind mine; we were two spoons nestled together. I took stock of all of him – hot belly, rhythmic exhalations against the back of my neck, hand slung over my hip possessively.

Sensing my wakefulness, he shifted onto his back. Yawned. Ping. Ping ping. Ping.

'What's that sound?' I whispered.

He yawned again loudly, in complaint, his muscles tightening, like a bear awakening from a winter's slumber.

I scooted my body back against him, waiting for him to settle, noticing, with satisfaction, a few drops of blood on the bedsheets. I hadn't told him it was my first time (or second, or third), but I wasn't embarrassed at the evidence as I had imagined I would be. I was sore but satisfied.

He settled back down, but the strange sound continued. I was absurdly awake. 'Is it a bird?'

'It's the halyards,' he mumbled. It was a metal pinging he was, apparently, accustomed to. The yachts moored only on this side of camp. 'Used to be all the masts were wooden.'

'So they didn't used to do that?'

He groaned. 'It's not even light out.'

We couldn't have slept for more than two hours. My eyes ached. But giddiness, and nervousness, and a creeping sense of distrust – not of Galway, exactly, but of what would happen next – were making it impossible to relax. I didn't know how to be this woman. If he fell asleep again, I was afraid that I'd lie here for hours or, worse, that I'd find myself slipping out of bed and tiptoeing away. I had no idea how I'd come back from that. I was pretty sure it wasn't possible.

Ev. How would Ev act on a morning like this? Would she talk to her lover? Would she hold on to the night's promise and insist the seduction carry over into day?

I turned and put my forehead against Galway's. The ancient box springs squeaked underneath us, and I realized, with a mixture of embarrassment and pride, how much sound we must have been making all night. The dawn filtering in through the rustling curtains brought with it the melody of the wood thrush. 'I'm starving,' I whispered, feeling my nipples harden against his smooth chest. I kissed him – his sleepy lips responding a split second behind mine. 'Let me make you breakfast.'

'No food in the house,' he grunted. I kissed him again with my mossy mouth. He tasted of me. He opened one eye and peered. 'You're peppy.'

I pulled myself onto one elbow. My hair was spilling down to my shoulders, loose and mussed. He reached one hand up and played with it, pushing it off my face, and I watched a fresh wave of lust wash over him. 'You're so beautiful.'

I found myself once again insatiable, joining my lips to his.

His body went slack. 'You made me want waffles.'

'You really don't have anything in the house?'

He whimpered.

I glanced out at the new day. 'We have only one choice.'

'Cannibalism?'

'We shall have to raid the Dining Hall,' I declared.

'There is absolutely no way I'll survive the journey.'

I put my head against his chest. Now that we were leaving, I regretted my earlier self. Had I been able to sleep longer, we could have stayed in bed, dopey and hungry for days.

'Suit yourself,' I whispered, placing one hand over his heart. I closed my eyes.

He stirred. 'I bet there's bacon.'

It was ending too soon.

Anyone who happened to peek out their window as dawn gave way to morning would have seen us streaming across the broad meadow and guessed what we'd been up to all night, but if they did, whoever they were kept the knowledge private, saving it in case it was worth something.

'Isn't Masha here?' I whispered, as Galway pulled me into the unlocked Dining Hall, which smelled of yeast and last night's brisket.

'She's visiting the grandkids.' He pushed me against the wall and kissed my neck before breaking for the kitchen. 'Forbidden meats!' he yelped in joy.

I hopped up onto the kitchen counter. He fed me. Bacon, crispy. Eggs, scrambled. Warmed blueberry muffins he found in the freezer and drizzled with honey. He slipped a honey-dipped finger into my mouth and then danced his hands up and under the sweatshirt I'd borrowed and thrown on over nothing. 'Not here,' I whispered, as he tried to wrap my legs around his waist. 'I see you've regained your strength,' I added, extricating myself and heading for the stairs. He followed me, as I'd known he would.

In that great vaulted attic room that held the Winslow secrets, Galway pushed the papers from the nearest table and ripped off the sweatshirt, took my breasts into his hands and lay me down. He put his lips between my legs. The table was cool against my back, his mouth hot at the very center of me until I came, hard and fast, and then, before I could gather myself, he entered me, until we were somewhere else, together, moving and crying out as one.

At the other end of lust, we held each other, spent. He helped me get dressed. I took in the mess we'd made of the papers and remembered he'd had some news.

'Right!' he exclaimed, now all business. 'I haven't told you. I asked the family accountant if I could look at some of the financial files – told him I was working on this project for the family tree – so he said I could stop by.'

'Where are they kept?'

'In the family vault.'

I raised one eyebrow.

'Yeah, it's ridiculous,' he said. 'But listen. I started looking back around the time of the bankruptcy stuff, and Banning Winslow almost filed.'

'I thought he did file.'

'No. All the paperwork was filled out – that's what we have – but at the last minute, it looks like he borrowed money or had some new source of income.'

'Who would have lent them money? No one had any.'

'Doesn't matter. What matters is that in May of 1933, there's a deposit made in the Winslow account of two hundred thirty-five thousand dollars. The Winslow debt is paid off immediately, with enough to spare to get the family through another month. And in June, there's another deposit: a hundred and ten thousand dollars. This goes on. Not every month, sometimes not every year, but, Mabel, the money grows and grows until they've got millions in there, earning hefty interest. They've got enough to invest and grow, and they make it out of the war just fine.'

'Where do you think they were getting that kind of cash?'

He shook his head. 'No idea.'

'How long did it go on?'

'What do you mean?'

'I mean, did the deposits end when the war did?'

His eyes darted warily away from mine. 'We should focus on the thirties. That's when it began.'

He was keeping something from me. But I saw that pushing him would only bring silence. 'You say Banning was the one who almost filed?'

He nodded. 'He was in charge.'

'I found something too.' I told him about what I'd discovered the night of our first kiss, how Bard was Banning's second-born son, and how quickly he'd come to power – ousting his father and older brother, Gardener, in the midthirties in one fell swoop. I explained how this upheaval of leadership led me to suspect that Bard was the one who'd single-handedly saved the family's fortune. He'd done something major to wrest the reins of control from a father who'd nearly ruined the family with his shaky investments of their trust.

How Bard had overcome his elder brother's inheritance of the family line was another matter, but I suspected that when Gardener saw how determined Bard was to overthrow their father, he'd willingly stepped aside. As I explained my theory to Galway, my confidence in it grew, and I felt sure that Bard was the one behind the cash deposits Galway had discovered.

'I just wish we could know what changed,' I mused, as Galway began to pick up the papers we'd pushed to the floor. Why had the money started coming in when it did? Why had Bard seized power when he had? 'What was Bard doing in May of 1933?' I continued.

'Well,' said Galway, holding up a piece of paper, 'in September of 1932 he got married.'

Right – he'd married Kitty. I thought of her journal, the journal Indo had insisted held secrets, but in which I could find almost nothing. It was too much of a coincidence to believe that Bard's sudden rush to power didn't have something to do with whatever secrets his wife's journal held. I just had to dig deeper. And tell Galway about it. He'd know what I should look for.

I was about to begin when he froze, putting a finger to his lips.

'What?' I mouthed.

He pointed downstairs as I heard the door to the Dining

Hall close. Manly footsteps marked their way across the wooden floor. We listened as they headed into the kitchen, then stopped at the sight of our dirty dishes.

'Hello?' came the voice.

'Stay here,' Galway mouthed, then called back, 'Hello?' I knew I was supposed to hide. I masked my footsteps in his, finding a spot in the far corner behind an old cabinet.

It was Birch. 'What on earth are you doing here?'

'Hungry,' Galway said.

'You've made a mess.'

'Which I intend to clean.'

I heard the water go on. I made out Birch's words: 'Good, Son. I can't be expected to clean up all your messes.'

After that, the old pipes began to moan, masking the voices of both father and son. I strained to hear Galway's response. But I failed.

CHAPTER THIRTY-FIVE

The Pile

I DON'T WANT TO SUBJECT you to their scrutiny,'
Galway apologized formally after his father left. He
helped me clean up, but it wasn't lost on me, as we placed
the discarded papers on the table where my naked body had
been less than an hour before, that he hadn't touched me
since Birch's departure. Galway planned to go back to Queen
Anne's Lace and sleep for a few hours, then head to Boston
in time for another busy week of work. I wouldn't see him
again until the weekend. 'We'll tell them soon,' he said, and
I thought of John and Ev's secret, part of me doubting we
would be any different. When he wasn't looking, I slipped
the Winslow family tree into the sweatshirt's center pocket.
An act of defiance.

I fell into bed smelling of the man who had made me
new. It was early in the day, but it may as well have been
midnight as far as I was concerned. I was grateful Ev was
nowhere in sight – I had no way to explain the transformation my life had just undergone, and slipped into a slumber
that seemed to last a hundred years.

I awoke to the clatter of something falling. A teacup, a
saucer. I was ravenous. I wrapped myself in the duvet and
fumbled out to the kitchen, searching for the shattered

ceramic, but there was nothing there. Maybe the accident had happened hours before, Ev had cleaned it up, and it had echoed in my head until my dreams could no longer contain it.

I felt as if I'd been in a cave. I burned a quesadilla, then wolfed it down so quickly I scalded my tongue. I drank three glasses of water and finally remembered to check my watch – it seemed probable it was late that Monday night. But it was 4:18 a.m. – I had slept for eighteen hours straight.

From the porch couch, I listened to the morning's arrival. First the wood thrush roused, then the nuthatch and the black-capped chickadees, and somewhere, far away, a woodpecker tapped on a trunk, until morning had gained its momentum and Winloch was brought fully into Tuesday. Only then did I wonder about Ev's whereabouts.

First, I called Abby's name. The dog usually came readily – one could catch the cheerful jingle of her tags as she ran up through the woods – but I strained to listen and heard nothing. I stood at the porch door and called again, then whistled. Nothing. Ev's tennis shoes were just where she'd kicked them off on Sunday evening before the skinny-dip. That seemed like months before, but I reminded myself it had been only thirty-six hours. I went back into the bedroom. Ev's bed was 'made' (the coverlet wrinkled and pulled up haphazardly, as close to neat as Ev ever left it). Heart beginning to flutter, I walked through the cottage, noting the unwashed cereal bowl in the sink, Ev's jacket hanging on the coatrack.

I went back into the bedroom and inventoried her goods. I couldn't put my finger on what was missing, but her usually overflowing drawers seemed to pull open too freely. I ran my hand across her bureau. How many times had I seen her sitting on the edge of her bed brushing her locks? She never went anywhere without her Mason Pearson hairbrush. But today it was nowhere to be found. I peeked under her brass bed. Her suitcase was missing. Ev had packed. She was gone.

Panic rose like bile. I obsessively circled the house, hoping to find a note, a map, some kind of clue. I turned up the couch pillows – perhaps she'd hidden something for me there (a promise to send for me? A gift? An apology?). But no such luck.

She'd been so happy the night of our skinny-dip, as though she and John had finally come to some kind of peace. How could I have been so stupid? They had made up. He had agreed to leave his mother behind. They had run away. As I raced through Bittersweet, I felt more and more sure Ev and John had proceeded with their escape plan.

I showered quickly, annoyed by having to wash. I scrubbed Galway off me, wincing at the raw parts of myself that had seemed badges of love and maturity only hours before. Already, I cursed myself for that night, rejecting its memory: if I hadn't been with him, Ev would still be with me. She'd been able to leave only because I hadn't come home. I should have kept my promise to Birch, and told on her. He would have kept her here.

I pulled on fresh clothes and headed out into the already humid morning. Now would be the moment to tell Birch his daughter had left Winloch. I had agreed to that, hadn't I? But then, I had no alibi for being out of the house during

Ev's departure and, given Galway's reaction to his father's near discovery of us in the Dining Hall, no good reason for telling him the truth about why I hadn't been able to stop Ev from leaving. And yet: I had promised. What if Ev was in trouble? I felt sure she was with John – I felt it in my sinking gut that she had left me, definitively, for him – but what if she wasn't? I could never forgive myself if Birch could have helped her but for my keeping her departure a secret.

As I strode over the hill into the great meadow, toward Trillium, morning sun warming my limbs, I remembered the tone of Birch's voice with Galway in the Dining Hall, how he'd ignored CeCe, his own sister, on Winloch Day, and the quick kick he'd deliberately delivered to send Fritz flying.

My feet diverted to Indo's door.

I checked my watch again. It was 7:30, a perfectly reasonable hour to knock, especially in a state of concern. Indo would be levelheaded, cynical even, about Ev's departure, and calm my nerves with her reassuring pessimism. I'd laugh when she called Ev a selfish little brat, and nod when she told me I was ten times the girl Ev was.

I knocked twice on the locked door to the kitchen, but the world was still. Fritz's familiar bark did not come. I tried again, this time on the window, my raps peppering back off the water. Nothing.

There was another door to Indo's, on the water side, up into her screen porch. I'd noticed that it, too, was lined with locks, but the wood of the doorframe was so punky that a sturdy push might break through. I knocked.

I heard a whimper in response – what I took to be an animal, but I'd been wrong before.

'Indo?'

Fritz raced from the bedroom hallway, through the living room, and onto the porch. He clawed at the screen. He wasn't being territorial. He wanted me to come inside.

I tested the handle and sized up the frame, then took in the rest of the meadow to see if anyone was watching. With one hefty slam against the door, the rotting wood gave way.

I followed Fritz into the cottage, back past the bathroom, and to the surprisingly elderly bedroom I'd glanced over that first day in Indo's cottage. As I pushed open the door, I uttered a silent prayer that I wouldn't find her doing what I'd found Athol and the au pair – or, for that matter, Ev and John – engaged in the last time I'd followed an animal-like sound. I was met with the single gruff woof of one of Indo's lesser dachshunds. I followed his nudge to the sight of Fritz pawing at a pile of clothing upon the pistachio rug. I stepped closer. Indo's favorite pup was licking frantically at the pile. And then I realized, from the graying braid sticking out from below the clothing, that the pile was Indo.

The next moments passed as though I were in a dream. I called Indo's name. Felt for a pulse. She was breathing, but her eyes remained closed. I called for help, but no one could hear me. I told her I would return, running back the way I'd come. As I vaulted off the porch I started shouting 'Help! Help!' and ran in the direction of Trillium – I could only imagine the expression of annoyance I'd meet on Tilde's face – when Lu and Owen bounded up the steps from Flat Rocks.

'Indo's unconscious,' I gasped, gesturing toward Clover.

'She collapsed.' Owen, resourceful boy that he was, declared, 'We'll call 911.' The three of us ran toward the Dining Hall. At Indo's cottage I peeled off, calling, 'She's in the bedroom.' They headed toward the only Winloch phone (why hadn't I thought of that?). Indo's hand was cold by the time I made it back to her side.

'Indo,' I said, 'Indo,' shaking her by the shoulder. Fritz frantically licked her ear, and I tried to gather him into my arms, but he was determined to help her. I inventoried her – intact arms and legs, no blood, no vomit, no urine. After an exhaustive tally, I watched her chest rise and fall, then touched her cheek – it was soft and worn, like a beloved children's blanket.

Her eyes fluttered open. 'Is it raining?' she asked in a dry voice.

I started giggling – hysterical, nervous, relieved. Pulled Fritz away.

'What happened?' She glowered.

'I found you here, on the floor. Lu went to call the ambulance.'

She tried to get up but couldn't even lift her hand.

'Do you remember what happened?' I asked to keep her speaking. 'Why are you here on the floor?'

She shook her head, baffled.

'The EMTs will be here to help you any minute.'

'No,' she said vehemently, 'I said I don't want any goddamn doctors.'

'It's okay.' I took her hand, as much for my own comfort as for hers.

'What time is it?'

'Eight in the morning.'

'What are you doing here so early?' she asked. Something had shifted in her questions – she was fully present now. She seemed to know who, and where, she was.

'I was having – I was just wondering if you'd seen—' I was going to say 'Ev,' but she cut me off with an exasperated growl.

'I can't hold your hand; you're going to have to figure it out for yourself.'

I took my hand off hers. I thought she was speaking literally. 'I just thought you might have seen—'

'You think I can give you my house if you don't have proof? Numbers and figures, written down and added up by men. They stole it, they grew it, they live off it and know the truth of where it came from. Blood money, blood money, blood money.' She moaned as if in excruciating pain. 'My poor mother! She made me promise – keep it a secret, keep it a secret – but I can't anymore. I can't. You can only cut out a tumor for so long before it simply infects the whole body. The time for sentimentality has passed.'

'You should rest,' I said firmly. I'd been wrong; she was not herself.

She lifted her head in a remarkable feat of strength and looked right at me. 'Mabel Dagmar, listen clear. I gave you my mother's diary because it tells the truth. The truth you have to find. If you want to be a Winslow you will have to change what being a Winslow means. You will have to take them all down.'

'The truth?' I asked meekly, as I heard an ambulance whining toward us through the woods.

'Pay attention to the when of it,' she said, her eyes rolling back in her head.

'But I've read it over and over,' I whispered, as the siren grew louder. She did not respond. 'What am I supposed to be looking for?' I might as well have been asking a wall.

The siren was met with a rising chorus of howling, barking canines drowning out the Winloch silence until the blaring vehicle halted outside. The EMTs descended upon us, shaking the little cottage with their efficiency. They rolled Indo out to the flashing vehicle, and loaded her in as bewildered cousins emerged from their cottages, grasping their robes around themselves. At the far end of the meadow, Birch and Tilde poked their heads out of Trillium.

As the EMTs closed the door of the ambulance and Birch started to run toward us, I put my arm around Lu's shoulder. Two words ricocheted through my head: *blood* and *money*.

CHAPTER THIRTY-SIX

The Threat

I TOOK INDO'S DOGS BACK to Bittersweet, tossed their hair-covered pillow onto the floor of the kitchen, and ordered them down. Fritz gratefully licked my hand, as though not a thing had changed. I thought, with a pang of sadness, of how much Indo doted on him. Sure, he'd stayed by her side when she collapsed, but he didn't seem to care now that she was gone.

Lu knocked sulkily on the door half an hour later. I didn't tell her Ev was gone, but she seemed to take it as a given; we both knew Ev would have never allowed Indo's mutts into her domain. I washed my hands and fixed us egg sandwiches and black coffee. Lu slumped dramatically on the porch couch.

'Indo's going to be okay,' I said, intending to comfort her, instead opening the floodgates. She sobbed, her salty tears falling on the crusts of the leftover toast. 'Really,' I said, 'you're a hero; thank you for calling, I didn't even think of that,' but still she bawled on. I took the plate from her. 'We did everything we could,' I said, rethinking all of it, telling myself we really had, when she mumbled something incoherent. I asked her to repeat herself.

'They're sending me to sleepaway camp,' she cried, 'in Maine,' wailing as another round of tears overtook her. She wasn't crying about Indo after all.

'Why?'

'Because of Owen,' she said, as though it were obvious.

'Start at the beginning.'

She wiped her nose on the back of her arm like a toddler. 'Owen and Arlo and Jeffrey took some stuff out to sell in the rowboat that night after we all went skinny-dipping. It wasn't a big deal – they were just doing it for kind of a joke. And okay, sure, they made some money. So they decided to do it again the next night, just mostly because they were bored. But then Daddy caught them or one of the Canadians complained or something and then Arlo and Jeffrey totally sold Owen out and said it was all his idea, and then Daddy lectured him about how bad it was to sell—'

'Why is it bad?'

'I don't know, May,' she said, frustrated, 'he just didn't want them to do it anymore – it was demeaning or some-thing. And then he told Owen he had to go home.'

'Demeaning to whom?'

'The Winslows.'

I rolled my eyes. 'Because Winslows aren't in sales?'

'Can you just listen?'

'Sure,' I sighed, equally exasperated. 'Why are they sending you to camp?'

'Owen was supposed to go home yesterday. But he didn't. He stayed. He was just going to stay a few more nights, we found a place for him to hide out, but then you were freaking out about Indo' – she sounded accusatory, as though in calling for help I'd plotted against them – 'and we were down on the rocks together but Owen heard you calling for help.' She shook her head. 'We shouldn't have come. They saw us together.' She crumbled.

I felt the worst for Owen; the rest of the parties involved, Lu included, seemed to have forgotten that Indo had collapsed, and that the boy was the one who'd called the ambulance. I thought of his sweetness that day at Turtle Point, wondered if Lu understood that he loved her, if she believed she loved him back. 'When are they sending you away?' I asked.

'Tomorrow,' she said, pouting. 'Mum called. It's all done.'

It was already late July. She'd survive.

She sat up straighter then, and did a frighteningly dead-on impression of Tilde: 'Off to camp, Luvinia. It's time to learn a lesson about consorting with the wrong sort of people.' She slumped back into her normal self. 'Unless.' I could feel her eyes on me. 'Maybe you could say something?'

'To whom?'

'Daddy's always talking about what a great example you are. Please, May? Just tell them you think Owen's a good person. That you'd trust your own daughter with him. Or whatever – you know what to say.'

I thought about it. Lu was a good kid, and I could tell Owen had the purest of intentions. Still, was it wise to butt into Tilde's affairs? Lu was only fourteen. If her mother wanted to send her to camp, that was her prerogative. But no, I thought, recalling the admiring way Owen had looked at Lu on Turtle Point, I should do what I can for love.

'I don't know why they care about his family anyway – it's not like I'm going to marry him,' she added derisively, swiping her arm across her nose again.

'You never know.'

'He's from the Bronx,' she scoffed. 'You think I'd marry someone from the Bronx?' The place name rolled off her tongue with a disdain that didn't seem the least bit manufactured. As though the word was falling from her mother's mouth.

Dear Mom – Now I'm lonely again. All these weeks I thought I'd found someone like me, or at least what I would be if I'd been born to the Winslows. But she is of them. Worse, she is like them. Willing to throw anyone under the bus, even her boyfriend, in favor of maintaining her position. I'll be doing Owen a favor by sending her as far away from the Bronx as I can.

'I'm sorry,' I said, 'I can't.'

'Please.' Lu pleaded with her puppy dog eyes.

'They're your parents,' I insisted.

She pulled away from me. 'Fine.'

'I've got myself to consider.'

'Right, I get it.' She stomped to the door, then turned and looked at me over her shoulder. 'Like what the hell you're going to do once I tell them Ev's gone?'

'Do you know where she is?' I asked, my voice shaking involuntarily.

She had the upper hand. She stood over me, looking just like Tilde. 'How long do you think they'll let you stay if she's not here to look after?'

I watched Lu run around the bend toward Trillium. I bolted the door. I didn't need some privileged child marching back into my home and threatening me for doing what was right. If she was going to tell, she was going to tell – there was nothing I could do about it.

I knew I should turn to Kitty's journal – Indo had been vehement, hadn't she? – but already I doubted my memory, and Indo's sanity. Blood money. That was what I was supposed to be looking for. But the last forty-eight hours seemed ridiculous enough without bringing some over-wrought family secret into the mix. What I needed was a conversation with Galway. He would set me straight. I'd quell the butterflies in my stomach with a walk to the Dining Hall and telephone him, girl on the other end of the line be damned.

I grabbed an apple and water bottle from the kitchen, *Paradise Lost* and a sweatshirt from my bedroom, and put them into a canvas bag I plucked from the peg on the porch. I placed my hand on the front door but held back, deciding, at the last minute, to take Kitty's journal from its spot under the bathroom sink. I unearthed the journal from its hiding place and wrapped it inside my sweatshirt, shoving the bundle into the bottom of the bag. I remembered the pilfered family tree and added it, then a beach towel, filling the stained tote that had once carried Antonia's library books and potato chips to happier picnics on happier days. Perhaps I'd find a peaceful spot in the world and have a moment of clarity.

Just then, there was a banging. Loud and insistent. I emerged from the bathroom to discover Birch's face against the screen, his fist pounding at the door that separated us.

I made an effort to say something welcoming, but I was

drowned out by the sound of his fist and a growl rising out of Birch's lips. 'Open this goddamn door right fucking now, you—'

'Birch!'

He stopped short at the sound of his name, called from behind. Over his shoulder I saw Tilde and Lu. They were panting, as though they had run to catch up. Tilde's hand was clamped tightly around Lu's wrist. The girl was crying.

'Birch, dear,' Tilde commanded again, as she might one of her dogs. The effect of her voice on the man was profound. He moved away from the door, down the steps. I was frozen, not allowing myself to think what might have happened had the bolt been unlatched, or Tilde not been on his tail.

'That's right,' Tilde said calmly, keeping a firm grasp on Lu, 'that's right, let the anger go. It's of no use to you. And look, here's your beautiful daughter, right here; you wouldn't want to lose your temper in front of her, would you?' Birch cast his eyes over Lu, who had finally managed to break free of her mother's grasp. He ran his fingers through his hair, appearing elderly for the first time in my memory.

Tilde looked up at me, peering at them from the porch. 'How about you invite us in?'

Inviting them in was the last thing I wanted to do. But was I really going to stand here in a locked house when my hosts had demanded entry? And what did I think Birch was going to do to me? Still, my hand shook as I undid the bolt.

We sat in the living room and pretended everything was fine, even as Fritz cowered in the kitchen. 'Have you heard

267

anything about Indo?' I asked, trying to make conversation, watching Lu rub her wrist as she pouted from the porch sofa.

'Why don't you apologize to May and she can tell us what she knows?' Tilde asked as she placed her fingers on the back of Birch's hand. He still looked distracted, not quite himself, but he nodded. It was hard to align this new version of him with the powerful man who had hosted me on his porch only a week or so before, or even with the man who'd just pounded on the door.

'What Birch wants to say,' Tilde told me instructively, 'is that Luvinia shared the news that Genevra seems to have flown the coop. Naturally, we were both concerned to discover this absence. But he forgot himself.'

'I understand completely.' I tried to sound convincing and not to glare at Lu for being a tattletale. I wondered if she'd known how angry the news would make her father.

'How long has she been gone?' Birch spoke, his voice shaky.

I replied carefully, wondering what my escape plan would be if he were to anger again. 'I discovered her missing this morning. I was on my way to tell you when I found Indo in her room.'

Birch swallowed. Tilde smiled her cool smile. 'See?' she said to her husband, adding to me, 'I knew you wouldn't keep such important news a secret.'

Birch was coming out of his foggy state. With every second, he seemed to become more aware of the world around him, to inhabit his body anew, to reinvigorate. 'Do you know where John took her?'

So he knew about them. I guessed they hadn't been too discreet. I shook my head.

'We'll find her,' Tilde said in a soothing tone. 'We'll make sure she comes right back home, now, won't we, dear?' To me, she added, 'It's so hard to love one's children as we love ours. It's easy to get . . . passionate.'

As Tilde rose to leave, the strangeness seemed to dissipate. Birch teased Lu that, if she kept sticking out her bottom lip, a bird would come perch on it, and tapped Tilde on the butt as though they'd been flirting all morning. I could sense relief in both Tilde and Lu, relief I recognized from my own childhood and, in truth, was feeling too. We were no longer under siege.

'Well then,' Tilde said, opening the screen door, 'we'll leave you to your day.'

I realized I was gripping my bag, which had held Kitty's journal the whole time.

Nearly at the door, Birch turned to me. 'As for Indo, we'll find it's another symptom of her downturn, I'm afraid.'

'Downturn?'

'Of the cancer.'

'Cancer?' The thought of Indo sick was a punch to the gut. 'She has cancer?'

'Oh, my dear,' he said, stepping toward me, pulling me into a hug I didn't want, 'I thought for certain she would have told you. It's spread to her brain.' I could hear the thud of his heart inside his chest. He smelled of mothballs. His sweater scratched. 'She has a month at the most.'

'I had no idea.' I tried to pull out of the embrace. But his arms resisted the distance, as though they were programmed to clasp me close. They only unclamped when I tugged hard against them. My feet launched backwards. I skinned my heel on the table beside the porch couch.

'I'm sorry to be the one to tell you.' Birch watched me as I rubbed the new scrape. 'I'm sure she's mentioned some batty ideas. Make no mistake, she is eccentric, but she's also, literally, losing her mind. I wouldn't take anything she's told you, or promised, to heart.'

Kitty's journal burned under my arm.

From out on the driveway, Tilde called to Birch, and he descended the porch steps toward her; Lu was already out of sight. Satisfied he was coming, Tilde walked on, out of earshot.

'Oh, and Mabel,' Birch said, turning just as he reached the driveway, 'I've been meaning to ask you. Have you called Daniel lately?'

My mouth turned to cotton.

'Your mother says the care he's getting at Mountainside is fantastic.'

I couldn't move, or speak, or think.

'I know your father works hard to keep him there. Let's remember your promise to keep me informed.' With that, he left me.

CHAPTER THIRTY-SEVEN

The Woods

I SHOOK AS I MADE my retreat from Bittersweet. The words Birch had used were innocuous enough, but they had shaken me. He'd been speaking to my mother? How much did he know about Daniel?

I cut into the pine forest behind the Dining Hall. I'd never wandered there before, and I welcomed the soft carpet of needles under my feet, the occasional pull of brambles across my bare legs. But in the shadowed woods, doubt pulled hard – if Ev was truly gone, if Lu was leaving, if Birch was threatening me and Indo was dying, and Galway coming only on the weekends, what was the point of staying here? But I had no money. And no place to go except horrible Maryland with my horrible aunt.

A rapid pounding echoed through the woods. With the day's sounds in play – the distant roar of a mower, the buzz of a motorboat – I couldn't distinguish whether the steady hammering was coming from a woodpecker or maintenance men. As I made my way deeper, downed, mossy trunks occasionally blocked my path. Above, the treetops rubbed against each other, a creepy, private sound, as though they were telling secrets about me.

Without warning, a great, primordial beast alighted on a dead tree only a few yards away. I froze. The creature's wingspan was massive, pterodactyl. I watched as it folded its wings, drew its red crest back, and proceeded to pound its beak hard into the rotting wood high above the forest floor. The sound was crisp and loud. The tree swayed.

I stood, enthralled, at the sight of the pileated woodpecker Lu had promised me, until he was done with his grubby snack and took off again. I could hear the rush of air through feather. I closed my eyes. I was being ridiculous.

Birch Winslow had been worried about Ev. A father should worry about his daughter; it was only because mine didn't that I'd thought his behavior odd. If he had threatened me – and I was starting to convince myself he hadn't – it was only to ensure I kept my promise to tell him of his daughter's whereabouts. Hadn't I been the one to break his trust by keeping mum on the matter? And anyway, wouldn't I want someone like Birch Winslow on Daniel's side? Hadn't that been part of the point of going to college, of all of this – to make connections that could better my, his, our life?

I almost tossed Kitty's journal into the forest. Whatever secrets it held, they weren't mine. It was the conceit of a dying woman, 'literally losing her mind,' that the journal even held anything of note. That's what Indo was saying, I told myself, when she talked about the tumor. Not about her family being infected. But about her body filling with cancer. Who knew what she meant by 'blood money,' but really, was it worth caring?

I hiked into the heart of the Winloch forest, slapping myself like a madwoman to kill the mosquitoes who'd found me. A couple of horseflies joined the swarm, and I draped the towel over my head to protect myself. Ev's flip-flops slipped on the forest floor, but I trod on. I'd run into a road someday, although whether I'd follow it was a question I had not yet answered. The crunch of pine needles gave way to rocky forest floor as, above, the canopy changed to maples and birch. I gave myself over to the chastising chatter of the brown squirrels, the far-off squawks of crows at play. I guessed I was walking in the direction of Mrs LaChance's house, so I cut back to my right. I didn't think I could bear her.

I wandered into a clearing, rustling a white-tailed deer out of a peaceful lunch. I froze. She held my gaze from the other side of the patch of grass, head lifted, smelling my human stink, until some indeterminate revelation about me sent her into the forest, her tail flagging long after the rest of her body was invisible. It was a sensible moment, a reminder that I was not a survivalist and could not stay in these woods forever. I looked up at the clouds breezing by, killed three more mosquitoes, and decided to follow the deer's trail.

Not that I had any idea how to follow a trail; I simply walked in her direction, cutting into my apple with an appetite it wouldn't long satiate. I thought of Eve and her apple, wandering in Eden. I walked on and on, until I started to feel tired and, frankly, bored. I nearly laughed at the memory of my former self, running from Bittersweet into the woods for cover. Ev would come home. Galway was my lover, not my boyfriend. And Birch was just a father looking out for his brood. Besides, my stomach was growling. I was about to turn back when I caught a phrase of music on the breeze. Motown. I followed the strains until I found myself in a clearing. There, before me, stood a cottage. A hand-carved sign over the door, straight out of the Brothers Grimm, read JACK-IN-THE-PULPIT. Deep inside, a radio played.

The cottage was standard issue, but it resembled Mrs LaChance's more than Indo's. Perhaps the buildings on this side of the bay, deep in the woods as they were, where the damp clung, were simply more prone to rot. 'Hello?' I heard myself call out, my mouth watering at the thought of the lunch that might be inside.

The radio switched off. If a wolf leapt out, or a raccoon, a vampire, anything, I would turn tail and sprint into the forest. Or maybe the creature would just kill me quickly, draining me of my blood, before I knew what hit me.

'Hello?' came the woman's voice as she stepped from the screen door, wrapping a shawl around her shoulders.

'CeCe!' I rejoiced with inappropriate familiarity. It was meant to be, I told myself. 'I'm Mabel,' I chatterboxed, removing the shroud from my head, 'Ev's friend? We met on Winloch Day. I guess I got lost! I was trying to find a good swimming spot.'

'There's not much swimming over on this side. You'd do better at Bittersweet.'

'Oh.' I tried not to show my disappointment. 'I guess if you could just point me to the road . . . ?'

She gestured down a pockmarked driveway I hadn't noticed. I nodded. Started walking in that direction.

'You hungry?' she asked after me.

I turned. 'Do you mind?'

'Just got supplies in town.'

CHAPTER THIRTY-EIGHT

The Sister

JACK-IN-THE-PULPIT was spotless inside. Every place had its thing and every thing had its place, but the whole building reeked of cigarettes – I felt my asthmatic lungs constrict the second I stepped inside. I realized this was one of the first Winloch homes I'd entered without a dog in it. My eyes lingered over the only picture on the living room wall: a clear-eyed, handsome soldier who resembled his cousins but would never grow old.

CeCe made us Campbell's tomato soup with three baby carrots each on the side. Her serving sizes were minuscule, and she nibbled at hers like a mouse. We sat at a rickety folding table in her large eat-in kitchen, surrounded by the same Vietnam-era appliances as in Bittersweet. The woodstove held court at the other end of the room. Above it, a wall that had once hung with several large frames still bore their outlines. The floor was scarred, as though the real furniture that had lived here for decades had crept out of the cottage by itself one night.

I ate slowly, trying to pace myself, but at the meal's end, my stomach growled. I assumed CeCe had heard the news of Indo's collapse, but she was surprised when I filled her in, if not very concerned. Indo was CeCe's sister, after all. But then, Indo hadn't been exactly warm to CeCe on

Winloch Day – in fact, CeCe was the only person I had ever seen Indo treat that way.

'Did you know about the cancer?' I asked, looking around. Even Mrs LaChance's house had felt happier than this – sadness seemed to have soaked into Jack-in-the-Pulpit as surely as the nicotine.

'It doesn't surprise me she'll die of it.' CeCe drew a pack of cigarettes from a kitchen drawer and lit up. The words were harsh, but she didn't say them harshly.

'Why?'

'Indo has fed on anger for years. Blame. Deceit. Makes sense she'll be eaten from the inside out.'

I must've made a face. CeCe looked briefly shattered, as she had on Winloch Day. 'Sure I'm sad,' she added. 'She's my sister.'

'She wasn't very nice to you on Winloch Day.'

'People living a lie generally don't enjoy the company of the one person who says the truth,' she pronounced cryptically.

I rose from the small Formica table. 'I should go.'

'Oh, please don't,' CeCe cried, grabbing my wrist with a clawlike hand. The smell of her tarred breath rose up all around me. 'You're the first person who's really talked to me in weeks.'

I sat down. 'Ev told me about Jackson. I'm very sorry.' I was, but I was also very curious.

She stubbed out her cigarette and lit another. The room had filled with a filmy haze. I felt my lungs tighten, but my cough went unnoticed.

'They claim they had nothing to do with it,' she said.

'Who?'

'Any of the Winslows. Anyone who keeps their secrets.' She narrowed her eyes at me.

'You blame your family?'

'I can blame anyone I want.'

'But he'd just gotten back from the war.'

'Shell shock,' she mused. 'People have been using that excuse as long as they've been killing each other.'

Silence hung over us for a moment. I made out the sharp ticking of a clock, somewhere deep in the confines of another room. 'But you don't think that was why,' I said leadingly.

'I know my son.'

'He didn't kill himself?'

'Of course he killed himself. But no one wants to talk about what he did before he put that gun in his mouth and pulled the trigger. That very week, he visited Indo at her place in Boston. Then Genevra at college. And the night before, he met with Birch. He had something pressing to discuss.'

Jackson had visited Ev at school? My mind raced. He'd been in my room. Jackson Booth himself. 'But you don't know what he wanted to discuss?'

'Au contraire, dear girl. I know exactly what it was.'

I sat forward. 'What was it?'

She lit another cigarette. Leaned back in her chair. Drew in with a long suck, then blew out a blast of gray smoke. 'I blame myself,' she said, as though she hadn't heard me.

'You shouldn't.'

'Were you there?'

I tried to think of something philosophical to say, but I

knew all too well that, if something terrible was your fault, it only made things worse when people tried to convince you otherwise.

The canvas bag was sitting at my feet. I knew Indo would kill me if she ever found out, but I couldn't help myself. I plucked my sweatshirt from inside the bag and unrolled it until Kitty's journal was sitting on the table between us. Indo was dying of brain cancer, and I was running out of time. I nudged the book closer to CeCe. 'Recognize it?' I asked.

She stuck the cigarette in her mouth and picked up the journal with both hands, examining the covers before opening it and carefully squinting over the pages.

She was taking too long. 'It's your mother's journal!' I crowed.

She delivered no reaction, simply turned page after page, then flipped forward to the opening of the book. She examined Kitty's name. Then placed the book back down. Removed the cigarette. 'That's not my mother.'

I opened the book again, pointing to Kitty's name. 'Yes.'

'My dear,' she enunciated, 'not everyone has children with their wives.'

'Oh.' I was flustered. 'I'm sorry.'

She waved her hand dismissively. 'I'm glad that monster's not my mother.'

I nearly blurted, 'Kitty wasn't a monster.' But instead I asked, 'So who was she?'

CeCe stubbed out her cigarette and didn't light another one. 'My mother's name was Annabella. She's the reason I look . . . Mediterranean.'

'But Bard claimed you?' I asked, mind racing. I started

278

searching the journal for the passage in which Kitty talked about Bard's affair – perhaps it was about CeCe's mother. But even before I found it, I remembered that the woman mentioned – 'the maid' – hadn't had a name that started with A. What letter was it?

'Someone tipped off the press. He had a choice – claim me, or be exposed as the sadist he was. He had to think of his business ventures. His reputation.'

'What happened to your mother?'

'She disappeared.' No emotion as she said this. Just the facts.

'Did Kitty claim you?'

'Kitty let Bard tie me to a kitchen chair and beat me whenever I got too "tan."'

Perhaps CeCe was the crazy one. I'd read Kitty's journal enough times to consider the dead woman a friend, or at least a reliable narrator. I wanted to press CeCe on the point of her mother, but I saw, as she lit another cigarette, that the subject was closed.

I searched for the entry that mentioned B.'s dalliance. Then pushed the journal toward Kitty's husband's illegitimate daughter: 'Friday, August 24th. B. has been carrying on with one of the maids, P. He has assured me it's over, but it is a mess nonetheless, one I shall be paying for myself, that weighs heavily upon me.'

'Who's that?' I asked, pointing to the P.

CeCe shook her head. 'There was no woman whose name started with P. when I was little.' She flipped through the journal, holding her place with her index finger. 'When was this written?'

'I don't know,' I said. 'She doesn't say the year.'

'That woman kept on task. I've never finished a journal I started.'

She read the dates to herself: Saturday, June 21; Sunday, June 30; Monday, July 14. She counted on her fingers and a smile began to form. 'Look at this,' she said, flipping back to the first and sixth entries. 'January second and January seventh are five days apart, right?'

'Yeah.'

'But she writes: Tuesday, January second, here. And here, she writes Monday, January seventh.'

'Okay.'

'Tuesday and Monday are six days apart. Not five.'

'Well, what does that mean?' I felt thick.

'It means that these two entries were written in different years.'

'Maybe it's a mistake.'

She shook her head. 'Trust me, Kitty didn't make mistakes.'

I took the journal from her hands. Something buzzed at the edges of my mind. If CeCe was right, perhaps that was why in some entries Kitty had noted the day of the week and sometimes she hadn't. I pored over the first week of entries – January 2 was the only date associated with a day of the week until January 7. Maybe this was a code to herself? A signal for when she'd switched to a different year? But why go to all that trouble?

'It looks chronological, sure,' CeCe said, growing excited for the first time, 'but it's not. She could have kept the journal over decades.'

I remembered what Indo had told me: 'Pay attention to the when of it.'

'So who,' I asked, flipping far ahead into the book and falling back upon the passage I had assumed was about Bard's infidelity, pressing my finger on the definitive P. mentioned there, 'is that?'

She took the journal from me carefully and leaned over it, squinting at the page as though it might reveal something new. And then, in an instant, I watched her figure it out. She dropped the journal and stood back, as though a thunderbolt had slammed her.

'Who is it?' I asked.

She pointed to her door. 'You have to leave.'

I gathered the journal, but I was desperate to understand. 'Just tell me who it is.'

'Don't tell anyone you have it. Promise.'

'I promise.'

'You weren't here.'

'I'll just tell them we had lunch.'

'No!' Her voice was sharp like a dagger. 'I'm not part of this.' She went to the door and held it open, her cigarette smoke blowing sideways in the wind. I shouldered my bag and made my way to the door.

'I won't tell anyone,' I said, disappointed. 'I don't know anything.'

She looked wistfully out the door, at a sky that had turned stormy. 'You'll figure it out,' she said, as though the inevitability of my discovery were the greatest tragedy in the world.

I passed out of CeCe's cottage and back into the day. Thunderheads rumbled. The smell of rain hung in the air.

She watched me walk down her driveway. I turned away from her then. I had nearly reached the road when I heard her footsteps. She was upon me in seconds.

'Be careful,' she whispered in an anguished voice, pulling at my shirt. 'They'll make you do things you don't want to. And once you've done them, you'll never forget because they won't let you. Don't invite them in. Don't tell them any secrets.' Her expression was childlike, damaged.

'I'll be fine,' I said awkwardly, trying to edge away. She grasped at me.

'No one is fine. No one is safe. Not here.' Tears began to pour from her eyes. Out in the light, her skin was gray, her teeth yellowed. I would have comforted another person, but her demented grief was grotesque. She began to sob as she doubled over.

I ran.

CHAPTER THIRTY-NINE

The Revelation

I SPRINTED TOWARD BITTERSWEET like a tornado, ready to cut down anyone in my path. I half expected to find the place gone – as disappeared as Ev – but the cottage was just as I had left it, seemingly untouched. I checked inside, greeting Fritz's hello with a biscuit. Satisfied that I was alone – and still clutching the bag with the journal inside – I made my way under the crawl space below the porch. On our cleanup day at the beginning of the summer, the day I'd put aside all those magazines, I had also bagged dozens of old wall calendars. Apparently Antonia Winslow had never met a free calendar – whether from the humane society, an insurance company, or the grocery – that she hadn't loved. But, unlike the magazines, the calendars were now intermixed with all the other recyclable junk, so I stooped in the cobwebbed space, rooting inside the sixteen garbage bags we'd tied and placed there, praying my hand would find only paper and not a nest of baby opossums, a colony of spiders, or a napping raccoon.

Anything that felt remotely like a calendar I piled beside me, until my back ached from bending over. After checking outside to see no one was watching, I carried as many as I could directly into the bathroom, keeping the journal with me. I repeated this a handful of times, until I felt confident I'd rescued everything that could be of use.

I called the dogs outside, insisting they relieve themselves before they were allowed back to their beloved pillow. Inside again, imagining Birch and Tilde occupied with the search for Ev, I bolted the porch door, fed the dogs, washed my hands, took a hunk of cheese, a bag of chips, and two more apples from the kitchen, and barricaded myself in the bathroom. How sweet was the sound of the second metal bolt slipping into place. I was beginning to understand why Tilde had thought them necessary.

I sat with my back against the door and tried to calm myself. I didn't dare let my mind wander to the vision of Birch pounding on the door or of CeCe collapsing in her driveway. Her family had done something terrible to her; that was all I knew.

I dove into the calendars, ordering them chronologically. I was lucky – they went all the way back to the midtwenties and ended in 1986, with a few years missing here and there. They were scribbled upon – 'Doctor's Appointment,' 'Buy Licorice' – but the dates were clear, which was all I cared about. Thank goodness Antonia Winslow had been a pack rat.

It was slow going at first, but I got into a rhythm. First I'd locate a date in Kitty's journal, then, using the day of the week mentioned, I'd sift through the calendars at hand and try to determine a year. If and when I did, I'd write the corresponding information on a piece of paper, so as not to mark the journal itself. Every year, she wrote in the January section, then the February one, and so forth, until she reached

December and started the cycle all over again. She denoted these changes in year only by mentioning the day of the week on which she was writing. It was an easy tool for her to decipher, but just as easy to throw off anyone less determined than I.

In this way, she'd created a journal that looked as though it had all been filled over twelve months but had, in fact, been written over the course of decades. My theory was backed up as I came toward the end of each month and noticed that her entries grew shorter, the margins narrower, the letters smaller. As the years went on, she was trying to cram as much as she could into a space that was invariably becoming cramped.

Kitty Spiegel was a woman who could have afforded a hundred journals. But she had rationed the space in this book instead. That was a clue in itself. Maybe Indo and CeCe were both right.

I forged on, cataloging January and February dates. I began to realize that calendrical years repeat themselves – 1928 was exactly the same as 1956, which in turn was identical to 1984. I could rule out 1928, since I now knew that Kitty and Bard were married in 1932, and she hadn't started the journal until she was ensconced at Winloch, but I couldn't rule out even 1984, since Kitty had lived until 1992. I had to write down two, or even three possible years for every date, which opened up a maddening array of possibilities. Every entry had to be read with multiple eyes, multiple imaginings of the year from which she might have been writing.

Now I understood why she hadn't mentioned salient details about what was happening in the world around her.

Not because she was ignorant or uninterested, but the opposite: she was crafty. She didn't want anyone to do what I was doing right now.

Part of me wishes that, after going through the calendars, and marking down all the possible dates on my separate piece (now seven pieces) of reference paper, I had chosen to close the journal and go out for a swim. Better yet, that I had hauled all the calendars outside to act as tinder and built a mighty fire, tossing the journal onto it, sending it into ash and oblivion. Or, had I needed to press on, that I'd thought about what Indo had said, about blood money, thought, too, about the maid's silence in front of the Van Gogh, understood the painting's true secret, and hopped down the rabbit hole Indo had dug for me.

Instead, I opened the journal to an entry I'd noticed once because it had seemed out of place: 'Wednesday, November 6th. B. has gotten a new pair of shoes and is putting them to good use. An adorable sight, to see him toddling down to Flat Rocks, towel slung over his little shoulders!'

In my first passes through the journal, the entry had struck me as strange because the words used – *adorable, toddling, little* – were words to describe a child, and Kitty used B. to stand for her husband, Bard. But in 1940 – the year I guessed this entry was from – Bard would have been in his thirties.

I dug out the family tree and smoothed it on the floor before me. I pored over the names of the Winslows, hoping one of them would answer me.

And then it hit me, like the cold current of a rushing, rapid river: there was someone else in Kitty's family whose name began with B. and he'd been eighteen months old in 1940: Birch.

My mouth went dry. I raced back to the beginning of the journal and picked through the entries with another identity in mind. In most entries, B. was obviously Bard: 'B. came home from Boston last night exhausted. Poor man, he works his fingers to the bone'; 'B. has obtained a new sloop to be docked at Winloch. I only hope he'll have time enough off this summer to enjoy himself upon it.' But then there were others in which the identity of B. was murky, or obviously not that of a husband: 'B. spent the morning studying Henri, and, over snack, recounted the "story" Henri had "told" him,' or 'B. continues to use the toilet while singing himself a little song.'

I had never heard a grown man described this way. Heart pounding, I raced forward through the months and years, finding mentions of this second, younger B. As Birch grew from boy to man across the carefully laid pages, it became harder to distinguish the entries about him from those about his father. Up until this point the content of Kitty's journal had been an exercise in history. Now I was reading about someone I knew. Someone very powerful.

Again, I could have stopped. I had devoured my snacks, and my thoughts were like dust. I could see, from the tiny slice of light out the high bathroom window, that the long afternoon was stretching into evening. I had calendars to hide, and decisions to make. But CeCe clung to me. More specifically, I couldn't shake the look on her face when she'd read the journal entry about B.'s affair with P. I flipped back to that entry and read it again.

'Friday, August 24th. B. has been carrying on with one of the maids, P. He has assured me it's over, but it is a mess nonetheless, one I shall be paying for myself, that weighs heavily upon me.'

I flipped back to my notes. I'd marked the entry's year as 1956, when Bard would have been nearly in his fifties. But what if the entry was not about Bard? What if Birch, his son, had been carrying on with one of the maids? A servant whose first name started with the letter P.

Maybe this entry had been written in 1984. A little more than twenty-five years ago.

And then, in a flash, delightful and horrifying, I remembered tall, mighty Aggie dashing across Mrs LaChance's screen porch at the sound of the sick woman's lament, trying to stop John's mother from saying something worse to Ev than what she'd already said. Aggie had used Mrs LaChance's first name only once, but it had burrowed into my ear and stayed there, waiting for me.

'Pauline,' she'd pleaded. Pauline.

CHAPTER FORTY

The Return

THE IFS LED ME down a path.

If I was right, and Kitty had written this journal so that all the events within it appeared to occur during one year but it in fact spanned as many as fifty, then there was much more information between its two covers than there appeared to be.

If she was writing about her family over such a long period of time, then sometimes B. stood for her husband, Bard, and sometimes it stood for her son, Birch.

If Birch was the one carrying on with a maid called P., then that P. could stand for Pauline, and Pauline was the first name of John's mother, Mrs LaChance.

If Mrs LaChance had had an affair with Birch twenty-five years ago, then her son, John, might well be Birch's son too.

If John was Birch's son, then John was Ev's half brother.

If Ev was pregnant with John's baby, then Ev was pregnant with her half brother's son.

I dropped the journal. I unlatched the bathroom door, hoping to gasp the fresh air circulating through the rest of the cottage. But I took in the whole place – the sagging couch, the yellowed walls, even the lake lying below the dusty kitchen windows – with new eyes. It was poisoned, stinking, imbued with an awful history that was now inescapable. Asthma began to tighten my chest. Did Birch know I had Kitty's journal? Was he watching me with hidden cameras, listening to me through planted microphones? My paranoia led to disordered thinking, but the outcome was the same as if I'd been rational: it was time to leave Winloch.

I would start running and never look back, and this time, I would take the road, so they would all know I was leaving. I wrapped the journal in its towel and thought of stashing it under the sink. But if someone knew where I'd been hiding it, they'd look there first. So I dashed through the house, rejecting hiding spots – under the bed, too obvious; under the porch, too exposed to the elements – before remembering the board John had been trying to fix. I dropped to my knees and located it easily, prying it up with a pen cap. Sure enough, it offered six inches of storage space below it. I wedged the journal, wrapped in the towel, into the new hiding place, stacked the calendars in the corner of the bathroom, and pocketed the family tree. I decided that the sheets of paper that held the true dates of the entries (as far as I could guess) were too dangerous to leave with the journal – since they worked as a decoder – but they were a dead giveaway for someone in the know, so I couldn't carry them myself. Nor could I destroy them – I had too much pride in my research. No, I'd take them to the Winslow paper stash in the Dining Hall attic; what better place to hide them than with a thousand other papers? Only Galway – I thought of him with a stab of pain – might recognize that they were new, might follow my bread crumbs, once he found the calendars and snooped around the house. Couldn't he?

I gathered up essentials – snacks, a toothbrush. Even though Ev had left a crumpled hundred-dollar bill on top of the dresser, I didn't touch it. I already owed the Winslows too much.

I poured as much dog food into the bowl as it could hold and let Fritz and his buddies gorge themselves as I left behind everything Ev had ever bought me.

I dashed out just as night descended. I don't know how far I thought I would get, with the mosquitoes already on my tail, no light, little food. With every step I took, I was stabbed by terrible fantasies – Athol would emerge from the bushes, a rifle aimed at my kneecaps; Tilde would hit me in the back of the head with a shovel. I was grateful when I spotted the Dining Hall, my last stop before freedom. Safely out of Winloch, I could call my mother, tell her I needed help, and pray she wouldn't deny me refuge just because I hadn't sent her one letter.

Masha was hard at work peeling potatoes when I pushed in through the doors of the otherwise empty Dining Hall. She lifted her head in the fluorescent lights of the kitchen to watch me dash up the stairs. In my state, I found her glance predatory.

On my way up, I flipped on the light, already feeling calmer as I readied myself to be surrounded by my old friends, the Winslow papers, just one last time. Maybe it was foolish to leave and I was wrong about the journal. Maybe Birch was just a nice older man and I had a dangerous imagination.

I mounted the final step.

The attic was empty.

Not just empty; spotless. Not a speck of dust or a forgotten paper, or a pile of unused furniture. Even the tables were gone, any trace of the project I'd embarked on completely eliminated.

The sound of my defeat echoed in the cavernous, empty space.

I took the stairs down two at a time and waved a quick good-bye to Masha, calling, 'Check on the dogs in Bittersweet,' without looking back to discover her reaction. It was good to have a witness. Someone who could report that I'd left as soon as I knew my place.

I sprinted onto the main road. It would lead me out of Winloch once and for all. I slowed my steps, remembering to pace myself; I had to formulate a plan. I'd run (or walk) the couple miles – it couldn't be more than six – to the country store we'd passed a few times on our way in and out of camp. They had a phone there. I'd call my house collect and hope my mother answered.

The roadbed moved from meadow into woods. I was glad for the cover, if not for the mosquitoes. In the still, thick night, they were hungrier than I'd ever experienced. I chose not to use my flashlight, lest I register how many of the swarming insects there actually were. Besides, I could sense my way from the rattle of gravel below my soles.

I heard the motor before I saw it. The whine of the radio carried through the trees before the headlights flashed around the bend. I ducked into the Winloch woods, grateful for their cover. I didn't need to go very far – anyone driving by would hardly be looking into the forest. I certainly didn't expect to see anyone for whom I'd willingly step into the road.

Galway – I would have stepped out for him. As the sound of the car drew louder, my heart leapt at the thought of the safety of his arms. Only yesterday, he had sheltered me. But he had retreated into the recesses of my mind, shimmering at the edges like a mirage. All it would take was his rounding the corner and I could be released from this paranoid fear.

The headlights flashed. I tried to temper my expectations. It was Birch, or one of the maintenance men in their little white trucks. It was Athol and the nanny. It was a dinner guest.

I saw it was a truck – higher than a car, filled with two bodies. John's truck. The windows were unrolled. They were listening to Chet Baker.

I stepped into the road before rational thought could stop me.

I felt the headlights skip over me.

The sound of the brakes. The purr of the idling motor.

I opened my eyes. Shielded them with an arm.

The driver flipped the lights off.

Then: the welcome sound of Abby's bark. Followed by the crunch of footsteps. And then: Ev's arms around me. The sweet smell of her. 'What's wrong?' she asked, the words biting me like the mosquitoes. 'You look horrible – where are you going? What are you doing standing in middle of the road? You smell like cigarettes. Have you been smoking? Are you okay? Mabel? Are you okay?'

The words growled up from deep inside me. 'You left me.'

She stretched out her left hand. 'I got married.' I registered the ring on her finger as she pulled me toward the truck.

'C'mon,' she said, 'let's get you into a nice warm bath.'

CHAPTER FORTY-ONE

The Proof

Ev was horrified by the state of the cabin – the dachshunds, the calendars, the riffled drawers – but she bit her tongue and took care of me. I can't imagine how wretched I must have looked to arouse such motherly impulses in her, or perhaps her new role as wife had planted the seeds of domesticity much more quickly than I would have expected. In any case, when I emerged, saner, from my bath, scrubbed as clean as could be in the silky, sulfuric water, dinner was waiting for me, and Abby and Indo's three dogs were lying at Ev's feet in harmony.

John wolfed the spaghetti down. 'Thanks, Evie,' he said, rising from the table, kissing her forehead, giving Fritz an affectionate pat.

'You're leaving?'

'I've got to see her.'

Ev almost retorted, then acquiesced in the way only a wife can. 'Are you going to tell her?'

He was sizing up the doorframe. 'Tell her what?'

'The plan.'

He looked down at her as though she were an after-thought. 'Foundation's sinking' was all he replied. Then he stepped out of the kitchen without a second glance.

'The plan?' I asked.

Ev sighed next to me. 'We're leaving again in a couple days.'

'Why?'

She grimaced at the need in my voice. 'My money finally came through. Daddy said if I came home it would be waiting for me.'

And here I thought I'd gotten her back. Foolish Mabel Dagmar. 'But you're going to leave anyway? You're going to go back on your word.'

Her reply was nasty. 'Not everyone can be as perfect as you.'

I left her in the kitchen and followed John to his truck. 'You're just going to let her leave me here?' I tried to keep my voice low so she couldn't hear me. 'You have any idea what they'll do to me once they discover you're gone? I'm supposed to be keeping an eye on her.'

He sized me up. 'I thought you believed in love.'

'There's a big difference between loving someone and taking her away from her family.'

'Remember, Mabel,' he said, as he opened the door for Abby, 'you're not a Winslow.' He looked more unfriendly than I'd ever seen.

I scoffed. 'It's not right,' I said, 'lying, hiding—'

'I've got a lot to worry about.' He sighed, world-weary. 'Please tell me I don't have to worry about you too.'

I hated how I sounded – petty and childish. Like Ev was a toy I was fighting him over. My heart started pounding when I realized I could just say, out loud, who I thought his father was, and win. If I even wanted to win. If that even was winning. But no, I needed proof first. 'Could you drive me to the store next time you head to town?' And then I needed him alone.

He got into his truck.

'It's the least you can do before you abandon me here,' I heard myself say.

He started the engine. 'You don't sound like yourself.'

'And who exactly do I sound like?'

He nodded toward Bittersweet. 'One of them.'

I wanted to tell him right then, tell him he was one of them, much more than I would ever be, but I bit my tongue. 'So? The store? Can you?'

He gave a single nod and pressed down the accelerator. He was gone in a flash, red taillights streaming out of sight.

I found Ev at the table. She had removed her wedding band. 'They'll let you stay here till the end of the summer,' she said. 'If you're worried about yourself.'

'I'll figure it out.' I cleared the table.

'It's weird you're someone's wife,' I said later, to break the silence, and remind us both that we were friends.

'I don't know why he won't tell his mother we got married,' she said, a grimace on her face.

'Now you want her to know?'

'It's not like she can keep us apart now that I'm his wife. So I told him we could just bring her along if he's going to whine about it all the way across the country. Why the hell not, if it's so goddamn important to him?'

I wondered what Birch was capable of. Could he find them? Would he blame me?

'Don't you even care where we're going?' she asked. 'Sure.'

297

'California.'

I could have found out why. Or when. Or how. Instead I asked, 'You're sure it's a good idea to take her with you?'

She slapped the table with both hands. 'No,' she said, her voice rising as her body did, 'but it's all I've got, Mabel. If I want to be with John, she's part of the package, and I'm okay with that. I don't really give a shit if you are.'

I sank my mind into the soapy, stinky dishwater along with my hands. I wanted to be rinsed clean, but I fiddled with the details of Kitty's journal. The logic carried over every time. There were a lot of ifs, but each brought me to the next, and every time, I concluded with John and Ev as brother and sister. Half brother and half sister, but what was the difference?

If I was taking on the task of telling one of them, I needed to know for sure.

'Anyway,' Ev said, drawing my attention, 'I'm not the wife you should be worrying about.'

'What's that supposed to mean?'

'Galway. He's married.'

I pulled my hands from the hot water and turned to her. She looked triumphant. 'Oh, I'd heard rumors, you know,' she said, 'but I couldn't believe anyone would actually want to marry him. Apparently, some girl from south of the border needed a green card, and I'm sure she didn't mind—'

'That's not true,' I said, my voice shaking. 'That can't be true.'

I knew she was a liar, but she wasn't lying this time. Her expression was honest, if mean, especially as it melted into a mocking frown. 'Poor, sweet Mabel's getting her bubble burst.' She shrugged. 'Guess you had to learn how the world works sometime.'

I felt it then – an angry devastation I had never before felt at her hands. Galway's lie was like a punch to the gut, but the dismissal in Ev's eyes as she hurt me was almost more unbearable. She searched my face to locate the pain she'd caused, and then, satisfied as she watched it bloom, left me alone.

I awoke the next morning pretending I'd never met Galway. My heart was a fortress. My body was a nunnery. My mind was a library. Proof would set me free.

'Masha?' I called into the Dining Hall kitchen.

The grandmother emerged from the walk-in refrigerator, wiping her hands on her apron. 'Breakfast?' she asked.

I shook my head. 'You've worked here for a while, haven't you?'

'Oh boy.' She squinted up at the ceiling. 'Thirty-six years?' Her accent was still thick, but her English impeccable. I thought, with sorrow, that Galway had probably had something to do with that. Unacceptable. I was not to think of him.

'Do you think you could remember back around the time Galway was born?' Galway was about the same age as John, and I knew the mention of his name would throw her from the scent while softening her. Still, it was hard for me to say it.

'About what?'

'About who worked here. Specifically the women.'

Masha looked alarmed.

'Oh, it's just for the research I'm doing. Upstairs, you know? The papers that used to be upstairs. Galway asked me to help him.'

She eyed me carefully for a good long while. 'It's hard to remember.'

'I know,' I said, feeling my heart thump. 'But it's okay if you do.'

Masha swallowed. She stuck out her bottom lip in a gesture of the difficulty of recall, but I knew she knew exactly who'd been working here.

I'd have to try a different tack. 'Did you know Ev is sleeping with John LaChance?' A look of panic swept across the old woman's face. 'They have a right to know if it isn't right.'

Masha's eyes darted around the Dining Hall. 'Please,' she whispered. 'Don't make me say.'

'You don't have to tell me the maids' names. Just how many women worked here back then whose names started with the letter P.'

The old woman began trembling before me. I was moved to touch her, to comfort her, but that would have kept me from the proof. I was in too far to stop now. I had to know. So I crossed my arms and waited.

'They have a right to be happy,' she pleaded. 'Please don't tell them.'

'How many women worked here whose names started with P.?'

Slowly, inevitably, Masha lifted her hand before her, like a secret, as if it held a terrible power, and from her fist bloomed one gnarled finger.

'Good,' I said. Not 'Thank you,' not 'Oh god,' but, because it felt like a relief to finally know I had been right, to know something for certain, however terrible it might be, 'Good.'

CHAPTER FORTY-TWO

The Good-bye

SOMETHING HEAVY PLOPPED DOWN on the foot of my bed the following morning. I rubbed my bleary eyes and took the room in. Ev slumbered soundly in the other bed. Even the wood thrush wasn't singing yet.

'I came to say good-bye,' Lu whispered.

'You're leaving?'

'Mum's driving me to the bus station.'

'How long will you be at camp?'

'I have not been informed.'

I sat up and swung my feet onto the cool floorboards. I put my arm around her bony shoulder. I was willing to forgive her for putting me in Birch's fierce path. She'd probably had no idea how he would react. 'It's been great getting to know you,' I said.

'I'm not dying,' she said and laughed, planting a kiss on my cheek. She sprang up from the bed and jumped onto a sleeping Ev, who groaned in complaint.

'Good-bye, old bat,' the little sister teased. 'Nice of you to come home.' Then she bounded out of the room, blowing me a kiss from the doorway.

John's truck pulled up soon thereafter, sooner than I expected. I waved to him from the kitchen as he made a beeline for the bedroom to rouse Ev. The door closed behind him. Abby sought me out in the kitchen, her chocolate eyes urging me to sneak her a bit of leftover chicken. Grateful, she licked my hand and trotted back out onto the porch.

I picked at my bowl of oatmeal and pretended to read *Paradise Lost*. But Lucifer's soliloquies offered no distraction. I allowed my mind to think about what I knew, and if it was right to tell. Would it make any real difference for John and Ev to know they were siblings? They had already gotten married. They had a baby on the way and were planning to move across the country to a place where they knew no one else. Was it just my selfish curiosity, my hunger to know what they would say and do once I said those words, that made me want to tell them? Or was it worse than that? I wanted Ev to myself, didn't I? Didn't I hope that this revelation might send John away? That, when he went away, things would go back to the way they'd been at the beginning of the summer?

Then again, maybe it was crueler to keep the secret, to withhold something so earth-shattering as the truth of someone's origins from him, origins he deserved to know. Surely John's paternity was why his mother detested Ev. If I didn't tell him, Mrs LaChance would only make their lives miserable, trying to drive Ev away.

I would have wanted to know.

Or at least that's what I told myself.

My oatmeal was cold when John emerged from the bedroom. He poured himself half a cup of coffee, which he drank in one gulp, spilling a bit down the front of his red flannel shirt. He took in my pajamas. 'You want a ride or not?' He whistled to the dog.

We barreled out of Winloch in silence, not because there was nothing to say but, at least on my end, because there was too much. My mind raced as we accelerated over the deeply pitted road, past the places I had come to know so well. First Bittersweet, with a sleeping Ev inside, disappeared behind a curve in the rearview window. We turned past the Dining Hall, empty but for Masha's constant watch. Then sped beyond the trio of cottages belonging to Athol, Banning, and Galway. As we revved past each well-worn building, I bid the place a kind of good-bye. I would be returning with a new perspective on things: I would have told John, or I wouldn't. I would have called my mother, or I wouldn't. Not to speak was as much a choice as its opposite.

We skidded around the curve where John and Ev had discovered me two nights before, and he cleared his throat as though the memory of me standing before his truck had jostled him.

'So California, huh?' I asked.

'I've got a friend out there. Does contracting. Going to help me with a job.'

I nodded, not saying any of the skeptical things racing through my mind – she'll leave you in a week, you aren't prepared to be parents, she's your sister for fuck's sake, why on earth would you bring your hateful mother along – and on the last count, at least, he seemed to read my mind, because as we passed the turnoff for his mother's cottage

– speeding past it even faster than we had anything else – he said, 'My mother's going to come around.'

'She doesn't seem to like Ev much,' I pressed.

'Yeah, well, she worked for the Winslows for a long time. She doesn't want to see me hurt.'

'Or she knows something.'

'What the hell's that supposed to mean?'

We burst from the woods, startling the goldfinches. They lifted up from the meadow and sped north, like a yellow arrow. 'What if she kept a secret, and the secret was meant to keep you safe, but now she can't keep it anymore because—'

John slammed on the brakes, and the cab swung forward, then back. Our heads bumped the backs of our seats. I craned against my seat belt to see the animal in our path, the reason we had stopped, but there was nothing there. Instead, John was staring me down.

'Ow.' I rubbed the back of my head, looking in the rear-view mirror to see if Abby was all right. She was gamely righting herself.

'I don't like it when people beat around the bush,' he replied.

'I'm not—'

'What do you know?' he pressed.

'I don't know anything.'

'May, I'm not an idiot. The Winslows have their dramas, but as far as I know we LaChances have managed to stay above all that. So if you know something about my mother, now's your chance.'

I was losing my nerve. 'John,' I said warmly, gesturing to the road, 'I just want to call my mom.'

'And I don't want Ev to leave here with any doubts. I'm not letting you get out of this truck until you tell me what you know. Because if you don't tell me, you'll tell her.' He shook his head. 'They hate each other enough as it is. I'm not pouring lighter fluid on that bonfire.'

The chirruping finches had come back to rest on the reeds gently rustling in the breeze off the lake. The sun was warm.

'You don't want to know,' I said. My eyes began to blur.

'You don't tell me, I'll find out. I promise you that. I'll find out the truth.'

Ever since I had suspected, then known, the truth of John's paternity, I had imagined telling him, but never what the words would be. In my imaginings, I had had the papers with me, spreading them across the seats, and I had taken him through every step – through Kitty's journal, and the entry naming P., and the calendars, and the research – so that, by the final if, he could draw his own conclusions. He'd be the one to declare the truth, and I'd be free of my terrible secret, but I wouldn't have to say it.

But in that moment, in that car, it was just as it had been with Daniel, in the river. Just as startling and clear: I was being asked to be the darkness.

The answer.

The executioner.

The one who did what no one else was brave enough to do.

'John,' I said, 'Genevra is your sister.'

CHAPTER FORTY-THREE

The Waiting

I THOUGHT HE WAS GOING to hit me, but his hand sailed by and punched open the passenger door. Not a word, not a look. I stepped down, he slammed the door closed and sped off, away from me and Winloch, sending up a cloud of brown dust. Once it settled, all that was left of him was the distant roaring of the motor and Abby's incredulous bark.

I followed on foot. Not because I wanted to catch up but because to go back into Winloch just then seemed an impossibility, and the road led only two ways. I didn't blame John for leaving me – I knew I deserved it. Just as it had been with Daniel, I would accept my fate. If I must be blamed, I must, but I believed now, from the vantage point of having told, that it had been the only thing to do. As I walked, the memory of Galway's body – the vividness of his limbs, the points of his hips, the succulence of his lips – swam back into focus. I trained my mind on the minutiae of our lovemaking, how it had felt, and tasted, and, in doing so, did not allow myself to veer off track and into the less appealing realms of his marriage, or John and Ev's future, or the family he came from – Birch, Tilde, CeCe, Indo – and the secrets they kept.

Not a car passed me, and I relished the country route

on my own, dreaming it would go on for miles. Thanks to Lu, I knew this world well, and I admired the Queen Anne's lace and chicory lining the gravel road, the familiar, identifiable chirp of the nuthatch. I felt my arms growing tanner in the sun and relished the sweat on my brow. I suppose I knew that to meet civilization again would be eventually, inevitably, to meet the consequences of my actions, so I was disappointed when the gravel gave way to macadam, and when I rounded the final corner to glimpse the corner store.

I had walked nearly six miles, ostensibly to call my mother, but as I drew closer to the telephone box, I wanted less and less to hear her voice. All this time I had planned to tell her I was coming home, but, as my steps carried me along, I realized I didn't want to. To do so would have been a gesture left over from some long-ago self who needed someone to tell her who to be. The daughter Doris Dagmar had spoken to back in June, dependent, repentant Mabel Dagmar, no longer existed. And I was glad of it. Liberated. I was a maker. Controller of destinies. If I had to leave, I'd cut my own way out.

I went inside and bought a box of red licorice. Then I turned around and walked home.

Ev glanced up from her book when I came in. 'Where's John?' she asked. I hadn't forgotten about him; no, the vision of his hand punching open the door was seared into my mind, but the long walk in the sun had done its trick of making the morning's conversation in his truck feel distant. I hadn't prepared myself for her inevitable question.

'Oh,' I said, taking a moment to gather my lie, 'he dropped me off.'

She craned her neck toward the driveway.

'At the store.'

'He made you walk home? That's six miles!'

'I'm going for a dip. You want to join me?' But we both knew she would say no.

Without Lu and Galway, with my knowledge now passed along to John, Winloch seemed empty, almost as though it were a forgotten place and Ev and I, once again, its only inhabitants.

We made collages. Not of the families we wanted, or the families we had, but for each of the mainstays at Winloch.

Indo: purple flowers, hats, galoshes, box collections, all crammed into one small piece of paper.

Birch: straight lines, a smoldering cigar, a sailboat.

John: Ev's sketch of his muscled back, set against a photograph ripped from a bikini catalog, so that it appeared John was sitting at the edge of an imaginary cliff face, looking out over a Tahitian sunset.

Melancholy settled over us. We must have eaten, we must have spoken, but all I can recall is the solitude of that night when it finally came – the crickets, the wheedling bats.

We were both waiting for John.

CHAPTER FORTY-FOUR

The Widow

A T SIX THE NEXT morning, Ev awoke me. She was fully dressed. Her drawers were open and empty. Far in the distance, I could hear the insistent barking of a dog.

'Are you leaving?' I croaked.

'John was supposed to be here an hour ago.'

I sat up. She sat down.

'Did he say anything?' she asked.

'About what?'

'When he left you at the store. It doesn't seem like him. Was he distracted? Did something happen?'

My pulse raced. 'We were talking about his mother.'

'I knew it,' she said, as her lovely brow furrowed. 'Today was supposed to be the day. They were picking me up before sunrise.'

'You were going to leave without saying good-bye?'

Her glower turned into an indulgent smile. 'You're a goose.'

But I knew she'd planned to slip off. 'Maybe they'll still come,' I said finally.

She shook her head. 'Sun's up.'

'Tomorrow then.'

'What did he say? About his mother?'

'Just . . .' I sighed. 'I honestly can't remember. He wants you two to get along.'

'It's so strange he didn't stop by last night. It's not like him.'

My heart was still pounding. I hadn't expected to tell him Ev was his sister and have life just go on as usual, had I? The truth had consequences. I hadn't wanted Ev to leave. But seeing her like this, worried, knowing that if she knew the truth she'd be destroyed, I found myself wishing I could go back. Still, if he didn't come, she'd stay. And I could stay with her.

'Get up,' she said, slapping my legs, pulling a pair of my cold jeans from the floor. In the distance, the dog's bark was relentless. 'You're coming with me.'

How can I describe my state of mind as Ev and I picked our way through the Winloch woods?

Safety at the weight of Ev's hand in mine.

Self-assurance that I had done the right thing in telling John – if I'd kept my mouth shut and they'd taken his mother with them to California, the truth would have come out anyway.

Apprehension about John's reaction to my presence – would he rail, or weep, or curse?

Relief at the possibility that he might have left her to me forever.

Ev and I hardly spoke as we made our way through the forest. The dog had not stopped barking – the persistent sound peppered the quiet morning air, disturbing the natural order of things. The light dappling through the pines was thin. I squeezed Ev's hand.

We passed into the clearing where I had met the doe, but she wasn't waiting for us. We cut back into the forest and scrambled up a slope of mossy rocks. Occasionally the road peeked through the trees, but no one drove on it. We were alone.

'Does that sound like Abby?' I asked, as the barking got louder. We were close enough to hear that the dog was tired. There was a crack in its voice.

Ev shook her head.

'Maybe his mother was sick in the night,' I said. I couldn't help expanding the story of my innocence, even though I knew all it would take was one explanation from John, and Ev would know what I'd done. Still, I thought, there must be a way out of her knowing I'd been the messenger.

We crept up a final rock, then had to cut back down its ridge to avoid a twenty-foot drop. From our height, we had the advantage of a view over Mrs LaChance's roofline. As far as I could make out, John's Ford wasn't parked in the driveway. The dog was still barking, and the sound was coming from the house. It was Abby. No matter what Ev said, I knew that bark was Abby's.

We scrambled down a last, wiggly boulder, only thirty steps from John's mother's door.

'Where's Aggie's car?' I whispered.

'John gave her today off so she wouldn't know we were leaving.'

Every footfall, every pop of a broken branch, every crunch of leaf cover, seemed to ricochet between the rock face behind us and the cottage before us. We had no way of knowing what was waiting inside, but, even today, I contend I could feel it as I stepped into its vapor; the air around us turned cold and sad.

'John?' Ev asked boldly. At the sound of us, Abby's bark turned more insistent. The dog whined. Her distress was coming from underneath the porch, I was sure of it, and I tugged Ev's arm in that direction, but she pulled me toward the cottage door. The screen was in place, but the wooden door was open, as though someone had stepped inside only a moment before.

'Ev,' I warned, but she opened the screen door and called John's name again.

'Mrs LaChance?' I said meekly, following Ev inside.

'He wouldn't leave her here alone.'

It's hard to remember, after all the questions, after replaying what was where it was supposed to be, and what was out of place, after the shock of the discovery, and Ev's mouth like an O, what those moments were like before we found her.

Were we afraid?

We walked through the living room and onto the screen porch. John's mother was sitting in her wheelchair, her back to us. I can remember thinking her head was at a funny angle. Ev was a half step in front of me.

'Mrs LaChance?' she whispered.

No response.

Ev placed her hand on the woman's shoulder, turning her toward us. Then Ev's hand sprang back. I watched it recoil, and my eyes found their way up to Ev's face, to her horrified expression, and then down again, scanning over the water view, to the death mask of Pauline LaChance.

The bruises around her neck showed exactly how the life had been squeezed from her.

'Oh my god,' Ev bleated, backing up, as I stood there, frozen. Directly below the floorboards we were standing on, I was aware of the sound of an animal crying, barking, trying to break free. The sound had been going on for a long time, but the buzz in my ears had drowned it out.

I turned. I saw the porch door behind Ev, hanging off its hinges. I pointed. She bolted out the door: 'John?' she hollered. I followed her.

Abby's bark was loud outside. Ev took off down the trail, but I called to the dog, and she answered me. I crouched to look below the porch and saw, through the cracks in the boards, that she was trapped under the steps – someone had placed an old door in front of the opening she usually used. She was frantic, scraping at the barricade, and I realized her paws were bleeding.

'It's okay, girl,' I said shakily, trying to move the heavy door myself. I could only lift it a little, so I used all my weight to push it aside and managed, after the third try, to make a gap big enough for Abby to squeeze out. She didn't stop to thank me or take comfort. Instead, she shot off down the cliff trail, straight after Ev.

Out onto the trail I sprinted, clipping at Ev's heels. We cut back and forth along the switchbacks. Somewhere ahead of us, where the trail met the air, Abby had started barking again. We raced to catch up.

We came abruptly onto the point. I suppose we both

believed that John would be standing there. That time was of the essence. That there was logic, and explanation, and that the end of the cliff held it all.

But it was just air above us. Below us, water. Out to the horizon, nothing but blue. Ev began to speak, but the words couldn't form themselves. They were like tumbling rocks, too heavy, too full of their own momentum to make sense, impossible to understand over Abby, whimpering and whining, her paws coming dangerously close to the edge of the cliff, stones slipping from underneath her bloody nails and onto the rocks far below.

I watched one as it fell.

There, at the foot of the cliff, his limbs at odd angles, lay John. He was on his back, looking up at us and the new day.

I thought, for a split second, that he was alive. That he might lift his hand and wave.

August

CHAPTER FORTY-FIVE

The Aftermath

ABBY WOULDN'T LEAVE. HER barks were like gunshots. Ev pulled at the dog's collar, pleading, cursing, commanding, bits of the earth cascading into free fall onto John below. Then it was my turn to pull at Ev, to gather her and tell her, in a clear, adult voice, that we had to go now. We left the dog behind.

Ev promised to stay in the Bittersweet bathroom. I pulled Fritz's pillow across the living room floor, ordering Indo's dogs to barricade the door. Straining to listen, I could hear Abby's barks echoing through the forest, sharp, distant cracks of terror that measured the distance between John's body and my ears. Ev began sobbing, and once again I commanded her to calm down; I was getting help. Keep the door bolted, don't talk to anyone. Fritz stood at attention below me. Ev's sobbing dwindled into a whimper.

I stood alone in the Dining Hall. Cupped the phone's mouthpiece with my hand. 'Come to Bittersweet. Something terrible happened.'

Back in the bathroom, Ev and I huddled side by side. 'It's

my fault' was her constant chant during those waiting hours. Abby's bark was growing fainter.

'It's my fault. It's my fault.' She didn't want to be told otherwise.

Galway must've driven from Boston like a madman. I stood on my tiptoes and peeked out the bathroom's eyebrow window, confirming it was the growl of his motor I was hearing on the breeze. Ev had dozed off. I met him outside.

Did I mention murder? What I remember is Galway dashing past me, into the house, to his sister's side, and feeling a sudden, powerful drowsiness descend upon me.

He made me oatmeal with raisins. He led Ev into the bedroom with his hand on her back. Out the kitchen windows, the sun blazed.

I was familiar with the near dead. With the rubbery skin of a half-drowned brother. With the quickness with which one could put life back into the lungs of people who'd seemed to draw their last breath. But I hadn't guessed how vast the difference was between that and death. Time pressed with the near dead; it ceased to matter when someone was already gone.

With panic, I realized the world was silent. When was the last time I'd noticed Abby's barking?

'John killed his mother.' These were the words, the thoughts, I repeated as that day turned to night, as our statements were taken, as Bittersweet became the eye of the storm. It was no coincidence that I had told John of his paternity on the day someone had slipped his hands around his mother's neck and squeezed out her life. That he had jumped to his death only cemented his guilt. That is what I was told, and believed, and said: 'John killed his mother.'

Whom did I tell?

Galway, Detective Dan, Birch, Tilde, Athol, Banning, not to mention the many cousins dropping by with well-timed plates of food, hoping to get a first-person account from the traumatized girls. I told the story (albeit sanitized to protect the innocent) dozens of times, each time, safely ensconced in that cottage – alone at the kitchen table, huddled beside Ev on the porch couch, and, once, from my bed, as though it were just a nightmare that could be swallowed again by blessed sleep.

The police were happy to get our statements at Bittersweet, Birch and Tilde by our sides, Galway taking notes. There was no talk of police stations, or official questioning. It was clear to me from the moment Detective Dan knocked on our door that, as a general rule, Winslows were not suspects.

'What did you see?'

I told them everything, everything but the fact that I had told John he was Ev's (and Galway's and Athol's and Banning's and Lu's) brother.

Or that he was Birch's son.

Or that he had married his own sister.

Or that she was carrying his child.

Galway was the only one who pressed me, that first day, in the kitchen. 'Ev told me you saw John yesterday.'

'He drove me to the store.'

'What did you talk about?'

'They were running away. To California.'

'What did he say about it?'

'I can't remember, Galway.'

'Try.'

I had told John of his paternity on the day his mother had been murdered. He'd slipped his hands around her neck, squeezed out her life, jumped to his death all because of me. So did I blame myself?

Well, why had he just taken my word for it? How could it be my fault if I'd simply discovered someone else's secret? Why on earth had he killed the mother he was so loyal to? And if he really loved Ev so much, how could he have left her and their unborn child behind?

I opened my eyes. 'I don't remember anything.'

Galway sighed. 'Mabel, it was yesterday.'

'And I've been through a lot since then.'

He watched me for a long moment. 'Okay,' he said, his voice soaked in doubt. He opened his mouth as though to speak, then closed it again.

'Yes?'

He hesitated. 'I hope you're not holding something back.'

For the first time since discovering the horror, I felt a white-hot emotion sear through my foggy state. It was the only time I felt anything so strong in those days, like a nail hammered into a single, unlucky nerve that had escaped anesthesia.

I rose from the table. 'Like a marriage?' I asked, my voice trembling against my will.

He looked perplexed.

'You're married, aren't you?' I said, my voice shaking. He

opened his mouth to explain, but I saw, in the wince in his eyes, that he was. Before he could speak, I railed, 'Get out. Get out get out get out.' And he did. He stood right up and he walked right out.

'Where's Abby?' I asked. I asked Birch as he stood in our doorway, Galway when he came back and wouldn't look at me, Detective Dan in the morning, Ev late at night, and, in between, the curious cousins, my voice rising in a panicked insistence as each of them, in turn, answered with a pitying look.

'Rest, dear,' Tilde said, offering me another pill. Her chilly fingers pressed into mine as she passed me the water glass.

They couldn't find John's truck. It seemed to have vanished into thin air. 'He wouldn't let that truck out of his sight,' Ev told the police. She believed, I knew, that someone else had been in that house, that someone else had driven off after committing double murder. 'Please find that truck,' she begged, but no one else knew it was the plea of a wife, and I didn't take up her cause.

Ev and I were never left alone. There was no place to whisper in that small, tight cottage filled with listeners. But I heard her mumbled chant – 'It's my fault, it's my fault' – in those moments when no one else was listening.

She did not say a word of her marriage, or of the baby, to anyone, so I followed her lead. I kept my mouth shut. I watched her carefully. I made sure she ate. I gave her full glasses of water and stood beside her until she drank them down.

———

One morning I realized the bolts were gone, from the porch door, bathroom, and bedroom. The holes the screws had made were filled with Spackle, sanded, and painted. Doubting my own memory, I wandered back to the safety of bed.

We slept long and hard. Adults swept in and out, their hushed concern carrying into our room. I relished how the world moved to accommodate our trauma, and I'll confess that, in the midnight hours, when I awoke, with a startle of new horror at what we had seen with our own eyes and the pressing questions about that vision – how John LaChance had been capable of committing such a terrible act, where Abby had gone in the wake of it, and whether I was responsible for the gruesome violence – I was comforted by a familiar sensation from my girlhood:

Dreaming a startling, awful truth, frigid water pouring down my sleeping gullet. My slumbering, drugged mind clawing at the surface of wakefulness, trying to burst out for air. Finally recognizing my surroundings. Stifling my cry, slowing my heartbeat, unclenching my fists. Willing myself to forget the whole truth of the terrible world in order to focus on what was happening in the immediate. Straining to hear the familiar sound of the grown-ups just outside my door, busy listening to the radio, full of plans and beliefs, made competent in the face of crisis. Their presence established, turning in my bed, pulling the duvet up around my neck, and slipping, once again, into the gift of night.

CHAPTER FORTY-SIX

The Row

I AWOKE WITH A START. It was bright in our room, but the specter of John's lifeless face looking up at me – the vision that now ended every dream and started every day – was seared into my mind. Ev snored in the bed beside mine; if the days preceding were any indication, she would stay out until sundown, awaken for a meal, then slip back under the covers after taking another pink pill. I didn't have the guts to ask her if they were safe for the baby.

It seemed as though I had been sleeping for months. I couldn't count the days anymore. But they had turned hot, I knew that much, and someone, some time ago, had mentioned it was now August. I forced myself out of bed before John could pull me down into another nightmare. I hated closing my eyes anymore; bruised and feverish, they were damaged by the weight of their slumber.

In the bathroom, I took a look in the mirror. Not a pretty sight (stringy hair, mossy teeth), although I had to admit that all the meals I'd slept through had made me look more like a Winslow than ever before (cheeks taut, belly flat). I passed lukewarm water over my face. Brushed my teeth halfheartedly. Forced on a pair of Ev's flip-flops and stumbled out the door.

Oh, the world. It was dazzling that August – every wavelet

in its place, every cloud passing along at a fast pitch; Winloch as Samson Winslow had imagined it. No sweatshirt needed, no sweat on the brow. The dust skipped up from underneath my heels.

When I arrived at the edge of the Dining Hall, I craned to see if Galway was coming from his cottage. But the road was empty and I wasn't going to seek him out. I hadn't seen him alone since that night I'd confronted him about his marriage. He'd been in Bittersweet on and off – he'd cared for us in person, and protected us by answering Detective Dan's questions about why it had taken so long to call the police (apparently 'traumatized girls' still worked as an excuse in rural Vermont). I expected an explanation, an apology, some kind of olive branch (which I would, on principle, have rejected), but he had been strictly professional with me, as though he were a social worker assigned to my case.

My stomach growled. I considered going into the Dining Hall for breakfast but couldn't stand facing Masha. She was the only person who knew that I knew of John's paternity. The only one who could guess what I'd told him in his pickup. Even if she kept her thoughts private, I couldn't bear the look of her judgment. She'd begged me not to tell him.

So there was only one way to go, into the great meadow toward Flat Rocks. As I crested the hill and cast my eyes over the rooftops, it occurred to me that I didn't want to see any of the Winslows. It had filtered down to me in spurts and whispers that Indo was back, but I didn't have the strength for whatever that conversation would entail. Nor did I have the fortitude to slap on a happy face for

Birch, or the wherewithal to fend off his suspicions. He had been watching over us like a hawk, and I had been sure to keep by Ev's side whenever he was near. So far, he'd seemed as baffled as the rest of the Winslows about why John would have done such a thing, which I took as a good sign. But I couldn't tell what he was thinking behind his fatherly façade. It was risky to come over to this side of the property alone.

It was windy in the Trillium meadow, closer to the water. The trees skirting the grasses bent in complaint, filling the world with a rushing conversation. The edge of the sky was tinged with purple, but weather looked a long way off. A few weeks before, this place had echoed with the sound of children's laughter, but even though the day was hotter than I'd ever felt it, perfect to spend around a lake, Winloch was nearly as devoid of life as it must have been in the dead of winter. Nothing to cut a summer vacation short like a murdered (and murdering) servant.

A swim would have done me well, but, once on Flat Rocks – just a natural place again without the plastic toys and damp towels – I remembered that I didn't have my bathing suit. Bittersweet seemed miles away. I took in the dinghies tied up on the dock. A shed above the waterline held life preservers and oars. I needed some perspective. Although I'd never rowed a boat in my life, I figured this was as good a time to start as any.

'Want some help?' a woman's voice asked ten minutes later, as I bobbed in the rowboat, trying to fumble its painter from the dock's cleat. The life preserver was cutting off my air. I had grown more and more seasick and indignant at the slippery line and rocking boat. The water splayed angrily along the shore. I squinted at the figure above me.

It was Tilde.

'Where are you off to?' she asked, squatting and undoing the painter in one easy twist of her wrist. She held it in her hand, looking down at me. I imagined, for a glorious moment, that if I rowed backwards I could pull her into the drink. 'Can I come?' she asked. Before I could reply, she stepped in, jostling the boat so that I had to hold on for dear life until she was seated behind me.

I started rowing.

We slammed into the boat next to us.

'You're seated in the wrong direction,' she said tonelessly. 'Turn around.' Her way made more sense; I should be able to reach the oarlocks. But I was afraid to start the rockiness all over again. So she coached quietly – 'There now, swing that leg over, don't fret, you'd have to jump up and down to capsize us' – until I was facing her. She pushed us from the dock.

I had been in the boat with Lu at the helm a good dozen times. I had imagined the work to be harder than it looked. Water was a strange substance, like memory – much to push against, but nothing solid to hang on to. But when, under my hands, the dinghy's oars dipped and dipped, and my arms pressed and pressed, propelling the craft felt easy. Before I knew it, we were farther out than I'd been on any of my swims.

I was so focused on getting it right that I didn't fully register, until we were far from shore, that I was now absolutely alone with a woman who seemed to detest me. I brought the oars up to rest on either side of her. Little rivulets spilled toward her white trousers.

'I just needed a break,' I murmured.

Her face was gaunt. Ev's nose. Lu's chin. Galway's forehead. 'Are you doing all right?' she asked. I supposed the deaths had made us as close to allies as we'd ever get.

I shrugged.

'It's awful.' She shuddered, showing the most emotion I'd seen from her.

We had started drifting back to shore. I took up the oars again and pulled against them, heading toward the point where Trillium sat. I had never been around it. She offered tips. 'Try not to turn your wrists.' Then, a minute later, 'Brace your feet here on the thwart below me, and you'll get more power.' My arms began to burn. We were nearly underneath Trillium now, its windows dark in contrast to the morning light.

I could feel Tilde looking up at her house with me. Then her focus shifted; I felt her eyes on my face. I turned to meet them.

'They found his truck,' she said quietly.

The whereabouts of John's pickup had been a real source of consternation for the police; they'd been searching for it in the three weeks since we'd found the bodies. Rumor had it Detective Dan was ready to shut down the case but for the missing truck. The Winslows were eager to have their speculations confirmed about John drunkenly ditching it outside a bar before walking home to commit matricide. Just as it had been comforting to blame Jackson's suicide on his soldiering, so would it be convenient to blame John's hideous behavior on drink.

'Where was it?' I asked, realizing the waves below us were rougher than they'd been when we set out. We were bucking.

'Canada. Some drug addict drove it north.'

I felt a momentary sense of relief – one I did not expect, that led me to ask hopefully, 'Did he have anything to do with the murder?'

She shook her head. 'He checked out of a halfway house the day after.'

'Where did he find the truck?'

'Bus station. He says he found it three days after you found John and Pauline. It was parked behind a shipping container, out of sight.'

Why on earth would John have left his pickup at the bus station?

All this time I had rejected what I knew about John as a sensible man and relaxed into the comforting tale I'd told myself from the beginning: it was an open-and-shut case. John had flown into a rage. Sometime during that long night he had choked his mother to death. Realizing what he'd done, he'd leapt to his death on the rocks below.

I believed this even though it was breaking Ev's heart.

I believed this even though I knew how much John had loved his mother.

I believed this even though people didn't jump off cliffs backwards. Every morning, in the split second between remembering his face below mine and fully waking, I'd ask myself: If he'd jumped, wouldn't he have ended up facedown?

But I had to believe that John had done it. It was better that way – neat, over.

A particularly strong wave bashed the side of our boat. Water poured in. Tilde hardly reacted; her pants were already soaked. I picked up the oars again and rowed harder, putting my whole body into each drag, fighting against the waves until we rounded the Trillium point and caught sight of the outer bay. The wind came hard, furrowing the water. I put my head down and rowed.

The howling gale coming off the lake rushed into my ears, sending my hair tumbling. The world was made of whitecaps. The little dinghy dipped and bucked. My oars were useless as the thrashing waves pulled us, inevitably, back against the shore. The rough sandstone that edged the water over here resembled the rocks onto which John had plunged, and I found myself rowing any which direction, panic rising fast, just to escape.

'Here,' Tilde shouted over the wind, leaning forward. I thought for a moment that she was going to offer to switch places with me, but within an instant I felt her hands on mine; dry, slight fingers curling over the backs of my hands where they gripped the oars. I pulled back as she pressed against me with surprising strength. Rowing together, we regained a buffer from the shore. Once we were a safe distance from the rocks, she helped me dip the right oar into the water until we were lined up, organized. Then, together, we rowed, heads down, parallel to the rocks of the Winloch shore, aiming for a little cove beyond us, where the water calmed.

As soon as we were in the protection of the cove, Tilde let me go, leaving a breeze on the backs of my hands. My arms were sore. We drifted. Then, from above, there came a rumble. The outer bay was the color of an eggplant. Thunderheads churned above.

'There's a weather alert,' she said matter-of-factly. She was facing me, not the lake, but somehow she knew exactly what I was seeing.

'Like a storm?' I asked, my voice rising involuntarily.

'Exactly.'

I realized, with alarm, that Tilde Winslow was probably perfectly content to see me dashed against the rocks. But if she knew the forecast, why had she joined me?

She gestured over my left shoulder. I rowed in that direction. We were soon in a smaller inner cove – hardly bigger than our boat. Within it, the water moved in a soothing lap. Tilde reached out and grabbed the low-hanging branch of a red pine to keep us in place.

'I met Birch when I was very young,' she said crisply. 'Too young to see the world clearly. He was handsome. Well-educated. Established.' A smile formed on her lips as she remembered. 'A Winslow. I was so swept up in the fairy tale that I didn't think about what marrying him would make me.'

She leaned forward. Her face was beautiful in the stormy light tunneling down through the trees. The strange illumination erased the harsh lines from her skin. She came closer and closer, and I thought, strangely, of Galway's face in the moment before he kissed me. I could feel her soft breath against my earlobe.

'Ask me,' she whispered.

'Ask you what?'

'What did it make me?'

'What did it make you?' I repeated obediently.

'A Winslow.' A thunderhead rumbled directly above. 'Do you want to be a Winslow?' she whispered.

Of course I did. Of course I didn't.

She took my silence for assent. 'Then do not mistake knowledge for power.'

'I don't know anything,' I said. My voice came out whiny and wrong. The flat sound of it rebounded off the rocks before the wind tossed it up into the air.

Tilde's mouth did not move from my ear. The hairs on my neck were standing at attention, but I couldn't tear myself away. She waited until my protest had drifted off before speaking again. 'And do not mistake silence for blindness.'

The world lit with a flash. I gazed upward to see a needle of lightning cut across the whole sky. It was followed too soon – far too soon – by a crack of thunder. Involuntarily, I squealed. Undaunted, Tilde grabbed my arm.

'Respect our secrets, Mabel Dagmar. Or even those you call friends will not be able to protect you.' She said this calmly, inches from my face. She did not look mean. Just honest.

I realized what this was. Fair warning.

I nodded, new electricity sizzling between us as the stormy light cast us in its silver glow. I might have expected anything then – to see Tilde sprout wings and claws, like some mythic creature, and lift me into the cracking sky; or to feel her fierce hands push me from the boat.

Instead, she looked up to the storm above us, then down to the water now sloshing, ever more greedily, under the bucking rowboat. 'Poor girl,' she remarked in her plastic tone, examining my face as though I were a specimen under a microscope. 'Afraid of storms? Switch places with me.'

It was unbelievable, the strength with which that slim, sinewy woman rowed us back to the Flat Rocks dock all by herself. Thunder filled our ears, lightning bolts tested themselves within the clouds above. At first, my terror was split between the hungry depths and the woman rowing, but she proved herself, rounding the point beyond Trillium, making a healthy dash back to the dock, the pull of the lake toward shore now an ally.

I turned to see a sheet of water racing toward us. Rain at its most devastating. The white wall moved across the world until it overtook us. I shrieked, but the storm ate my voice. Still Tilde rowed, almost there, until I grabbed happily for the dock, tied the painter, and dashed for shelter.

By then it didn't matter where we stood, outdoors or in. We were already soaked to the bone.

CHAPTER FORTY-SEVEN

The Picnic

I WOKE THE SLUMBERING BEAST. She did not give in easily, but relentless show-tune singing brought her about, as did the smell of percolating coffee and the promise that she'd get caffeine only if she emerged into daylight.

The Ev I'd met almost a year before had been flawless – perfect skin, hair like ermine, slender but curvy. The Ev who emerged from the bedroom that morning was a haunted shell. She had acne and eczema, straw for hair, skinny limbs that jutted from her torso at the wrong angles. She stooped when she walked. Her eye sockets were hollow.

'I'm sleeping,' she mumbled into the kitchen, shielding her eyes against the sunlight blaring off the water. She was wearing an oversize sweatshirt so I couldn't see her shape. I wondered about the baby, but I knew better than to ask. Every time I looked at her, the sound of her anguish ('It's my fault, it's my fault') played in my ears.

I pushed aside the guilt gnawing at me and wrapped the final cucumber sandwich in wax paper. 'We're going for a picnic.'

She didn't even have the strength to roll her eyes. I decided it was to my advantage that everyone had been telling her what to do. Now it was my turn.

'Sit down,' I commanded, handing her the promised coffee. I checked the wall clock. 'We're leaving in forty minutes.'

Ev – who would have disdained my alpha stance only a month before – sat and ate, chewing the scrambled eggs obediently, sipping at the coffee even though it had burned my tongue. I told her to put on some clothes; she retreated to the bedroom and dressed. I gathered together our discarded shirts and pajamas, underpants and jeans, and filled our laundry bags for the regular pickup we had missed for weeks now. 'Brush your teeth,' I commanded. I found her lingering upon the toilet twenty minutes later. 'Did you pee?' I asked, as though she were a potty-training toddler. She nodded obediently and followed me outside.

We walked up the same familiar road. I led by a few steps; she lurked at my heels – I had the sensation of dragging along a reluctant child. When I turned to confirm that she was with me, her face was a mask, her expression impenetrable. I couldn't remember how long it had been since she'd been outside.

'Where are we going?' she asked as we came in sight of the Dining Hall.

'Bead Beach,' I answered nonchalantly. Back in July, she had talked of that place with pleasure, and I was hoping the mention of it would reinvigorate her and force her forward, especially since I had no idea where it was.

'But we're going the wrong direction,' she replied with more vehemence than I'd heard from her since John's death. Mission accomplished.

———

We hiked into the Winloch woods behind the Dining Hall. I resisted the memory of the last time Ev and I had wandered under those trees together. Tried to push aside the horrible sound of Abby's entrapped bark under Mrs LaChance's porch, to forget the fact that no one would tell me where the poor dog was now. Ev must have been replaying the same terrible memories – the hideous sight of Mrs LaChance's death mask, the wretched surprise of John's body far below us – because she cut us away from Echinacea before we were at risk of seeing it, skirting a path closer to the water. The going was rougher nearer to the lake – large rock faces to scramble up; treacherous, weed-choked terrain at the damp, low spots where Winloch's small streams fed into the vast blue; and, at one point, right in our pathway, the sturdy, rusted-out hull of a long-abandoned Model T.

Ev and I hardly acknowledged each other, save to hold a snapping branch, lest it spring back and hit the other. Above us, pine limbs rubbed with a nervous squeak; far off, able to fly wherever he desired, the pileated woodpecker knocked insistently upon a grub-filled trunk; and below us, on motorboats and yachts, other people enjoyed their summers – sunblock, water skis, lemonade.

All at once, Ev cut down toward the lake. She used the trunks of the pines to brace herself against the slippery, needle-covered slope. She disregarded me, pushing ahead, her long legs carrying her farther in one stride than I could make in three. This was how it was supposed to be.

In sight of the beach, Ev halted. I had given up on being graceful, finding it much more effective to slide down on my bottom, and now pulled myself to standing a few feet above her, stumbling and slipping into a tree trunk by her side. She pursed her lips. Already I was thinking how hard it was going to be to scale back up the eroding hillside, but I told myself it didn't matter.

'So where are all those beads?' I asked in a chipper tone, eliciting Ev's grimace. I tumbled down onto the marshy sand and didn't turn back to check that she was coming. A moment later I felt her soft footfalls behind me.

Bead Beach was as Ev had described it – an exposed, sandy expanse, with hearty reeds growing from the clay deep below. Looking out upon the outer bay, I realized we stood somewhere on the shoreline between the Trillium point I'd rounded with Tilde and the horrible rocks on which John had met his end. Though the terrain surrounding us was rocky, the beach itself was a peaceful place – Winloch's soft belly. Lu had explained to me, what seemed like a decade before, that wind swept in off the outer bay and churned clay up from the lake bottom and tossed it onto the reeds that dotted the beach. The clay dried in droplets around the long, thin plants, hardening in the sun, leaving gray beads with perfect, reed-thick holes in their centers. If one put one's fingers around the dried orbs and pulled up delicately, they were easily collected, for stringing into necklaces and bracelets. Looking out across the sand, I found it easy to imagine feral, girlish versions of Lu and Ev, nature's beads strung over their milky torsos, pretending they were the original inhabitants of this land.

Ev and I explored each end of the beach by ourselves. At first I was shy about collecting the beach's fruit, but I noticed Ev carefully hunched over the tops of the reeds on her end of the sandy waterfront. I studied her form, noting how gingerly she plucked the small balls from their homes. I found a particularly sturdy-looking spattering of dried clay and tested it. The first few beads crumbled in the force between my thumb and pointer finger. I softened my grip, and they came more willingly. I collected a ripe handful before noticing that Ev had found a spot to sit on a fallen tree and was gazing out at the open water.

I remembered her weeping over John's body, how fragile she'd seemed, and broken. I made my way to her, lugging the canvas bag that held our picnic. 'Lemonade?' I offered her the thermos, but she shook her head and kept her eyes on the lake before us. I followed her lead and took in the soft wind upon my face, the caplets of fresh water licking up at our toes, the swish, in and out, of the water upon the shore.

I felt light-headed. I didn't know if I could do what I must. But then, I thought of Tilde in the rowboat: 'Respect our secrets.'

Say Tilde knew, somehow, that Birch was John's father – perhaps an explanation for why she was unfriendly; the realization that one's husband had cheated with a woman now living in his care would harden anyone. Still, Tilde hadn't exactly been good to Ev or Lu, as far as I had seen, had she? She'd been cold – mean, even – to everyone I liked at Winloch: her daughters, Indo, CeCe.

And she didn't want me to tell the one secret I knew.

If she knew the secret, it wasn't mine anymore, was it? Nor was it hers. Neither of us could control it anymore. It could pass along to anyone it wanted.

It wasn't that I thought knowing would make Ev feel any better, certainly not. But as awful as it was that John had left her, and in the way he had, wasn't it confirmation of how impossible their life together would have been?

'Do you still think it's your fault?' I asked. The moment Birch and Pauline had conceived a child together, something awful and inexorable had been set into motion. Something even the love John and Ev shared couldn't have stopped. 'It isn't. It never was.'

I was the executioner.

Ev didn't move a centimeter, but I knew she could hear me.

'Ev,' I said, examining her in my peripheral vision, 'your family has a lot of secrets. I stumbled across one of them and I told it to John.' My pulse was rising, sweat gathering in all the parts of me that were terrified. I didn't want to tell her, and maybe I wouldn't have to. Maybe she wouldn't ask.

'Which secret?' she asked.

I cleared my throat. 'I think . . . I mean, I'm pretty sure, because I did a lot to check it out, and I don't think there's any other explanation, but I think, Ev, I think John was your half brother. I mean, that your dad and Mrs LaChance . . .'

I let my voice trail off into the wind, and, as it did, I turned and looked at her, slowly, carefully, to see what the realization would bring. Would she collapse, weeping? Would she banish me?

Ev's breath rattled in and out of her chest. And then, oddly, a smile formed on her lips. She turned to look at me. We were inches apart. 'Why,' she said carefully, 'do you think Jackson killed himself?'

This was not the reaction I'd expected. But she was talking, and that was a good sign. 'Depression,' I answered. Her eyes darted over my face doubtfully. I went on. 'Shell shock. Something was wrong with him.'

She shook her head. 'Someone told him Daddy was his father.'

I tried to let the news sink in, but it was impossible. Every time I thought I'd figured it out, my understanding faltered. I wanted the family tree in front of me, so I could understand the slipknot of what she was saying. Then I finally realized what she meant.

Birch was CeCe's brother.

Birch was Jackson's father.

'Wait,' I said, my face turning down in involuntary disgust, 'CeCe and Birch are brother and sister.'

'Half. They're only half.'

'Does that really make much of a difference?' I scoffed.

'Of course it makes a difference.'

Then it hit me: Ev was talking about herself.

'Wait,' I said, starting to feel panic rise inside myself, 'you knew? You knew John was your brother?'

'Oh, don't judge me, Mabel, it's awful when you make that face.' She spoke nonchalantly, as though we were discussing the grocery list. 'Everyone knows my father has a problem. He's not— He can't control himself. It's a sickness, really. CeCe's the one who made it hard, saying she didn't want all that attention. And it's not as if the family hasn't been good to her, or to John's mother. I mean, god knows, it would have been so easy for Daddy to put Pauline out on the street, but he housed her, and promised John a lifetime of work.' She looked back out to the water. 'John was beautiful, wasn't he? I saw you looking at him. It's funny, isn't it? All he ever wanted was to be one of us, a Winslow, and all that time he was – he just didn't know.

'Well, I guess until you told him,' she added coldly.

My mind was racing. 'Ev,' I said, ready to hear something horrible, 'has your father ever touched you?'

'No! You think Mum would let something like that happen?'

I thought of the bolts on the insides of the doors. Of Tilde yelling at little Hannah on Flat Rocks. Perhaps I had Tilde all wrong. Perhaps she was the one who was keeping this place from dissolving into chaos. Perhaps she really had been trying to protect me.

Before I could respond, or close my horrified mouth, Ev stripped off her clothes, piece by piece, revealing her lithe, scrawny form, the little tuft of dirty-blond pubic hair, the purple disks of her nipples. Her belly was flat as the day I had met her. She dropped her clothes onto the ground without regard and waded into the water. The lake swallowed her up, step by step – first the backs of her knees, then her hips, the swell of her buttocks, her sacrum, her wing-like shoulder blades, then shoulders – until just her head was visible, and her hair spread out upon the surface of the water like a hand. She swam then, straight out, in a line toward the horizon, not once looking back. I couldn't take my eyes off her. I wanted to. I wanted to leave her there. But with every stroke she took away from me, I felt a gasping kind of pain.

Just when I felt sure she would drown, and I was contemplating ripping off my clothes and going in after her (which would have ended with us both going under), she turned and started back toward shore. It was only then that I could stand. I climbed back into the woods, pulling myself forward with the help of every tree trunk, until my arms ached, and my legs screamed out, but I kept going.

CHAPTER FORTY-EIGHT
The Key

I POUNDED ON INDO'S KITCHEN door until I heard Fritz's yap. I didn't wait for Indo to come – I didn't even know if she was able – just pushed, hitting Aggie with the door as she reached for the handle. The woman's face registered surprise, anger, concern, all in a matter of seconds, and she stepped back when she recognized who I was. She reached out one hand. 'Sweet girl.'

'Is she here?' I asked.

'I'll never forgive myself.' She began to cry. Fritz nipped at my heels, hurtling himself against me with abundant energy. I didn't have time for either of them. 'I shouldn't have gone home that night,' she moaned. I stepped out of her grasp, around her, passing through the jumbled kitchen, as Fritz frantically pawed the backs of my legs. 'Please,' Aggie pleaded, 'please,' in that tone people use when they want a piece of your tragedy. This time, I ignored it.

I marched through Indo's rooms as though surveying them from above. I knew, from experience, that even a pile of clothes on the floor could be a person. But she wasn't in the crimson living room, huddled in the Indonesian cushions on the rickety couch, and she wasn't hunched in one of the creaking, precarious chairs on the screen porch. I circled back around, into the living room, toward the bedrooms, when Aggie stepped before me from the kitchen. Her whole being was need: 'Mr John was such a good boy, I can't believe he killed her, ohhhh.' And there were tears and she wanted to touch me, to pull at my clothes, so I dodged her again – grief seemed to slow her down – and slipped into the hallway that led to Indo's inner sanctum.

The door was halfway closed, but I wasn't shy. I pushed it open. Indo's bedroom hadn't changed since the last time I was there: rosy pinks, medicinal pistachio. She was propped upright, head turbaned, mosquito net pulled back at either side, as though she were a queen holding court in a tropical deathbed. She looked so much older. Her skin was waxy, her cheeks hollow.

I heard Aggie coming. I shut the door, slamming her and Fritz out. The dog barked and she cried. I turned the brass key in the lock. It made a satisfying click.

'You're a sight.' Indo's voice was like ripped paper.

'Congratulations,' I growled. 'I found out your brother likes to fuck everything in sight. I suspect you already know he raped your own sister – excuse me, half sister – and Mrs LaChance and god knows how many other helpless women. So what? You're all just going to let him keep doing it, aren't you? You'll scream at your little girls to cover themselves and pay off your maids to keep their mouths shut. So what I don't understand is why, if you sat by all these years and let it happen, now you want me to be the one who gives a fuck. That journal isn't proof anyway, Indo. No one's going to believe me based on that – no one who's going to do anything about him.'

Indo sat patiently through my tirade. 'I have no idea what you're talking about.'

A cruel laugh rose up through me. But her expression didn't change. 'Come on,' I said. 'Blood money? Kitty's journal? You kept throwing me bones, and I did what you wanted – I fucking found out the secret, just like you wanted me to, and for what? She already fucking knew, Indo. Ev already knew John was her brother and it didn't matter. Do you understand me? She's as sick as her father. She knew John was her brother and she still wanted to have his baby.

'But John didn't know. So you know what I did? I told him. Just like you wanted me to, I fucking told him what I'd found, and you know what he did next? He murdered his crazy old mother and he killed himself and I'm supposed to have that on my head?'

I was crying now, wiping the tears away with my bare arm. 'No,' I answered myself. 'No,' I said striding to the bed, so that I was near to her neutral face. 'No, I know who wanted me to tell, and it was you, and so I told, but now, Jesus, Indo, now what the fuck was any of it supposed to mean, why would you do that to them, why would you do that to me?' And my words were swallowed by angry sobs that racked my body, and I felt an instinct to make the marks on Indo's neck that had been around Pauline's, but I restrained my hands. I wouldn't give her the satisfaction.

I hugged my arms around myself to calm down, trying to find some sense of quiet in the midst of Fritz's yapping and Aggie's racket and the storm within me, but it took a long time before I could form rational thought.

Indo blinked up at me calmly. 'My dear,' she said thinly, as though she was an unwilling adult forced to lure a child out of a tantrum. 'I see that you're terribly upset. But I'll confess your thoughts sound . . . muddled. You've been through a hideous ordeal, and no one can blame you for having disordered thinking, for mixing up the truth with gothic fantasy.'

It was as though I was speaking to a different woman here, in this pastel dowager's room. The feisty Indo I had met on the path only two months before, swearing at her dogs as they swarmed me, hardly seemed to exist anymore.

She went on. 'My brother is unscrupulous. But to accuse him of such unspeakable acts . . .'

I couldn't understand why she was so blind to her brother's proclivities. Ev's unquestioning acceptance of her father's rapes – or seductions, as she might have called them – though alarming in and of itself, at least confirmed I'd been right about Birch. But how Birch's own sister, who'd lived only a few hundred yards from him for most of their adult life, and shared a home with him as a child, could be so oblivious to his violations of his own family was beyond me.

And then I realized: he had probably violated Indo too. As his sister, she was likely one of his first victims. Maybe it had happened so long ago, when they were both so young, that she had buried those memories deep, and all she could remember about them was that she hated her brother.

There was a pounding on the bedroom door just then. 'Ms Linden! Ms Linden! Are you all right?'

Indo sighed and rolled her eyes at the door. 'Don't mind us, Aggie,' she pronounced, before putting her hand to her forehead. Her eyelids fluttered and her mouth seemed to suck at the air like a fish stranded ashore. I sagged with pity for the old, dying woman. She loathed her own brother and couldn't allow herself to know why or what that knowing would mean.

On the other side of the door, I heard Aggie's and Fritz's retreat.

'Indo,' I said, softening my voice, feeling weary myself, stifling a desire to crawl onto the foot of her bed, 'if it wasn't who Birch raped, what on earth did you want me to find?'

She sniffed haughtily. 'It hardly matters now.'

'Why not?'

She raised her hands as though it was the most obvious thing in the world. 'I'm dying.'

'But you were dying at the beginning of the summer.'

'Exactly. I only had a few months to take what I know and find the proof to back it up. Sure, I've got memories and tales, but those don't mean much without hard physical evidence.' She sighed. 'But I didn't have the stamina. Naturally, I thought all was lost. That I'd missed my chance to bring this corrupt family to its knees.' She pointed her finger at me. 'And then you waltzed in, bright-eyed and bushy-tailed, and I thought: aha!'

'Aha, I'll give her my house?'

'Once this family crumbles, someone else will have to live here. Might as well be you.'

'Why not just punish Birch with whatever you know? Why take them all down with him?' I had no idea what her bombshell was, and suspected that it would prove inconsequential in the face of Winloch's reach. Still, it seemed awfully harsh to want to punish every Winslow if only Birch was at fault.

'Because the cancer has spread to all of them!' she shouted, strong now. I remembered her earlier words to me about cutting out a tumor, had come to assume, given her diagnosis, that she had been talking about herself. But now I understood that she was speaking metaphorically, and she meant the Winslows. 'It was different when Mother and Father were in charge. We made sacrifices. We kept secrets. We didn't marry the people we loved because they were the wrong sorts of people.' That last sentence seemed to take the wind out of her, and she slumped back against her pillow. 'But under Birch's watch . . . There is no order. There is only corruption . . . So little appreciation of how those sacrifices must be repaid.' Tears began to form in her eyes. 'My painting . . .'

I felt moved by her great need for that beautiful thing. I still had no idea what proof she needed, or what I would do with it if I found it, but I wanted her to know there was still time. That I could help her get some peace. Before I could say so, she spoke, her strength regained.

'Maybe if you weren't so blinded by greed, you'd—'

'Greed?' I balked.

She ticked off her fingers. 'My house. Galway's bed. Ev's friendship. Pauline's secret.' She held them up triumphantly. 'You're covetous. I thought that flaw would help my cause – that your desire to own our secrets, to collect shiny treasures like a crow, would give me my proof. But I was wrong. You never wanted to help me bring my family down.' She narrowed her eyes at me. 'You only wanted to assimilate.'

'I just want to help you,' I said quietly, giving her one last chance.

She gestured around the room. 'The funny thing is, none of this is even mine to give.'

I took it all in – the dresser lined with enamel boxes, the small painting of Clover and the cove below, a crocheted shawl slumping over a useless chair. I was dizzy. And confused. And angry. And exhausted. 'Fine,' I said, walking toward the door, done with her.

'Stop.' The command was sharp. 'Wait.'

Even though I wanted to have the will to leave, I wanted answers more. So I did as I was told.

Indo sighed. 'It's not mine to give you because it's all stolen.'

'You'll have to do better than that.' My hand was upon the door.

'My mother's journal kept track of it all in the beginning,' she said. 'What was stolen. When. And where it went.'

Even though I couldn't pin down exactly what she was saying, she was telling more than she ever had. My mouth began to water. I let go of the door handle. 'In the beginning?'

'I don't want you to think ill of her. She was a good woman. The moment she became a Winslow, she loved this brood with all her heart. But it was this particular single-mindedness, this loyalty, that led her to come up with the idea. You have to understand, the Winslows were in trouble. After Samson lost his marbles, my grandfather Banning nearly ran the family into the ground with bad investments. We stood to lose everything, even Winloch. But we didn't, thanks to my parents.' What she was saying was consistent with what I'd guessed at, from the bankruptcy papers I'd found to Bard being behind some kind of windfall that had changed the Winslows' fate. I let her go on.

'What they stole, how they stole it, became a kind of instruction. A way of life for the Winslows. First we took goods. Then ideas, deeds, investments. I won't lie and say I regret it. My parents saved us. I truly believe that, Mabel. Perhaps I should be ashamed that it has taken me a lifetime to acknowledge my forebears' sins. To understand that they did wrong even as they were doing right.'

She sat up straighter in bed. 'But I see that now. And I'm the only one. You think Birch gives a damn? You think he's doing anything to stop this dangerous legacy? Not a bit. He's ten times worse than my parents were. More sophisticated. More greedy. My parents were saving us. He just wants to get richer.'

'So he's stealing too.' My mind was swirling with all she was implying, even if I wasn't yet able to pin her down. I wanted to know how, exactly, the Winslows had stolen what they had, and from whom, and when it had begun, and what they were stealing now. 'Who—'

'My dear,' she pronounced in an almost bored tone, 'there are always parts of the world in disarray. Just as there are always people willing to better their lot by helping unload what their countrymen no longer need. It's not half as hard as you'd imagine to locate what is no longer being appreciated. Most folks are desperate to trade their worldly goods for freedom.'

'Like where?'

'Over the years? Everywhere, really. The Far East. Darkest Africa. Central America.'

'I'll need dates.' My mind was racing. 'Specific countries. What was stolen. If you give me something I can trace, I'll start digging.'

Her vigor drained as soon as I tried to pin her down. She leaned back upon her pillows like a sullen child. 'I already told you. I don't have any proof. I asked you to find it and you didn't. So there's no point in trying to stop him anymore.'

'Indo,' I began to plead, desperate, 'you have to tell me something more if you want my help.' My mind grasped for an incentive. 'The Van Gogh. You want it back, right? Well, let me help bring your brother down and you can have it back.'

She began to laugh then, right in my face, a mean laugh as though I was the biggest idiot in the world. I felt my face turn hot. I heard the sound of Aggie and Fritz back on the other side of the door.

'I mean it,' I insisted. 'I can help you.'

'Oh no,' Indo yelped, overcome by a manic cackle that filled the room, 'oh no, my dear Mabel, no one – not even you – can help me now.'

I tried to talk to her again, but her laugh filled the room, drowning out my voice. She was as crazy as her niece and brother and everyone else in this godforsaken place. She wasn't going to help me, even though helping me would help herself.

The door handle started jiggling below me. I could hear something metal jimmying the lock. I had to get away. I needed air, and space to think.

When the key fell to the floor and Aggie and Fritz

burst through the door, I hurtled myself toward the opening, angling around them and out of the room as they rushed to Indo's side. Their needy combination was like poison to my ears as I ran from the cottage and out into the afternoon.

CHAPTER FORTY-NINE

The Theft

WHERE COULD I GO? To whom could I turn? Indo drained of knowledge, Ev gone mad, Galway revealed to be unfaithful, I had no one – not at Winloch, not anywhere. As I tore away from Indo's cottage and over the hill – running simply because my feet had to keep moving or I might lose my mind – I realized that, in the span of a summer, Ev's family had swallowed all knowledge I had of who I was and what I believed. I wasn't whole anymore, I thought, before realizing, with chagrin, that I hadn't really ever felt whole. This terrible realization stopped my feet short. I was young, still so young, that I thought my lack of wholeness was somehow my fault. I had no idea everyone feels this way – that the most essential part of growing up is figuring out where your empty places are and learning how to fill them by, and for, yourself.

I was at the base of the hill now, Dining Hall in sight, on the road that would lead me out of Winloch. I could hear the faint rumble of a motorboat, the drone of a lawn mower, the chattering of the chipmunks bustling in the undergrowth beside the road. But any immediate human sounds – save my own – were few and far between, and I realized, with a startle, that the only person with whom I had ever felt close to whole was my brother. Even before the incident, he'd been sheltered from the facts of life by a brain both too big and too small for what the world required, but what he knew of me was essential, pure. True. He believed I was good. He believed I was kind. He believed I had the answers.

For the first time that summer, I wondered: what would Daniel do?

Daniel wasn't afraid of anything, which is a nice way of saying he would wade into an icy river if you commanded him. He sought out justice, which made him impossible to lie to. And he was pigheaded, a nasty way of saying he never let a question out of his grasp.

I had to find out what the Winslows had stolen. Were stealing, if Indo was to be believed. I was furious at her vagueness and sad she was going to die. But I couldn't let that affect my search. Call that greed if you must (Indo had), but it was the only thing I knew to do next, because it's what Daniel would have done, had he been able. I wasn't doing it for Indo anymore; I was doing it for myself.

I had to look at Kitty's journal again. 'In the beginning.' It held answers.

I raced toward Bittersweet, sure Ev wouldn't have dried, dressed, and made it back from Bead Beach so quickly. I would pry the journal from its hiding place under the porch's loose board, head for the woods, and gather my wits. Knowing it documented what the Winslows had stolen would surely give me new eyes with which to read it. Once I found what Indo had been alluding to, I would figure out how to use that information. I would find the proof she wanted.

I was almost to the steps when I spotted Ev sitting on

355

the porch couch. She was flipping through a magazine, her back to me, oblivious to my gaze. The sight of her head – blond, tousled – was so familiar that my memory called up the smell of her salty scalp. Affection tugged at my heart.

But then I remembered what she had told me at Bead Beach. All this time, even when I'd learned she'd been lying to me about the inspection, or using me to hide her true intentions to leave Winloch with John, I'd believed there was still something strong at the core of our friendship. That we shared a moral universe: don't marry your brother, rapists are evil, et cetera. But on Bead Beach, she'd declared who she really was. I realized, in one, tragic, honest, relieving rush, that Ev and I were never really going to be friends again. That maybe we'd never been friends to begin with.

I'd used her too, hadn't I? Hadn't I believed that aligning myself with her would better my lot? That I deserved what she had? It was hard to know what was real about any of our friendship now that I knew how far apart we were. Was she even pregnant? Had she ever been? Had I liked Galway only because he was part of her world? Did it matter anymore?

Wait, I told myself, it won't do any good to chew it all over – there will be time enough. Later. So maybe we weren't ever friends. So what?

I had to get that journal. I had work to do.

I pushed open the screen door. She glanced up at the sight of me. 'Where'd you run off to?' As though none of what had been said between us on Bead Beach had occurred.

'Are you hungry?' she continued. 'I asked Masha to bring sandwiches.' I remembered the picnic I'd abandoned. My stomach growled. Ev smiled. She knew the way to my heart.

I calculated whether I could retrieve the journal and keep the secret of the hiding place in the time it would take Ev to, say, go to the bathroom. I glanced down at the loose floorboard, only a foot from where she sat. My look to the board was fleeting – a split second at most – but that was all it took. Ev followed my gaze.

She straightened her impossibly long leg and pressed her big toe against the loose board.

'What happened to the baby?' I blurted, desperate to win back her attention.

She set her foot flat upon the floor, shifting her weight onto it.

'Ev,' I said, 'did you lose it?'

She crouched. I stepped into the cottage and let the screen slam shut behind me. I couldn't let her find the journal. Indo had entrusted me, and me alone, with Kitty's secrets.

'There's nothing in there,' I said unconvincingly. But Ev was lost to her discovery. She used her index finger to jimmy at the side of the board and, just as I had, decided she needed a tool, grabbing, from the side table, the same ball-point pen I'd used.

She uncapped the pen and levered it so that the board yawned open. A few more forcible thrusts, and the loose wood popped from its home.

I stepped forward. I'd grab it the second she pulled it out. She leaned over the hiding place. Frowned. Placed her

357

hand inside and felt around. Only then did she look up at me, startled. 'There's nothing in here.'

My heart started hammering. I craned to look inside the cranny where I'd so carefully hidden Kitty's journal. 'Where is it?' I asked.

'What is it?'

'I mean it, Ev, what did you do with it?'

She shrank back, just a fraction of an inch, for just a moment, but I saw it: I'd scared her.

'Just give it back to me and we won't have a problem,' I pressed.

'Seriously, Mabel, I have no idea what you're talking about.' She was pulling herself to standing. The second she did, she would have gained the upper hand.

I placed my hands on her shoulders. I pressed down as hard as I could. She shrieked. 'Stop it!' Dodged my attempt to pull her back down. 'Ouch, Mabel! Stop!' She slipped through my grasp and stood tall above me. Brushed her shoulders off. Tossed her hair, loosening the ends with her fingertips, regaining herself. She wagged a finger at me as she headed toward the kitchen. 'Honestly, Mabel, sometimes I have no idea what the fuck is wrong with you.'

Dear Mom,
Things have gone a bit off the rails since I (didn't)
write you last. Suffice to say I hadn't imagined a world
in which an incest-committing, possibly psychopathic
roommate is the more appealing of two options, the other
of which is that someone has been spying on me day and

night, found out I have, in my possession, a family
journal full of dark secrets, and has stolen it from me.
I've considered sleeping on the couch, but Ev's been
acting perfectly like herself since dinner, as though she
didn't knowingly marry her own matricide-committing,
suicidal brother. Frankly, I'm afraid to deviate from the
norm lest it set her against me. We will pretend that
everything is normal. Thanks to you, I've had plenty
of practice.

That night, I watched Ev swallow two sleeping pills, and kept my eyes on her until she was sound asleep. Only then did I close my eyes.

But it didn't matter where I lay my head. I turned it all over in my mind, trying to come up with a game plan for when daylight returned – where would I find Kitty's journal? What would I say to Indo to get her to tell me more? – until I began to lose consciousness and my memories became jumbled, and John's face became Daniel's and Daniel's face became my own.

Just as I was finally drifting into slumber, a regular pinging started to pull me back to the waking shore. I tried to ignore the sound, but it came again, then again, until I found myself sitting up in bed. Across the room, Ev slept heavily. But the window above her bed rang out with a regular rhythm that I realized, after a few disorienting moments, was the sound of gravel thrown against the pane.

I stood and hunched between my bed and Ev's, peering out into the pitch-black night, when a flashlight flipped on, and a ghoulish face appeared. I yelped, but Ev didn't stir. I put my hand over my mouth to stop myself from making any more noise as I squinted out at that face. The flashlight shifted, and what seemed to be the stuff of nightmares proved to be only Galway.

I tiptoed out of the bedroom, snuck onto the porch, and cringed at the screen door's squeal.

'I need your help,' he whispered.

I wasn't much interested in helping him, and my face must've told him as much.

'It's Lu,' he pleaded.

CHAPTER FIFTY

The Director

W HAT WOULD YOU HAVE done if Ev woke up?'
I asked as we drove out of Winloch. Galway
steered more cautiously than John had; less to prove, or
he didn't want our departure to be advertised, or both. The
aroma of his car was good, like the sweatshirt I'd long
since squirreled away under my bed. I prayed to lose my
sense of smell.

'Ev sleeps through fire alarms,' he said, 'and I figured if
she did wake up, she'd leave us alone.'

The sentiment clung to us; we had unfinished business
that even Ev would respect.

'Are you going to turn on the headlights?' I asked, once
we had passed onto the meadow – he'd been using his
parking lights. It was a night lit by only a sliver of moon,
but out here in the country, that was enough to pretend by.
He flipped on the real headlights, and we headed toward
the highway. Once on it, we took an exit onto a back road
that, by my calculation, led us east. 'Is Lu at camp?' I asked
finally. All that urgency and then nothing. I was starting to
wonder how important this really was.

Galway cleared his throat. 'Whatever happens, we have
to keep it a secret, understand?'

That sounded familiar. 'That depends what happens.'

'It could be a matter of life and death.'

I actually knew what that meant now. 'I'll do my best.'

Satisfied I could be trusted, Galway grabbed a used envelope from the dashboard. 'Masha got a phone call tonight, from the camp.' He handed me the paper, scribbled with directions. 'Rocky something. It's in Maine. Anyway, it was the camp director, Marian. Very upset. She was calling for Mum and Father, and she didn't know she was getting the Dining Hall. Masha took the message and' – he handed me his flashlight – 'see for yourself.'

I made out Masha's loopy handwriting. My eyes stumbled over the words as I tried to decipher their meaning.

'Read it,' Galway commanded.

'"Your daughter is very sad. She has attempted suicide. She say she saw something terible. She beg me not to call you. But three weeks of this, I have no choice. Please come."'

Galway hit the steering wheel. 'Three weeks,' he said in disbelief, and I wondered what we were in for.

It was a long night and a longer road. The disdain I'd felt toward Galway in recent weeks began to loosen as we sped around the curves of rural Vermont. The road took us through the verdant alpine meadows leading to St Johnsbury, then down into New Hampshire and through Crawford Notch State Park, and steadily away from Winloch. Our headlights illuminated farmsteads, one-room schoolhouses, and empty high schools. The whole state seemed to be aslumber.

Galway's concentration was fixed on the road. He was clearly worried about his little sister. It was hard to stay angry with him.

The specter that haunted us was those three weeks. For I realized, as I did the math, trying to grasp hold of a time that had turned elastic and strange, that it had been three weeks to the day since Ev and I had found John's and his mother's bodies.

'When did Lu leave for camp?' I asked. It didn't seem possible she had said good-bye on the same day we'd discovered the bodies, but as I did the math again and again it seemed likely, even though I was unable to pin down the exact chronology of that terrible week. I tried to connect the memory of Lu's weight upon the bottom of the bed – I'd been frustrated at her for some reason; there was a lingering sense of disappointment – and she'd jumped on Ev, and Ev had been drowsy. I'd been dreading something, but nothing terrible had happened yet. And then I connected it – Lu had left for camp on the morning of the day I told John who his father was. She was on that bus long before murder had sullied Winloch.

'Did anyone tell her about John?' I asked.

He shook his head. 'They wanted to protect her.'

I let out a sigh of relief. 'It probably has nothing to do with him then. You know what it probably is, it's Owen, just normal teenage girl stuff.' I mused on Owen, what his life in the Bronx was like, if he'd heard about the murders, if he and Lu had been corresponding. 'I'm sure that's it,' I repeated, but Galway didn't respond.

Galway swung the car into a gas station on the other side of the road. He knocked on the window of the convenience store. A weary-looking mechanic opened the door and, after a bit of conversation, let Galway in. They chatted inside for a good while, as I watched stripes of light paint themselves on the distant horizon. The sky was pink by the time he emerged with two coffees and a pair of packaged Danishes. He placed them on top of the car while he filled the tank. I could feel his eyes on me through the rearview mirror but avoided his gaze. At the first taste of the coffee he handed over, weariness nipped me.

He buckled his seat belt with a definitive click. 'It's too much of a coincidence, Mabel,' he said, picking up where he left off. 'The timing of it. Anyway, she's not the kind of kid who gets caught up in boy stuff.'

I opened my mouth to argue. But we'd find out soon enough.

'Look,' he said, without starting the car, 'I'm sorry about what happened between us. I know my apology probably means shit to you, but I really am. I didn't tell you I was married—'

'You lied to me—'

'Okay, if you want to call it that.'

'Yes, I do. Because you're married.'

'But not like you think. That marriage was a legal contract, something I did to help someone. And I don't expect you to forgive me for it, but I do want you to know' – and here his voice broke – 'that I've never felt about anyone the way I feel for you.'

'Please don't say things like that.'

'I have to,' he said, looking down at his hands. 'I'm not good at lying to you.'

It was another two hours before we pulled out the map and found our way down a dirt road wide enough for only one car. It was not unlike the Winloch road, winding and narrow, but the forest was thicker, filled with fir trees, lending the light a smoky haze. We drove for miles with no sense if we were headed in the right direction, but just as we were about to stop in the middle of the road and do a fifteen-point turn, we came upon a fork with a small wooden sign nailed to a tree: CAMP. An arrow.

Galway followed the sign. He took the road more slowly now, saying, 'Let me do the talking.'

The camp was a collection of mossy, shingle-covered cabins. It was sleepaway camp as I had only ever imagined it: lakefront, canoes, arts and crafts, a fire pit. It was hard to imagine Lu thriving in such a damp, enclosed place.

I followed Galway into the administration building, where a wan girl lay on a cot in the corner of the room, under a thin wool blanket. We were met by a concerned-looking woman with thick spectacles and a beak of a nose, who nodded sympathetically as Galway explained the phone call we'd received, that his parents were indisposed and they'd sent him instead. She squinted at me. 'And she is . . . ?'

'My wife,' Galway said, taking my hand. I withdrew my fingers quickly, as though they had touched fire.

She dropped her gaze to Galway's offered identification. 'We're not in the habit of handing children over to just anyone.'

Galway nodded vehemently. 'In any other circumstance, I'd agree a hundred percent. But this sounds like an emergency. Naturally, my mother wanted to send someone as soon as she could. And I am Luvinia's brother.'

The girl coughed from her cot. The birdlike woman

reluctantly handed back the license. 'I'll get Marian,' she said doubtfully, rising from her small oak desk and disappearing into an inner sanctum.

An effusive, meaty woman came out hardly a minute later, offering her hand to Galway, then to me. 'Thank you for coming.' She led us outside. The other woman scrutinized us from the doorway.

CHAPTER FIFTY-ONE

The Camp

M ARIAN LED US PAST cabins, and then along the back of the Dining Hall, inside which, thanks to a wall of windows, we saw a handful of capped, pale, foreign-looking women toiling in an industrial kitchen. Marian noticed my glance up at the working girls and said, 'It's great experience. They get to come to the States for the summer.' Yeah, I thought, and cook for a bunch of rich children. Galway tried to put his hand at the small of my back as we crested a steep slope, but I darted from his touch.

We climbed a stairway set into the hillside, toward another set of cabins. Out of breath at the exertion, Marian huffed, 'This is where the counselors stay,' explaining the towels drying on the porches, hand-me-down boom boxes, and half-broken folding chairs set up outside. It was chilly under the dense evergreens; even though it was a warm August day, one could sense October on the air. A few girls my age passed, nodding greetings to Marian as they headed down to the Dining Hall in their hooded sweatshirts and cutoffs. One looked over her shoulder at us, and I sensed she knew exactly who we were there to see.

As we made our way uphill, Marian lowered her voice, speaking confidentially to Galway. 'I hope we did the right thing. My instinct was not to call the police, since the girl did no damage to herself, but not everyone agreed with me. And I didn't call you before because – well, because she begged me not to. I've never met a child who seemed so . . . terrified.'

'You absolutely did the right thing,' Galway replied confidently. It was strange to see how well he wielded authority in this world. 'Father wouldn't want anyone getting hold of this information. When young girls make mistakes they shouldn't be haunted by them.'

Marian nodded a frantic assent. She was wrapped around his finger. 'Well, here we are.' She gestured up to the last cabin in the encampment. 'I don't know the state you'll find her in. Some days she's inconsolable, others she joins in. I've tried to spend as much time with her as possible, but I have other girls to care for.' She checked her watch. 'And I'm due at assembly.'

'Just one question,' Galway said. 'Do you know what set her off?'

Marian shook her head. 'Whatever happened, she's been through trauma.' Then she headed back down the path without us.

The Winloch cottages, with their casement windows, slender doorways, and well-appointed views, seemed positively fussy in comparison to the sparse, hand-built cabin we found ourselves stepping into.

It took a moment for my eyes to adjust. As I discovered my surroundings, I realized that, deep in these dense woods, this was the most light that penetrated on a sunny day. The gloominess was made worse by the design of the building; where there might have been an abundance of windows, instead the walls were lined with utilitarian bunks. There was no sign of Lu.

For the first time since we'd arrived at camp, Galway seemed indecisive. Just as I was about to take charge, a toilet flushed from behind a closed door, and a counselor emerged.

'We're here to see Lu,' I said.

'I only left her because she was sleeping,' the girl apologized, gesturing toward the second bunk room.

'Why don't you head to breakfast?' Galway suggested, regaining himself. The girl eagerly gathered her sweatshirt and headed outside. We stepped into the room she'd gestured toward.

At first, I thought the counselor had been teasing us – there was no sign of human life. I squinted my eyes and examined the empty bunks again, until a shape that I had taken to be a pile of linens stirred on one of the bottom bunks – I was reminded of finding Indo collapsed on the floor. I pointed. Galway followed my gesture, creeping closer. When we were within arm's reach, her face appeared. She was ghostly, pale. Pulling her long, brittle body into standing, she dashed across the remaining space between us, then clamped her arms around me, squeezing the air from my lungs. She was scrawnier than the last time I'd seen her, but her weight loss hadn't seemed to diminish her strength. I tried to find air.

She shook and keened and pulled Galway into the embrace. I was sandwiched between them, and tried not to enjoy the press of him against my back.

A knock on the door ended the moment. Breakfast sandwiches for each of us, delivered by a curious camper. She craned her neck to see inside when I took her food, but I blocked her gaze.

We ate, stooped, on the bunks. There was just enough light to notice how Lu barely picked at her food. She was close to emaciated, but her appetite didn't show it.

Galway finished his sandwich first. He leaned back in the bunk, folding his hands around his lifted knee. Watched Lu like a hawk as she nibbled. Chewing and swallowing were feats of will.

She finally met his gaze.

'So?' he asked, not very gently.

Her lips turned down. I saw she was about to cry. I set down the remains of my breakfast and left my bunk for hers. I grabbed her hand. 'Just tell us what happened.'

'I'm sorry,' she whispered, dissolving. We sat through that round of tears, until I asked if she'd rather be alone with one of us.

She shook her head. 'I only want to tell it once.'

So we waited. And waited. I could sense Galway growing impatient, and I understood now why he'd insisted I come along. I squeezed Lu's hand. 'Did you hurt yourself?' I asked.

Lu's eyes opened wide. 'I didn't mean to,' she said. 'I mean, I meant to, but it was only to stop remembering. I was so afraid because I thought they knew, and they would come, and . . .' She shivered as though she were repulsed. 'Thank you for coming,' she said. 'Do they know?'

'Who?' I asked.

She looked to her brother.

'Masha's the only person who knows we came. She won't tell anyone unless I ask her to,' he answered.

She shut her eyes in relief.

'Why don't we start at the beginning?' I suggested.

I could feel how afraid she was. 'The last time I saw you was the morning you were going to camp,' I prompted. 'You came to Bittersweet and said good-bye.'

She reluctantly began her tale.

CHAPTER FIFTY-TWO

The Witness

UNBEKNOWNST TO THE REST of us, for the week prior to Lu's forced departure, smelling something inevitable on the wind, she and Owen had been scheming to beat the system. They believed themselves star-crossed lovers, and saw her parents' resistance to their union as only further evidence of their entwined destiny. They were wise to the fact that they wouldn't be allowed their dalliance much longer. 'You know that abandoned cottage above Turtle Point?' Lu asked Galway, avoiding my gaze.

'That thing's still standing?'

I knew now what she and Owen had really been up to out on Turtle Point.

'The plan was, Mum would drive me to the bus station, but then instead of getting on the bus – since she never stays to actually make sure – I'd hide out. Then I'd call camp and pretend to be Mum and tell them I wasn't coming after all – I do a really good impression of her, right?'

I nodded, remembering how effortlessly Lu had impersonated her mother the morning Indo had collapsed, when she'd tried to get me to talk her parents out of sending her away.

She went on. 'Marian doesn't ask many questions, and I figured if I dropped Daddy's name enough times she'd believe me. Then I'd get back to Winloch and meet Owen at the cottage above Turtle Point, and we'd just get to be together. Arlo could bring us food from the Dining Hall, and, since he has a car, he could drive us into town every couple days. We figured we could hole up there for a while before anyone would notice I hadn't made it to camp.' She looked back and forth between us. 'We weren't hurting anyone. We just wanted to be together.'

I nodded sympathetically at the lunatic teenage logic of it. I could see Galway's foot bobbing impatiently out of the corner of my eye.

'So what went wrong?' I asked.

'Nothing,' she said. 'Mum dropped me off at the bus and I just didn't use my ticket. I called Marian at camp. She totally bought it.' Her eyes welled. 'And then John came to pick me up.'

'John?' I asked. She might have no idea what had happened. But her tears told me otherwise.

She sniffled. 'I'd asked if he could help us, a few days before my bus. He asked if we loved each other.' Lu paused.

'And what did you say?' I tried to ignore the lump welling in my throat.

'I told him I thought so. He said he didn't like going behind my father's back, but "love should get its chance."'

I glanced at Galway, filling with emotion.

'Go on,' Galway urged.

'Anyway, it was an easy job,' Lu said. 'All he had to do was swing by the bus station. I'd hide under a tarp in the back of the pickup. I know what you're going to say – it's not safe – but it wasn't even on the highway, and it was only from the bus station to his mother's house.'

I replayed that day. John had been with me that morning, until I told him Birch was his father, and then he'd sped off. He could have gone anywhere from there. 'When did he pick you up?'

'I don't know. One?'

A good three hours after he'd abandoned me on the Winloch road. 'How did he seem?' I asked selfishly.

'We didn't really talk. I just climbed in back and he drove me home.'

'So you were hiding in the bed of his truck because you didn't want anyone to see you come back.'

She nodded. 'I was supposed to stay in there until after dark. Because we didn't want anyone to see me, and, you know, Aggie works there.' She caught herself. 'Worked.'

Galway and I exchanged a look. She had seen something. I felt sure of it now.

I rubbed her hand reassuringly. 'Whenever you're ready.'

She took a deep breath. 'He brought me a peanut butter sandwich for dinner. He made it look like he was getting something from the truck, but he was really making sure I was okay. Not too hot and stuff. And he made me promise I'd be out of the truck right after it got dark. Then he told me not to worry, he was letting Aggie off early, so as soon as I heard her car leave, I could sneak off without being seen.' A new round of tears bubbled up. 'He was really nice to me.'

'Lu,' Galway said, obviously irritated that she wasn't getting to the point, 'what happened next?'

She shook her head. 'I went back under the tarp and waited some more. It was impossible to tell what time of

374

day it was, and, you know, I was under there a long time, so I started to get cramped. But then I reminded myself I could be dying of boredom here at camp, instead. So I just waited.'

'It got dark?'

She nodded. 'I heard Aggie say good-bye. She got into her car and drove off. So I thought, you know, I'm free. I waited a few more minutes, and I was just standing up when one of the maintenance trucks came down the driveway. I ducked. It actually parked really close to me, and I thought whoever was driving had seen me but . . .' She shook her head no. She was gripping my hand now.

'I thought, I'll just hide under here until they leave or whatever. But they didn't leave. Not for, like, a really long time. And then I heard shouting. From inside the house. And barking. The barking kept going on and on.' My fingers were losing feeling under the pressure of her grasp. 'So I decided to climb out of the truck. It was really scary, like, so hard to do, but I figured if I could hear shouting, then no one would notice me running away, because it meant they were inside. It was really dark out, but there was all this light coming from John's mom's cottage, so I could see enough to get out of the truck.' She stopped to collect herself. 'I started to run away. But then I heard . . .' She began to wheeze. Her fingers clenched mine. 'I heard, like, a scream. Like a scream in a movie.'

'And what did you do?'

'I went toward it. I couldn't help it. It sounded so scared, that scream, and I thought, I don't know, I thought I could help or something.' She shook her head at the futility of it.

375

'So I go to the cottage. Like, I creep, on my hands and knees around the side of the house, toward the porch, 'cause I figure there I can hide better in the trees and see more. Everything's quiet.' She shuddered. 'I shouldn't have looked, but I did.'

'What did you see, Lu?'

Lu's eyes were fixed on her brother. 'He was standing over her. He had his hands around her neck. He was squeezing her so hard. I could hear her choking, her body was moving, like, back and forth, but he didn't stop, he just pressed and pressed and pressed until she was still.' Tears were streaming down her face, but the words came easily.

'John?' I asked. 'You saw him killing her?'

She frowned. 'No! John was just lying on the floor. But then he woke up. He saw what was happening and he lunged, but he couldn't save her. And then they began to fight, and John ran out, and then he did too, right past me, into the forest, up the path. I followed them. I knew I couldn't stop them, but I couldn't just let them go either, so I followed them, and I hid in the bushes by the point. They were yelling at each other, punching and stuff, and then all of a sudden he pushed John, and John lost his balance, and then . . .' Her little hands released mine, sailing up into the air like doves. 'Then John was gone. Over the cliff.'

'Who was it?' Galway pressed, sitting forward. 'Who killed them?'

She nodded at the tragic inevitability of her answer. 'It was Daddy.'

CHAPTER FIFTY-THREE

The Jailbreak

G ALWAY DIDN'T LOOK ALL that surprised. But neither did he offer Lu any comfort. I realized then that he was calculating:

Motive.

Damage.

Our next move.

I put my arm around Lu's shoulder as she told us what had happened next: terrified and disoriented, the world filling with Abby's barks, she watched her father drive away in the maintenance truck. When she realized she was alone with two dead bodies, she first thought about running back home. But she wouldn't be safe near her father, and anyway, her parents already thought she was at camp. Neither could she go to Turtle Point with Owen as she'd planned; she was sure her father would find her there. John's keys were in the ignition. She'd driven Arlo's car a few times, and John's truck was an automatic. So she found a pair of work gloves in the shed, hopped into the driver's seat, and, heart racing, drove to the bus station without leaving her fingerprints on the wheel. She hid the truck behind the shipping container and waited for the morning bus to camp. Camp was the only place she would be safe. But coming hadn't made things any better, as what she had witnessed haunted her more with each passing day.

I whispered, between her sobs, that she was so brave, and nothing was going to hurt her. She pulled back from me when I said that. 'If he knew . . . ,' she said, and she began to make a shrieking sound, high and quick, adding, 'What will I do if he finds out I saw?'

I took her face in my hands. 'Shhhh,' I said, 'shhhh,' and it was as though I was talking to my younger self, the part that had believed my life, too, might as well be over.

The girl calmed. I thought, I'm going to tell them now. All about what I did when I was a girl, and how it made me better, and more honest, and how I had felt so worthless but now I felt strong. But as I opened my mouth to begin, Galway stood. 'I'm going to find Marian,' he said. 'Have a chat, make a phone call or two. You girls okay here?'

'Galway,' I chided, 'tell her it's going to be okay.'

He frowned at my tone, then knelt before Lu. He wiped her tears with his hand.

'Horrible things happen in this world,' he said finally, 'but I'll do everything in my power to keep you safe.' She hesitated a moment, then wrapped her arms around her big brother. The look on his face as he comforted her was so wounded that I was forced to remember his own sister had just told him she was witness to their father committing double murder with his bare hands.

Once he was gone, we folded her clothes into her small suitcase. 'I can't go back to Winloch,' she repeated again and again. I assured her that we would work something out, although I had no idea what Galway had in mind, and, aside from offering her a spot on my parents' couch

– where Birch would find her in about five minutes – I had no resources.

I brushed her limp, greasy hair before the mirror, and realized she and Ev had deteriorated in much the same way. How quickly the Winslow girls had become nearly weightless. Translucent. As if trauma had swallowed their lives and bodies.

We heard footsteps on the path. I smiled at Lu in the mirror. Galway poked his head in the door. 'You can put that down,' he instructed me. He meant the suitcase in my hand. I frowned in incomprehension. 'Can we have a minute?' he asked.

I kissed Lu's sticky, tearstained cheek and blinked back out into the day. I leaned against an old fir tree, searching the cabin's windows for a sign of what was happening inside. Galway emerged alone. He hopped down the steps. Headed onto the path that led to his car.

'What about Lu?'

He turned and caught my eye. 'It's time to go.'

My voice raised to a cry. 'We can't abandon her, Galway. She needs us.'

'Trust me.' He walked on.

I glanced back up at the cabin, where, presumably, Lu was now watching me choose. I could stay here with her, but I had no money, nothing to offer but the comfort of my embrace. Still, to leave would be to pretend I didn't care at all. Was Galway really this cruel?

A breeze skipped in off the small lake, lifting a clatter of girls' voices from one of the full canoes skimming its waters. I was suddenly, terribly cold. I thought to go back, to tell her I was sorry, to tell Lu I was no use to her here, but out there, I would figure something out. But I knew that an apology would be worse for her, because it would have been worse for me. So I ran down the path as fast as I could, catching up with Galway, glad the cabin was out of sight and her eyes were no longer boring, longingly, into the back of my head.

In the car, Galway's foot pressing the accelerator, I felt bile rise.

'We left her there,' I shouted, already regretting my decision a thousand times over. 'We shouldn't have done that, Galway, you should have taken care of her.' But on he drove.

At the fork in the road, instead of continuing on, which would have led us back to civilization, he turned. 'I asked you to trust me,' he said.

'What the hell does trust have to do with it?'

We skidded to a halt. A boulder, brought by some glacier millions of years before, sat on the other side of the road. It was the only landmark for miles.

Galway strained to see into the woods. 'Because,' he replied, 'you'll really have to trust me in order to swallow what comes next.' As he spoke, I watched a white dot weave in and out of sight from behind the tree trunks. It grew larger and larger, revealing itself to be a T-shirt worn by Lu, as she sprinted from the forest, spotted our car, and ran to us.

The girl flung open the back door and tossed her suitcase across the seats. She brought the smell of the pines with her, a mossy dampness permeated by sweat. 'Go!'

'Buckle up,' Galway insisted, turning the car as quickly as he could.

I looked between them as we accelerated. 'You mean this was a plan?'

'It had to seem like you were really leaving me there,' Lu explained. 'In case my father asks, because they'll suspect you for taking me.'

'But won't Marian just sound the alarm?' I asked, feeling hurt.

'Everyone knows Marian has gambling problems,' she went on, 'so all Galway had to do was tell her he knew about her "financial issues"—'

'And offer to make an anonymous donation to the "charity" of her choice,' Galway added.

'And then as soon as you guys left, I could just run down the other side of the mountain, and she gets to say I was a runaway, but she'll keep her mouth shut for a while because she wants the money—'

'But we get to leave with Lu.' Galway laughed, hitting the steering wheel triumphantly. 'Everybody wins!'

Were they actually enjoying this?

'Mabel,' Lu said, leaning forward in her seat, putting her hands on my shoulders, 'I told him not to tell you. We want to put Daddy off the trail. You're not the best liar, you know, and it has to look to everybody like I just ran away so he believes them.'

I started to laugh. I was exhausted, and angry, and scared. Unhinged, perhaps. Overwrought. Underestimated. I was many things, but a terrible liar wasn't one of them. The laugh encompassed me.

They exchanged a bemused look in the rearview mirror. 'Are you okay?' she asked. My stomach muscles began to hurt. I gasped for air. Another round of laughter overtook me. Then, as the sheer ridiculousness of all of this abated, I slapped Galway on his leg. 'You could have told me once we got in the car.'

He rubbed at the spot. 'But you're cute when you're mad.' I almost punched him in the jaw.

CHAPTER FIFTY-FOUR

The Memory

L U CURLED LIKE A kitten in the backseat. Soon, her snores were filling the small car. 'Where are we going?' I asked.

Galway didn't answer. I was sick of his insouciance in the face of all this tragedy, but I noticed, as I fumed beside him, that his hands were trembling on the steering wheel. He had turned pale.

'Are you okay?' I asked.

Galway checked Lu in the rearview mirror.

'She's out,' I said.

Only then did he let down his guard.

'When I was a kid,' he began in a low voice, 'Father used to get in these rages. He'd belt us, that kind of thing. I assumed all fathers did that, you know?'

I did.

'But this one time' – he paused, confirming, once again, that Lu wasn't listening, then lowered his voice as an extra precaution – 'I was down at Flat Rocks with Mum and all the kids. Ev was little, so I must've been, what, six? I'd forgotten my comic book up at the house, and Mum said I could go get it by myself. I was in my room looking when I heard these strange sounds coming from the bathroom. Athol'd been telling me stories about raccoons, so I became convinced it was one, and I picked up a baseball bat and crept to the door, and listened, and then, when I knew for sure something was in there, I tried the handle, and the door opened right up.'

I wasn't sure I wanted to know what that little boy had seen.

'And there, on the floor of the bathroom, was my father, with his pants down, one hand over the mouth of our au pair, the other pinning her down. Raping her, Mabel. She had this single tear . . .' He shook his head. 'I can still remember the look on his face when he saw me – if he'd had a gun, he would have used it. I ran downstairs. He didn't follow me. And I was a kid, you know? So I just decided I hadn't seen anything. I didn't even know how to say what I'd seen.

'Days passed. Nothing. I almost believed it hadn't happened. But then a week or so later I was playing cards with Athol, and he accused me of cheating – he always accused me of cheating – and Father' – he swallowed, reliving it – 'Father just appeared. With a poker in his hand. He came at me. Beat me, like a farmer beats a stubborn donkey. He broke my ribs, my wrist, my ankle. Athol just stood there, watching. Mum came home in the middle of it, but that was by chance. She stopped it, but it didn't matter. I knew, once and for all. He would have killed me, easy, with no remorse.'

What invisible lines had Tilde drawn in the sand to justify staying with that man? He could rape the maids but not his daughters? In the rowboat, she had told me that marrying Birch had made her a Winslow. I wondered how she felt about that. How Galway felt about the blood running through his veins.

I kissed my hand and put it back on his leg. Let it grow warm there, between us, as he wept.

We rode on like that for a good while, until he cleared his throat and tried to talk in a businesslike tone. 'What I don't understand is what he possibly could have been doing there. At Mrs LaChance's. Why would he drive a maintenance truck out there? And why on earth did he kill them?'

'I told John something that day,' I said carefully. 'Something John might have wanted to confront Birch about. Maybe he invited Birch that night, so they could end it.'

'But why did Father drive a maintenance truck? Why not just come in his own car?'

'If the murders were premeditated, the maintenance truck was the perfect foil. No one would guess it was Birch behind the wheel. Especially if he drove over after night fell.'

Galway let this sink in. And then he asked the question I knew was coming. 'So what did you tell John?'

I withdrew my hand from his leg. And then I told Galway what I had told his sister, and half brother, before him. 'That your father was his father.'

Galway took the news stoically. 'How'd you find that out?'

I told him about my discovery of the P. in Kitty's journal, and how Masha, against her will, had confirmed John's paternity. I told him of Ev's pregnancy, and seeing John and Ev making love, and their subsequent elopement and planned departure. I told him I couldn't bear to think of their life together not knowing who they really were to each other, and I told him, not quite knowing how to tell any more – but feeling that I must – that Ev had already known, that she had wanted, somehow, to be with her own half brother in that way. I told him that the way Ev had guessed John was her brother was that Jackson had come to her, and asked her if she knew that CeCe and Birch were his real parents, because someone in the family had confessed Birch's sexual secrets, that he had raped his sister – and who knew what other relatives – not to mention the maids, and that that was the real reason Jackson had committed suicide. The knowledge that he was the product of a brother and sister's miserable incestuous union had been too much to bear.

I told Galway almost everything, but held back the part about Indo insisting Kitty's journal offered more secrets, or what those secrets were – that the Winslows had stolen, and been stealing, from others for years. It wasn't that I didn't trust Galway, it was more that, riding beside him, I couldn't imagine delving into anything unproven. My throat was raw from talking. I wanted to leave it all behind – Indo's dying wish, and what the journal might offer, and who had stolen it, and how I might be able to use it to prove a much deeper conspiracy than Birch's rapes. I felt as I had when they had pulled me from the river, my body cold, my heart colder, but relieved, lighter, now that I had released my darkness into the world. I just wanted to believe that the truth, enough of it, had set us both free.

Galway slowed to the side of the highway. Chunks of macadam ticked under the belly of the car. I wondered if he was going to throw me out as John had. I would have accepted my fate.

But instead, Galway opened his own door. The traffic rushed past us, someone laid on a horn, the air in the car suctioned in and out, and at the changed pressure, the girl in the backseat stirred and grumbled.

Galway swayed at the edge of the rushing traffic. I knew that he was considering changing his fate. A Mack truck would make his departure quick, if painful. I undid my seat belt and placed my hand on my door, knowing I wouldn't get there in time if that was what he chose. But instead, he crossed in front of the car, lurched toward the forest line, bent at the waist, and vomited.

We stopped for a late lunch on the outskirts of a small town. Galway made Lu wait in the car so we wouldn't be seen together, which I thought was a bit overzealous – we were hundreds of miles from Winloch, a nondescript family riding in a nondescript car – but she was game, folding herself under a blanket in the backseat. Now that she was safely in our care, she seemed giddy at the intrigue of our situation, as though we were in a spy novel. As I sipped my chicken soup and kept an eye on the car from our window booth, my heart almost broke with the thought of what she'd been bearing alone, and what she'd have to face once all this action was over.

'So what's the plan?' I asked Galway. He had regained his color and will. As he sipped his coffee, I pushed away the realization that he looked like a younger version of his father.

'White River Junction,' he said.

'What's in White River Junction?'

'Someone's meeting us,' he murmured, summoning the waitress for the check, ordering Lu a gyro.

CHAPTER FIFTY-FIVE

The Handoff

WHITE RIVER JUNCTION LIES at the confluence of I-89 – connecting Boston to Burlington – and I-91, which runs from Canada down to New Haven. The signs leading toward the town, as we made our way south on 91, seemed to advertise it as a bustling metropolis. But when we curled down the off-ramp and Galway turned in to the parking lot of an abandoned-looking warehouse, I'll admit to feeling disappointed. We pulled behind the long, wide building so we were invisible from the road. Then we waited.

Galway checked his watch. Turned to address his little sister. 'You sure you want to do this?'

'I don't have a choice.'

'Do what?' I asked.

'You won't be able to come back until he's either in jail or dead,' he said. 'You can contact me, but the rest of them—'

'I don't want to see the rest of them. I don't want him to ever know where I am. But I want him to know there was a witness, Galway. I want him to be afraid I'll tell.'

Galway nodded as a navy pickup came around the back of the warehouse. I could make out a black-haired woman at the wheel. She was alone.

She parked nose to nose with us and hopped down from

the truck. Her gait was easy, her legs long, her hair glistening. She sauntered over to Galway's window. He unrolled it. She leaned in and smiled.

'Thanks,' said Galway.

'I owe you big-time,' she purred. Her voice itched at me – I had heard it before. I knew who she was, but it seemed impossible he would have asked her here without warning me. She caught the look on my face and smiled again, sympathetic. Stretched out her hand. 'Marcella.'

I touched her fingers. They were warm.

'And you,' she said, turning her smile toward the backseat, 'must be Luvinia.'

Lu straightened and smiled. 'Thank you for helping me.'

'Like I said,' she gushed, eyes casting over her husband again, 'big-time.'

She got in the backseat. They schemed. It seemed Marcella, as Galway's wife, had access to his trust. She would use it to obtain the necessary documents and tickets to ferry Lu out of the country. 'She can pass for eighteen,' she said, appraising Lu, 'if we cut her hair.' With a careful eye, I watched this woman who had shared Galway's bed, and realized the seriousness of what we were discussing. Worry began to gnaw my gut. 'We'll set you up,' she said. 'You can trust us. Your brother has helped a lot of people.'

I kept my mouth shut, but I wondered what exactly 'helping' people meant. Smuggling children out of the country? Because that's what Lu was, after all.

'Want to take a walk?' Marcella asked, bringing me out of my reverie.

Lu and Galway deserved time alone together, but that

didn't mean I had to talk to Marcella. I slammed the door shut behind me, crossed my arms, and made my way to a loading dock, littered with disintegrating cardboard boxes. Marcella got a cigarette from her truck, lit up, and smoked, her long throat tilting toward the sky.

She came toward me, inevitably. Leaned against the concrete. She smelled delicious. 'Galway helped my mom and me get to this country. I admired him. Then he offered to marry me, see if he could pull some strings, get me a green card.'

'And did he?' I asked miserably.

'I'll tell you a secret: I even thought I loved him.'

That was a secret I didn't want to hear.

'But then, right after we got married, I met someone. Like, the someone. I admire Galway. But I'm not meant to be his wife.'

This made me feel only slightly better.

'He loves you,' she offered. I could feel her eyes darting over my face. 'I'd know even if he hadn't told me.'

I kicked at a pebble with my foot. 'Oh, you would? How on earth would you know?'

'How he looks at you.' She stubbed out her cigarette. 'I speak from experience: don't waste your time being afraid of love.'

Lu flattened her palm on the passenger window of Marcella's truck, a smile tucked bravely in the corners of her mouth. We had already cried, and hugged, and established that she'd send me an untraceable e-mail, as soon as she was safe, with the word *turtle* in it, so I'd know she had made it. I can still see her face in the moment they turned out of view, when Galway and I became just us two.

We sat in silence together. He started up the car.

'Let's not go back,' I suggested.

He sighed. 'I always knew what a monster my father was. But then, you know, I believed in Winloch more. In the Winslows. I thought we were sane. Honorable.' He shook his head. 'I have to stop him. I have to try to save our family.'

We paid cash for a bed at the HoJo's. Lay down beside each other.

'What happened to Abby?' I asked as the shadows grew long.

Tears filled his eyes. He waited for them to abate before he spoke. 'When I got over there after you called me . . .' He began again. 'Look, she was aggressive. She wouldn't let anyone near her. Father came over— I know,' he said, as I startled. 'I called the police, and got Father, just so someone with authority was there, but when Abby saw him, well, she went . . .' His eyes opened wide with admiration and sorrow. 'She charged him. I thought it was just a dog who'd witnessed violence and snapped. I had no idea she was attacking her owner's murderer. We called animal control.'

'They killed her?' I cried, my body dissolving into full sobs. Some part of me had known all along, but it was too much to bear.

We slept hard: like babies, like rocks, like the dead.

CHAPTER FIFTY-SIX

The Service

W E REACHED WINLOCH BY early afternoon. We were fortified and ready: we would confront Birch in broad daylight, in front of Tilde – what was he going to do, murder all three of us? We'd tell him we had a witness, the person who'd driven John's truck out of Winloch and disappeared for good, but we wouldn't reveal the witness's name. Sometime tomorrow, he and Tilde would receive a call that Lu had just run away from camp. By then, Lu and Marcella would be long gone, with the lead time of a full day and a half. Birch would eventually suspect that Lu was the witness to his acts of murder – if he didn't already – and, if he really was as much of a monster as he had already proved himself to be, would begin to hunt his daughter down the second he suspected she might speak against him.

As far as I was concerned, Tilde was our insurance policy. As unfeeling as she seemed, I had started to believe that her warning in the rowboat came out of a desire to protect me, just as her barking orders to Hannah to cover herself on Flat Rocks came from a need to shield that child. Tilde was the one who'd stopped Birch from breaking down the Bittersweet door. The one who'd insisted we put up the bolts in the first place. I was starting to believe she was in the business of protecting people from her husband.

If offered the choice between Lu and Birch, I was betting that Tilde would choose her daughter. That she would keep her husband at bay as long as she could, give Lu the chance to run. Galway wasn't sure of this – he had become a nihilist overnight, sure he knew nothing and could trust no one (save me) – but I held fast to the promise of Tilde's benevolence, because it was all we had.

It was another blinding late summer day, but we had brought Maine's chill with us. Through my unrolled window the lake wind flowed. I wrapped my arms around myself as we turned the corner where Ev and John had discovered me the night I'd tried to run away.

Galway caught sight of the Dining Hall and exhaled. On a normal sunny afternoon like today, the building would be abandoned, quiet, the Winslows lost in outdoor pursuits. But today, the road leading to and from it was lined with cars. We slowed, parked at the back of the line, and got out.

As we walked toward the Dining Hall, Galway took my hand. We were going to end this, once and for all.

We mounted the steps quietly, but it was obvious, as soon as we swung open the doors, that every Winslow I'd ever met – Ev, Athol and Emily, Banning and Annie, the Kitterings, even CeCe – was gathered there, dressed in black and seated in makeshift rows as though to create a congregation. The crowd was facing the closed, gated kitchen, in front of which Birch stood, hands folded, head bowed. He lifted his eyes at the sound of us. And then they all did, the great herd of the great family, the young and the old, each and every one, lifting their blond heads and casting their blue eyes upon us.

Birch gestured to a seat that had been saved for Galway in the front row. Galway squeezed my hand – I thought it was a temporary good-bye – but he held his ground, and the doors came to rest behind us. Panic settled on me; were we about to be indicted of something? Why else would they all be here, waiting for us? I nearly dropped Galway's hand, longing for the virtual anonymity I'd enjoyed in my early days at Winloch. I felt the impulse to apologize, then run.

The Winslows turned back to Birch, but his eyes stayed upon us. A faint smile grew at the corners of his lips. I couldn't bear to look at him, but to look away would be to show my fear.

'I trust you received the message I left in Boston,' Birch's voice boomed across the space.

Galway didn't skip a beat. 'Yes, Father. We came as soon as we could.'

Birch dismissed us in a glance. Then he spoke to the gathered group. 'As I was saying, she was a strange woman, but her oddities didn't detract from her unique vision of the world. She was funny. She was stubborn—' At this, there were some chuckles from the family, and a dissolve, from a woman on the left, into a sob.

It dawned on me that someone had died. That this was a memorial service.

'Linden was my sister,' Birch solemnly intoned, confirming my fears, 'and death won't change that. I'm glad the end was quick—' His voice cracked as he fought back crocodile tears.

So Indo had finally died. A stunned, numb sadness settled in my chest. As Birch pretended to struggle, letting his shoulders quiver enough to gain sympathy, but not so much that he was rendered speechless, I realized how perfectly in control he was. He was playing the convincing part of the devastated mourner, and nearly everyone believed him.

He had won. She had lost. I believed, without a shadow of a doubt, that it was partly my fault that she had given up, and that he held all the power now; I had been unable to find the proof she wanted, needed, to expose him. That I had failed her only meant he was now free of her. I'd even lost Kitty's journal; worse, someone else – probably Birch – had it in his clutches. And now Indo was dead and her horrible brother was standing before a roomful of his followers, smugly eulogizing her, tasting victory, and there was nothing I could do about it. Fury mounted inside me, at my own incompetence, at the cancer that had eaten Indo up, at the horrible man before me, tricking everyone with his false grief.

'My sister was a materialist,' he continued, his supposed sorrow ebbing, his hands gesturing animatedly, as though he were running a PowerPoint presentation. 'She loved beautiful things. Not expensive things, not necessarily, not diamonds, not lavish vacations or caviar, but little boxes she collected from her travels. Fabric from the souk. Photographs taken on a backpacking trip to Machu Picchu . . .' Birch went on, but something he'd said caught, like a fishhook, at the corner of my mind.

Indo – a materialist. That was certainly true; her small red cottage was packed to the gills with collections and whimsy, an abundant stockpile of too-muchness. She loved her things. And then, I thought of it – the Van Gogh. In her bedroom, on the last day we'd spoken, she'd cried out for it: 'my painting.' But when I had tried to use the Van Gogh as an incentive to tease out more information, she had started to laugh maniacally, insisting it was too late for her. I'd thought her mad. But maybe there was something more concrete at play. Maybe she had started laughing – and wanted the painting in the first place – because it, in itself, was important.

I had to get to it. Perhaps it could tell me what Indo had not.

Birch droned on. The congregation grieved. But I knew that to truly memorialize Indo wouldn't be to sit in a closed room listening to someone she hated speaking in platitudes about her. To honor her would be to carry on her cause.

Knowing it would cause a disruption, but not caring anymore, I pulled my hand from Galway's and backed out of the double doors behind us. I would run as fast as I could.

CHAPTER FIFTY-SEVEN

The Truth

I SPRINTED DOWN THE STAIRS, up the road and over the hill, into the long meadow. Past Clover and the other cottages, and toward Trillium. I dashed to the screened-in porch. No one seemed to be inside. I placed my hand on the screen door and yawned it open, heart pounding, bracing for a gun, or a bear, or a vampire, but then I was just standing on Birch and Tilde's porch. The summer room's doors stood open, and the Van Gogh waited for me like a piece of ripe fruit ready to be plucked. I walked toward it.

'Lovely, isn't it,' came a reedy, small voice the instant I stepped in line with the painting. I wheeled around. There, in the chair where Athol had caught me the night of the wedding, sat Gammy Pippa. She was as small as a girl, wrinkled, knobbed. She listed to one side. The scent of talcum powder wafted off of her.

'Good gracious, dear,' she replied, 'you look as if you've seen a ghost.'

I shook my head stiffly.

'I couldn't stand all those hypocrites talking about Linden as though she was some kind of saint,' she remarked, blinking up at the masterpiece. I watched her eyes dance over the lines of the painting, before they searched the world beyond me, out on the porch. 'The light comes off the water just as it did when I was a girl.'

She was only an old woman. Strange, nosy, but aged enough that I could speak to her of sentimental things, admire the room, flatter her family, and she wouldn't know I had come to see the truth, once and for all.

She examined me carefully, looking me up and down. After a moment she asked, 'Who are you?'

Even better. 'I'm Mabel,' I said, extending my hand. Her small palm gripped mine. Her knuckles were knobby. 'We met the night of the wedding. Mabel Dagmar. Genevra's roommate.'

'I know your name, Mabel,' she said, irritation creeping into her voice. 'But who are you?' She was hot to the touch, her pulse throbbing through her veins, as though her whole hand was a living creature with its own tiny heart.

'Who are you?' she asked again, this time, her words ringing with playful demand. She pulled at my hand with surprising strength. 'Who are you?'

I felt the same strange sensation as when she had touched my face in the tent – of transparency, light-headedness. Of her looking deep inside me and seeing what I wanted to keep hidden.

'My grandnephew Jackson,' she began, her words spilling forth buoyantly, 'came to see me the day before he died. He'd asked everyone to tell him the truth and no one would. "Who am I?" he cried over my kitchen table. "Who am I?" So I asked him, just once, what he thought the truth would do for him – why he wanted it so badly. He told me he believed it would set him free.'

The old woman's eyes sparkled triumphantly. 'So I told him,' she said, her jaw tightening. 'I told him exactly who his parents were. I told him the truth – the truth everyone else was too afraid to tell him. "There," I said, once it was out in the open' – she chuckled to herself, as though this were an anecdote that brought her great joy – '"now you know, your father is your uncle, does that set you free?"'

My mouth had gone dry.

'Depending on what you believe about the afterlife,' she prattled on, 'I suppose you could say that the truth did set him free, out into the great expanse—'

'How can you say that?' I said, tearing my hand from her clutches. 'It was because of what you told him that he killed himself.'

'Wouldn't you have done the same?' she asked slyly, looking straight into my eyes. And I realized: she knows. Somehow, she knows what I told John. She knows I am partly responsible for his death.

'Don't feel ashamed, girl,' she said, answering my thoughts. 'The truth is a noble grail to seek. But if you're after it, you must imagine, first, what it will mean to get it. The truth is neither good nor bad. It is above evil. Above morality. It doesn't offer anything besides itself.' She nodded resolutely. 'I'm proud I told Jackson the truth. I'm glad he died knowing who he was.'

'The product of brother-sister rape?' I balked.

The old woman shut her eyes, as though exasperated at my histrionics. 'My dear, it would be best for you to decide now whether you are strong enough to know the truth, especially if you're going to be a part of this family . . .'

My heart pounded. I wanted Galway, didn't I? Didn't being with him make me a Winslow? 'I don't know,' I said vaguely, unable to tear myself away from her even as she horrified me. 'I don't know what I want.'

'Well, you better make up your mind,' she said impatiently, looking back out toward the porch. 'They're going to wonder where you ran off to.'

I swallowed. 'I want to know about the painting.'

'The truth?'

I nodded.

'Go on,' she said, her gnarled hand pointing up at the Van Gogh. I looked back to the masterpiece – trees, sky, and meadow. It was beautiful. But it held no answers beyond itself. 'Go on,' she said, pointing in agitation, irritation creeping back in her thin voice, 'take it down.'

It was a priceless work of art. I laughed. One sharp, incredulous laugh. 'I can't.'

She struggled to her feet then, hoisting herself up with the help of the armchair. I looked back to the painting. It was three feet long and at least two feet high. The frame was gilded and heavy – I imagined I would just barely be able to lift the work off the wall, and wasn't sure I'd be able to get it back into place. But I feared it would crush her. 'This is silly,' I said.

'You want to know the truth, I'll show you.' She was still struggling to stand. She'd barely make it to the painting, let alone lift it.

'Sit,' I insisted, stepping before her. She narrowed her eyes and obeyed.

The story the Van Gogh told changed up close. Instead

of long, fluid lines that made a picture, it was globs of paint. Midnight blue, magenta, and gold rippled with skill and effort.

I lifted my hands to perch along the edges of the frame and lifted. It was heavy, but not as heavy as I'd thought. I tottered backwards, unsure of how it was attached to the wall. It unhooked easily. Pippa pointed to its back.

I balanced it down onto the floor. Turned it so I could see its reverse. Even then, I was doubtful I would find anything worthwhile.

But I was wrong. For there, on the back of the Van Gogh, was an official-looking stamp, the words in German, surrounding a swastika.

CHAPTER FIFTY-EIGHT

The Curse

B ACK IN SUMMER'S FIRST days, in mid-June, I had found myself strolling, alone, past the Dining Hall. I was in search of Ev. We had passed the inspection, Winloch was filling with residents, and I didn't yet know that she was sleeping with her brother. All I knew was that she'd promised me a swim and, while I was getting ready, had wandered off, this on the day that my catalog bathing suit had finally arrived. I was incredulous. Irritated. Greedy for her attention.

In sight of the Dining Hall steps, I spotted Indo just as she spotted me. The older woman was perched on the wooden boards like an awkward bird, angled toward the sun, dressed in a purple sweater and wide orange pants. She lifted a hand and shielded her eyes and called to me in stentorian tones.

"'Of Man's First Disobedience, and the Fruit / Of that Forbidden Tree . . .'"

I had no idea what she was talking about. Then followed her gaze to my crisp new copy of *Paradise Lost*; I'd reluctantly resolved to head back down to the Bittersweet cove for a bookish afternoon if Ev was nowhere to be found.

'Such a wee scholar you are, Mabel Dagmar,' the older woman intoned in a Scottish accent as I detoured toward her across the emerald lawn. I didn't know whether she was teasing or flattering me. 'You do realize, my girl, that most nincompoops have no idea what the Fruit of that Forbidden Tree actually was. Most people believe the apple merely represented Knowledge. But we know better. It was the Fruit of the Tree of Knowledge of Good and Evil. Nothing less than the curse of consciousness. Of moral responsibility. Of always, ever after, having to choose between what is right and what is wrong.'

This was long before I truly knew the Winslows; before I discovered the worm at their center. I had only just begun the search for Indo's proof, but I knew nothing of Kitty and her journal, or a swastika on the back of a Van Gogh.

Indo guffawed as an early summer breeze skittered over us. 'Knowledge! Knowledge.' She shook her head. 'As far as I'm concerned, there is such a thing as knowing too much for your own good. Don't you agree, Mabel?'

I can't know for sure how I would have responded, but I sometimes wonder if it could have been the truth. That early in the summer, it might have been a relief to unburden myself, to confide that, yes, I already knew too much, entirely too soon. To confess I had come to Winloch to forget. That I believed her family, beautiful and rich, would deliver me from the bitter knowledge of my own making.

But instead I heard Ev calling my name.

I turned to see my friend emerging from behind the tennis courts, Abby nipping at her heels. 'I've got to run,' I said, watching Ev's hair halo in the sun.

Indo's eyes followed mine. 'Beware Lucifer's rhetoric. He'll seduce you with charisma.' She smiled. Tapped my book.

I glanced down at it. 'I haven't really started reading yet.'

'Well then,' she said crisply, 'perhaps you'll know what I mean by the end of the summer. How darkness infects those among us who can't resist a juicy tale.' Her eyes lit up impishly: 'Beware. You look like such a girl.'

This was the scene I recalled as I climbed those same steps one last time, the Dining Hall looming above me, the Winslows gathered inside to eulogize poor Indo in their way. Had my wild-goose chase of a summer been orchestrated by Indo? Had her introduction of the Winslow papers into my life, and the promise of a manila folder she knew wasn't there, and the whetting of my appetite for the Van Gogh, and her handing over of Kitty's journal, all been part of an elaborate test of my fortitude and stubbornness, leading to my inevitable search for proof of what the Winslows had stolen? Did she really believe that I, alone, could bring them down? That I'd want to?

She'd been right on the money; a juicy tale was my weakness. Perhaps she'd been correct to call that hunger greed. Despite my best-laid plans, I was now drowning in the cursed Knowledge of which she'd warned me. For better or worse, I was about to walk through those double doors and share it with as many Winslows as cared to hear it.

But then what?

I opened the doors to the sound of chitchat. The service had broken up, and the family was milling about, murmuring in low, respectful tones, snacking from the spread Masha had laid out at the far end of the room.

Even the children were subdued that morning, sulkily

sucking their thumbs. One small girl noticed me, and then the next Winslow saw me, and the next, until it seemed as though the eyes of every one of them, young and old, had clapped upon me and wouldn't let me go.

Birch conversed with a cousin on the makeshift stage. When news of my arrival reached him, he, too, lifted his head and took me in, his face revealing nothing. Beyond, Ev and Athol and Banning were gathered, and when they, too, noticed me, they showed me nothing beyond recognition. Ev and I were no longer what we'd been. At least I had Galway.

'Are you all right?' he whispered. His words upon my neck set off warning bells, just as my stomach lurched with the questions the stamp on the Van Gogh insisted upon: How had the Winslows acquired that painting? How many people had died because of its acquisition? And, most pressing to my selfish mind: did Galway know about the swastika?

The Winslows bid one another solemn good-byes. No one spoke to me. But their reproachful glances as they headed out into the day were enough, as though they were the dead and I had invaded the underworld. In a few years' time, when chronology and memory proved slippery, it might be easy to blame it all on me, on the outsider who'd infiltrated Winloch: Jackson's suicide, the murders, Lu's disappearance. But for now, I was just inconvenient.

The doors clapped shut. We were the only people left: Birch, Tilde, Athol, Galway, Banning, Ev. And me.

Galway cleared his throat.

Tilde lifted her head at the drinks table. She looked straight at me, sharp eyes piercing. The words she had uttered in the rowboat came back: 'Do not mistake silence for blindness.'

'Wait,' I warned Galway. I didn't want to stop him, not exactly, but I had a feeling this wasn't going to go as planned. My time with Gammy Pippa had unsettled me.

But they were already upon us, five sets of eyes spanning the large room – father, mother, brothers, sister. And Galway was unstoppable – I could see it from the set of his shoulders. No amount of cautiousness from me would seal his mouth, not after years of biting his tongue, not anymore. The best I could do was stand by his side.

'We know what you did, Father,' he said, voice trembling.

Birch laughed dismissively, spurring Galway to advance in hate across the wide room. 'We know that you murdered John and his mother because John found out he was your son, that you raped Pauline, Father, and you bought her silence by—'

'Stop it,' Athol snapped, stepping between Galway and their father, clenching his iron jaw. Shock had settled over Ev. I wished I'd had a chance to tell her, in private, how John had met his end.

'We have a witness,' Galway continued, slow and steady. 'Someone who saw you put your hands around Pauline LaChance's neck, Father, and wring it until she died, who saw you chase John LaChance onto the point and push him to his death—'

'Stop it!' It was Ev's voice now, high-pitched and frantic.

Tilde held her back. It was the first time I'd seen those women touch more than glancingly.

'It's true, Ev,' I said, my mouth going dry. 'Birch murdered John.'

'Don't,' Ev spat, her face turning ugly. She was angry, I could see that. But I was just the messenger. In time, she would understand. I stepped toward her, to try to explain, but she cursed at me, spewing rage. She'd never looked at me with hate before.

'And the women, Father,' Galway continued, undeterred by our interaction. 'Your sister, our maids, rape, incest—'

Athol struck Galway across the face.

'Children, children.' Birch chuckled evenly, as though breaking up an argument over a toy. He stepped between Athol and Galway, clapping his eldest son on the shoulder.

Galway dodged his father's touch, taking my hand triumphantly, even though I could sense he'd lost momentum. 'We're going to the police. We're telling them everything. That you're a murdering, raping pig.'

'Birch,' Tilde said sharply, eyes darting between her husband and sons.

Ev pulled away from her mother. 'She's written terrible things about us, Daddy,' she blurted, winning her father's attention. She was pointing at me like a village girl in the Salem witch trials. 'She wrote letters to her mother, Daddy, I read all of them, about her plans to steal our money.' I opened my mouth to protest, to explain, but her eyes narrowed. 'I can't believe I let you sleep in my house. She's some kind of lesbian, she always wants to borrow my clothes, she's probably been spying on me when I shower, who knows, maybe she wanted to skin me and eat me and make me into some kind of coat.'

Tilde murmured a doubtful response, and Ev pulled free, wagging her finger at me as the words cascaded forth. 'And she made these collages – these sick, weird cutouts that she spent hours on. She made me do them too. Of everyone here, everyone in this room, making fun of all of you. There's something wrong with her. She's obsessed with us.'

Strong as I believed I was, prepared as I had been for Birch's wretched words, Ev's betrayal took me by surprise. I didn't think I could bear her hatred. 'Ev,' I began, stepping toward her with my arms up in a gesture of surrender.

'Don't let her near me!' Ev shrieked like a banshee.

Galway tugged my hand. 'Let's go.'

But I couldn't leave, not yet. I turned to Tilde. 'I'm concerned about Ev,' I pronounced.

'Oh?' Tilde asked.

'I should tell you in private.'

'Anything you have to say to Tilde you can say to all of us,' Birch said shrewdly.

Ev's growl was hardly human.

Let her loathe me. I was protecting her from herself. Not to mention defending that baby. 'She's pregnant,' I announced. Even as I said it, I doubted if it was true.

A yelp sharpened out of her. She doubled over. I felt wretched, if justified. But as we all looked to her, it dawned on each of us that she was laughing. Laughing so hard she could barely breathe. Ev gestured to her belly, trying to get words out as she giggled riotously. Finally she managed, 'Do I look pregnant?'

'Ev,' I said firmly, remembering her flat belly on Bead Beach, 'if you had a miscarriage, you should go to the doctor.'

'I'm not fucking pregnant, you psycho!' She was full of rage.

The world was beginning to buzz. 'John was so excited.' I was starting to wonder if she'd even been pregnant. If she'd made the pregnancy up to keep him loyal, to get him to agree to run away with her. If she'd just been lying to him, using him, all that time. 'She and John eloped,' I tattled.

She lunged for me. Galway shielded me. Her brothers caught her.

'Darling,' Birch said calmly to Tilde, until mother pulled daughter away, 'why don't you take Ev outside?'

But Ev and Tilde both shook their heads. Ev flung herself down along one of the couches and hated me from there.

Galway tried to regain the room. 'We're going to the police.'

'Son,' Birch replied, 'think long and hard. Is that what you really want?'

Galway nodded decisively. 'I want justice.'

CHAPTER FIFTY-NINE

The Chaperone

JUSTICE.' BIRCH SAVORED THE word like a fine scotch. 'Justice.' He smiled with grave benevolence, like a long-suffering priest, heartbroken by the sins of man. This stance exerted a strange power over us all. Athol and Banning stepped back and settled into chairs to watch from the sidelines. Ev pulled a pillow into her arms. Tilde leaned against the snack table, but not before she poured herself some wine. Was it my imagination, or was her hand shaking as she lifted the glass to her lips?

For the first time that afternoon, Birch honed in on me. 'Mabel Dagmar.' His voice filled with false wonder. 'Your parents assured us you were a sweet girl. Humble. That you'd perform well in the position we offered. They understood that your placement here was delicate. That, for all sorts of reasons, Ev wasn't ever to know she was being chaperoned—'

'Daddy!' Ev declared sharply.

'My dear,' he chastised Ev, hardly lifting his eyes from me, 'you're the one who wanted to stay behind.'

I tried to understand what he was saying.

Chaperone.

Position.

Placement.

My ears were starting to fill with a cold, familiar, rushing sound. My soles felt cemented to the floor, as if stuck in the tarred, black mud that lined the river.

'You must admit, Mabel, you've done a terrible job on all counts! Seducing my married son!'

He interrupted himself, turning to Galway. 'Poor Marcella,' he tsked. 'Don't you think even the illegal daughter of a whore deserves fidelity?' But before Galway could respond, Birch came back at me. 'Nosing about in the business of my terminally ill sister! Allowing Ev to elope— Yes, Ev,' he chastised, diverting again, 'I know about your little side trip, although, if you reflect upon it sensibly, do you really think a judge would be available for a marriage at ten thirty at night?' He turned to Tilde and chuckled. 'They forget how many people I know.'

So he'd sabotaged John and Ev's wedding and known about Galway's wife? I felt myself shrinking in the face of Birch's power, in how it made the world what it wanted. It was alarming to hear the scope of his reach. Especially when I thought of the swastika.

But he wasn't done with me. 'Not to mention spreading insidious rumors about my family. Dear Mabel! Your parents will be appalled.' He made a fist and frowned at it. Pulled a Swiss Army knife from his pocket and cleaned his nails methodically. The blade glimmered in the light filtering through the double doors.

Galway grabbed my hand. His fingers were a tourniquet. 'It's time to go.' But I was rooted to the spot.

Birch flipped the blade closed and pocketed the knife, secure in my attention. 'This used to be a common arrangement.'

Galway pleaded, 'Mabel—'

'An unmarriageable girl – an ugly girl – would serve as companion to the one with prospects. When it worked for the best, the situation could last a lifetime.'

'They wouldn't do that,' I mumbled, but I didn't believe myself. I remembered my mother's phone call: 'Be sweet.' I had taken those two words as an assurance. But what if they had been more exacting? What if she had only let me believe Ev was my friend so she could get her handler's fee?

A look of calculated alarm crossed his face. 'Oh dear, I see I've upset her.'

Was that what I was? Upset? The river was roaring now inside my head, chilling my body as the cold current seemed to rise around me. Somewhere, in the back of my mind, I remembered that Galway and I had had a plan, and that I had knowledge I could use against the Winslows, know-ledge Indo had instilled. But what it was, what it had been meant to accomplish, I could hardly put my finger on anymore. The only thing I could hold on to, despite my best efforts, was the concise, conniving sound of Birch's rhetoric.

'Did your parents fail to mention our financial arrange-ments? Why, you've earned more for them this summer than they've made in the past year with that little dry-cleaning endeavor of theirs.

'It was Linden, old bat, who gave me the key. That pretentious tome you're always carrying! I asked her what on earth a girl like you was doing with such a book, and she replied, "I suspect her fixation betokens a fascination with sin."'

'Beware Lucifer's rhetoric.' That's what Indo had said that day, long ago, upon the Dining Hall stairs. I realized, too late, that she had been talking about her own brother. For he had rooted me to the spot – I was staying to find out how all this ended.

'Remarkable,' Birch continued, shaking his head as though in disbelief. 'Remarkable that you would accuse me of unspeakable crimes!' He pulled his eyes from me and turned toward his family, passing his earnest gaze from face to face. 'Your court documents are sealed. But you can't walk away from what you are.'

'That's it,' said Galway, forcefully taking my hand and pulling me toward the door. 'Mabel,' he said sharply, grabbing my chin in his hands, 'we're not going to stay and listen to these lies.'

'Lies?' Birch said incredulously. 'You mean to say she hasn't told you? Oh, Mabel, whatever damage you inflicted upon your poor brother, Daniel, is between you and God. But why would you drag my son into it?'

Galway's need was just one more current, dragging me along in its cold-fingered insistence. If we got out onto the steps, we would leave the Dining Hall, then Winloch, and then what? We might go to the police. Lu might make it to safety. But Galway would always wonder to what his father had been referring.

It was going to be a relief. The truth. At last.

Birch prompted me. 'Daniel had never quite been right. Slow from birth, but Mommy and Daddy had to work full-time at the cleaner's just to make ends meet. Poor Mabel here was stuck with an older brother who could hardly tie his own shoes. It was humiliating. Your parents working all the time. You had to take him with you everywhere, didn't you?'

Galway slackened his pull, acknowledging the futility of his efforts. I wrapped my arms around myself.

'From what I've heard, Mabel here was quite the mommy dearest. She fed him, changed him, even bathed him. And one day, she decided she was done. Asked him if he wanted to go for a little swim, didn't you, Mabel?'

I was fighting against memory and losing.

'She brought him down to the river. Pointed to the water and said she'd be right behind him. He trusted her, more than he trusted anyone else. He got into the water. She stayed on shore and let him be swept away.'

'It was a mistake,' I heard myself say. That's what I had told myself all these years. A misunderstanding, the exhaustion after a day of care for someone who could not be contained. Who would not stop asking questions. Demanding the world.

'He didn't die, did he?' Birch said. 'It was even worse than that. He lived. Dumber, needier, than before.'

I could feel it, the icy water rushing over my head, in the instant I saw Daniel swept off, in the moment I realized I wanted him back, that there was something worse than the burden of servitude, and it was the sin of killing, and that to hate someone so good was pure ugliness. That I had to save him so I could save myself. I dove into the frigid waters again and again, trying to find his big, bulky body, every so often seeing his gasping mouth in the waters above me as we were swept downstream, until the men pulled us out, and made Daniel alive again, until I confessed, and the hospital and the counseling and my mother weeping and my father raging . . .

I looked up. The Winslows – Galway, Ev, all of them – were far away, a family in which I had no part.

Galway tried to justify it. 'You were a child.'

I met his eyes. 'I tried to kill my brother.'

'And this,' Birch boomed, 'is private property and you are trespassing.'

'We know what you did,' I said, my voice weak. I met his eye. 'I'll walk right into the police station and tell them—'

'Given your confession, and apology, and the fact that your attempt to murder your brother didn't exactly pan out, you managed to avoid being put into a home for girls, didn't you? A mental institution,' Birch explained to his captive audience. 'I suppose it goes without saying that any young girl would be miserable in a place like that.'

'Father,' Galway said briskly, finally coming to my aid, 'I'll back her story up. You can't have her institutionalized for telling the truth.'

'Of course not, my good boy. No. I only mean, let's say this witness you claim to have up your sleeve, let's say she can be . . . located. Let's say she's boarding a flight to Mexico City, under a pseudonym, at three ten this afternoon. She's using false ID to board an international flight – isn't that a federal offense? I'm sure it wouldn't be hard for someone to stop her from getting on the flight, for a psychiatrist to prove her unstable enough to send her somewhere she'd be locked forever.'

He had found Lu. Sweet, lovely Lu, who fought for turtles

and made me bracelets, who was still mostly child. Lu, who smelled of sweat and honeysuckle. 'You wouldn't,' I said, voice trembling against my will.

'Wouldn't what?' Tilde asked. She'd been sitting there so quietly. But her ears had pricked up when Birch alluded to their daughter, even though he hadn't named her.

I had to make a decision now. Promise to either keep what a monster Birch was a secret, or tell, and send his daughter to certain misery. She'd already attempted suicide once. She wouldn't last more than a few days in any place he'd send her.

Galway tried to touch me, but I pulled away. I couldn't think clearly with him muddling my mind.

'And if I go,' I negotiated with Birch, 'and I keep the murders to myself, you'll let her go?'

'Let who go?' Tilde pressed. 'Birch, what does she mean?'

'Don't let him intimidate you,' Galway warned.

'My dear,' Birch replied, taking on a condescending tone, 'everything will be as it was.'

'He's lying,' Galway said.

'Birch,' Tilde pleaded, 'tell me right now what she means.'

'No.' I put my hand up. I'd seen the way Galway had looked at me when his father told him what I'd done to Daniel. 'No.'

To Birch I said, 'She's going to contact me to let me know she made it. If I don't hear from her, and hear exactly the code word she was going to use, I'll go straight to the police. Do you understand?'

'She's very emotional, isn't she?' Birch quipped to his audience, but I could tell he was considering my offer.

Tilde was pulling at him now, but he was ignoring her. 'You remember your promise to me,' she said through gritted teeth. She was speaking in the voice I remembered from that afternoon at Bittersweet, when Birch had nearly beaten down the door. Only this time, her command didn't work – she was no longer in charge. 'You remember your job, Birch. It's your job to keep your children safe.'

'Do you understand?' I pressed.

He hesitated for an infinitesimal moment. But then, as he brushed his wife aside, ignoring her urgent pleas, I saw I had won. Not everything. But it was victory enough to gain Lu's freedom.

Birch approached me briskly, then, like a birding dog pointing out its prey. I wondered if he would strike me. Or pull the knife from his pocket and stab my carotid artery. Or simply put his hands around my neck and squeeze the life out of me while his family looked on.

But instead, he extended his right hand.

I took it.

We shook once. A business agreement, sealed. Then Birch Winslow strode out the double doors.

Galway shook his head as he watched his father leave. His annoyance, or disappointment, was useless to me – all he seemed to care about was whether he had bested the man who'd intimidated him for his whole life.

'She's a little girl,' I reminded him, my eyes beginning to well, thinking of Lu's feet dangling in the water off the swimming dock, hair tucked behind one ear. I wasn't going to have a hand in destroying her.

I turned to leave. I heard Galway's footsteps behind me, as Tilde and Ev and Athol and Banning all began to speak at once, among themselves, trying to draw some meaning out of all that had just occurred. At the door, I turned back to Galway, stopping him in his tracks. 'Where are you going?' I asked.

'With you.'

'Did you know there's a swastika on the back of the Van Gogh?'

He didn't have to tell me either way – I saw his answer in his eyes. He probably also knew what the Winslows had been doing for decades, beginning during Hitler's rise to power, when they'd started to steal from Kitty's countrymen. Hadn't Galway hedged when I'd tried to pin him down on how long money had been coming into the Winloch coffers?

'That's all right,' I said crisply. 'I'll find my own way out.'

June

CHAPTER SIXTY

The End

MORNING COMES EARLY. COLD toes on my shin. Crumbs spilling onto the duvet. They pull us into the waking world. There are costumes to adjust, fairy wings to fix, and what am I doing with my hair, and is Daddy wearing makeup again this year?

There is hardly a chance to catch a glimpse of our view, but I insist upon it: the watery cove, the vista, through the trees, onto the expanse. Every day, I make a point to drink in our heaven. I braid their hair, wipe jam from their fingertips, and ask myself: What if Adam and Eve had figured out how to stay in Eden after they ate of the forbidden fruit? Say our first parents were skilled in the art of negotiation, instead of newly formed. Savvy instead of obedient. Imagine they'd looked God in the eye and stood their ground, having learned something from Lucifer about the linguistic art of persuasion: 'No, we are not leaving. We belong here, and here we shall make our home.'

And then I smile.

For where they failed, I have triumphed.

I was self-righteous and smug as I strode from the Dining Hall that August afternoon. I felt liberated – from my history, from Ev's coldhearted betrayal, from Birch's accusations, even, to tell the truth, from Galway's need.

With every step I took, I convinced myself that I wanted no part of their lunacy. Better yet, that I had played them. For I had sworn to keep my mouth shut about only the murders. I hadn't made any promises about the swastika, or what I knew it meant.

As the road wound around the forested curve where John and Ev had found me so many weeks before, I quickened my pace and formulated a plan. Indo's words resounded in my ears: 'Blood money.' I was beginning to understand.

I would call my mother collect. For the first time in months, I realized I could face my parents, knowing they had sold me off. Somehow, it made them more bearable, as though they had finally admitted how dysfunctional I had always known we were.

If I shuddered to think of the nameless, uncountable girls I might be leaving to Birch's rapacious appetites, didn't I tell myself I was doing no more harm than the rest of them, keeping my mouth shut? I had no physical proof. I had saved Lu – that was heroic enough.

Besides, I was going to do even more than that. My chest swelled with self-congratulation. As I strolled, my mind raced: over Kitty's German upbringing, and the money that had saved Winloch and the Winslows from financial ruin, which had, conveniently, begun to flow just as Hitler ascended. The financial records Galway had alluded to, which showed money starting to come in in the early thirties. I would bide my time. Do my research. And then, almost certainly, if I asked the right questions and found the right records, I would be able to prove – or at least provide a compelling argument – that the Winslows had stolen from murdered and encamped Jews. Blood money made off the backs of Kitty's massacred countrymen.

But that was just the beginning. A drop in the bucket. Because if Indo had been right, what the Winslows had gained from the wartime slaughter was not only financial but – probably even more fruitful – an instruction, the blueprint they had been able to apply over and over again as time pressed on. What had she said? 'The Far East. Darkest Africa. Central America.' I didn't know my history as well as some, but I knew that war had ravaged the world in the twentieth century. Birch's words played over in my mind: 'They forget how many people I know.' The Winslows had been making money off the world's misery. They had taken from the disenfranchised and displaced by siphoning money and goods from those parts of the world where no one would notice them missing.

Perhaps I'd be able to provide the evidence for a legal case against the Winslows, but, even if not, I could at least mar their reputation. Make it so Birch could never do business again. Get the IRS involved.

By the time I heard the motor coming up the bend behind me, my pace was almost a run.

The girls flit around my ankles like chickadees, chirping as we lay out the feast. I shoo them off halfheartedly. Once they lift away, I shield my eyes from the midsummer sun and watch them stream toward the tennis courts, laughing as they go, wishing I was still a girl myself.

This is, at last, the place I imagined it to be that first bright morning I awoke in Ev's bedroom and watched the shadows play over the ceiling. The place in which children can and should run free, and the fears that haunt a mother's heart – a slippery footfall, going out in a dinghy without a life preserver – are reasonable.

Adam and Eve could have stayed in Eden only had they done their best to forget what the serpent had taught them about each other, and themselves. One cannot grow and thrive when the sun is clouded over, or drink from a well when it is poisoned.

I lift my eyes as our matriarch descends the hill, a bucket of black-eyed Susans in her arms. She is an older woman now, and plumper in a way that pleases. Her cheekbones could no longer cut glass, but then, she no longer needs to. No one rushes to assist her, knowing she would swat away our arms, cluck violently at the suggestion she needs our help.

She doesn't.

It was Tilde's white Jaguar that pulled up behind me. I thought of darting into the forest, then laughed at my dramatics. All I had to do was move into the ditch, and she'd pass me by, gunning toward wherever she was headed.

Instead, the car crawled to a halt beside me, its motor idling gently.

She rolled down the passenger window. 'Get in?'

It was not a demand. I weighed my options. What was she going to do, mace me? I placed my fingertips against the metal handle and opened the door.

The climate was supple in there. The air smelled of leather. Tilde had driving gloves on – I didn't even know they made those anymore.

'I know about the swastika,' I began. I considered going on, but I figured that was enough. A threat to break the silence.

We sat together for a moment. I wondered if she was going to drive me somewhere, but no. 'I hope you'll reconsider,' she replied.

I shook my head. 'I'm telling.'

'Not about telling, goodness. About leaving.'

I laughed. I couldn't help myself. Had she been paying attention to any part of my agreement with Birch?

'I like your influence upon my children,' she explained.

'That's not how your husband sees it.'

She removed her sunglasses and tilted her head, examining the pines swaying in the breeze above us. 'Birch has his way of seeing things,' she said carefully, 'but the world is not so black and white.'

'What he said is true.' My heart was pounding. 'About my brother. I tried to kill him.'

She closed her eyes and rubbed a slender finger over her temple. 'Why,' she asked calmly, 'do you think I requested you as Ev's freshman roommate?'

It took a moment to get my mind around her response.

'Oh, dear girl,' she continued, 'you think Birch is the only one who knows people? I wanted you the second I read your file.'

I shrank from her. That is the only way to describe what I did in that car – I wanted to get out and run, my mind racing. She had known all along I'd tried to murder Daniel? And she had picked me – knowing I had applied to Ev's college, gaining access to my sealed court document, intuiting my innermost secret – because of it?

She surprised me with her vigorous laugh. 'Everyone makes mistakes,' she said warmly, as though my past were a mere trifle; an attitude, I supposed, central to surviving a marriage to Birch Winslow. She lifted a finger. 'But not everyone has a conscience.'

'Galway does.'

That only made her laugh harder. 'My dear, who do you think has been footing the bill for his exercise in slippery borders?'

My jaw dropped.

'Galway talks a noble game. He believes in helping people, yes. But he is his father's son. Everyone can be bought, my dear. Every single person on this earth has a price.'

With it all laid out like that, it was tempting to think of turning around and going back. But I shook my head.

'It's the painting, isn't it?' Tilde said, sounding perturbed.

'It's that you participated in the theft and murder of millions and who knows what else!'

'Well, I didn't.'

'It doesn't matter whether you actually did. You've been profiteering, knowingly, for decades.'

She smiled. 'She told you, didn't she?'

'Told me what?' I should have kept my mouth shut.

'You weren't the first person she tried to enlist. Poor Jackson, he was so mixed up in his final days. He came to me, one night, weeping, telling me she'd told him the

Winslows were rotting from the inside. That it was too late to cut the tumor out, that the cancer had spread to us all. Of course, I had no idea what he was going to do' – she shivered – 'that poor boy. There were others too, others she tried to lure over to her side, to the notion that, if she couldn't get her own way, she'd bring us all down.'

I swallowed.

'You don't agree with her, do you?' she asked. 'You don't think we're all bad?'

'I don't know what you're talking about.'

'Of course, someone would need proof.' She sighed. 'And my guess is that, although Indo had plenty of rumors, and suggestions, and fairy tales, she didn't give you much in the way of solid evidence.'

'That painting's not yours,' I said, trying to sound confident, 'no more than it was Indo's, or her mother's.'

'So if I returned it, would you come back with me?'

I snorted. 'Who would you return it to?'

She waved her hand dismissively. 'We'd locate the descendants, have a ceremony, start a foundation. You could run it! Don't look so gloomy, that's how these things are done.' She turned up the air-conditioning. It whirred below her voice. 'Dear girl, think of your education. Of Daniel. Bind yourselves to us, and doors will open. Leave, and what will you take with you – a rumor about a painting we've already given back? If you think you'll get access to our taxes or bank records, you're much more naïve than I thought.'

My heart sank.

'Yes,' she mulled, watching my face carefully, 'I think that's

427

just what we'll do. I've been wanting to redecorate the summer room anyway. We'd save so much on insurance . . .'

If they gave back the painting, and condemned their ancestors' actions, I had not a thing to hold against them. For she was right; what Indo had told me, by itself, proved nothing.

'Come back,' Tilde purred. Then she lifted her purse onto her lap and removed a familiar journal. Kitty's. 'Under the floorboards – you think you're the only one to think of such a hiding place?' She flipped through the journal. I caught the handwriting and felt a lurch of nausea at who Kitty had really been. 'I wanted to destroy it. I wanted to end Indo's assault against this family once and for all. But then I thought: why do away with something that can be put to work?'

She fumbled open the journal and searched for a moment, then thrust it into my hands, her finger gesturing to an entry I'd read a hundred times: 'We are being joined this week by Claude, Paul, and Henri. B. and I are so looking forward to offering them shelter until they decide where to settle.'

I searched her face. 'So?'

'Surely you know about the other paintings?'

I realized what I had been missing in that journal. 'Claude' was not a person. He was a painting. A nickname Kitty had applied to a pilfered work of art, likely by Claude Monet. 'Paul' might be a Paul Klee. And 'Henri' – perhaps one by Henri Rousseau.

My mind raced over the dozens of such entries, naming 'guests' and their arrivals and departures – to New York, San

428

Francisco, Chicago. Just as Indo had promised, this journal was the key to tracing the locations of hundreds of stolen works of art.

Tilde smiled. 'Think of the difference we could make.'

I understood, in a flash, that this was what had been done for her. A recruitment. A mother-in-law – Kitty, in Tilde's case – luring back her son's mate, making promises for a life Tilde could have only ever imagined. She was paying me the favor that had been extended to her. The invitation.

But then I thought of Birch. The locks that had disappeared from Bittersweet's doors as soon as he realized he'd nearly lost his power over Ev. The horrifying childhood scene Galway had described, of opening a bathroom door to find his father plowing the nanny. I wouldn't be able to sleep at night, knowing that man was roaming the grounds. Besides, going back to his domain was, if not an implicit approval of his actions, then an idiotic move – hadn't I promised I'd leave forever? If I left, I would know Lu was safe, and I wouldn't have to be afraid anymore.

'No,' I said sharply.

Tilde cleared her throat. There was a catch in the sound, something odd. I glanced at the steering wheel and realized, with surprise, that her hands were shaking. I followed the lines of her arms, up to her shoulders, and there, upon her face, I saw something I never could have imagined: tears. She spoke unsteadily. 'If it's Birch you're worried about, I'm taking care of it.'

'What does that mean?'

'For years, I've been the only thing standing between him

and everyone else. I signed up, you see, and I believed, in order to have this life, I had to endure everything being married to him requires of me. That I, alone, could keep my family safe.'

She wiped a tear from her cheek. 'But then you came along. I've never seen someone so small as you, someone who he underestimated so much, stand up to him. I suppose, in watching you, I began to realize that all I had justified – his violence, his cruelty – was not necessarily what I deserved. Still, I could bear his . . . attacks, if that's what you want to call them, if it meant my babies were safe. He always promised me he'd never lay a finger on his children. But then he killed John. John, after all, was his son. So that worried me. But still, I thought, well, at least my children are safe. But then . . .' She shook her head in disbelief, and fury. 'He threatened to go after Lu. Our baby . . .' Her sentence ended in a gasping sob.

I waited for her to calm. I felt certain I was one of the only people in the world she had ever spoken to so honestly, at least in recent years. I didn't want to waste my chance. 'So what will you do?' I asked definitively.

'He thinks he won,' she said, her jaw tightening. 'But I know people too. I am people.'

And in that moment, I realized two things. First, that Tilde and I were more alike than I had ever imagined. And, second, that Winloch would be a very different place without Birch in it.

She brings the flowers to the table. 'Where's Galway?'

'Getting the sawhorses.' I unfold the tablecloths Masha

430

insisted on bringing down from the attic all by herself. I spread them across the lawn to air them out just as she instructed me, knowing the ancient woman is watching my every move from the Dining Hall. I know better than to cross Masha.

Tilde checks her watch. 'They'll be here soon.'

I place my hand on hers and squeeze. 'And we'll be ready.'

And so it comes to pass that the Winslows descend upon the Midsummer Night's Feast as they have for generations, spreading the cherry pies and watermelon and cucumber sandwiches across the groaning board. The winged children come, and the dogs, and the girls return, swirling about me with their needs and complaints. I kiss the tops of their sweaty heads and draw my arms around Galway's waist, nuzzling gently at the back of his neck until goose bumps form.

We came to our reconciliation over time, after he explained that he had learned of the swastika – and his family's ongoing theft from the world's saddest places – only after I sent him digging into his family's fiscal history. He had been waiting to tell me what he knew, but all that had happened with Lu and his father had gotten in our way. It took me time to forgive him, to listen to his first wife's advice about letting myself love. But then I did, and, in a life full of many choices, it is the best I've ever made.

It was strange, and sudden, an extra burden and tragedy for this storied clan, that one early Saturday morning at the end of that very same August when John and Pauline LaChance were found dead on Winloch grounds, Birch

Winslow decided to swim out to the far point all alone. He was in tiptop shape – he'd had a physical only a few months before – but when he hadn't been seen for a few hours, his devoted wife, Tilde, put out the alarm, and the cousins went looking in a rowboat. The Coast Guard was called. They searched and searched, first from the surface of the water, and then with divers. The next day, his bloated, ghostly body washed up near Turtle Point.

A heart attack.

In the days afterward, Tilde and I kept our silence. A pill, I thought, a pill to make it look like that, was that even possible? She knew people. She had promised me, he would pay.

And then, at the September funeral, yellowing maple leaves shaking above us, Lu weeping, and the minister waxing poetic, they lowered his bulky coffin into the fertile earth. Tilde's eyes swept mine, and in that flinty moment I knew.

'We find ourselves together again,' she says, her voice lifting clear above the din, until, one by one, we turn to her. 'Another year gone by. Another decade. And yet the Winslows keep on. Can't get rid of us.' Laughter ripples the crowd like a breeze off the cove.

From behind the food table, Athol sulkily sips his gin. He has become sharp-edged and reedy, Emily long gone, even his children desperate to be away from him. He wants to talk business with me, has been trying all week, desperate for information on the foundation, and whether I located the Degas, and if I'll be flying to Berlin again, and how much money has been budgeted for the annual fund-raiser.

To ingratiate himself and prove himself invaluable to the Winslows' cause is now his prerogative, since, funnily enough, upon Birch's death, the Winloch Constitution seemed to have vanished off the face of the earth. A will was found in its stead, a will that reverted the entire estate not into the hands of Birch's one presumptive heir – Athol, his firstborn son – but to any person with Winslow blood flowing through her veins.

They surround us now, the 132 equal owners of this property, who, the year after Birch's death, voted in over-whelming majority to create the Winslow Foundation, dedicated to tracing goods stolen from honest people by the craven Winslow ancestors, and returning them to whom they rightfully belong. The majority vote came about, as these things do, because of some behind-the-scenes wrangling; namely, the hideous threat that, if such a foundation were not established, and Winslow funds not put into it, our name would be sullied forever. Damning evidence existed, somewhere out there, that would bring us all down. So we could choose – hold on to our hoard as it was ripped from us, or take the first step in generosity, having discovered such atrocities in our past, and become leaders, experts, lauded philanthropists in a field that had been so underfunded and so ignored.

It worked. Jolly Banning, whom we affectionately call the Mayor, shows off the new Labrador puppies; Arlo feeds his six-month-old a bottle so that his wife can enjoy a night of relative freedom; CeCe Booth sips her glass of Sancerre.

'Aunt LuLu! Aunt LuLu!' the girls cry, and here she comes, braid all atangle, carrying a bucket of frogs for the children, smelling of the water. Her overalls are damp and her forehead is smeared with mud.

'Sorry I'm late,' she apologizes, and I tease her, for she is always late – Luvinia Winslow, Ph.D. – especially now that she has the lake to study, her degree as a freshwater marine biologist serving to solve the mysteries of her childhood: the dead turtles, the disappearance of the otters, the spread of invasive duckweed. Now a woman, Lu still frets at night about our changing world, the rising waters, the spreading droughts. Some evenings, she lays her head on my lap and I offer up a thanks that she is safe.

As the stage is cleared, and the blankets are spread upon the ground, as the children reapply their glitter makeup and the men slip off to don their Pyramus and Thisbe costumes, I catch sight of a solitary figure across the lawn, leaning against the Dining Hall.

She is not unlike her mother once was: brittle, unpleasant. She keeps herself apart, from us and the world. I suppose she could still have a life, children, a husband if she wanted them. But something irrevocable happened to her that summer – she was stunted by it, by John's murder and her father's death, by the fact that the skewed moral universe she'd been born into, and adhered to, was dismantled the day Birch died, by the truth that, even had she been able to escape Winloch, she would always have Winslow blood in her veins.

She observes the children's antics, the dogs tussling over a piece of ham. They are all a bit afraid of her, the quiet aunt who wears a mantle of sorrow. But I am not, even though she believes I am responsible for what is broken in her. Or at least I am not afraid enough to keep myself from remembering.

Under the canopy of birch, pine, and maple branches, sun dappling down, I can pretend it is a lifetime ago. If I didn't know any better, I could believe we are back in that first summer, when it was just the two of us, alone, in an undiscovered kingdom. It is a dangerous, slippery wish.

I was meant to become one of you, I think of saying, but she can't hear me across the lawn, and yet, I know, when she nods, that she means to say, yes. She means to say she knew I would be a Winslow before I did. I think I will go to her, will say just that into her sweet pink ear, when the children parade out, and the applause begins.

I look for her again. She is gone.

So I sit with my daughters and celebrate.

And I do my best job of forgetting.

ACKNOWLEDGMENTS

Although only my name is on the cover of this book, there are dozens of others who inspired it, believed in it, strengthened it, and worked on making it what you now hold in your hands. I am humbled by them.

Thank you to Jennifer Cayer, Tammy Greenwood, Heather Janoff, and Emily Raboteau, for their keen eyes and honesty; to Elisa Albert, Daphne Bertol-Foell, Caitlin Eicher Caspi, Amber Hall, Victor LaValle, Luke McDonald, Esmée Stewart, Mikaela Stewart, and all the many folks I'm blessed to call friends, for their faith, generosity, and encouragement; to Rob Baumgartner, Mo Chin, Joyce Quitasol, and everyone at Joyce Bakeshop, for being a second writing home; to Amy March, Cathy Forman, Amy Ben-Ezra, and Farnsworth Lobenstine, for their generous support, which has made much of my work on this book possible; and to Lauren Engel, Sherri Enriquez, Martha Foote, Sandra Gomez, Margaret Haskett, Elizabeth Jimenez, Shameka Jones, Krissy Travers, Olive Wallace, Patricia Weslk, and everyone at PSCCC, for caring for my boy so I could write this book.

Thank you to Maya Mavjee, Molly Stern, and Jacob Lewis, for welcoming me with open arms; to Rachel Berkowitz, Linda Kaplan, Karin Schulze, and Courtney Snyder, for taking the book international; to Christopher Brand, Anna Kochman, Elizabeth Rendfleisch, and Donna Sinisgalli, for giving it such a beautiful face; to Candice Chaplin, Christine Edwards, Jessica Prudhomme, Rachel Rokicki, Annsley Rosner, and Jay Sones, for introducing it to the world; to Susan M. S. Brown and Christine Tanigawa, for tightening my prose; to Sarah Breivogel, Nora Evans-Reitz, Kayleigh George, and Lindsay Sagnette, for being such supporters; and to Rick Horgan, for giving me his sage advice, and for twice now encouraging the bookmakers to gamble on me.

Thank you to Anne Hawkins, for standing by my side and believing this would come again (and for all our delicious lunches); to Dan Blank for teaching me so much about what it is to be a writer these days and helping me lead the charge; and to Christine Kopprasch, who knew exactly how this book should end (and in knowing, showed me she was meant to be my editor) and for all the hard work she's put in since. She is wise, enthusiastic, and kind, and I am proud to call her my friend.

Thank you to Kai Beverly-Whittemore, for listening to my first tangled idea and insisting I start writing, for reading, for believing, for suggesting, and for loving me no matter what; to Rubidium Wu, for being such an example of patience and fortitude (not to mention demonstrating feats of strength with the young prince); to Robert D. Whittemore, for reminding me that the isle is full of noises, sounds, and sweet airs, and teaching me about that natural world so I could breathe life into Winloch, and for carrying on the legacy of his father, Richard F. W. Whittemore, who loved the land so much that he passed along its stewardship to his lucky descendants; to Elizabeth Beverly, who endured (and claimed to enjoy) many, many drafts of this book, including listening to me read it aloud, and for the ancient motherly truths that are so much bigger than their pithy names, like love and pride and strength – thank you, thank you, thank you.

To my two loves, David M. Lobenstine and our SPERO, I say: my heart is full. I knew our lives together would be a beautiful adventure, but you have exceeded every expectation. I am so blessed to call you my own.